Praise for Leo Dark's *Lucifer Sam*!

"Leo Darke has created a heavy metal nightmare made of hard-driving prose, a dark sense of humor, and a jovial nod to 1980s horror fiction. There's sex, gore, and suspense to spare, and it all unfolds to a heavy metal beat. An enjoyable read."

—Ray Garton, author of *Crucifax* and *Ravenous*

"Just like the punk rock era that it so finely evokes, Darke's tale is edgy, dangerous, thrilling, unpredictable, and scary. Lucifer Sam rocks. Hard."

—Stuart R. West, author of *Twisted Tales from Tornado Alley* and *Ghosts of Gannaway*

"Death Metal has a new vanguard band—and a literal meaning. This band's music is truly Killer."

—Mallory A. Haws, The Haunted Reading Room

Other titles by Leo Darke

Lucifer Sam
Pandemonium

Writing as Mickey Lewis

Walking Shadow

SAWNEY BONE

LEO DARKE

A
GRINNING SKULL PRESS
Publication
PO Box 67, Bridgewater, MA 02324

PART ONE

HOLE

Father's shout.

Eat the world—and the cave stinks of horror.

I sees the sun spurt blood over the deathless sea. I squints at the rocks with their *hoods o' weed skulking on that goriest o' shores. I sees the world in my head, and I'll eat it all.*

The grisly man crouches at the mouth of the cave and scratches irritably at his rank beard. *Eat. I'll eat 'em all.*

Across the sea, the mound of Ailsa Craig drips with blood from the wounded sun. The grisly man gazes at the blood, can taste it on his lips, feel it ooze down his jaws. He stretches gnarled hands toward the sun, thirsting for redness.

Behind him, from the depths of the cave, comes the pig-stuck roaring of his spawn. He snarls back into the darkness. If any are unwise to venture near him now, he'll scoop them up by their chicken-bone ankles and slap their brains out against the roof of the cave. He hears his hag of a woman spit and curse and the sound of stone on flesh. It excites him; he wants part of the violence. He is about to scamper into the throat of the cave when a sound reaches his sensitive ears.

His grotesque head tilts upward, nostrils working eagerly. His body, clad in a filthy jerkin and a loincloth of rotting seaweed, stiffens; a man of rock with death screaming in his mind. He listens, breath stilled. The echo of hooves can just be detected from far above.

He moves.

Like a human crab with scabbed flesh and slimy hair, he sidles over the rocks beyond his cave, swarms over piles of sick, pale weeds, and sprays through the first tongues of the advancing tide. He needs be hasty.

The carriage road winds toward the edge of the world.

The cliff tops hang above a gulf of twilight. The horizon is a band of blood, splitting the dark of the sea from the dark of the sky. Blood. The old woman at the Inn talked of blood and other horrors. Her ghoulish babbling gains more credence as the evening sucks light from the heavens.

Beware the cliffs of Bennane.

The knotted crone burbled gleefully upon the subject, and the words have taken root in his head, will not be tugged free. Now they grow with his fear, take on awful shape.

Folk disappear, lad.

A shriek swoops at him from over the lip of the crags. His heart stammers. A seabird, wailing horribly as it circles its cliff-top nest. The traveler urges his horse onward, the steady tattoo of hooves on the rough road mingling with the agitated screams of the gull. Far below, the sea pushes hungrily against the rocks.

He must reach Stranraer before dawn, and this guilty road is his only route. Why should he fear?

The gull ceases its mournful cries. The hollow trembling of the sea below... Night seizes him.

Father's shout.
Mother's scream.
"Derek, mind the road, for God's sake."
Gulls.

HOLIDAY

1972

Father's shout.

One large hand left the steering wheel, formed into a fist, swung around into the back seat, pounding the boy's right arm like a fleshy demolition ball. The Avenger veered dangerously across the coastal road.

Mother's scream.

Father twisted round again to confront a big, blue vista of sea filling the windscreen. He bore down hard right on the steering wheel. Tires screamed in agony. The car bucked madly, barely managed to cling to the narrow road, and pulled away from the cliff edge.

The boy rocked against his brother, who elbowed him viciously back onto his own side of the seat. As the car steadied itself again, the boy nursed his arm, fury building, out of control like his Dad's driving. "Bastard. *Bastard.*" He shrieked the colorful word—it sounded so good, so *right*—at the back of his father's bullish neck. Father's oversized head (Freak. *FREAK!*) began to swing toward him again.

"Derek, mind the road, for God's sake," Mother whinnied. The boy watched his father's profile as it swiveled to confront him, his bulbous left eye bloodshot with rage. The boy leaned forward and stabbed the index finger of his right hand into that mad bull's eye. Then he was scrabbling at the back door of the Avenger, ignoring the bellow of pain from his father, the frenzied octaves of his mother. The door swung open, the gray surface of the road ground past. The horizon of sea and sky beckoned him on. He took one quick look back, saw the gloating expression on his brother's young face. *Go on,* his expression read. *Do it. We all hate you. Jump.*

The boy jumped.

He hit the grassy verge at the side of the road, and the breath left him with a punch more brutal than those even his father regularly dealt him. His body rolled on, tossed by momentum, plunged through the rusty web of an old wire fence and down, down. Sea, sky, and bracken, merging crazily. Down. A rock thumped his left kidney, bounced him into the air, winded. He landed in thick ferns, his frame suddenly numb. The sea rolled closer.

Something was leaning over him, preventing him from falling farther: a tall, white object that reared incongruously up from the bracken. It rocked when he collided with it, but it did not fall. The boy wondered dimly through his pain why a refrigerator should be stuck out here on this wild slope. Perhaps the seagulls kept their fish fingers in it. Not funny. Too much *hurt.*

Unconsciousness beckoned, but he wasn't going to let it take him away. The hurt kept him alert. Far, far away it seemed, he heard his father's bellows as he searched for his son.

The boy's agony urged him to be sensible and wait here until his father found him, but his hate forbade it. Instead, he forced himself to his knees and crawled away from the rusting fridge, away from the sounds of searching.

A glimmer of sand: a beach lurked beneath the tumbling hillside. He could hide there. The bastard with the swinging, balled fists wouldn't find him there. Ever. And then they would all be sorry, he promised himself as he half-crawled, half-rolled down through the ferns onto the dirty, white beach. He thought of his mother's careworn efforts to stop the violence; the jagged bursts of fury into which his father would ignite, chasing him round the kitchen table, chasing him up the stairs, always chasing him.

And when he caught him...

Waves rolled in. Spears of sunlight glanced off rocks that rose from the beach like petrified monsters. Seaweed was strewn thickly over the sand, off-white innards bloated by the surf. Gulls mourned.

The child heard more cries from above: his father's angry voice fading, to be replaced by his mother's pleas. Was he supposed to believe she really cared? The boy wasn't going to fall for that one. He knew what would happen if he let himself be found. The rage of his father unleashed, an unstoppable thing. He considered crawling onward into the wall of waves ahead, allowing himself to float off into the glorious burst of the setting sun exploding across the sea. He inched forward, sobs chugging up from his chest.

When the surf licked at his hands and his knees, bare below his shorts, he knew he couldn't go on. The cold pulled him back from the brink. He stood shakily. The bastard mustn't find him; he must keep that thought uppermost at all times. His legs wobbled as they carried him along the shore, but the pain was not so fierce now, although his left kidney felt as if it had been flattened. But he would not cry anymore. That was all over.

As he limped on, the heather-covered slopes surrendered to sheer cliffs. Gulls rose and fell around the tops of the crags, white and gray confetti scattered by the wind. Their sad cries mingled with those of his mother, the pounding surf a steady backbeat.

The beach ended where an arm of rock pushed out into the frothing sea. Automatically, as if he must keep as much distance between himself and his parents—his *family*—as possible, he began climbing around the outcrop, and the cave was suddenly there.

He forgot to breathe. A hole like a screaming mouth gaped from between shoulders of rock in a dry, narrow inlet. Above, the cliff face bulged out into a stern forehead, sweeping up, up, so the boy had to crane his neck to follow it. His gaze leaped back to the mouth of the cave, from which a spew of boulders dribbled down a slight incline of shingle and weeds toward him. The weeds were thicker here, piled like ripped white bellies on the rocks, and the violent stink of it prised his nostrils wide. But his eyes were wider. The boulders formed an ogre's staircase leading up to adventure.

The hole pulled him. There was no choice, really; even if he had wanted to turn away, he couldn't. Not now. There was something here for him; he knew that somehow. Something special. He clambered up the boulders toward the screaming mouth, sliding and slipping over the weeds clinging like wet hair to the rocks. The crack widened to greet him as he neared it, then closed abruptly over him. The sobbing of the sea faded.

The cave was dark, and it was full of horror.

The ten-year-old could smell it. He could taste it. But he could see nothing beyond the first few yards visible in the faint light from outside. The cave opened into a fairly large chamber after the constricted opening. Then, as he groped his way onward, hands outstretched, nothing but blackness. He felt the damp roof lower over his head and the rough walls squeeze him in as the opening chamber gave way to a narrow tunnel. Now and then, his hands would sink into cold emptiness as they traveled along the walls, side passages leading into deeper mystery. Terror squeezed him like the walls as he ventured farther in, and he wondered why he should savor it so. He sucked it inside his lungs, breathing it deep.

And it was the best thing he had ever experienced in his life.

With the pulse of the sea distant now, he eventually reached the end of the cave. Here, he felt the tunnel open up into another chamber, smaller than the first, where a wall of rock prevented further progress. On an impulse, the boy squatted on the cold ground, small, alone, drinking in the delicious wine of this new fear he had discovered.

Bone.

He had been sitting for several minutes, his hands distractedly exploring the floor of the cave around him when his fingers slipped across the smooth, brittle object. His heart inflated with a burst of horror. His subconscious mind identified it before his rational one would dare. He tried to focus his eyes on the find, but the dark would not let him, as if the object should remain unseen, hidden.

Bone.

Yes, a bone, a special kind of bone. And it refused to pull free from the crack of rock in which it was embedded, so he applied both hands, laughing wildly.

The double row of jagged teeth rasped against his palms as he wrenched, as if nibbling his skin in welcome, or hunger. The shape of the football-sized bone seemed oddly malformed, he thought as he caressed the bulging forehead and poked his fingers into the hollow sockets, which surely were set too far apart. His special fear rode him, spurring him on, and so intent was he on his efforts that when he heard the voice, he wasn't sure at first whether it was merely the sound of his own excited breathing playing tricks on him in the cave. A drip of water from the roof, the wind beyond the cave mouth? Then it came again: his name whispered through the dampness and the dark.

He paused to listen, but only the wailing of gulls reached his ears. Had his father followed him down onto the beach, was he calling him still? But it hadn't sounded like someone calling, more like someone sighing. He returned his attention to his find and, with a final exertion, managed to pull the skull from the crevice.

He cradled it eagerly, his heart stamping so loud that it could have been the heartbeat of the cave itself. And over the beat, the whisper came once more...

A whisper coaxing him with secret words. He bent his head to the filthy jaws and listened to what they had to tell him.

Beyond the mouth of the cave, the gulls mourned ceaselessly.

The family holiday was over.

"Father..." the child breathed, sitting in the dark.

PART II: THE SLAUGHTER

1993

CHAPTER ONE

"I want the sickest film you've got," the man said.

Jack had watched him enter the video library. He was the first customer of the day (always the worst?), and Jack had never seen him before. He was quite sure of that. He wouldn't have forgotten a face like this one in a hurry. A sly face, long, and somehow uncomfortably handsome in a bitter kind of way, as if the features were only reluctantly good-looking and tried to twist themselves slightly out of true to spite the man to which they belonged. There was a flick-knife viciousness in the eyes, which were so dark as to be almost black. The cut of his thin lips was dangerous. The man's eyes slid over the tightly packed video shelves lining the narrow passage leading to the counter.

Jack took in the long, dark overcoat, the square-toed biker boots emerging from the turn-ups of his black jeans. He looked as if he'd edged violently into his thirties and was lean and sharp as a pirate's cutlass.

I don't like you, Jack thought as the stranger approached the counter. *Nope. Not at all.* He felt himself worm under the nasty chisels the man used for eyes.

The stranger slicked a blade of jet-black hair away from his eyes. There wasn't a trace of color anywhere on his body; from his frost-white face to the heels of his dark boots, he was every inch Veidt's Cesare, nightmare-walking into Jack's life. His lips tilted into a serial-killer sneer.

I REALLY *don't like you.* Jack's guts tensed, and his teeth clenched the way they always did when he found himself in circumstances he wasn't happy with.

"I don't mean just sick," the man continued in a voice laden with grave dirt. "I mean *vile.* Mind-bendingly repulsive." He spread his hands on the counter and cocked his head forward. Jack noticed how long and thin his fingers were, all rough and grimy like raw, stringy carrots, the sort of vegetable fingers you'd stuff in the sleeves of a scarecrow.

Jack summoned a cheery grin that read: *Love to help, mate, even if you are the most unappealing creep I've ever been forced to serve,* and said, "I'm afraid we don't stock mind-bendingly repulsive films, chief. Not even merely vile ones. Sorry." He *was* actually, or rather, always had been up to this point. He loved horror films. But right now he was suddenly quite happy with the situation. "This is a clean shop. No under-the-shelf nasties here." He marveled at his own smugness.

The man wiped one hand idly along the countertop, his eyes never leaving Jack's. The sneer remained. *He's going to flip into violent mode any minute.* Jack performed a rapid mental check of the video library for possible weapons with which to defend himself. Unless he was prepared to fight off the sick bastard with a copy of *BEE Movie* that leaned patiently against the computer waiting to be put to bed, there really weren't many options.

The stranger turned around to survey the shelves of the small video vault that, with its low roof, narrow passage, and subdued lighting, resembled a fox's bolthole. *I'm trapped in here,* thought Jack. *Shut in with Mister Mind-Bendingly Repulsive. How was that for typical Tuesday afternoon entertainment?*

The dark man pulled a video box down from a shelf. The naked light bulb shimmered on the plastic cover. Jack read the title and wiped his mouth nervously. *The Boogeyman.* Mister Vile weighed the box in one hand as if deliberating whether or not to rent it. Jack could feel a ring of sweat under his collar. *This is stupid. So he's unpleasant and creepy, but that doesn't necessarily make him dangerous.*

"Evisceration," the man breathed. "Decapitation. Dismemberment..." He drew out the last word lovingly as he faced Jack again, and his snarl was pure Jack-O'lantern.

Jack knew he was as pale as the stranger now. He groped for

reassuring reasons for the man's behavior... A joke? Some ridiculous gag dreamed up by his mates to freak him out? He dismissed the idea. His friends didn't have the imagination to come up with something like this.

So why was this happening to *him*? He'd never done anything to deserve this persecution. The only comforting thing he could think of was that if the man wanted to see a film, he was going to have to become a member, and to do that, he would have to do normal, mundane stuff like producing a driver's license and bank statement. Safe sort of things. Of course, he could already have joined when Jack wasn't working, but even then, he'd have to show his card, and Jack could fix something on him, like an address that would make the man just a customer and not a homicidal maniac.

"Do you think this might give me what I want?" the man waved *The Boogeyman* at Jack.

Jack steadied himself. *Get a grip, you prick.* "Depends what you're looking for, I suppose."

"I just told you what I'm looking for. Grotesque mutilation is all that will satisfy me. I'm looking for blood; I'm searching for guts."

Blood. His slug-black pupils were swollen like they were gorged with the stuff. *You're freaking yourself, Jack.*

His voice came out through a dry crack. "Well, you won't find much in that film." He was determined to keep some kind of customer-friendly slant to the conversation, to pretend he wasn't disturbed at all by the man's behavior. No way, no how. If he showed fear... The Video Shack had never seemed more like a fox hole than right now. He forced the bravado. "It's been cut, mate." *Wrong choice of words.*

"Cut?" The man might as well have slavered like a hound, he was that delighted as he closed on his prey. "Like a throat? Like an eyeball peeling before a razor?" A grim smile. "No, you mean censored, don't you? Our sanity and senses protected by moral guardians. The butchery butchered. And that's a sad irony because I'm in the mood for a little dismemberment right now. I need inspiration."

Jack looked away quickly. The man's eyes were so dark as to be impenetrable. If the man was playing, there was absolutely no way of telling. "Never mind," the stranger continued, "How's about..." He trawled along the horror section near the till and came up with a find. "This one?" He held it up for Jack. *The Mutilator.* The cover showed some backwoods retard wielding a bloody big axe.

"Nice title, don't you think? Just rolls off the tongue."

"This is a wind-up, isn't it? Either that, or you've got a serious problem." *So much for the pretense of normal customer service.* The words were meant to be bold, but Jack's voice carried an embarrassing wavering note that spoiled the illusion.

The pumpkin grin vanished. The long face tautened like a whip before the crack. Silence for a fistful of sweaty seconds while Jack swallowed dryly.

"Does it look like I've got a problem? Don't I look perfectly in control to you?" He pushed *The Mutilator* across the counter toward Jack. *By pick, by axe, by chainsaw … Bye, bye,* the cover blared luridly at him. Jack glanced at the misanthropic hillbilly straddling the tagline and went right off the film. He'd watched it twice himself and thoroughly enjoyed it—horror films were the reason he'd chosen to work here, after all. He got to see all the latest releases free-of-charge. But he'd suddenly lost his taste for this one.

He turned his attention toward the computer sitting on the counter before him and nudged the pad on the keyboard in an attempt to defuse the situation. The customer index file flickered up on the screen. "Are you a member?" he asked with reasonable calmness. "If you want a video—mind-bendingly repulsive or otherwise—you need to be a member."

The stranger didn't answer. Jack looked up, and the man nodded once, slowly. *Progress of a sort?* "So, what's your name?"

Nothing. Jack drummed his fingers nervously on the keyboard, but he wasn't going to look up again. He could wait here all day, if it came to it. He was being paid to sit here.

"Bane," the dark man said finally, and his smile would have given a crocodile bad dreams. Jack looked up. He could see his own pale, lugubrious face echoed in the stranger's bulging pupils. He snatched himself back from the brink and punched the name into the computer. A response leaped up instantly: MISTER BANE, THE SLAUGHTER INN, BUCKINGHAM ROAD, BRISTOL.

Jack blinked stupidly at the entry. Maybe it *was* all a gag, after all. But if it wasn't his mates pulling this stunt, then what about Mary? Mary being the blonde Video Vault worker *Jack* had been trying to pull for the last year. The Slaughter Inn, for Christ's sake. *Mister* Bane, the man with no Christian name. Everyone had to give their Christian name. It was library policy. No exceptions. So, this *was* just a prank, after all. Of course, it was. Hilarious. He should have been annoyed, but the relief felt too good. Mary, bless her. He smiled at the dark man with confidence for the first time. Where did she find *this* geezer? He had to admit he'd fallen for it brilliantly, what with the horror-video angle and the sicko in search of a macabre fix and everything. If Mary hadn't made the joke too obvious with the Slaughter Inn gag, he'd never have cottoned on.

Except as he beamed foolishly at the dark man, he suddenly knew it *wasn't* a joke. No way, no how. Which just made the whole thing grotesque. Ghoulish.

As if reading his thoughts, the stranger pulled a pack of Death cigarettes from his coat pocket and lit one.

"I live just down the road from you. Isn't that nice and cozy?"

For a moment of pure panic, Jack was sure the man knew where he lived. Then he realized the stranger must be talking about the video shop. Buckingham Road was indeed just down the road from here. But as Jack lived roughly opposite the shop, it didn't make a whole load of difference.

"I...never heard of it," he stammered. The *Slaughter* Inn. *Jesus.* He pulled himself together and rummaged through the A–Z drawer of tapes behind the counter, found what he was looking for, and stuffed *The Mutilator* cassette into the plain plastic customer box with *Video Vault* emblazoned on it, and then pushed this across the counter to the man. The sooner he got what he wanted, the sooner he would go. Hopefully.

The man sucked hard on his Death cigarette, which was as black as his hair, and tossed three pound coins down beside the film. He scooped up the box and turned to leave. *He's going*, thought Jack, feeling like he was ten years old again and morning was coming after a long, scary night. But the stranger *wasn't* going. Not yet, anyway. He stopped halfway down the aisle and turned his unnaturally dark eyes on Jack once more.

"Tonight's Opening Night," he said, flashing Jack a farewell rictus grin. He bent his head slightly as he strode toward the door, and his boots clicked hollowly on the wooden floor.

CHAPTER TWO

Neighbours was just finishing when Dennis announced his return to the flat with the usual demonstrative slam of the door. Jack twitched awake in his black plastic armchair, the one he'd rolled a mile from where he'd found it sitting in the rain outside a house on Ravenscourt Road. Why? Because he'd fallen in love with it on sight. And he was way too tight to buy a new one. He yawned with a mixture of relief and irritation. Irritation because he'd fallen asleep in front of *Neighbours* again, and relief that Dennis was home so he could discuss the day's bizarre events with him.

"I keep telling you... This shit cheeses your brain," Dennis grunted, flopping onto the threadbare sofa and looking more than a little aggrieved that he'd missed it himself.

"I like to keep tabs on reality," Jack told him.

Dennis began to roll a cigarette, bored with the conversation already. He was a funny-looking bastard, and Jack never tired of telling him so. Although the electrician was only twenty-nine, he already had the face of a world-bitten East End villain from the 50s. His small eyes glinted only occasionally now with a fading memory of their former juvenile mischief. More often these days, they were cloaked with cynical bitterness. Back in his adolescent days, when he had something to prove, mainly that he wasn't a prick despite his name, he changed his hair color from week to week, and often he would have to bend low to get his comical spiky coiffure through doorways. That was the Dennis Jack always looked for and very rarely found of late: the manic, dare-all, bumbling rebel without a clue who was always there for his mates and always got them in trouble. In the last decade, he'd wised up, cropped his hair, and lost the joke. Now he looked like his Dad, Dennis Senior, who was also an electrician and who also resembled one of the Krays' bodyguards, but without the bitterness. Dennis's old man was a jolly, innocent soul; Dennis was dangerous.

Jack watched the Six O'Clock News for a while. Dennis said nothing. Jack guessed his old friend was already plotting some new adventure that would take him off and out of himself to some distant haven for a short period and then return him here again, more cynical and disappointed with life than ever. Four years ago, Dennis had done what Laurel and Hardy had done to more amusing effect before him and ran off to join the Foreign Legion. Ran, as in chased. The police wanted to chat with him about certain things. Petty things, on the whole. Nicked car stereos, the odd bit of B & E. Oh, and, of course, his girl had left him. The clichés made the man, but Jack wondered if he might not have done the same himself if a girl like Sam had dropped *him*.

Dennis had left his family, his friends, and his drugs far behind to find himself caught up in a nightmare of his own making. Wild adolescence had received a good kicking, and a bitter man had emerged on the other side. During the first week in the Legion, he spent every night tied up in a closet with a pair of soiled Y-Fronts for a gag as part of some disgusting initiation ceremony. Seven nights breathing in someone else's shit. *What was that like, Dennis?* Jack had often wondered. Unsurprisingly, it wasn't Dennis's favorite topic of conversation. No wonder he was a different person from the naïve, boisterous clown he used to be back in the good old carefree days. "I'll tell you one thing the Legion did for me," he once said in a matter-of-fact tone: "I'll never be scared of anything again." Jack rather envied him that quality, if nothing else.

After a year or so, Dennis found himself promoted and in charge of a tank unit ordering the shelling that obliterated a nest of Iraqi snipers in the Mother of all Wars, and he became the recipient of a Legion d'Honneur as a result. He'd come back on leave a hero. Jack always thought that was quite strange, really, when he remembered the drunken wreck Sam had turned him into by giving him the elbow a few weeks before he took off for Tangiers. They used to use him as a doorstop down at the Crown. You'd always find him lying on the floor at the end of the night (and often at the beginning) with a bottle of Famous Grouse clasped in his paw. So he came back a hero, and suddenly the sun shone where he shat. He didn't like to talk about his heroics, and Jack respected him for that. It's funny what they gave you medals for, and Dennis obviously thought so, too; he deserted while on a tour of Canada a few months later.

"Fancy going out tonight?" Jack asked his flatmate. A strange excitement had seized him ever since the dark man left the video library. His uneasiness only intensified it.

"*Coronation Street*'s on," Dennis answered without apparent irony.

"There's a new pub opening tonight in Buckingham Road. Sounds interesting." Jack stared at the *Clockwork Orange* poster on the wall above the TV, and the anticipation was thick in his belly like hot soup.

Dennis nodded wisely and puffed on his rolly[1]. Anna Ford told them about rape in Paisley and tins of dog food laced with arsenic placed in many chains of a well-known supermarket.

Jack flicked the channels with the remote control—*Batman*, *The Addams Family*, *Home and Away*—then flicked back to Anna. Baroness Thatcher was shaking hands with Jimmy Saville. "Something pretty scary happened today..." Jack trailed off. It wasn't that interesting to anyone but himself, really, as evidenced by Dennis's total lack of response. Saville's face filled the TV screen. "Twisted bastard tried to put the frighteners on me," he continued regardless. "And then invited me to his pub's opening night." He mimicked Saville's creepy voice. "'Ow's about that, then? And wait 'til you hear the name of the place..." Dennis gave all the signs of being able to wait a very long time, so Jack put him out of his misery: "The Slaughter Inn. Crazy, eh?"

Dennis turned his head slowly to look at him, then turned back to the television. Jack's pulse was quickening just from saying it aloud. Alex the Droog met his gaze from the poster on the wall. One eye winked at him, laden with false eyelashes.

"Just as long as it's dangerous," Dennis mumbled around his roll-up. "I need some danger tonight. I need reminding I'm still alive, now and again." Which sounded pretty funny when he'd just been looking forward to *Coronation Street*. He exhaled smoke at the TV screen, obscuring a particularly hideous political correspondent. "And as long as there's women. I don't care what sort, just as long

---

[1] Hand-rolled cigarette

as there's some sort."

"You never know your luck, Dennis; Sam might even turn up."

Dennis yawned to show his huge indifference to the subject of his ex. "Better make sure I get into a beery mess, then; I wouldn't want her to think I'm getting all civilized these days."

While Dennis lumbered about in the bath, Jack made a couple of phone calls. The night was definitely beginning to sound promising; Joe was free from delivering pizzas that evening and would see them there, so Jack wouldn't have to cope with Dennis alone. He thought of ringing Nigel but decided he wanted to enjoy himself for once. So he phoned Sam instead, after first making sure Dennis couldn't hear a thing; the ex-Legionnaire didn't take much provoking these days.

Sam was doe-eyed, svelte, possessed the most luscious mouth in the known universe, as well as mahogany curls that ivied down around her small, perfectly shaped face. Along with Mary from the Video Vault, she was the most eminently desirable female Jack had never gone out with. He'd kissed Sam once at a Christmas party when Dennis was unconscious in the toilet, and he'd remembered the taste of her ever since. She'd made it quite plain the next day that it was a drunken kiss only and gave him the "just a friend" speech. But he'd never given up hoping. She'd dumped Dennis when she realized he was an electrician with an attitude and was never going to change, and there was no reason why a video clerk should have any better luck. But he would never give up, even if Dennis had wisely seemed to do just that long ago. She was dating a property developer these days. Jack hoped she wouldn't bring him along tonight.

"Oh, it's you, Jack," her voice purred along the line.

Don't sound so thrilled, he thought, but batted on regardless. Yes, she agreed finally, she would come: The Slaughter Inn sounded pretty off the wall. She asked Jack if he minded her bringing Thomas ("My name's Thomas, *not* Tom") along, too. "Of course not," Jack answered in a strangled voice. The telephone went dead to her husky Honor Blackman farewell.

He took his place in the bathroom. Dennis had left him a gift. No, he'd been more than generous and left him two: one unflushed in the toilet bowl that greeted Jack as he lifted the lid to take a leak, and another made of pubic hairs forming a nest in the bath as he stepped in to take a shower. He whizzed the wiry hairs along the bottom of the bath and down the drain with the shower head, then turned the lukewarm jet on himself, the water becoming rapidly colder with each second, just so he wouldn't forget Dennis's third gift.

He wiped the steam from the mirror and examined himself as he toweled his body. *Hey, good lookin'.* Well, almost, if you were *especially* forgiving, as his mother used to say in her tired way. It was the closest she'd ever come to joking with him, and with the memory came a sense of wry pain. But she was right; his face was a little too long and his nose a little too large for him to win many beauty contests, but hell, it showed character, didn't it? Maybe a dash of gaunt attractiveness if he held his head at a certain angle. His brown eyes held a slightly lost look. "Is that acid casualty with the bewildered hair a friend of yours?" a female wit once asked Dennis in a pub. His flatmate had taken particular delight in repeating *that* one to anyone who would listen for the next six months.

Jack entered his bedroom and began drying his hair. Whenever he tried to impose a style onto it, he failed miserably. Its natural state was a brambly anarchy, and short of cropping it completely, there was no way of getting around that fact. He reached into the wardrobe and chose his favorite shirt—a black, silky number fraying slightly at the cuffs and collars from overuse—and pulled on a clean pair of crisp black jeans. He made an abortive effort to brush some order into his hair and gave up when it looked worse than before he'd started.

"Hurry up, ladyboy," Dennis hollered from the hallway, already opening the door to the flat.

Jack shouldered his way into his leather jacket, hunching it around until it felt good. He patted the twenty quid note stuffed in his back pocket and joined his friend at the door. Dennis looked him over with undisguised amusement, a roll-up jammed between his lips. He was dressed in his usual casual get-up of brown suede jacket and faded blue jeans. "Where d'you think *you're* going? The High School Prom?"

"If I am, I don't think much of my date." He was ready.

For the Slaughter.

The phrase repeated itself inside his head as he strode down Southley Road and turned onto Buckingham, while Dennis stomped moodily along at his side.

CHAPTER THREE

Thomas arrived early. It was an annoying habit of his. No, strike that; it was one of many annoying habits. Sam hadn't finished applying her make-up, and she did not want to have to do it while he prowled around her small flat, distracting her with inane comments like: "Still slapping the cement on, Samantha?" She *hated* being called Samantha. He only called her that when he was in an irritable mood. Well, that made two of them now.

"Why don't you make yourself a coffee and watch telly for a bit." She knew that would get him; he hated waiting.

His expression clearly showed what he thought of that idea. "You said you'd be ready by eight," he said reproachfully.

"It's only ten to. Sit in the lounge and stop panting down my neck." She watched his reflection in the dressing table mirror. He was rooted behind her now, staring at her back, and it didn't look like he was going to shift. "Please?" He wavered, hands in the trouser pockets of his Armani suit. It *had* to be Armani. Thomas never liked to disappoint in the unoriginality stakes. He was almost at the door when he turned back.

"Are you sure you want to go to this pub?" he said, leaning against the bedroom door jamb.

Sam sighed and put her eye pencil down. He wasn't going to give her any peace. "Of course. It sounds a laugh."

"It sounds like torment. It'll be full of ugly people with bare armpits and music to make your head bleed."

She regretted asking him along now, but who the hell else could she have turned to? Her best friend Sue was out with her boyfriend (as usual), and she couldn't go on her own. No, she had to drag Thomas with her, if only to spite Dennis and show Jack she always had *some-one* on her arm. But that suit...

"Couldn't you have come more casually dressed? How many times have I told you to loosen up? There'll be nobody there *you'll* want to impress."

"I *am* loosened up. And I don't need to impress anybody. I just like to look good. What's wrong with that?"

"You'll look stupid." She picked up her lipstick and tried to dismiss her irritation. It was a hard job. She could see it staring back at her in the mirror. There must have been a time when he didn't annoy her, but she'd be damned if she could remember when that was. But she only had herself to blame. What did it say about her that she needed to go out with people like Thomas? Self-centered high achievers who liked control. Did it make her feel in control, too, to run with the ruthless executive set, when all she would ever be to them was just another asset? Is that what she really wanted?

He was fidgeting with the door handle now, pushing it down and allowing it to spring back up again noisily with the impatience of all greedy people. He obviously had something on his mind. She could wait.

"When are you going to grow out of them, Samantha?" he said after a pause.

She put down her lipstick. There it was. It had been a long time coming, but it was something between them they both knew was there, although neither had openly acknowledged the fact before. It had been gnawing away at him ever since he met her. Now, at last, he was letting it out. She turned around, and he was pouting sulkily the way he always did when he didn't get what he wanted. His swept-back, pure Gecko hairstyle had a little too much Brylcreem, his eyes were a little *too* sweet, his chin a little too infirm, she thought, and wondered why it had taken her so long to see it, or so long to admit it. Tonight, she could see him naked and it wasn't as appealing as it used to be. He was a selfish little boy, and she was growing tired of little boys.

He waited for her to respond. When she didn't, he pushed on regardless: "I mean, they're not exactly your type, are they? They've got no style. No class."

She considered stopping him right there but decided to let him run on, have his little say. Then she could have hers.

"I mean, what *are* they exactly? An electrician with a criminal record, a rental clerk who gets off on video nasties...and a pizza delivery man, for Christ's sake! Worse, a pizza delivery man who thinks he's Brian fucking Jones. It's as if they're all competing to see who has the worst job. You should have moved on, Sam. You really should. A long time ago. You're just clinging to them from some deluded sense of—I really don't know what—surely not loyalty? It's embarrassing. They probably despise you anyway for trying to improve yourself. They're really not your problem anymore. You've got new friends, a different set. Let them go."

She crossed her arms, her face expressionless. "All done?"

He shrugged, but she noticed he couldn't look her in the eye. He had been compelled to say it, she could see that, and now that he *had* said it, she could suddenly see just how big the block really was he carried on his shoulder.

"They threaten you, don't they?"

He met her eyes; they were small, bewildered, and, yes, a little afraid. He put on a complacent grin. "Yeah, hell, I just can't compete..."

"That's just it; they worry you because *they* don't *have* to compete. They don't think a fat salary and a fast car are that big a deal, and that really *bothers* you, doesn't it? That sort of undermines everything you believe in." She got up, and she was feeling good for the first time in... Yes, she was feeling—what? Clean. She eased into her black suede jacket. "And you're wrong. They might be beer-guzzling slobs, they might never be achievers, and they might not speak with the right accents, but they'll *always* have class. It's something you wouldn't understand. Now, take me to the ball; we're late."

She swept past him down the short hallway to the door of her flat. He stayed where he was for a minute, digesting everything she'd said. She looked at him quizzically and realized she didn't have to worry about rushing back before midnight; the pumpkin had already appeared, and she was taking him with her.

CHAPTER FOUR

Fiery leaves dropped from the oaks guarding either side of the Inn. It had been a small hotel, but now, in its new incarnation, it made for an impressively sized pub. Eight bay windows faced the busy Buckingham Road. Only those on the ground floor were lit, and lit in a particularly eerie fashion, splashing blood-red glare onto the pavement where Jack and Dennis stood gaping.

The building had undergone quite a transformation since the last time they had strolled this way, back in the warm vacancy of early summer. Then it had sulked forlornly behind For Sale signs, boarded windows, and a bad case of peeling paint eczema. The ivy that crept over the walls had looked incongruous and scruffy; now, tamed and burning with autumn glory, it contributed elegantly to the gothic facade the building had assumed under its new ownership. Once-flaking shutters newly excavated from the ivy were painted black along with the rest of the exterior; Victorian lanterns swung from the eaves; a brass wolf's head knocker snarled from the heavy oak door. The red paint on the door gave it the look of a wound cut into the dark flesh of the Inn. It should have looked tacky, but somehow it worked. The entire building was one big Halloween trick.

Music beckoned to them to step in out of the late September chill. It didn't tempt many other passersby, who glanced timorously or disdainfully in the direction of the skull-bludgeoning row that scared the leaves from the trees and promised a crowd of dubious character

"

beyond the Victorian bay windows. Dennis perceptibly brightened at the raucous sounds, but Jack was more fascinated by the wooden pub sign hanging above the door.

THE SLAUGHTER INN was splattered in deformed red letters that twisted in and out of the hollow eye sockets of a skull perched on top of a pint glass. The contents of the glass were red, too, while more blood oozed from between the skull's jaws, down the side of the glass, and onto the table beneath. A grisly company of rogues hunched on stools around the table.

"A nice family pub, then," Dennis said brightly. Jack nodded approvingly. He was transfixed. His gaze crept from the sign to the bold white letters set above the entrance to the pub: BANE, LICENSED TO SELL BEERS, WINES, AND SPIRITS. The Man with No Christian Name—the initial had either fallen or been taken away, and had Jack really believed the dark man would be anything other than the landlord?

Dennis indicated the garishly illustrated villains on the sign. "You should feel right at home, Jack."

"So, what are we waiting for?" Jack's excitement was a wild thing, spreading through him like burning radiation.

The music hit them hard as they pushed their way into the bloody gloom. Scarlet lights glowed through banks of dry ice that swirled and prowled around the large interior, swallowing tables packed with revelers, then crawling eagerly on in search of fresh prey. Jack and Dennis posed stupidly in the doorway. Whatever they had expected, it wasn't this.

"We just walked into the London Dungeon, mate."

Dennis wasn't exaggerating. Jack could only stand there with his mouth open, a child at Christmas gaping at a heap of presents underneath the tree, and think: hold this moment and frame it. He had walked into a dark, delicious dream. While Dennis scraped at the imitation cobweb that clung to his face with some irritation, Jack wanted to applaud. He wanted to shout. He almost wanted to cry.

It was like entering a bizarre gothic cave. The red lighting splashed on folds and buttresses of fiberglass rock. Tables nestled in cobwebby nooks and crevices where lovers flirted over foaming candles; small TV screens were embedded in the faux cave walls at various positions, soundlessly relaying dodgy horror movies to anyone inclined to watch them, rarities, too—Jack spotted *At Midnight I'll Steal Your Soul* and *Devil Story* flickering in a couple of dark crannies and could only admire Bane's taste. Many of the pub's customers were marveling, too, hardly believing their eyes as they followed the onscreen carnage and obscenity.

A stage was built opposite the entrance: microphones shrouded in cobwebs, a couple of leaning guitars and a drum kit, cymbals drenched in gore under the scarlet lights. Skeletons in gibbets hung on walls or drooped from the low, cave-like ceiling; a hooded executioner lurked in a corner, axe up for a permanently delayed chop; Jack the Ripper leaned over a table, seemingly chatting to a couple of spike-haired female Goths, his eyes wicked wax, lusty blade poised above their smiles. The bar stretched along the wall to the right of the stage, crafted to look like one super long teak coffin, complete with brass handles. Two gruesome bouncers guarded the bar: Frankenstein's Monster (the Karloff version, of course), arms outstretched, frozen mid-lurch in a pool of green light, and Chaney's Wolfman crouching over a torn woman of wax.

"It's different, I suppose," Dennis barked over the horror punk screaming from the speakers. They headed for the bar, Jack expecting his alarm clock to pluck him rudely from sleep with every step. Passing a cave mouth that yawned beside a table of bright young students, he almost leaped into Dennis's arms when a lull in the canned music allowed a gurgling roar to burst from the dark hole. Dennis grinned, but the sound effect had momentarily made him lose his cool as well. Jack glimpsed the flare of panic in his eyes with something like satisfaction.

Mary Shelley's creature groped for them as they leaned on the bar and waited to be served. Dennis eyed the monster dubiously, but his enthusiasm cranked up a few notches when he caught sight of the seven Real Ale hand pulls bristling along the bar top. All were equipped with gleefully morbid names and designs on their oval labels. There was The Impaler, Spot of Gore, and Cannibal's Sup, amongst others. Dennis went for Old Corpse when he realized after patient scrutiny of all seven beers that it came up trumps on the OG score. Jack plumped for a pint of Zombie's Bite and realized with a stab of pleasure that the raven-haired barmaid, clad in a Morticia body stocking, was staring at him intensely.

He found himself blushing under her gaze. She flashed him a smile that could take him down whole, boots and all, watched him carefully as she pulled his pint. He smiled back, refusing to be abashed. Her eyes were a crafty green, and Jack sensed mayhem lurking in their depths. No, more than mayhem: cruelty. Her arrogant nose added to the impression, while morbidly hollowed cheekbones accentuated the skull beneath the white flesh. The tattoo above her left breast made her cleavage sinister, dirty, and irresistibly desirable: a crow perched on a bloody skull.

Dennis was also eyeing the tattoo. The woman ignored him, her attention riveted on Jack like a blackbird sizing up a worm. His confidence began to leak. Her intensity reminded him too much of —

"Where's the Landlord?" he blurted, more to dissipate the tension than from any genuine desire to know. He certainly didn't want to see Bane again in a hurry. Who was he kidding? Of *course,* he did— Bane fascinated him. Like most dangerous things, the dark man possessed an unhealthy appeal, like walking right to the very edge of a precipice and leaning over.

Jack scanned the bar. The rest of the staff consisted of a dumpy skinhead girl and a ponytailed biker in his forties. Bane, however, was conspicuous by his absence.

"What's it to you?" Morticia gave him an adder smile.

Jack reddened. "I...just wanted to know if he...liked the film he rented." Beyond lame.

"You work in the Video Vault." It wasn't a question. She knew. He felt flattered and disturbed in equal measure, and, as her eyes continued to nail him, a little turned on. Make that a *lot.*

"Bane came in this morning," he muttered. Where was this stilted conversation supposed to be going? He felt like a fake, talking about Bane as if the man was a great mate instead of the creepy stranger who had completely freaked him out earlier.

He plunged on regardless. "He told me about this place. I guess he invited me." *As if he'd known I would be hooked, unable to resist.* The thought dove on him from nowhere.

"How nice for you." She turned away to serve a couple of bikers, leaving Jack both deflated and anxious without knowing why. He was determined to put the barmaid to the back of his mind, so he concentrated on sipping his pint. Dennis shrugged at him, looking just a little peeved that he hadn't been included in the conversation. He was usually the one the girls chose to speak to, after all. He could charm, when he wanted to. Put on his Devil-may-care guise and let them come. How else had he ever won Sam?

Joe appeared out of the drifting dry ice. His large, inscrutable eyes homed in on the two flatmates. His helmet of blond hair flopped around his face in a fair imitation of the Stones' Brian Jones. He was wearing a ridiculously rumpled Paisley shirt riddled with cigarette burns and splodged with old beer stains. He was only five foot four, and his shapeless overcoat trailed around his old army boots. He rarely smiled, and he didn't do so now as he greeted his two friends.

"Pepperoni and Mushroom, no garlic bread," Dennis welcomed him dryly.

"Let's have a go on yer phone, mate," Joe replied with equal dryness. The lines were the same verbal routines that always played out between the two, and while they had long ago ceased to be funny (had they ever been?), they were nevertheless an essential introduction to any evening's drinking where Joe was concerned. It was pure ritual and meant that everything was right in the world. Joe drove a custard-yellow Fiesta with *Luigi's Pizzas* emblazoned on the doors and bonnet. The car also sported a giant glow-in-the-dark plastic telephone on its roof. Joe was constantly being assailed with requests by abusive teens to use the silly phone as he drove through the city. Dennis and Jack often joked that "Let's have a go yer phone mate" would make a great epitaph for Joe.

"Just up your street, eh, Jack?" Joe surveyed the pub impassively. He didn't seem at all impressed by the theatrical surroundings. He wore stoicism like a charm; it shielded him from an uncaring world and steered him admirably along his odd path in life. It would take a lot to fluster Joe or to move him to any degree of emotion, for that matter.

Jack nodded at his friend. "The chickens have come home to roost," he said and blinked stupidly.

Joe nodded back with piss-taking complicity while Dennis spluttered over his Old Corpse. "And what the fuck is that supposed to mean?"

"I'm not sure," replied Jack truthfully and blushed.

Joe coughed as a wave of dry ice enveloped him. "Gives you cancer, this stuff," he said, rolling a cigarette, his pint perched on the wax breasts of the Wolfman's victim.

Sam arrived, and heads turned in her wake. The Property Developer scowled behind her. Dennis bared his teeth and downed his pint in one noisy gulp. He lurched off to the bar to get another round. Sam looked exquisite in her suede jacket and tight 501s, but then she would have looked exquisite in a boiler suit; it was something she really couldn't help. Jack smiled at her, and she smiled back. Thomas, her fashion accessory, also smiled, with all the practiced integrity of a store dummy. The smile sank a little as he offered it to Joe and received a stonewall stare in response. Gamely, he tried to salvage his self-image as a popular social animal by attempting to engage Joe in a male-bonding conversation involving cars and football. Joe gazed back deadpan as the young property developer waxed lyrical about the performance of Bristol City away against Burnley, his fifty-pound haircut glistening with little beads of sweat as it became increasingly apparent from Joe's silence that he was beyond bonding. Joe waited patiently for a punchline. When it didn't come, he carried on staring, expressionless. Sam looked embarrassed.

"Hello, Jack," she said, turning away from the awkward scene.

"Hello, Sam," he said back. They stopped there. He sensed she was going to describe her trying day at the insurance office and suddenly realized that he didn't want to hear it tonight. This came as something of a shock. Normally, he hung on her every word, not so much out of interest in what she was saying, but simply to enjoy the closeness to her that conversation brought, her luscious lips forming words just for him. Right now, his attention was drifting already, and it struck him that he hadn't tucked Morticia away at the back of his mind after all. Not at all; she was just behind his eyes, splendid bust revealing its morbid tattoo in the privacy of his own head. He suddenly envied Dennis, who was still at the bar, and turned to follow his progress. He was glad to see his friend was being served by the biker with the ponytail. Morticia was dealing with a couple of female students; he knew they were students from their affectations of poverty, which came equipped with Doc Martins, ripped jeans, and £10,000-a-term schooling. He turned back as he realized Sam was talking to him, raising her voice over a sudden resurgence of canned noise.

He experienced a pang of guilt when he saw the slight hurt in her green eyes. Green eyes, yes, but a safe, calm green, unlike the snaky guile of the barmaid's. He tried to focus on what she was saying. What the hell *was* she saying? Oh yeah: work. Her boss was all hands and slobberings. *Think I've heard this one before, Sam, but I love you anyway.* He nodded for her to continue, a nagging voice in his head asking why he *should* bother listening anymore; she never showed him the favors he really wanted. The thought shamed him but stayed with him nevertheless.

Joe was still staring dully at Thomas, the property dummy. The poor yuppie was drowning helplessly in his own words. All conversation seemed superfluous with Joe. The pizza delivery man dragged on his cigarette, his gaze inexorably drawn to the chunky mobile phone peeking out of the developer's breast pocket. Jack waited for the inevitable and wasn't to be disappointed: Joe interrupted the developer in mid-gush, "Let's 'ave a go on yer phone, mate," and Jack could relax, able to return his wandering attention to Sam again. Her lovely puffed lips were still twisting in disgust as she described Boss Blubber's attempts at touching up her friend Sue behind the filing cabinets.

"I see Sam's keeping everyone riveted as usual," Dennis butted in, three pints squeezed between his hands. His tone was nasty, as nasty as the music bursting from the speakers, and Jack sent him a look of repudiation that bounced right off the electrician's thick hide. The trouble was, Dennis was right; Jack couldn't focus on Sam tonight, and thanks to Dennis's callous remark, he couldn't even look her in the eye now. *You invited her, you look after her.* But she had Thomas for that, didn't she? She certainly didn't need Jack.

Dennis slurped messily at his pint, playing the pig to maximum effect. The music belched literally to a stop, and Dennis's voice was loud in the relative quiet.

"I see you brought your new toy with you, Sammy, dear." He grinned at Thomas.

Sam ignored him—or tried to. She resisted for a whole ten seconds before biting back. "Actually, I've left all the really childish things behind me these days."

Dry ice shrouded them. Jack coughed and tried to step away from the pall. A figure loomed in front of him, blocking his way. Thick spectacles, a fat greasy head, the neck folded into the collar of his shirt like the thread of a screw. A flat face, with pin-prick eyes scarcely magnified by the heavy lenses. The man paused in the artificial fog, grotesquely incongruous amongst all the horror rock trappings in a shapeless brown suit. Then he heaved away into the mist, momentarily reappearing again at a table near the roaring cave, where he took a seat. With a jolt, Jack realized everyone at the table was looking in Jack's direction. He took a nervous sip of his pint. They were still watching him; the fat man and two young women with identical clothing, hair, and features. Twins. Jack liked them even less than he liked the fat man. There was something disturbing about their synchronized immobility as they stared, their blonde hair shoulder length, their faces insipidly pretty in a curiously unnerving way, their dresses black and somber. Dry ice hid them away, and then the show began.

The band came on.

Joe stared inscrutably. Sam pursed her lips, her eyes wide and a little worried. Thomas frowned. Dennis said, "Fuck," and Jack could only agree.

The "musicians" were beasts dragged from rock hell, and they didn't look pleased to be here. They were an outrage, an affront to peace of mind, dignity, and everything that is secretly cherished, even by the depraved. They weren't a rock band in any accepted sense of the term. They were anti-music, anti-optimism, anti-life. Decency fled like a ghost when the singer strode on stage. He was Dirty Harry mutating into a werewolf, hard stubble bursting from his chin, hair grubbed up and out in a shabby punk bouffant, while wraparound shades mercifully obscured his eyes. He wore leather jeans held up by a massive, spiked belt and a medieval codpiece; his naked arms were like white tree trunks diseased with tattoos. He was carrying an axe.

The singer stalked to the edge of the stage, scanning the pale faces upturned in the false mist. "I fuckin' hate your guts," he growled like a Grizzly through a gobful of blood, and everyone in the room knew he really meant it. The bassist took up his position to the left of the stage, an ogre with hands the size of most men's heads. The guitarist wore a tramp's top hat, the crown hanging loose on a shred of material like a hinged lid. His face was gaunt, nasty, scurvy with stubble. The drummer was behind his kit now; he looked like a dark-skinned terrorist in leathers, wearing biker boots that came up to his knees. The stink of the band was almost visible.

But the noise was worse.

Thomas tried to drag Sam away after the first obscenity of a number. She didn't want to go. Like Jack, Joe, Dennis, and most of the audience that had risen from their tables to cower before the stage, she was rooted. Something about these monsters connected. Jack felt the guitar riffs slink into his soul and paint it black.

The vocals carried a shameful hook that couldn't be dislodged. Bass and drums pumped up the adrenaline of fear. Jack could see it in Sam's eyes. He could feel it in the shudder of revolted delight roller-coasting down his spine. Bad things popped into his head and wouldn't go; things he'd tried to shut away, things he'd believed hidden for good. Now they were out and frolicking gleefully in his mind.

He was thinking of his parents; what they had done to him. What he could do to them. What he could *do* to them... He was thinking of hate in a way he'd never thought of it before. And it was liberating, glorious. He rolled the thought around in his head, letting it gain momentum. Evil could be good if you just let it out. Let it have its say.

"Good God, Sam, let's go!" Thomas gasped after the third number. There was something like true panic in his eyes. Jack had seen that look before. It was the green rottenness of inner terror splashed across the face of an acquaintance he'd once introduced to the delights of magic mushrooms. Naked, private horror; the sort that lurks in those nasty places in the dark of ourselves that should never be shared. Sam's boyfriend wanted out. Jack didn't try to stop him.

Thomas looked back once to see if Sam was coming with him. Her eyes were following the singer, her lips slightly parted. He made as if to say something, but he had to go. The dry ice snatched him before he made five yards.

The singer swung his axe in a vicious arc. "The ultimate weapon," he snarled. The band lurched into an atrocity ballad with lyrics eulogizing hate and nihilism. And Jack suddenly felt nauseous. He swayed, almost passing out, and Sam put out a hand to support him. He stared into her eyes, and there was fear there, too. Perversely, it eased his own panic. He clutched her hand as if for salvation and soon was breathing calmly again. The insecurity was beginning to fade from her own eyes, and he would have kissed her then, oblivious to the consequences: her discomfort, perhaps; Dennis's resentment, certainly. He would have kissed those slightly parted lips and held her lithe figure and everything might have been all right.

But as he moved closer to her, he noticed a figure behind the bar, hollowed eyes fixed on him. *That's the last time you'll feel this way*, a voice slithered in his mind. *The last time you'll want HER.* The same mocking smile played on the barmaid's lips, and she undulated slightly to the repellent music, a vile, sexy cobra.

The chickens have come home to roost, Jack.

That's the last time you'll ever want HER.

He snatched his gaze from her witch eyes. Across the room, he saw the twins were watching him, too.

The chickens have come home...

CHAPTER FIVE

The twins were watching him.

They found him fascinating—the conflict of self-confidence with self-consciousness expressed awkwardly by body language. The moods of the physical were something they understood well.

Sweat delineated the muscles on his slim torso, glistened in his belly button. He was obviously aware of their presence and was playing up to it in some macho, self-deceiving way. They enjoyed watching him strut along the scaffold planks, clenching his fists to pump up his muscles, then leaning oh so casually against a pole as if entirely oblivious to their presence in the school window five feet behind him.

They watched the sun work sweat from him, wondering how much more—sweat, and other things—*they* could wring from his body.

Behind them, their classmates were chatting quietly amongst themselves, also pretending to be oblivious to the twins, but for very different reasons. They had learned the hard way. Free study period was the most dangerous time, when the small class was left untutored to its own devices for an hour. It was an hour of dread, unimagined by parents, unheeded by teachers. The sort of black, consuming dread experienced first and most keenly in the classroom.

The twins, had they been just a little more sensitive, might have picked up on the wave of hate emanating from the subdued fifteen- and sixteen-year-olds. As it was, there was only one emotion they could sense, only one they were interested in.

They fear us.

It was like the power their father wielded: he bullied school governors, they bullied the children. Bullied? It was more calculated than that, more meaningful. They were playing with sensibilities here: shaping girls' lives. Because the twins knew instinctively that the girls they persecuted would bear the memories of their school years with them for the rest of their days. The twins could mark them forever. That was power. That was fear.

Fear hung in the classroom like stale perfume. Old fear. They had no time for that right now; they could smell *new* fear from the young building laborer on the scaffold planks outside the third-story window. This was a different fear; it was insecurity mixed with desire. Lust fear. They wanted to smell some more of that.

Charles Morton wiped his nose with the back of a grimy hand.

"You'll never make good laborers," he pronounced grandly, convinced he was consigning Mike and Will's futures to oblivion.

Mike, who, at twenty, was bursting with a voracious hunger for life, could only heartily concur. He leaned back against the wall of the wooden hut and munched his cheese and chutney sandwiches. Next to him, Will studied the opposite wall like a guilty schoolboy. Will was nineteen and, like Mike, was serving time on the building site during the summer break from college.

Morton's disgust was evident. Boys sent to do man's work. A bunch of tight, grubby curls hedged in the bald apex of his rugby ball head. His spectacles reflected the promise of bright daylight from the small window as he sat forward to emphasize his point, his belly easing out like blancmange[2] between his belt and the hem of his thick wool shirt. "Lazy bastards, afraid of work. I know your sort."

Will snorted over his sarnie[3]. Mike grinned broadly at the site foreman. "And what sort would that be?" He imitated Morton's thick West Country burr as he spoke, challenging the foreman with an open stare.

"Think you're better, don't ya? Fuckin' college boys playin' at workin' men's jobs. Spend three weeks on a building site pretendin' to be workin' class, and then run off back to college to finish your

---

2 The British equivalent to an American pudding or custard
3 British slang for a sandwich

dissertation. That's the fuckin' sort you are, sonny."

A dollop of ketchup dropped from Morton's egg sandwich onto his open-necked shirt. *Like a gout of blood,* thought Mike. He kept his eyes fixed on Morton's. The foreman hadn't finished yet. He hefted himself out of his plastic seat, which was ingrained, like the seat of his cords, with dried mud. He extended a finger the size of a Cumberland Porker[4] at Mike, his face flushed pink as undercooked bacon.

"A degree don't mean fat bollocks these days, my lad. It certainly don't mean a career. You'll end up on the dole heap with all the other lazy, whingin', lefty scroungers that's bleeding workin' men dry."

Mike sighed. "And here I was, hoping to turn out just like you."

Morton yanked open the door of the hut, and bright sunlight slipped in eagerly. His belly was heaving with anger. "Couple of chimneys need demolishing on the east wing. I want it done before four o'clock, or I'll be up there to kick your lazy ass off the scaffolding and all around the yard. Hear me, college boy?"

Mike was tempted to let him do just that, if only for the opportunity of seeing Morton put some effort into something for once, but wisely, he didn't say as much. Morton crashed down the two steps from the hut and swaggered off toward the scaffolding that tightly embraced the imposing private school for girls Vernon and Sons were contracted to renovate. Will stood up sheepishly and began to follow him. Mike took his own good time.

Up on the high roof of the east wing, Mike wielded his sledgehammer against the old brick chimney to devastating effect. He thought of Mucky Morton as he swung. He despised the foreman. He was everything Mike loathed about certain workers in the building trade; he was stupid, bigoted, sexist. And despite all his belly-heaving proclamations against Mike and Will, he was the laziest bastard ever to swagger onto a site. He loafed around, issuing guttural commands and cracking lewd jokes about the schoolgirls as they left the building to be collected by their wealthy parents. "I'd like to break that filly in," he'd chuckle as a fourteen-year-old stepped past, eyes downcast, an innocent glimmer of flesh revealed between skirt and stockings. When nobody laughed at his filth, he'd bark out aggression and extra duties for his long-suffering laborers. He always made a point of not venturing onto the high scaffolding, preferring to lumber around on ground level, more often than not slinking off to

---

[4] Pork sausage

the hut to "do some paperwork." Mike had often spied on the foreman in there, sharpening his intellect on *The Sun*. He wondered what effect would result from his blobby, middle-aged body pitching from the top scaffold. He imagined the blood would easily reach the little hut farther down the drive.

The sledgehammer pounded into old brick. Chips spun in the air. Half a brick separated from the stack to loop over the edge of the roof. Mike pulled the sledge back for another blow. Two more bricks exploded across the sloping slate roof. *Smash it up.* Mike grinned, began singing the punk anthem in time to the beat of his sledgehammer. *Ooo-ooh, smash it uuup!!* He was enjoying the anarchy of demolition. But five minutes of furious destruction later, his anarchic impulses began to tire, and he was looking for a break.

He leaped down from the edge of the roof to the scaffold planks a few feet below and leaned over the pole railing. The makeshift work yard far beneath him was a mess of skips, cement mixers, and grubby wheelbarrows. He could see Will returning from the temporary workmen's toilet box situated at a discrete distance from the select school. The sun tingled on the back of Mike's neck and arms. He peeled off his T-shirt and draped it over the rail, ruffled his mop of peroxide blond hair back into shape, and turned to make his way down the ladder toward the ground.

As he reached the third floor, he paused as he often did. A window overlooking the scaffold platform on this level opened onto a classroom usually packed with post-pubescent schoolgirls. He sucked in his slightly paunchy stomach and stepped onto the planks, posing with mock nonchalance as he strode past the window. He glanced casually inside.

The classroom contained about fifteen girls. Only two were looking at him. They were sitting beside each other on chairs near the window, identical pairs of blue eyes regarding him from identical oval faces. A shiver of unreality surfed through him; two attractive, well-developed blonde clones were smiling subversively suggestive smiles at him. Twins. He blushed a little under their unflinching gaze. They let their eyes rove over his slim body, which, although not exactly bronzed, had benefited somewhat from two weeks laboring, often shirtless, under a hot June sun.

Mike had to look away eventually, as they didn't appear to be inclined to do so. A sheepish grin spread over his smooth features. They looked sixteen at least, their white school blouses pushed forward by the well-defined bulges beneath. He felt the crotch of his jeans push forward in appreciation. *They're schoolgirls*, he chided himself and walked on, past the window to the end of the scaffold planks. So what? He was only twenty himself. Despite his excitement, he paused at the corner of the building, reluctant to pass the window again. Their stares had been disconcerting as well as teasing. He'd felt they were looking beneath his skin, dissecting him almost. Still, they were horny as hell. He'd have to go past the window again to reach the ladder, but this time he wouldn't look in at them. He had to keep some cool.

He looked in as he passed the window. The twins had disappeared. Feeling a little deflated, he swung onto the ladder and descended to the ground.

The twins were in the toilet. They had taken Sally Davis with them and weren't going to let her out until they had worked off some of their frustration.

She was pleading with them pitifully now. She knew what they were capable of, and as a result, she had lost all her dignity, all her daintiness.

"Please let me go. I wasn't looking at him. *I wasn't.*" A vicious belly punch snatched her voice away. She stumbled into one of the stalls, sprawling on moist tiles.

"Scream a little louder," ordered one twin. Sally stared up into the beautiful, impassive mask leaning over her, trying to second-guess her tormentor. She scrabbled on her knees, her back against the toilet.

"Scream," hissed the other twin. Her eyes were sharp and blue as broken pottery.

"*Why* were you looking at him?" The first twin pushed Sally's head back until it banged on the toilet pipe. "What was going through your mind when you looked at him? What did you want to *do*?"

"I wasn't...wasn't looking at him. Please." She broke off into sobs, head lowered, not daring to meet their eyes.

"Shall we show you what you wanted to do to him?" Sally was no longer sure which twin was speaking; she had never been entirely sure of their identities over the whole year she had known them.

Now they were two implacable instruments of torture blending to make a single terrifying entity of pain and evil. And they *were* evil. She had heard what happened to the girls they took into the toilets. She had seen the victims afterward. The shocked, raped look of them. The *lost* look of them. It had always chilled her. The way everyone was too terrified to breathe a word about the outrages the twins performed on their classmates. Except for Sheila the Skunk, of course.

The thought of Sheila made Sally shake uncontrollably. Why hadn't anything been done? Why hadn't anything ever been *done*?

"Shall we?" The twin to her left speaking, her lips shiny with lust. "Shall we do the things you wanted to do to that boy but were too scared? I think we should." Her cultured voice was low, almost guttural with excitement. While one twin held Sally, the other tore at her clothing, and something glinted in her hand. Sally tried to focus on it, but her assailant kept it just out of her vision. *Don't struggle, and they'll let you go. They didn't all end up like Sheila; she must have struggled, made it difficult for herself. Just let them do it, get it over with, just let them be quick, oh God, just let them be—* The object in the twin's hand lifted for her to see, and Sally opened her mouth, not to beg anymore, but to scream. Scream for God. And what was the point of suffering all those Sunday school mornings if, in the end, there was nobody to help her when she needed it? Hadn't she always been good? Not like Sheila. Sheila the Skunk. She was smelly; she had a funny white streak in her hair. Maybe she deserved to be sent weird like that. *Oh God, what did they do to send her so weird?*

There was no scream. It was strangled by the toilet chain wound repeatedly around Sally's neck by one sister while the other pulled away the last of the victim's clothing and moved in, the long, glinting object held tightly in one fist.

Sally looked into their eyes as she choked, and there was something missing there. She didn't know what it was, but its absence was truly awful.

Slipping around the side of the building, Mike sneaked along a path between old Birch trees and down a slope into the dense woodland guarding the rear of the exclusive school. He looked behind once to check if Mucky Morton was on his tail and, satisfied that the coast was clear, strode into the cool sanctuary of the woods.

He followed the track through the sun-stippled trees, a June breeze caressing his bare chest. The fresh, clear embroidery of bird song, wanton greenery abounding; summer had settled on this quiet pocket of the Cotswolds, and every moment was ripe with hedonism, so Mike settled himself on the grassy bank beside the path to enjoy it.

A squirrel gave him the eye from a muscular branch above him, spoiling for a fight. He smiled at it and withdrew a slightly bent joint from his back pocket. He straightened it tenderly, and flicking a match alight, he caressed the corkscrewed end of the spliff[5] with flame.

The sweet, harsh smoke tingled through his body. He felt his nerves stand up, his senses stir and recoil. He was young; he was desirable and alive. The world was beautiful, and his.

"Fancy a toke?" he asked the squirrel, raising the joint toward the beady-eyed rogue The squirrel trickled up another branch and slipped into the thick green foliage. Mike leaned back into the shrubbery behind him, resting his head on a pillow of soft sward. Magical purple smoke curled up into the ceiling of leaves. A crow remonstrated with him, hidden by thrusting boughs. He laughed at the scratchy *rawk-rawk* and sucked on the joint, let the sound float into his ears, into his head. This was a secret, wonderful place.

By the time he had finished the joint, it was ten to three. He'd been gone nearly forty-five minutes. Morton would probably be looking for him, but hell, he didn't really care. On the other hand, he thought ruefully, the prospect of spending the rest of the afternoon with Mucky on his back was not an endearing one. Especially when he was stoned.

He heaved himself up, and stretching elaborately, sucking in the summer now that the dope was gone, he loped back along the path toward the school.

Morton was nowhere to be seen as Mike came from behind the toilet box. Probably relaxing in his bloody hut again, wanking over page three. Ah well, we all kick against the inevitable in our own little way, he found himself pondering in a charitable fashion. Hell, he was almost softening toward the fat creep.

The ladder vibrated beneath him as he lunged up the side of the building. Sunlight splashed across the window on the third floor, preventing him from seeing inside. Impulse tore him from the lad-

---

[5] British, informal, a joint

der and onto the scaffold. He leaned against the rail in front of the slightly raised window, pretending to look down at the yard. He knew they would be looking. Life was for grabbing.

A wolf whistle mocked him from the window. Turning slowly, Mike saw petite hands heave the casement fully upward. The twins were there and staring at him. He stared right back.

They leaned on the sill, mouths slightly parted. Glancing past them briefly, Mike saw the classroom was otherwise empty now. Hot lust was busting at his zip. And then his eyes were dropping away from theirs as self-consciousness robbed him of his cool. Words didn't fit his mouth right now. He couldn't get his tongue around any.

"Hey, sex machine." The blonde on the left spoke quietly, her voice laden with dirty promise.

"All right?" Mike offered, still crippled by hopelessness. The joint had blown his glibness into the clouds. His cheeks burned even fiercer than his sun-lashed back.

"Hey, Mister Laborer, how would you like to labor on us?" This time the twin on the right spoke, her voice educated, knowing. She winked and shook her shoulder-length blades of corn hair back from her face. The buttons of her blouse were undone, and Mike could see the lacy white cups of her bra peeking through the gap. He glanced from one to the other, very conscious suddenly of his own semi-nakedness. They were identical, and they were gorgeous, albeit with an overly glossy beauty. The plasticity of their good looks frightened him a little, and he didn't know why. He chased the unease from his mind. This moment was burning too brightly for shadows. He held the moment, relished it.

"Where would you like me to start?" he said, his shyness momentarily conquered. Life was for grabbing. He moved toward the window. One of the blondes slipped long fingers around his neck and pulled his head toward her. He had to stoop to take the kiss. He returned the girl's passion hungrily, absently pondering the consequences of Mucky Morton spotting him now. The idea perversely delighted him. And let's face it, he thought as his tongue toyed with the blonde's, he wasn't exactly inconspicuous, leaning against the window three floors up in broad daylight, snogging a schoolgirl. Hah! Life was for *grabbing.*

It wasn't until the two girls helped him through the window that he noticed one of them had blood smeared on her hand.

They had gone too far.

And wasn't it good.

Evil: what was that?

If evil meant releasing things others feared to free, then it was good, not bad. Healthy, not sick. And they were untouchable. Like Daddy, they were untouchable. The Skunk had shown them just how much. Her parents had tried to make a fuss, but money silenced everyone. And Daddy had lots of that. Enough for the Skunk's parents, enough for the governors, enough for Miss Smarm, the headmistress. She'd probably greased her knickers a few times to get where she was. And Daddy helped keep her there. For a little compromise here and there, of course. Like mollifying irate parents.

Not that there had been many of those; the twins' victims were usually too traumatized to breathe a word. They knew damn well what would happen if they did. Even the bloody educational psychologist knew they were untouchable. Tea and biscuits, and a blow job. That's all he meant to them. That's all anything came down to in the end: sex and hypocrisy.

But maybe this time they had gone *too* far. Maybe just a little.

Or perhaps they'd simply grown up. They were mature women now, and it was time they left this place. They passionately believed that beyond this fold of timid sheep there lay pastures of lust and torture where they could frolic, indulging their needs endlessly. Just let them open the gate and run free.

And God help *anyone* who got in their way.

Poor Sally Davis, pretty, little Sally Davis. More tea and biscuits for the twins. Because Daddy was a politician, Daddy was untouchable.

The twins could *never* go too far.

CHAPTER SIX

Corpses found under plumber's garden; armed maniac shoots six in gun siege; pensioner beaten and left for dead in own home.

Dennis watched the news without seeing it. Instead of Anna Ford's flaking beauty, he saw a desert lit by blooms of flame. His eyes were glazed, wide. A cigarette was held to his lips by fingers that did not tremble. Smoke crept around his hardened profile. The BBC commentator's voice droned on, the Alice in Acidland clock on the mantelshelf ticked, hesitantly it seemed. The sound of a radio could be heard from the flat next door. The day held its breath, and a huddle of Iraqi boys flew into ragged, smoldering pieces.

Boys with guns. Didn't even know how to use them properly. The Mother of all wars, killing its children. Dennis pulled the cigarette stub free of his lips and savagely extinguished it in an ashtray on one arm of the sofa. It didn't bother him; he could stub out the images. Easily. He yawned and blinked at the TV screen. Grief and cadavers at teatime. Lately, it had become more apparent that he needed glasses, but he'd be damned if he would concede to the fact. Glasses would make him feel trapped.

He heard Jack enter the flat, and his mood lifted slightly. He'd beaten the bastard home from work for once. It always irritated him to find Jack lounging in front of the television with a complacent air hanging over him like a cloying perfume. What the hell did he have to make him so content? What good had he ever done in this world?

Jack came in slowly, almost cautiously. He glanced at the television before he glanced at Dennis, as if acknowledging his best friend first. He said, "Make us a cuppa, seeing as you're home early."

Dennis didn't look up, giving the comment all the attention it deserved, but Jack obviously wasn't expecting a reply. He crossed absent-mindedly to the Georgian window and gazed across the road at the ugly mass of gray steel and concrete that housed the Bristol University Student Union, now sinking slowly into the dusk. It was one of those architectural atrocities from the 60s, when functionalism was not as closely bound to aesthetics as later, more prescient decades deemed it should be. It was a monster, six floors of sullen metal pierced by banks of windows through which students could be seen scurrying like self-important ants. Dennis often claimed that one day soon, as the students poured out of the building around midnight, a roaring, self-indulgent ejaculation of pampered youth, he would take up a Kalashnikov and pick them off slowly, patiently. Jack had always assumed he was joking, but it was increasingly difficult to tell with Dennis.

"Fancy going to The Slaughter tonight?" Jack asked as if they had been going there for the last five years or more.

"No."

"Not your scene, eh?"

Dennis groped for another cigarette and then reluctantly shoved it back in the pack. He wasn't going to chain-smoke, no matter how enjoyable it would be. "I fancy a quiet night in."

"Hiding away with the soaps and sitcoms... Becoming a habit, isn't it? Hardly the Dennis I used to know." Jack disappeared into the kitchen to make a cup of tea. Dennis pulled a cigarette anyway, and his depression deepened as he lit it. A train had jack-knifed off its track in India and disgorged its bloody insides. So many corpses. Dennis watched them blankly until Jack returned with his tea and popped an old video cassette into the VCR. Distraught relatives were replaced by video flak. Dennis continued to stare as if the picture hadn't changed at all. The tempest of electric snow filled his mind, blotting out everything. He didn't blink when the screen cleared to reveal a lurid yellow scream of a title: *Absurd.* Italian credits fought to be deciphered over the graininess, and then, after a tear in the tape had rolled up and down the screen for a breathless moment, the film began.

Dennis, never a critical viewer at the best of times, gazed vacantly as a gigantic inmate with uncoordinated eyes and bad taste in pajamas escaped from a hospital for the criminally insane and proceeded to inflict atrocities on innocent bystanders, which included bisecting a meatpacker with his own bandsaw and forcing a babysitter's head into a kitchen oven. When the doorbell chimed, Dennis didn't move. Jack swore and placed his tea to one side. He scooped up the entry phone in the short hallway, his irritation smoothing out when Sam's voice greeted him.

"Who is it?" Dennis' voice was flat, without curiosity.

"Your beloved ex," Jack delighted in telling him, coming back into the living room. Dennis frowned, but Jack could see the hope light up his eyes.

Sam was immaculate in a chic leather jacket and pressed 501s. She trailed a long leg over one arm of Jack's PVC armchair as she sat and smiled cautiously at them.

"It's no good; I won't take you back," Dennis said drily, shaking his head.

"Dreams keep you sane, I'm told," she replied tartly. "But don't get excited. I didn't come to see *you*."

"That makes me the lucky one, then." Jack was unable to keep the surprise out of his voice. The thought would have sent him into orbit a few days ago. Now it just made him feel...what? Confused?

Sam unhooked her leg from the chair arm and sat up. She was blushing. He'd made her feel awkward. For once, she looked lost for words.

Dennis brayed with cynical laughter. "Got nothing better to do than call on a no-hoper like Jacko. My, your social diary must be *very* empty. Don't tell me Gecko the Geek's dumped your sorry arse?"

"I'll make you a cup of tea," Jack said quickly. He ducked through the archway from the small lounge to the smaller kitchen. Sam followed him out, and as she moved hesitantly to stand by the window, Jack saw the twilight fill her eyes and realized for the second time in two days just how vulnerable and insecure she really was.

"Did you enjoy the gig last night?" he asked to lift the tension.

She was partly turned away from him, her profile ghostly beside the darkening windowpane.

"*Enjoy?* No, of course not." She paused thoughtfully. "I've never seen anything like it. That band..." She fished for the right words.

"They made me feel... like I didn't want to breathe the same *air* as them."

Jack smiled. He knew exactly what she meant. "But you didn't want to leave either?"

"No," she admitted.

It all sounded a little absurd now. But it was also disturbing to hear her expressing the same emotions he'd felt at the time. "Your boyfriend didn't seem to feel the same way. He scuttled like a kid who's just smoked his first fag. Green as moldy cheese." Of course, Jack had been just *fine,* hadn't he?

"He's not really my boyfriend," she said quickly, then gave Jack a conspiratorial smile. "He *is* a bit of a prat, isn't he?"

Jack stirred her tea. The hyperactive score of the video nasty playing in the next room reached a peak as some poor soul bought it in a particularly unpleasant manner. The drill scene? Or the pickaxe through the bonce[6]? He suddenly realized that an uneasy silence had fallen in the kitchen.

"So... Why are you here, Sam?" He was beginning to guess, but he wanted to hear her say it. Something about the gig at The Slaughter had touched her somewhere she didn't want to be touched, and perhaps she'd sensed a similar uneasiness in him. Maybe she wanted to rationalize her feelings with someone who might understand.

"Would you rather I left? It's obvious you want to get back to your film." Her insecurity snapped suddenly into irritation. "What's wrong with you today? Can't I call on a friend without there having to be a reason?"

Guilt made his words rushed and clumsy. "It's just... Well, you've never really bothered before. Always so wrapped up in the latest Mister Wonderful."

She blushed angrily. "Bloody hell! Anyone would think you don't want me here. It's you who's always phoning me all the time, begging me to come out."

He wasn't handling this very well. He *did* want her here, just not quite as much as he might have a couple of days before, that was all. He felt as if something new had reared its ugly head in his life, and he hadn't realized it until Sam turned up on his doorstep claiming kinship. But what the hell was it that was niggling at him? Bane? His morbid barmaid? Or was she his lover? There was more

---

[6] British slang for head or skull

than a professional link between them; he was sure of that. Maybe something else was bothering him, something closer to home. Something he'd found out about himself? Forget it. Concentrate on something that makes sense, that's wholesome, sane. Like Sam.

Sam was tapping her teacup distractedly. "Perhaps I've decided not to forget my roots, that's all. You and Dennis were the first friends I made in Bristol." She paused, thinking it through, confused. "Or maybe I came to see you because I realized last night that you were different, Jack. Different from Dennis and Joe. And Thomas. It's taken me all this time to realize there's... I don't know...more to you than I thought, I suppose, and...and I don't know why I'm saying this, and I don't know what the bloody hell I *am* saying, and I think it would probably be a good idea all around if you go back in there with your mate and watch that delightful video. Sorry." She was blushing madly now. She put down her teacup and zipped up her jacket. She couldn't look him in the eye. Jack watched her helplessly and was strangely relieved when Dennis loomed in the doorway.

"Now, isn't this nice and cozy?" Jack could sense the deep resentment in his flatmate. Sam sighed and folded her arms.

Jack desperately thought of something to say to dissipate the tension and didn't do a very good job at all. "Sam's missing her roots." It sounded mocking, and he really hadn't meant it to.

"Stop dying your fucking hair, then." Dennis sneered, then disappeared back into the lounge. They heard the video nasty die a horrible death, and soon *Ziggy Stardust* was crashing from the speakers.

"Thanks for that, Jack. We really must do this again sometime."

He flinched at the hurt in her eyes. "I'm really sorry, Sam. Look, can we meet up for a proper chat? Soon?" He reached out instinctively and seized her hand. She responded with a confused frown and removed her hand from his, then made her way out of the kitchen to the door of the flat. He closed the door on her and stood in the hall for a moment, lost in a profusion of thoughts. Then he shrugged and encroached on Dennis's Bowie defense line.

"So what's made you so popular all of a sudden? Can't be your looks, and your personality wouldn't win you any prizes either. So come on... Give your Uncle Dennis the secret." He was smoking again, sitting on the sofa and gazing at the rectangle of darkness pushing against the windowpanes.

"I think I can safely say it certainly isn't down to the company I keep, Dennis, my old mate." Jack shut the lounge door firmly on

Dennis's braying laugh and went into his bedroom. He sat in the old rocking chair by the window and watched the lights bloom across the city. The dark seemed to be watching him, as if waiting for something.

CHAPTER SEVEN

He wasn't entirely happy with the idea of meeting her in The Slaughter. The place made him uncomfortable, and yet it pulled him, too. It was like a pub he'd dreamed of, and the dream had turned into a nightmare mid-way through. Good to bad. Just as he'd felt when the band started to play, until he'd forgotten which was good and which was supposed to be bad.

He arrived early so as to have some time to himself, and as he walked up to the door, excitement and trepidation wrestled inside him. *She* was there. No longer dressed in the Morticia body stocking, but in a smart, black trouser suit hitched in around her slim waist by a belt with a large brass buckle forged into Medusa's head. Her dark hair coiled around her face with a mysterious coyness. She poured him a pint of Old Corpse and looked straight through him.

He shuffled in his pocket for change, blushing like a school-kid. His mind angled for words, but nothing would bite. She obviously didn't want to make conversation and retired to sit on a stool at the far end of the bar, bored by the slow lunchtime business.

He felt inexplicably crushed.

He retreated to a table by the roaring cave, now silent. The sound effects had been turned off, as had all the video screens. The pub reminded him of Blackpool's Golden Mile in January; rejected, desolate, the attractions gathering dust, their glamour fading. The Frankenstein Monster looked sad and a little silly in the cold light of day.

Jack could see the joins. The Wolfman was just a rather amateur-ishly painted dummy without the dry ice to imbue it with menace. Jack the Ripper leaned sleepily over his table like an overworked waiter.

He listened to the music (Radio *1??)* and waited for Sam. But it was Nigel who turned up. Jack desperately pretended to be inter-ested in the plastic cave wall behind him, but he was backing a los-ing horse; Nigel spotted him immediately, collected a drink, and made his way over to join him. Jack pretended to be pleased to see his oc-casional colleague, but he was very quick to point out he was ex-pecting Sam at any moment.

"Mary at the Vault said you'd be here. Nice girl. I wouldn't mind—"

"Don't even think about it. I don't want you harassing my work-mates. Look, Nigel—"

"She'll stand you up, mate. Don't you ever learn? Sam's out of your league."

Jack tried not to rise to the bait but could feel himself grow-ing irritated already, and Nigel had only just sat down. Nigel was a living, breathing paradox; he oscillated between Dr. Upwardly Mobile Jekyll and a council estate Mr. Hyde. He'd never been able to make up his mind which was the real Nigel, and his personal dichotomy confused not only himself, but everyone he met. He regularly hopped from one end of the social spectrum to the other. One evening you'd find him in a wine bar clinging to the coattails of the bankers and in-vestment brokers he wanted to call his "friends"; the next, he'd be slumming it with the redneck building laborers from the severely downmarket B&B where he lived, out for a dozen pints, a curry, and a city center rumble.

The last decade had not been good to Nigel. While his success-ful acquaintances of former years moved on to haul in salaries of fifty grand and up, Nigel pocketed a hundred and fifty pounds a fort-night. Nigel was on the dole, but he tried not to let it stop him from com-peting. When he was with his executive chums, it was all Latin Ameri-can bistros he couldn't afford and attempts at chatting up women who wore more money on their fingers than he claimed a year. When he was out on the town with his laborer mates, it was twenty-quid massage parlor blow jobs and cheap nightspot pickups.

Nigel's cultural dilemma was reflected in his physical appear-ance, if you cared to look closely enough. A high forehead fell away to small, desperate eyes that could gleam with vulgar bravado on cue; his nose tilted up like a penguin's bill above an indecisive mouth; his clothes were Country Man casual, his accent wavered alarmingly from sophisticated yuppie to South Bristol Lad, depending on whose company he was keeping. He was a social chameleon who was more and more frequently forgetting when to change color.

"So that's why you drink in this morgue." Nigel was gazing appreciatively at the barmaid as she sat patiently on her stool. "Fancy a bit of Ingrid Pitt, eh? Not bad, but not really my cup of tea. More up your graveyard, mate. Unlike Sam. Take my advice and forget her."

"Like I said, Nigel," Jack said with an edge to his voice, "I'm expecting her any minute. Have you heard the one about two being company?"

"And Sam would make a crowd. Yeah, I see what you mean. Never mind: if she does turn up, hopefully she won't hang around for long." He went for his pint in a big way. When he'd finished gulping, he clomped the glass down on the table and exhaled bad breath in Jack's direction. "Actually, I came here to do you a service, mate. We've got some work coming up."

Working with Nigel meant a few days of driving around the major cities of the South West, popping into all the music retail outlets and buying bag-loads of CD singles just to "help" them along in their journey up the charts. It was sporadic and unreliable employment, but when it appeared, the money was good enough to induce Jack to give his boss at the Video Vault some implausible excuse or other so he could hit the road with Nigel instead. Jack considered this new information briefly. Nigel considered his watch.

"She's blown you off, mate."

Jack was beginning to agree with him, and he didn't know how that made him feel. He glanced over at the bar. Morticia had disappeared, the bar left unattended, there being only a handful of other customers in the pub. He swilled the last quarter of his pint around in his glass. He decided to buy another drink, reluctantly asking Nigel if he wanted one, too. To his relief, Nigel shook his head, his glass still half full.

The landlord appeared from the back of the pub as Jack strode toward the bar. Mister Bane.

Jack froze in the act of placing his empty on the bar top. He felt a queasy knot twist his gut. Bane was clad in a T-shirt black as a beetle's carapace and dark jeans. The flesh of his arms was pale as fungus, lean as old dock rope, and scribbled with scars. His eyes held no light as he looked at Jack, the cruel smile digging at his nerves.

"Corpse?" the landlord asked, and Jack's eyes dilated with strange fear until he realized Bane was referring to the beer.

He nodded, floundering for something cool and assertive to say while Bane worked the hand pull. The best he could come up with was: "I hope the video was repulsive enough for you."

Bane didn't reply, his unblinking gaze leveled on Jack. It looked as though the man had no irises, just small, black planets floating against white. Jack tore his gaze away and looked down at the pint Bane had filled. Bane's hand was clasped over the top of the glass, as if trying to keep a trapped moth inside. Jack went to take it, and Bane lifted his hand with a scarecrow smile.

"It's Slaughterin' Time."

Beer frothed over Jack's hands as he picked it up. He ignored the weird comment and made his way back to Nigel.

"What's his problem?" Nigel asked, having noticed the way Bane stared at his friend.

Jack looked at him vaguely, as if he hadn't heard him.

"Creepy guy behind the bar," Nigel prompted.

"Your guess is as good as mine." *Slaughterin' Time.* Jack drank deeply, the dark, treacly liquid falling heavily inside him. The taste seemed slightly different from his last pint; something familiar about the new, subtle flavor nagged at him, staying just beyond identification. Bane had put his hand over the pint. Why? Had he wiped something on the rim, or... "Your pint taste okay?" he asked Nigel.

Nigel smeared a hand across his lips. "It's got some poke, this stuff," was his only comment.

Jack shrugged and took another gulp. Something slipped down his throat along with the beer, something gritty and slimy, like a knot of earthworms. He gagged. Retched dryly. But whatever it was had dived down his throat and was already swimming in his stomach.

He stared at the thick, black surface of his pint. Nothing there. He looked up at Bane, the blood leaking from his face as his imagination began to storyboard revolting images. Worms in his pint? No, perhaps not; whatever it was had been very thin and stringy. Maybe a few soggy blades of grass that had somehow gotten into the barrel.

Bane was leaning on the bar, giving him the evil eye, smoking a Death. *Yeah, I get it: you're baaad.* Jack began to seriously contemplate drinking elsewhere in the future. But he'd paid for his beer, and grass in it or no, he was bloody well going to finish it.

It wasn't until fifteen minutes of aimless chatter with Nigel later—when Jack had almost reached the bottom of his glass—that he began to feel it.

Panic bolted through him. His mind stretched, then *curved*. The sensation was unmistakable. He stared into the depths of his glass, and his fears crystallized: a small nest of bedraggled tiny mushrooms with slender stalks and ominous nipple caps was piled densely on the bottom of the glass like a ball of wet hair. Jack stood up, and the pub carouseled crazily. His heart was a basketball thudding repeatedly off a wall. Nigel's dozily inquisitive face distorted as he rode the merry-go-round pub table, glass tilted to his lips. His friend's features began to run like an ice cream cone left in the sun too long.

"What's up, Jack? You look as if you're going to chuck, mate."

Jack swiveled to face the bar again. Bane's grin was a hard-edged crack in pale plastic. For a horrible moment, the grin was all that was left of Bane, hanging there without a face or body, an ogre Cheshire Cat smirk that had slipped its moorings and wanted to grind him with yellow tombstone teeth. Jack stumbled away from the table, heading for the door. Nigel gaped at him, a little more concerned now.

"Where you going, mate? You haven't finished your beer."

Jack changed direction suddenly, causing the pub to heave around him as if he were braving the deck of a storm-locked galleon. Bane was back in focus, rocking with the swell behind his bar. His grin was in place again, though distorted and unreal, as if painted on his head by Hieronymus Bosch. Jack's thoughts were folding and bending nastily. A psychopath was making origami with the contents of his head.

"You...bastard," he croaked, pointing at the landlord.

"Slaughterin' Time," Bane repeated.

"*You're out of your mind,*" Jack hissed. The handful of drinkers scattered throughout the pub were looking at him warily. He was conscious of their eyes pricking him like hypodermic needles.

"No," the landlord replied calmly. "I think you'll find that's you."

The Frankenstein Monster lurched at him, gray Karloff face snarling; Red Jack sniggered through a mouthful of wax and turned, knife raised to rip; the Wolfman poised for a spring.

Jack fled the pub.

He staggered along Buckingham Road like a drunk wading upstream. The outside world closed in on him in a barrage of tangible light and noise. Normality was slipping off him like skin shed by a lizard: a girl cycling past in a vivid multi-colored anorak was a rainbow on wheels; cars were grotesque steel monsters steamrolling along the busy main road. Too much. Too *much.*

He sought the haven of a quiet side street, a fox going to ground, pursued by the reality hunt. He collapsed against a lamp post, fighting for calm. He hoped Nigel wasn't following him; he couldn't face his friend now. Couldn't face *anyone.*

He regained a measure of composure and left the lamp, following the side street as it opened onto a large, square space filled with the artificial green hump of an inner-city reservoir. It reared above him like an ancient burial mound, boxed in on all four sides by the peeling backs of houses. Jack closed his fists around the railing of the iron fence protecting the reservoir and wondered what the hell he was going to do now.

Bane had dropped magic mushrooms into his beer. While his eyes fixed Jack like a rabbit to a road, his hands had slipped him a psychedelic pint.

The reservoir was a stirring behemoth, lifting its back to stretch. The blank houses seemed to shuffle closer together, trying to squeeze him in. Claustrophobia clamped him. His flat was just up the road, he reassured himself. Dennis wouldn't be back from work for hours yet; he could lie low there until the effects wore off. But how long would that be?

He could tell these were extremely potent mushrooms, far more powerful than the occasional few he'd taken before (voluntarily, too—he must have been crazy). He was crazy now, that was for sure. Or soon would be. The disorientation was becoming stronger with every minute as the psilocybin tobogganed around his nervous system. His mind was sledding downhill, too, and there was no way of slowing. Faster now. Out of control. *Faster. STOP!* he screamed silently, squeezing the railing until he imagined it collapsed within his grasp. *Slow down. Slow* down*!*

The realization hit him that he could be in for six to eight hours of hell. Possibly longer, if these were as potent as he feared. He pulled himself free of the railing, his fingers unwilling to leave the iron bar as if they'd been glued there. As he headed for his flat, the monotonous homogeneity of the streets and houses contained him in an endless maze of brick and concrete repetition. Rounding a corner, he faced off against a fat woman with a mustache who was propelling a pram toward him, pregnant with threat. Her bare arms were bunched like

Popeye's thews; the baby was a gargoyle leering wickedly at him from a nest of grubby swaddling.

Somehow, he reached his street, and the bright September sunlight fractured around him; he could see, *feel* the splinters cutting his skin. The brownstone walls of the buildings crumbled like cake under the blasting shards of light. He made for his door, the blare of the hunt still after him. His keys were a jagged clump of alien artifacts in his hand.

Inside the main hall, the morning's post lay spread out on the doormat where he'd left it. He hopped over the bright envelopes as if they were landmines and hared up the two flights of stairs to his flat. He locked the door behind him and pressed his head against the cool wood.

But even here, he wasn't safe; the cluttered rooms mocked him, cruelly reminding him of his altered state through their sheer banality. All his personal items seemed mundane to the point of viciousness; his old punk CDs with their rebellious covers sneered at him from their pile on the carpet; video nasties leered from their shelves like intruders. Were they really his? Had he degenerated this far? He fled to the bathroom. The small room boxed in his fears to a greater degree; the mirror showed him swollen pupils (*just like Bane's*) and mottled, ghostly skin.

He lurched from room to room, desperate for some relief from his turmoil.

And found none.

Sam hesitated for a second or two before entering The Slaughter. Did she really want to go back in there?

She wished Jack had suggested somewhere else for them to have a drink, but he seemed fixated on the place. She didn't like it at all. She didn't like the violence kicking out from the speakers; she didn't like the tacky wax monsters leaning around as if waiting for life; she didn't like the stupid, bad-taste names of the beers or the pub itself, for that matter.

But most of all, she didn't like the bitch behind the bar.

Not. At. All.

She pulled herself together and entered the pub, and the bitch was the first thing she saw. She clocked Sam, too, and the same hostile mask with which she'd served Sam the night of the gig immediately fell into place again. Malice oozed from her as she watched Sam, her eyes sharp and nasty.

Sam turned away and scanned the pub for Jack. She saw Nigel instead and groaned. She would have walked quickly out again, but Nigel, casting his beady little eyes around the pub for someone to latch onto, beamed delightedly as they snagged her. He waved her over. Resigning herself, she went to join him.

"Have you seen Jack?" she cut in quickly before he could make any pathetic attempt at seducing her. The guy just couldn't help himself.

"You just missed him. He left about ten minutes ago, in a bit of a bad way, I might add; looked like he was about to show me his guts, so I didn't try stopping him. Can't hold his ale, I s'pose, though I don't know why he blames the landlord for *that*."

Sam let that one past, not in the mood for dallying. "I was going to meet him here, but I got held up at the office," she explained. "Has he gone back to the flat?"

Nigel shrugged. It didn't interest him. "Look, how about you let me buy you a drink. A sophisticated guy like me knows just how to treat a classy girl like you."

She had to choke down a laugh. He really was grotesque. Lurching into yuppie gear, he was trying to impress her with a weird attempt at a public-school accent, cruelly undermined by his South Bristol breeding.

"How about I *don't*," she told him firmly. "If Jack comes back, tell him I'm sorry I was late, and I'll see him again soon."

Nigel nodded slightly, but Sam got the feeling her message had sailed completely over his head; Nigel's gaze was fastened unswervingly on her chest, and there was only room in his head for one thing right now. She pulled her coat together, conscious of her slight bust, even though it was adequately hidden by her sweater. Nigel's eyes still seemed to see right through to the skin somehow.

She tilted her jaw up a little defensively as she left the pub, knowing the barmaid was watching her. What had she done to inspire such animosity? Perhaps it was just a mutual instinctive dislike. As far as Sam was concerned, she'd hated the bitch as soon as she first set eyes on her. It was that simple.

Leigh Woods. He would find sanctuary there. No people, no bustle. Just trees and birds and soothing nature. But reaching the woods proved to be the most demanding and disturbing journey Jack had ever made.

Above all, he had to feign normality. He was sure every window contained a suspicious spinster, her fingers already dialing 9-9-9 as he slipped past the twitching curtains. He must look as bad as he felt, and although taking magic mushrooms was not, strictly speaking, illegal (though drying and preserving them was), the mere thought of being questioned by the police in his present state shook him with horror. And there were his video horribles to consider: many banned and outrageous gore titles sitting cockily on his shelves. The police would have a whale of a time rifling through them after dragging Jack back to his flat. They'd start implicating him in every unsolved murder in the South West. No, he would have to play Mr. Straight and try not to imagine what his eyes (black holes) or his face (spook white) must look like. *Can I help you to some paranoia, sir? I'm already being served, thanks. Can't you see it in my thousand-yard stare?*

Crossing the main road separating Clifton Village from the broad stretch of grassland that swept up toward the cliff tops of the Avon Gorge, Jack spotted a policeman heading his way. Think of one, and he will surely appear.

Jack was Mr. Normal, going about his legitimate business, acting one-hundred-percent natural. He swerved into a ninety-degree turn like a clockwork robot and lurched stiffly toward a red phone box. He hid inside, pretending to thumb coins into the slot. Nice one, Jack, *very* smooth maneuver. He glanced nervously over his shoulder. P.C. Plod was proceeding unhurriedly along his way, enjoying the autumn sunshine.

Jack left the box reluctantly. He felt safe in there, but he couldn't improvise a six-hour phone call. As he stumbled across the bright grass, he felt the mushrooms seethe inside him like a clutch of vipers in his belly.

The blades of grass glowed with health, sheathed by sunlight beneath his boots, but Jack was in no mood to appreciate the beauty. His head was a vortex. He made the suspension bridge as the day turned plastic around him and time fell apart. Inside the small window of the toll booth, the collector sitting before a portable TV receded into his own little world at the inverse end of a telescope. The gorge plunged away beneath the bridge as Jack ventured across it; insecurity rushed at him from out of the gulf. He was walking a frail rope bridge across the gaping void of eternity. Brightly colored rock climbers were pasted like flies against the bulging cliffs, wriggling vaguely. Jack watched them until giddiness threatened to suck him over the rail and over the edge of the world.

At the far end of the bridge, he fought to regain his breath and his sanity. He heard the sharp clatter of plodding hooves behind him as he drooped over the rail. Don't look round: it'll be a mounted policeman. He looked round. The officer locked eyes with Jack briefly while a million volts blasted through him. The horse plodded on. Jack forced himself to leave the rail and set off on the last leg of his journey.

To reach Leigh Woods, he had to venture through the most exclusive district of Bristol. Massive houses crouched in groves of ash and birch, guarded by dogs that clamored at his passing. He felt very conspicuous in his leather jacket and Damned T-shirt. People with money were perennially insecure; they didn't like anyone without near their property. Jack knew his eyes would give him away if anyone spoke to him. And so, devoured by paranoia, he reached the country lane and the stile that stepped over onto a footpath leading into deep woods.

The trees were Roman candles of frozen, golden flame. Drifts of Autumn-burned leaves exploded with reflected sunlight as he crackled through them. It should have been beautiful; he should have felt safe alone with nature and all its discretion.

Instead, a morbid pallor of decay diseased everything. And the mushrooms in his gut twisted like knives.

As his vision began to darken, he realized he might have made a bad mistake coming here. He blinked madly, and the fog lifted; the trees around him seemed to draw back guiltily, as if they had been shifting nearer in the temporary darkness. He could die out here with nobody to help him. He staggered aimlessly deeper into the woods, losing all sense of direction. The blackness continued to fall over him, yet at times would suddenly lift, as if someone were playing with the lid of a coffin while he lay inside. He tried to regurgitate the contents of his stomach but could manage only dry heaves. He was a specter of himself, white and shaking, creeping between skeletal trees, hopelessly lost.

By the time he stumbled upon the Bronze Age burial mound hidden away in a clearing at the heart of the woods, Jack was reaching the peak of his trip and the nadir of his life. Terror throttled him. He felt certain he was going to die. Bane had slipped him lethal mushrooms, not the mind-expanding psilocybins he'd once nonchalantly picked on Clifton Rugby Pitch while burly men collided belligerently around him. *These* were killers. He could feel them dry and harsh inside him, sucking his life juices. His breath was a death-rattle rasp. The darkness came again, like a black mist shrouding the trees, but not the figure that appeared amongst them, strolling toward Jack with gloating eyes.

Bane, stepping between rows of tiny gravestones growing like toadstools beneath his feet. The landlord knelt, picked one, and lifted it for Jack to see, his own name etched on the lichened stone.

The hallucinogenic image mercifully faded, but Jack could feel the poisons in him continuing to spread, squeezing his nervous system dry. And what was there to live for anyway? He thought of Sam and remembered sitting in The Slaughter, waiting...a lifetime ago. But had he even really wanted her there? Did he want her here now, to see him transformed into a husk? He didn't know what he wanted, what he'd ever wanted. The barmaid? Why think of her? He didn't even know her name, and thinking about her made him feel even more poisoned. Now *she* was drifting toward him through the trees, her cruel, desirable face framed by midnight tresses, pale worm fingers beckoning to him. She had known he was going to die today, and it had bored her. She hadn't even looked at him.

His mother replaced the barmaid's image, hunched and twitchy beneath the shadow of an ash, following him with suspicious eyes. And anger burned through Jack's fear, turning swiftly to hate as his father joined her, both staring at him as if he weren't really there, as if he'd never been there. Never important. Just an object to be ignored or abused depending on what mood took them; just another victim. His hate made them fade like old photographs, and the mist went with them until he could see trees and leaves and nothing more.

He stumbled toward the mound, ghostly under a down of Old Man's Beard. Silence thick as the mist had been pressed around the eerie hump. Jack's fevered imaginings conjured moldering warriors, dead before Jesus was born, stirring in the hollow dark beneath the turf. They tilted time-worn faces up toward him, watching Jack through the soil and the purple brambles with punch-bowl cavities for eyes. Dry heaves wracked him again. His lungs were parched bags.

Jack wondered why he couldn't turn away, and looking down at his feet, he saw them disappearing into the grass. He was taking root; soon, he would be just another bone protruding from the earth, like the bare trees bending crisp and white as ribs over the mound.

He perceived his fate so clearly that when he intensified his struggles to move, it came as something of a surprise that his feet obeyed him so readily. He staggered closer to the mound, as if nearing the end of a terrible quest. The mound had a doorway, and he wondered why he hadn't seen it before. It was as if the hole gouged into the end of the mound had opened just for him like an earthy mouth, drooling wisps of Old Man's Beard and choked with leaves. Toadstools ringed the mouth, rotten teeth that left a trail of saliva on his hands and face as he knelt and crawled inside. He *had* to go in. It wasn't a conscious decision, just instinct pushing him like a firm hand. Silence mourned him as he hunched forward into the darkness. Even the birds had died.

And now he knew he must be mad. Why else would he crawl into a hole like Alice chasing the White Rabbit? The hole wasn't there; it was a figment of Lewis Carroll's imagination, of his own imagination. But he could smell the earth. And something more. At first, he thought it was the fetid stink of the toadstools, and as his eyes became adjusted to the gloom, he could see scores of the evil fungus sprinkled around the floor of the chamber in which he found himself. But the smell came from something else entirely.

He was no longer in the barrow but standing in the garden of his parents' house. He was staring at the stiffening paw sticking up like a root from the rose bed where Puff lay, strangled and half buried. And as he dug frantically, the tears mingling with dirt on his face, he smelled Death's odious breath and saw its agents boiling inside cold fur.

He imagined his father's huge hands seizing the terrier by the throat, probably in a pique of fury when the little dog wet the kitchen floor or wouldn't stop barking at the night. His mother had probably been glad to rid her proud house of the dirty creature. Jack had spent years putting the pieces together in his head; Puff was just one more thing he could never forgive them for.

Jack was panting in the dark of the burial chamber, his fists clenched so tight his fingernails had caused his palms to bleed. Still no sign of the White Rabbit. Only Death waited for him in here. The Puff smell was strongest ahead of him, where the chamber was darkest. He had to go and take a look, a boy once more advancing across the lawn.

The barrow was wide and deep, and there was plenty of room for him to stand upright. He stepped through the speckled toadstools until the dark was a solid wall before him. Fear stopped him in his tracks, and even the madness that had pushed him into this hole couldn't push him any farther. His foot nudged something soft. His breath was a hollow rasp as he bent to touch the object. His hand slipped over a cool, porous surface, his fingers finding a moist hole ringed with—

He cut loose a shriek that blasted his ears in the confined space. He leaped away from the face at his feet, lost his balance over a heap of bodies piled in a frozen orgy around him, and toppled backward into a cold embrace. He struggled wildly, but the stiff arms only hugged him tighter. He felt rigor mortis lips kiss his face, and the sounds he emitted were the strangled yelps of a puppy. *It's not real, not real, not real!!!*

He was lying on the cold earth floor of the barrow. He rolled, got to his knees, almost vomiting with relief. Nothing there. Of course not. *Just tripping.* He turned back to the barrow entrance, a patch of daylight beckoning him, and dragged himself toward it, crying now, the sobs snatching at his breath. He was almost there when he sensed a movement behind him.

A shadow was detaching itself from the dark at the rear of the barrow. Jack knew instinctively it was responsible for the heap of human jackstraws he'd fallen into (and had he *really* just imagined them?) and knew it intended to add him to the pile.

He could smell the shadow; a rank cocktail of blood, offal, and decay came off it in waves. But Jack had reason on his side; he was tripping, and this was just an ogre who lived in that trip, and nowhere else. The shadow couldn't harm him. Jack had reason on his side, oh yes...

...but reason wasn't working. Not today. His breathing stopped, too.

The shadow was closer. Soon it would shuffle into the faint light from the entrance, and Jack would be able to see it. Panic threw him forward. The shadow wouldn't let him go; it gripped his jacket and held him fast. He twisted around and fought wildly, releasing a guttural croak of fear and rage, his hands beating, ripping, until the shadow was just a part of the darkness, and the darkness was fading.

The darkness was gone. Had never been. Jack was slumped against the brambly slope of the mound, and there was no hole. No black ogre clutching him, but a coil of brambles fastened to his jacket. His hands were tightly clasped around something small and torn and warm, pressed into the turf of the mound. It had stopped wriggling now as the *mother* of all hallucinations passed, and Jack's eyes bulged from his head at what he was doing. What he had done.

He let the limp squirrel drop to the grass and staggered back from it, bludgeoned by horror. The animal's neck lolled limply beside a sporing dandelion. Several seeds detached themselves and settled on the body. Dead beady eyes peered up at Jack, their mischief all squeezed out.

"No..." he pleaded. Tears of anguish pricked his eyes as he knelt beside the squirrel, stretching out the hands that had killed it in supplication. He was ten years old and cradling Puff in his arms. Earthy, stiff Puff with his mouth locked in a grin as if he still wanted to play.

Jack ran.

The clocks had been stopped, and only now the hands began to lurch into motion again. Precious seams of normality opened in his mind, as welcome as dawn after a bone-chilling nightmare. Loping madly along the woodland path, Jack felt the waves of psilocybin begin to withdraw from his body. The tide was going out. The relief was strong enough to make his eyes tear again. He emerged from the brittle clutch of trees as if he'd just broken free from the grave. He leaped over the stile, felt the sun warm on his face, and his adrenaline began to calm at last.

He walked along the country lane, and his lungs filled with freshness. By the time he was back among the houses, he could feel the invigorating surge of health fighting off the last of the toxins in his system. A postbox pillar gleamed a cheerful red; a blackbird's clear trickle of song filled his breast with hope. Across the bridge, getting better. The city sparkled on the far side, a Mecca clean and bright with possibilities. He would ring Sam, make another date. He would *live*.

He realized he really needed her: her healthy beauty, her cheerful wit, her vivacity, most of all. She made him feel alive; he could see that now. Other things...he would drive them from his mind. Think positive.

Through Clifton Village, into Victoria Square, nearly home. The faces of passersby vivid with optimism, their clothes throbbing with color. The cobbled pathway through the park was an artery leading him back into the heart of life.

The horrors of the day were illusion only. He'd left them all behind.

Bane hadn't finished him with his poison. He was just a creep, like Nigel had said. Nothing to be scared of.

He'd come through.

And Jack actually found himself whistling.

CHAPTER EIGHT

He woke in the night with a single thought. Hadn't it felt good?

The animal under his hands. The freedom to kill, just for a moment. How his father must have felt with the terrier twisting and dying in his grip.

Hadn't it felt...*good*?

He blacked the thought out, repelled. Shut his eyes and the shadow man was there waiting for him, in the hole, in the darkness, and now he could see the man's face. His *own* face.

The shadow was Jack. And Jack was killing a squirrel.

Jack loved animals. But hadn't it felt...?

He lay stiff and sweating until dawn pushed against the thin curtains of his window like the pale gray face of a giant.

Then, at last, he slept.

Mary had covered for him at the Video Vault. Luckily, the manager had not been in the previous afternoon while Jack was wandering like a ghost through Leigh Woods. But now he owed Mary a big favor.

"I suppose you want a pound of flesh," Jack said as they lounged behind the counter, waiting for customers.

"I wouldn't touch it if you paid me. How many times does a

girl have to say no, Jack? It's getting embarrassing." Her pampered face had broadened slightly over the year he'd known her, and one day that baby fat cuteness would stop being so cute, although her tawny, sun-flake eyes would always be alluring. She seemed oblivious to the encroaching danger to her curvacious figure, however, as she gleefully tucked into a Mars bar.

"Ho ho, Mary." *That would make a good epitaph for her,* he thought. Her attempts at humor were as pathetic and repetitive as his previous advances toward her. At least Jack knew when to stop.

"So, what *do* you want?

"Hmmm..." She deliberated grandly, scanning the walls and ceiling for inspiration. "I'll think of something over lunch."

"You've just *had* lunch."

"I have?" She widened her eyes in mock innocence. "Are you *sure?*"

Jack sighed. "All right. Take off."

She leaned forward and pecked him on the cheek. He reclined in his chair and watched her go, and now that he was alone, he remembered how tired he was. He remembered other things as well and promptly began fishing around in some of the dustier boxes at the back of the shop to keep his mind occupied. Blood on his hands. He could see those dead beady eyes watching him still. It was an *accident!* He wasn't in his right mind at the time. He couldn't be held responsible.

His hands were shaking as he delved into a box of dusty video cases, searching randomly for something to watch, not really bothered over whatever it might be. Snatching the first that came to hand, he slapped it into the VHS player behind the computer, and soon the small television set mounted on a shelf above his head flickered into life. Mary had kept him busy, kept his thoughts off things he'd rather not think about. He hoped the video would take her place.

He sat back and tried to concentrate on the TV as the video began. *Doctor Who,* for Christ's sake, in black and white. Shit. Not in the mood for that silliness. He was about to eject it, but after a few minutes of fidgety viewing, he began to fall under the spell of the old 60s relic.

The screen showed a deserted pebble beach. A thick gas pipe stretched across the shore. The bleakness of the scene got into Jack's pores. He continued to watch, forgetting where he was.

Another scene, this time inside the impeller shaft of a gas refinery. One of the actors was trapped in the dark shaft as seaweed hissed and writhed around him. It should have been silly, but the uneasy claustrophobia was palpable. Jack began to feel a little uncomfortable. The confined space, the darkness, and the stifled air of terror all reminded him too much of the day before.

"Am I disturbing you?"

The voice snatched him away from the screen. Jack's first reaction to Bane's mocking civility was a whiplash of fear. Then he remembered he had overdosed on fear the day before, and it was time for anger.

Here was the man who had turned his life inside out and upside down on a whim, sent him on a day trip that was nearly one way. His fury kicked him up and out of his chair.

"You crazy bastard!" he shouted hoarsely, his voice knotted with outrage. He wanted to do something to that smug, dangerous face, but fear—it was still there, would *always* be there when this man was around—held him back. And that made him even madder. Bane was the last person he'd expected to see after yesterday. Couldn't he even let Jack lick his wounds in peace?

"What the hell did you think you were doing? You could have killed me, you sick—"

Bane slid a video case along the counter toward Jack. He had a folded newspaper tucked under one arm, and his lips were puckered into a parody of reproof.

"Don't you think you're overreacting just a *little*?"

Jack resisted the urge to hurl himself over the counter. "I went through *hell,* you bastard!"

"Then I envy you; it's a place I long to revisit."

"You poisoned me..." His words were weak and pathetic, incapable of expressing the outrage he felt.

"Was the beer too strong for you?" He watched Jack carefully, perhaps hoping his gibes would stir Jack into more fury.

Jack's pent-up breath left him in a frustrated gasp. "You're mad. A real Hatter. I think it's about time I called the police."

Bane looked genuinely disappointed. He turned away slightly, offering his dangerous profile to Jack. It was sharp and hard-edged, like the ridge of a crag. His fingers played idly over the spines of video boxes on the shelf beside him, and when he spoke, his words played nastily over Jack's, too. "Oh, I wouldn't do that," he said casually.

Jack hesitated. Bane was beyond his understanding, beyond all rationalization. He was stamping on Jack's noisy bravado with the softest of words, and Jack was a toy in his hands, a stick of seaside rock waiting to be snapped. He feared this man. "And what would stop me?" he asked lamely. "You?"

Bane pulled out a film from its groove on the wall rack. He showed it to Jack. *Eaten Alive.* The cover depicted a rabid cannibal sucking on a human limb. Bane smiled, and his eyes bulged black, obscene.

"You went too far. Those toadstools were bloody lethal!" His last word rang out across the video library as the shrieks from the screen behind Jack were silenced.

Bane took the folded newspaper from under his armpit and tapped the countertop. "Lethal?" He considered for a moment. "Yes," he said at length, "I suppose I am."

He tossed three gold coins onto the scratched wood surface of the counter. Jack caught them as they rolled. He paused, preparing to refuse to serve the man, and then thought better of it almost immediately. Why cause himself more grief? And what had Bane done, really? Given him a trip, that's all. Dennis would say he should be thanking him, not grassing him up to the cops.

Slowly, in an effort to be as defiant as was possible within the confines of such a servile act, he issued Bane the video and entered it on the computer. Bane took the film, and his eyes probed Jack's.

"It's really not me you should be afraid of," he said, and he was no longer smiling. "But I think you already know that, don't you?"

Jack met his gaze. It hurt. Like staring into dark, endless space and knowing it would send you mad. "Why?" he said quietly. "Why did you do it?" And the one thing he really needed to know was, "What the hell have I ever done to you?"

Bane scratched his stubbly chin with a corner of the VHS box as if deliberating whether to answer. Jack's question hung between them. At last, Bane turned slowly, and without another word, he walked down the aisle and out of the shop.

Jack felt his nerves retreat from the edge, and that made the anger return more strongly. His impotent rage needed an outlet. Something to smash, destroy. His eyes alighted on the newspaper Bane had left on the counter, and he seized it eagerly.

On the point of tearing it apart, his attention was caught by the grainy black-and-white photograph on the front page. The lurid headline kicked in a second later:

KILLER TWINS RELEASED AFTER ELEVEN YEARS

Horror crushed his fury. He was staring again into two pairs of duplicated empty eyes, at the blandly attractive faces he'd seen at the Slaughter Inn. But younger, wilder versions, their voluptuous menace caught by the photographer in the first black-and-white blooms of womanhood. Beneath the main picture, two smaller ones depicted a pretty young girl, smiling shyly, and a peroxide-blond lad, his grinning appetite for life frozen forever. Beneath them, the captions ran: *They tortured her to death in the school toilets.* And: *They made love to him before blinding him with a chisel.* Jack devoured the main story hungrily.

When he had done, he folded the newspaper calmly. So what if they drank in The Slaughter? So what if they had killed people? That was eleven years ago; they were disturbed kids then. They wouldn't have been released after all this time if they weren't thought to be safe now. Cured.

He took another look at those hollow eyes, filled in with monochrome grain, and imagined the young student laborer looking into them and seeing...what? His own death? He felt ashamed at the little thrill that mixed with the horror.

He toyed nervously with the video Bane had returned, trying to rid his thoughts of the desirable, disgusting killers, twin Myra Hyndleys with sex appeal. On impulse, he flipped open the box and withdrew the tape. Bane had kept it for three days; Jack should have charged him for overtime, but the idea seemed extremely petty.

Bane was baiting him, that much was obvious. He'd left the newspaper behind to freak out Jack, knowing he'd seen the twins in the pub. Were they friends of his? *"It's not me you should be scared of."* Did Bane mean the twins? He looked at the cassette in his hand. There was no label on it. He studied the box again. *The Mutilator* was stenciled on the spine (by Jack himself). Now what? Bane had switched tapes, which meant he still owed them a film. Jack ejected the *Doctor Who* cassette and popped the one Bane had returned into the machine instead. He didn't know what he expected to find, and after a few seconds of blank hiss, he was just about to remove the tape when it happened.

There it was. Proof that Bane was one sick puppy indeed.

It was hard to tell what was going on; the home video footage recorded on the VHS was cellar-dark.

Bane was playing snuff.

Or was he? All Jack could distinguish was the occasional glint of what he guessed was candlelight on the blade of a hand axe as it climbed and then dived, accompanied by disturbing sound effects as the chopper dug into some soft object. Once, there was the briefest of hints as to what that object might be. Jack rewound that part several times, but it was impossible to define clearly. Jack could play guessing games, though, and the wriggling in his stomach tangled into a big, BIG knot. What sort of scary shit was Bane playing at? *Playing?* Was this another stunt like the horror-themed pub and the mushroom trip to freak out specially favored customers? Or was this for real?

He thought about it for a minute. His hand wandered toward the telephone. Old Bill or Richard, the manager? The police were somehow not an option. Not yet, anyway. Richard, then. He dialed. This was wanton theft of Video Vault property, if nothing else—substituting a twenty-pound video cassette for a cheap home recording—it was something tangible with which to nail the bastard, get him banned, at least.

The phone called out to an empty house. Jack slung the receiver back in its cradle just as Mary waltzed through the door. He ejected the tape and replaced it casually in its box, then shoved it away under the counter. It could wait.

"Been watching dirty movies while I'm out?" Mary flounced up to the counter and spotted the newspaper. "This is more than six months old," she said disgustedly, indicating the date. She tossed it at him. He caught it as the paper flapped toward his face and, for a second, was treated to a close-up of the twins. He threw the paper into the waste bin, as if it was distasteful to the touch.

"You all right?" chirped Mary, dropping her pudgy buttocks onto the seat next to him. She popped open a bag of Hedgehog Flavor Crisps—she still thought that was a cool gag—and offered him one.

He declined with a shake of his head. "Why shouldn't I be?"

"You look a bit of a gloom pig, that's all. Cheer up, Jacky; it might never ha—"

He clapped a hand over her mouth before she could complete the irritating phrase.

After a period of mindless chatter from Mary, which he volleyed dully, he put *Doctor Who* back on. Patrick Troughton's comically grave face reassured him somehow. And that was ridiculous, really, because the Doctor looked scared out of his wits.

CHAPTER NINE

"This is all a bit sleazy, isn't it?" Sam muttered as they stood in the foyer of Camden's Parkhouse Cinema. Jack grinned and hefted his box of video nasties defensively.

"I'm just trying to make an honest buck." He had finally summoned the courage (after years of lusting and yearning, as she well knew) to ask her out. He'd done it over the telephone, casually, as if ordering a pizza, and when it finally came to the crunch, it hadn't seemed such a big deal. As far as he was concerned, she could either say yes or no. Yes was good for him, no was embarrassing, but that was all there was to it. Simple. As it happened, when she answered the phone and listened to what he had to say, she had thought about it very briefly and then said... Well, she'd said yes. Maybe realizing she sounded a little wary, a little unsure what she was getting into, but Jack would have to take that, wouldn't he? She'd said yes. And the thing that struck her as most surprising of all about the whole thing? It *was* no big deal. Jack was Jack and Sam was only Sam, after all. It might work, it might not.

And now Sam was definitely uncomfortable. The titles of some of the films Jack was selling made her blush—*Shriek of the Mutilated* for one, had failed to charm her.

"When you asked me out on a date, I had something rather different in mind," she said a little peevishly. "Dinner in some waterside restaurant, or tickets to a big show. But funnily enough—and you might think I'm being overly particular—I hadn't really considered spending my Saturday night at a gore film festival."

"No?" Jack said innocently. "I thought you might find it interesting."

"Jack, just so you know for the future: flogging violent obscenities to emotional retards is *not* my idea of interesting." She picked up one of the garishly illustrated video boxes. "I mean, *Nightmares in a Damaged Brain*? Hardly inspiring, is it?"

"It inspires this lot." Jack nodded toward a bunch of young men coming their way, dressed, like the majority of the festival attendees, in leather jackets, lurid T-shirts proudly displaying various forms of violent death, and grubby jeans.

"That's what I'm worried about. Inspire them to do what, exactly? Go on, come clean: this is some weird kind of test, isn't it?" Sam watched the uncouth horror fans shambling about, probing at the contents of his large shoebox.

"Test?

"Like an endurance test. To see if I can share your interests. To see if I fit into your dark world."

He grinned but was prevented from answering by a stunted youth with seaweed hair, his face half eaten away by acne, waving a video in front of Jack's nose. "Is this cut?"

"No," he lied smoothly. "It's all there. A real bloodbath. Mind-bendingly repuls—" He hesitated for a moment. Maybe it was his conscience pricking him, Sam thought. Then he plunged on, a splatter salesman waxing lyrical: "Pure gore, mate. Buy it, cherish it, put it on your shelf to impress your mates. We're talking a bloody collector's piece here, and all for twenty quid."

Sam eyed Jack quizzically. He was in his element, eyes glowing, smiling like a wolf prowling amongst the flock, and she was seeing a flip side of him hitherto buried. It was more than a little sordid.

The dwarf with the polluted hair scanned the video cover dubiously. *Zombie Creeping Flesh*, the title boasted, superimposed over a scene of three putrefying heads emerging from the sea, their expressions promising wholesale antisocial activities once they reached the shore. The youth sucked snot down his throat and coughed a blast of foul air over Sam as he deliberated.

A man with a gut like a church bell, wearing a *Nekromantik* T-shirt, pressed a crisp twenty note into Jack's eager hands and tucked a copy of *The Texas Chainsaw Massacre Part Two* inside a carrier bag. Sam sighed. Easy money. Unless one of these ghouls turned out to be an undercover Trading Standards officer. Then there would be *real* horror at the festival.

"Why do they want these tatty old videos?" she asked, deciding she ought to feign a little interest. "Why don't they just buy them new from HMV or somewhere?"

Jack brightened. This was obviously a subject he enjoyed discussing. "They wouldn't be collector's items, would they? These old 'tatty' things, as you call them, are worth loads now. Lots of nostalgic value. Plus, they're uncut. The new vids you get in the shops are trimmed to get a certificate."

"If you say so. I think it's all a bit sad. Not to mention unwholesome."

Now he looked disappointed in her. Oh well. With the break between films over, the eager punters retreated into the screening room again, leaving the merchandise dealers looking rather pleased with themselves. Hugging his box of delights protectively, Jack led Sam toward a large stall guarded by a stocky man dressed completely in leather. His head was as bald as a light bulb, the fluorescents bounding off his waxy pate. Sam waited patiently while Jack conversed with the dealer about their shared "unwholesome" interest.

She turned quickly when the foyer doors of the cinema pushed open behind her, pricked by a dart of fear, expecting to see a squad of policemen with gore detectors at the ready. The man who entered was much more disturbing; Sam had never seen an uglier guy than the one now striding across the foyer. As she watched him, she knew she had seen him before. The fat, jolly butcher face without the jollity; the thick spectacles behind which tadpole eyes squirmed unnervingly; the flabby neck folded into the open collar of his shirt. Yes, she recognized him. But from where? Jack saw him, too, and broke off midsentence. Sam saw a flicker of uneasiness tug at his features, but he was looking past the fat man now, at the two identical blondes who strode stiffly behind him like guards.

The odd trio paused at a stall not far from Jack, ogling the splattery merchandise. Jack felt queasy.

They made love to him...

He tried to prevent the rest of the headline from popping into his head. They were after *him* now.

...before blinding him with a chisel.

No, of course, they weren't. He was just being paranoid again.

"What are *they* doing here?" He was talking to himself in a hoarse whisper, but Carl, the bald dealer, took it upon himself to answer.

"The fat dweeb's a horror writer. He's a festival guest. You know... Roderick Whassisname."

"Bolton? *That's* Roderick Bolton?"

"Not very pleasing on the eye, is he? His books are all right, though."

Jack glanced dubiously at his friend. Carl wasn't renowned for his sophisticated taste in literature. Come to that, neither was Jack. But Roderick Bolton... His novels were unrelievedly nasty, the characters vile, the plots twisted in the extreme. Jack had felt sordid and bruised after reading *Night Scum,* like he'd been given a good kicking. It wasn't an experience he'd been in a hurry to repeat.

"Now I think of it," Jack mused, "he does look like how I'd expect him to, sort of like a fat sea slug with bad taste in suits. But I bet you don't recognize the sexy twins."

Sam gave him a disdainful look. "I'm seriously beginning to wonder why I bothered coming."

Carl pulled at his chin with one hand, the closest he could get to looking thoughtful. "Should I know 'em?" The two blondes were skimming through a magazine with a bisected head on the cover, wearing the same long black dresses they'd worn to The Slaughter. Bolton was inspecting some videos arranged on a dealer's table with the air of a disappointed connoisseur.

"Don't you ever watch the news?" Jack said as if he was diligent in that respect himself. He pushed his unease deep down. Buried it. Why should *he* fear? Just because they drank in his...local? Could he really call it that? Did he even *want* to think of The Slaughter in such cozy terms? He didn't fear the twins. Bane had been wrong if he supposed Jack did.

They repelled him, but he didn't *fear* them.

"So, who *are* they? The new *Blue Peter* presenters?" Carl's popout eyes were bulging more than usual as he inspected the twins' voluptuous bodies.

The twins were walking away from the stall now, heading in Jack's direction, Bolton leading them like a bizarre pimp. All three were watching Jack as if they not only recognized him, but were unsurprised to see him here. As if they'd...followed him? Jack's mouth was dry.

"I don't like the look of them," Sam hissed as they approached. "They seem more your type, though, so I'll leave you to entertain them." She ducked off to the Ladies.

"Talk about bedroom eyes," Carl whispered, gaping at the twins.

"Try slaughterhouse eyes instead," Jack answered, and then they had reached him, freezing like wax dummies, as if waiting for Bolton to give them leave to speak.

As Sam hovered above the wet toilet seat, flesh writhing at the squalor of the cubicle, she remembered where she had seen the fat man.

She flushed the toilet by using her foot to depress the dirty handle, then pushed open the door. One of the few other females present at the horror festival was gazing at her sorry reflection in the mirror. Her skin was dirty white, like slush. She wore black jeans, a black sweater, and a black leather jacket, while a broom of dyed black hair sprouted from her head. She resembled a swollen maggot squeezed into a fancy gothic dress. Sam washed her hands next to the girl.

"Hi," Sam said brightly.

The podgy Goth looked her over moodily. "Not gory enough."

"Sorry?"

"The festival films. Tame as fuck." Her eyes were dim, her mouth forming the words without stretching, like a morbid glove puppet.

"I really wouldn't know."

"The world's too safe and bland. Sanitized as fuck. Even our films have been neutered. It's the McDonald's syndrome, ain't it? No fuckin' heart. Have a nice day, although I fuckin' hate your guts. Let's see more *real* guts."

"I'll pass, if you don't mind." Sam didn't want this conversation. Thanks awfully, but no.

"That's what we're here for, ain't it?" The Goth's small rip of a mouth twisted disconcertingly into a sneer. "I suppose you just like a good story." She watched Sam washing her hands thoroughly.

"As a matter of fact, yes." Irritation flared in her voice. Irritation with the seedy festival, the tragic Goth next to her, but most of all with Jack for bringing her.

"Of course, you do." The maggot girl sniffed. "So why are you here?"

Sam shook her hands dry. There was no towel or drying machine, naturally. "A good question. Give me five minutes, and I won't be."

As Sam made for the door, the girl called after her. "I used to go out with him, you know."

Sam stopped, hand on the doorknob. The girl looked lost and pathetic by the grubby wash basins. "Who?" Sam asked. Dismay grounded her. The girl couldn't mean Jack, surely?

"Oh, you know...*him*. Disgusting, ain't he? I don't know how I could have done it, really."

Sam waited for her to continue.

"We've seen you in The Slaughter. What a coincidence we should find you here, too." Bolton's voice was faintly tinged with a Brummie accent. The twins flanked him silently.

Jack didn't reply, didn't know how to. Bolton was shifting through Jack's videos, offering the odd comment as he did so.

"You have some films the press like to portray as nasty," the writer said, hitching up his brown trousers slightly. "But we know otherwise. Hardly a remarkable selection by any means." His tiny eyes burrowed deep into their pockets of flesh as if trying to hide from life. Jack had the unnerving impression that the longer he stared into them, the smaller they became, like whelks shrinking to the touch. His own face peered back at him, reflected in Bolton's spectacles.

Carl wouldn't let that comment pass. "What's unremarkable about *Bloodsucking Freaks* or *The Anthropophagous Beast*? Choice bunch, mate. Cream of the crop."

Bolton ignored him, still watching Jack carefully. "As I said, unremarkable. Safe, I might even venture. However, I know somewhere you might find a rather more esoteric collection to which the word 'safe' hardly applies." A flash of a twisted smile. His eyes emerged from their holes for a second, briefly excited, before retreating again. Jack looked away and met the gaze of the twins. Blue, blue eyes. Xeroxed eyes. Even their blinking was in chorus.

"You might wonder why I'm telling you all this," Bolton continued condescendingly. "I am moved, if you like, by an urge to broaden the viewing experience of those who share my interest. I wouldn't like for you to have to dull your mind on such...mediocrity." He glanced down scornfully at Jack's video box. "I can promise you *genuine* thrills." Again, that unhealthy smile, as he waited for his words to sink in. Jack waited, too, feeling like a butterfly pinned to a board.

"Would you like me to tell you where to find these unholy grails of the video age?"

"Too bloody right, mate," said Carl.

Sam was fascinated despite her distaste. "So why did you get involved with him? He's hardly a looker, is he?"

The girl rasped. Sam realized with a twinge of unease that she was laughing, although her eyes remained empty and dark.

"He's fuckin' *hideous*. Inside and out. But there's an attraction, too."

"There is?"

"He knows things. He...I dunno...has a feel for dark things. I...liked that."

She had dropped the sound bytes now, as if she realized she no longer needed to pretend she meant them. They were lines she'd diligently learned, but now that's all they were. The meanings had left her along with the one who'd taught them.

"But if he used to..." Sam hesitated. "...do sick stuff to you, why didn't you just walk?"

"He twisted my soul right. Twisted it like..." Metaphors failed her, but Sam, staring into her burned-out eyes, could form her own. "But there was a kind of thrill to it all as well. Can you understand that?" She looked up hopefully at Sam, then lowered her gaze again. "No. You probably can't. But there was, at first. Then there was just degradation. And fear." She reached out and played with one of the taps, turning it on, then off again. "He told me if I ever left him, he'd do worse stuff to me."

"So, how did you get away?"

"Oh, he got bored. He found others more like himself. Sick, nasty."

Sam forced herself to withdraw from this private, sordid world the girl was sucking her into. She craved daylight.

"They're out there with him now," the girl said, rasping with bitter satisfaction. "Talking to your boyfriend."

The twins hadn't said a word. Bolton was doing all the talking. And now he had finished. He put his pen away in a jacket pocket, pressed a torn piece of paper into Jack's hands. Jack stared at the hastily scribbled address. Carl craned his neck for a look, too, and Jack folded it away into his pocket. "Thanks," he said, unsure quite how to react.

Bolton smiled. And Sam stormed up to them, her face flushed with anger and disgust.

"We're out of here," she barked, throwing a withering look at Bolton and the twins.

"Hang on. I haven't finished selling my—"

She knocked the box out of his hand with a fury he'd never seen in her before. Videos tumbled onto the floor. *"Now!"*

Carl had a silly grin on his face. Bolton nodded slowly in farewell and ushered away the mannequin twins. Jack, face burning, stooped to collect his precious films.

Outside, Jack turned on Sam as she waited by his car. "What the hell was that all about?"

"It looks like I failed your sordid little test. Now don't talk; just drive."

Jack started the engine. He was angry himself now. "I could have made a packet in there!"

"Thanks for the date," she replied stonily. "I'll treasure it always." She stared straight ahead into the darkness, all the way back to Bristol.

CHAPTER TEN

Joe's roll-up was poised in front of his lips, his eyes blinking slowly. He seemed to be listening, but Jack couldn't tell for sure. He had to talk loudly to be heard over the babble of students filling the room. The Sunset Café was near to one of Bristol University's many residence halls and was always crowded during term time with exuberant students finding out what the game of life was all about now they had left their parents and the security of childhood behind. Jack envied them their optimism. Jaded and cynical already, and still only thirty! Perhaps Dennis was right, and it was watching all those videos that had killed his zest for life. Then again, Dennis was hardly one to talk about zest.

Weak sunlight made the world look tired and dirty through the windows. Passersby wore a washed-out, dusty look. The dust crusting the panes rimed the inside of Jack's head, too, and Joe's blank stare only intensified the staleness. Jack looked past him, watching The Slaughter Inn, which could just be seen on the far corner of the opposite street. It looked desolate, stranded in midday, craving the coming of dusk.

He'd been telling Joe about meeting Bolton and the twins. He wanted to tell him about Sam, but it hardly seemed worth the effort when it came down to it. One date and it was over. He wanted to tell Joe about the silent journey from London, about how he'd leaned forward to say something, *anything* to her as he pulled up outside her flat; how she'd slammed him out of her life with the simple words: "Forget it."

Forget it. Perhaps when he thought about it, it didn't seem such a hard thing to do. Yes, perhaps it was best to bury Sam. After all, he'd only gone out with her for one date. *And had fancied her for years.* He sipped his tea, feeling edgy and irritable. He couldn't explain any of this to Joe; you didn't talk about *relationships* with Joe.

"Fancy going to The Slaughter tonight?" he said to break the silence that had fallen between them.

Joe inserted his roll-up between his lips, took a long pull. It was his day off; he was determined to take everything slowly, and that included answering. "Why don't you just pack your bags and move in?" he said finally.

The idea made Jack uncomfortable. "I've only been in there twice!" Was Joe getting at him? He *had* been droning on a bit about the pub's infamous clientele. Did Joe think he *condoned* the twins drinking there? Sod him. He talked about the pub because it interested him. Bane interested him; the barmaid interested him. All right, it was more than interest; there was a healthy dose of fear involved there, too. But he wouldn't be scared away from the pub (and if that was all Bane was trying to do, why invite him in the first place?) because it offered something he felt he needed, although he didn't know what the hell that was. Perhaps just something to kickstart his boring life.

"You don't like it, do you?"

"Don't like what?" Joe's concentration had wandered again.

"The Slaughter."

Joe thought about that. "It's all right. Lost pub for lost boys and girls. I like any place where there's a chance of losing things."

Was that supposed to be profound? "Like your mind, you mean?" Jack hadn't told anyone about his little experience with the mushrooms. Nigel had phoned him the morning after to check if he was still on for work the next week and to grudgingly relay Sam's message. Jack had blamed his odd behavior in the pub on gut rot. Nigel had swallowed it, but then Nigel was stupid. Jack didn't want to discuss it. If there was some kind of crazy feud going on between him and Bane, then he wanted it to remain a private one for now. So why did he want to go back?

"That'll do, to begin with," Joe replied after a mighty pause so that Jack was left trying to remember what he had said to him in the first place. Joe was an incongruous sight, sitting in the café amongst so many bright young things. It wasn't his tatty psychedelic shirt and soiled overcoat that stood him apart so much as his stolid disinterest in everything around him. You could tell by his bagging eyes and his droopy, stoic expression that he had lived through a few things and would probably live through a few more, and all of them would be more genuine and meaningful than the accumulated experiences of every shallow-headed youth in the café. He could have been a Buzz Aldrin or a shell-shocked 'Nam vet. He could have been a singer in a rock 'n' roll band who could tell you a thing or two about hard living. He could have been a user, a loser. And really, he was all of these things and none of them. He was Joe, the Pizza Delivery Man, and he *could* tell you a thing or two. The trouble was, he never did. You could see all this in his calm but worn features, and Jack had always envied him for being so bloody cool. Sometimes he was so cool he was irritating.

Jack glanced at his watch. Fascinating as this lunch with Joe had been, he only had twenty minutes before he was due back at the video library, and he badly wanted to take a walk, get some fresh air. He was about to inform Joe when something happened to make him change his mind.

He saw two figures leaving The Slaughter, heading this way, and even though they were some distance away, he knew who they were. He stiffened with excitement, promptly forgetting all about Joe, and even Sam. There was something about this woman that he could not shake off. He watched her approaching the cafe, the singer of the band that had played in The Slaughter lurching by her side, and he was sure they were going to come inside. She wore a shiny leather jacket that tapered around her narrow waist and a long black skirt. Her hair was piled on top of her head, leaving her aesthetic cheekbones dangerously on show, honed to kill. They walked past the café, going about their own strange business.

Jack began to droop. There was something cruel about her, and he'd vowed to put dark things out of his mind, but—

She'd seen him! She had glanced casually through the window as she strolled past, and now she was stopping, watching him expressionlessly. Jack stared back. He was on the edge of a dizzy plunge, waiting to be pushed over. Then she was stepping toward the door and entering the café.

The singer followed obediently. Jack glanced at him nervously. Without his wraparound shades, he looked hunted, wary, his eyes pale and weak. In his dirty leathers, spiked belt, and big boots, he looked like a man playing at being a teenager, and in the light of day, he knew it. He shrugged off the dusty custard sunlight and closed the door behind him, hunched, sheepish eyes darting around the crowded room self-consciously. Stripped of his stage act, he was just a social misfit with a chip on his shouldder, not the terrifying moral rapist he'd been a few nights ago.

The barmaid stopped beside Jack's table. He stared at her, fascinated. Her lips were pursed coquettishly as she measured him up. He had to say something cool. He *had* to.

She spoke instead. "Been on any good trips lately?"

Jack wilted. His eyes fell away. He was a school kid, derided by a sarcastic teacher in front of his friends. She rested one hand on his arm as she spoke, and he could smell her perfume: autumnal musk. Her eyes were cruel, but he wanted her then despite everything. He wanted her badly, a deep need, uncomplicated by reason. So he looked up again, straight into her eyes, and he would have said something very cool indeed, but this time Joe beat him to it.

"He went to Weston Super Mare for the day in June. Does that count?"

Jack suddenly hated his friend. Joe didn't even smile as he said it.

The barmaid flashed him a look that would have shriveled any normal man, but not Joe. Her hand traveled up Jack's arm a little way, and electricity blasted through him. She knelt beside the table, her face level with his, while the singer strode awkwardly to the counter and ordered two teas.

"Was it bad?" she said simply.

Jack took control. He could almost have believed her concern was for real had it not been for her eyes. "Nothing I couldn't handle," he lied. He sucked in a breath. "Why did he do it?"

She tilted her head like a puzzled dog, although he knew she understood him full well.

"Your boss. Bane. Why did he do it?"

She smiled, showing glistening white teeth sheathed in strawberries. "My *boss?* Oh, he's a lot more than that..."

Jack flinched. Of course, he'd expected as much, but it still made him feel unaccountably numb. He made as if to shake her hand off his arm, but she squeezed tighter.

"Bane *does* things," she continued, answering his question at last. "He *likes* to do them." As if that explained everything.

Joe watched and listened incuriously. His saucer eyes took it all in, but he showed no sign of understanding their words, nor of wanting to. Jack was suddenly grateful for his incurious nature. He looked up at the dark woman, and anger struggled with his inexplicable desire.

"Tell him that *I* don't like the things he does. And I don't like *him*."

She chuckled, and it was a 3:00 a.m. sound, the hour that marked that loneliest, bleakest stretch of the night. Despite Bane, despite everything she was, he still wanted her; and maybe, just maybe, he could see something in her dark green eyes that showed some interest in him, too. Or was he deluding himself again, like he'd deluded himself that he and Sam might have something together.

The barmaid drew close, so close he could smell her warm, musky breath. She stroked his sleeve and said, "If you don't like Bane, why don't you tell him yourself?" Abruptly she straightened up and left him, sauntering up the aisle to join the singer at a table near the counter.

"She seems into you," said Joe. Was there a note of wonder in his phlegmatic drawl? And Jack, already disquieted by the barmaid's words, felt even more uneasy. He watched her chatting with the uncomfortable-looking musician, noticed the way the man answered her questions with politeness and respect, although Jack couldn't hear what they were saying over the general café chatter. Respect often came from fear; Jack knew that. But was it the barmaid the musician feared, or Bane?

Joe rolled another cigarette. "It might be safer snogging Myra Hindley," he said after a while.

Jack snapped his gaze away from the far table. "Safer than what?"

Joe's mouth tilted up at one end, the nearest he ever came to smiling. He shook his head.

"What *are* you on about, Joe?" He got to his feet, on the point of leaving. He felt irritated and turned on in equal measures. Then he shrugged and sat down again. "No one in their right mind would mess with a girl like that."

"That's why I'm warning *you*. Be careful out there."

Jack laughed him off. "Got too much pizza in your brain, Joey." But he had taken in every word.

Be careful out there.

CHAPTER ELEVEN

He hadn't heard her come in. He was busy watching an old black-and-white Universal horror film when the voice cut through his dream.

"You into wild sex?"

That woke him up and fast. She was leaning against the video racks that lined the left wall of the passage. Her black hair was messy, sleepy, creeping enigmatically over half of her long face, obscuring one eye. She was wearing a black lace bodice and tight blue jeans. Stiletto spikes held her high.

"What's that?" His mind repeated the question just to make sure he'd heard it right.

She wasn't fooled. "Well?" She blinked at him slowly, coquettishly.

He thought: *Am I...? Would I?* Hot excitement revved through him at what she was suggesting.

"Depends who's offering it," he said eventually.

Be careful out there. He remembered Joe's words.

And then he forgot them.

She took him through the back door of The Slaughter. He felt spiked with unease and hot with lust. She might be taking him to see Bane. But he couldn't have said no if he'd wanted to now. He was on the trail of wild sex, and he was hooked.

But was he the hunter or the prey?

She led him up a darkened flight of curving stairs. *Was Bane waiting for him at the top?* They passed a small window, which gave him a snatch of daylight, and carried on up to a landing and a deep, deep black carpet that sucked at his feet. She held his hand, her cold fingers coiling around his. She hesitated outside a door, glanced back at him as if checking to see if he was brave enough.

Be care—

Shut up, Joe.

He smiled at her with what he hoped was cool nonchalance and said, "Why me?"

She arched her dark eyebrows and pushed the door open. *Why me?* The question chased around inside his head. *Why not?*

He lay on the black-quilted bed and watched her undress, and each item of clothing she took off peeled away another layer of excited panic inside him. *This is ludicrous*, he thought. *These things just don't happen. Not to me.*

Old paintings of mostly obscure origin adorned the crimson walls; in pride of place above the headboard—above Jack's head—a framed print of Goya's *When Reason Sleeps*. Jack gazed at it and breathed in deeply. His heart was running downhill, gathering speed. The carpet and curtains, like the walls, were steeped in blood, a vibrant, screaming scarlet. The effect accentuated his desire—and his fear.

His brain told him this really wasn't a good idea; Bane could return at any moment. His body told him to lie back and enjoy it.

"Aren't you even going to tell me your name?" he said as she unhooked her bra. His eyes were firmly fastened on her, unable to look away. The crow and skull tattoo quivered and was freed. He couldn't leave now.

"Is it important?" She slid out of her jeans and stood over him, naked but for her black panties.

No. "*I* think so," he said. *Bane. Where was Bane?* She'd said he was out of town for the day. She could have got it wrong. She could be lying, playing dangerous games. And what if the barman who'd been serving downstairs should see him leave through the back door? If anyone found out he was messing with Bane's woman... His eyes fled toward the door. His lunch hour would be over soon. *Get out. Now. Before you get in too deep.* Who was he fooling? He was in as deep as it got. She knelt on the foot of the bed and stalked toward him on all fours. *Get out!*

"I don't," she purred, closing the door on that subject. She nuzzled his neck as she began undoing his belt, then sat back and pulled off his jeans.

The girl was smiling coyly at him as she peeled off her blouse. Outside, he could hear crows in the trees; they made him feel cold and afraid, and he couldn't remember why that was. She was laughing at his shyness, yet he knew she was frightened, too. This was a new experience for both of them. He was lying on his bed, and she was kneeling beside him, naked now but for her little white bra and panties. Her blonde hair fell over her left eye and half of her mouth. Her cheeks were red, as red as his, but she was braver. He was in too deep to stop now, and his heart was slamming against his naked chest. She took one of his hands in hers and placed it against her naked stomach, began to slide it up toward her bra. "Come on," she said, "There's nothing to be scared of..."

But there was. There was.

They hadn't heard him below them. They hadn't heard him creeping up the stairs. He shouldn't have been there. But he was. He was. The bedroom door swung slowly open, and a shadow blocked the doorway.

The girl looked up, not understanding at first. Then her face was falling apart in utter terror.

But the boy couldn't see his father's face. It was lost in shadow like the rest of his body.

A shadow that didn't move.

Outside, the crows filled the endless stretch of time with their black sound. The house held its breath.

He was helpless. Locked in sudden terror. He stared into her eyes as she leaned over him, a woman with hair like the night. He was choking, suddenly unable to breathe, then her hands were caressing his face, calming him. He closed his eyes and sucked in breath like a drowning man.

She unbuttoned his shirt, kissed his left nipple. Stroked one hand down his thin chest. *Maybe it was all right...this time.* The fear lingered, but the lust was stronger; it was thick and sweaty, driving away doubt and memory, urging him on, a remorseless thing that would not be ignored.

"What about ..." He found his voice, but his words sounded lame, pathetic. "You got something I can wear?"

She lifted her head from his chest and gazed at him mockingly. "You want to slip into some pajamas?" She laughed that bleak 3:00 a.m. sound again, kissed him, and a demon came alive inside his mouth. Her tongue darted in, out. Her breath tasted of something strange, indefinable, at once unpleasant and delicious. His hands crept to her breasts; the panic was just a faint shadow of memory, and he no longer cared. About anything.

She withdrew her mouth from his, arching her neck back like a cobra poised to strike, momentarily holding back the killing bite. "Sex and Death: two sides of the same coin. Do you want to toss for it?"

He blinked up at her uncomprehendingly.

She shook her tousled hair until one eye disappeared beneath the black tendrils. "You have to ask yourself: does this girl fuck on empty? Or is her chamber loaded? To know life, first, you have to rut with death." Her hands crept up her own body, over her cheekbones, slid into the depths of her tangled hair. And pulled. The black wilderness came away smoothly. She laid the wig on the bed beside Jack, and her head was as bald as the moon.

Jack's breath expelled slowly. Her baldness accentuated her cruel, desirable features. He felt his passions soar.

"My name's Lila," she said, and descended on him fiercely.

CHAPTER TWELVE

He woke to the sound of crows, and they made him feel small. Small and lonely and scared. Black velvet croaking, rain tapping the window impatiently. Crows? Their ugly sound scratched away the remaining veneer of sleep. The first thing he saw upon opening his crusty eyes was a pair of Y-Fronts draped over the bedside lamp. As he stared at them, the hangover kicked in. He blinked, rolled over, trying to summon the oblivious cocoon of sleep again. The crows wouldn't let him. Nor would the prolonged drill of the doorbell as it sounded for the second time.

He groped out of bed, head blank, swaying, fished his underpants from the lamp, and stumbled into them. His alarm clock lay on its side in the middle of the room, one leg in the air as if it, too, had enjoyed a wild night. Its blank face seemed somehow disapproving as it showed him the time: 12:30.

He wavered, listening to the bell and the crows and feeling very unclean. The inside of his head needed a rinse. He thought of Lila. *All* of him needed a rinse. But he'd have to answer the bell first.

He scooped up the entry phone, throttling the bell in mid-whine. "Yeah?"

"The day's old. Time to do something." Joe, and the pizza delivery man's words could be a comment on Jack's whole life.

"How do you know I'm wasting it?" He clawed a hand through his hair, his mind a turgid mess of dirty memories.

"It's Saturday, or so my Mum said when she brought me my breakfast in bed. Which means last night was Friday. Which means we were pissed out of our swedes[7]. Which means you're almost certainly still in—"

"Yeah, all right. Spare me the bloody deductions, Sherlock." Joe could be a real pain. Jack thumbed the button to unlock the door and dropped the phone back on its hook. He climbed into his dressing gown[8] and waited for Joe to reach him.

Dennis had left half a bowl of cornflakes on top of the telly in his usual rush before work. The electrician loathed working Saturdays. Jack stared out the window at gray skies while the preceding day's events shunted slowly along his memory tracks. Lila's bedroom, a hungry red mouth; escaping The Slaughter at last; slinking guiltily back to the Video Vault an hour late from his lunch break; Mary's prying questions; Joe; the pub. Not *that* pub. He had been quite firm on that score. Joe had been puzzled, but Jack had wanted to *drink* and wasn't in the mood for explanations. He felt unclean then, he felt unclean now, and all the beer in the world had been unable to wash away the stain.

His mouth was a fetid swamp. And he missed Sam. *Can't make up your mind, can you?* You have delirious sex with a crazy, wild woman—*Bane's* woman!—and now you're running scared, clutching at safe memories of Sam, safe because they never meant anything.

He missed Sam.

Joe nudged his way into the flat, rain glistening in his hair. He was carrying a big parcel the size of a hatbox. "Wise man bearing gifts," he said, his round face expressionless. Jack blinked sleepily at him. Joe was still wearing the same clothes as last night, a stretched red jumper that would have suited a reprobate Rupert the Bear, a frayed overcoat, and a pair of rumpled jeans. His eyes were puffy saucers. Jack had never seen anyone who looked less like a wise man. The idea forced a chuckle from him.

"What the hell have you got there?"

Joe shrugged, handed the box to Jack. "Dennis must have let it in," he said as if he were discussing the household cat.

Jack held it. JACK BREEN was scrawled in spidery script on the address sticker. A finger of unease poked him in the back as he

---

[7] British slang, head
[8] Bathrobe

examined the handwriting. It was jagged, spiteful. He tore away the wrapping and opened the box.

Both of them gaped at the object revealed inside, stunned into silence. Nausea chugged up Jack's throat. Fear picked at his mind.

A skull sat in the box.

A human skull. Soil clogged the eye sockets, stained the teeth. And between those teeth, held firmly like a sandwich, was a video box. Jack could read the Video Vault label and the title, *Eaten Alive,* on the spine. Something moved in one of the caked eye sockets: a maggot, creamy tip quivering through a tunnel of soil and bone.

"Do all your customers return their films like this?" Joe asked after a while. He lit a cigarette and sat back, studying the grisly object impassively.

Jack breathed in deeply, found his voice. "Only the sick ones."

"A novel form of hate mail. I like it. So, who's it from?"

"Bane," he answered in a small voice. He still hadn't told Joe about the landlord's little pranks involving swapped tapes and mushroom trips. He hadn't mentioned his tryst with Lila either. Dark secrets had to stay buried.

"Mister Slaughter Inn?" Joe digested this information. "D'you think he's trying to tell you something?"

"He's just trying to freak me out, that's all."

"Doing a pretty good job. What have you done to him? Slept with his mother?"

Jack said nothing. If Bane knew about his little tryst with Lila, it would explain this latest stunt, but not the previous things he'd done. Whatever the reason behind this madness, Jack was undoubtedly neck-deep in some very bad stuff, and he wanted out. Gingerly, he pried the video from between the soiled jaws. Then he slammed the lid over the hat box.

"Bit of a head-case, I'd say," Joe said. "Or is this some sort of code you horror fans indulge in? D'you have to send him back a severed foot?"

"What do you want anyway, Joe?" Jack was scrutinizing the video box. He flipped it open.

"What do you think I want? It's Saturday."

"We've already been through that bit. So what?"

"So, let's drink."

"We did that last night."

"And we can do it again today. Keep doing it until we get it right."

Joe couldn't take a hint. His eyes were leveled on Jack, measuring him up. When Joe looked at him that way, Jack always felt like those big, sadly comic eyes were inside his head, rooting through the contents. He was going to have to be firm.

"No, Joe. Not today. Do me a favor and drink on your own. I've got things on my plate."

"In your box, more like."

"How about if I say please?"

"If you don't want me around, you be sure to tell me now." Joe continued to relax in his seat, calmly smoking. Jack waited for him patiently. When he finally got to his feet, it took him an age to move to the door. He looked over his shoulder at the box as he left the room. "I can see you'd rather play with a dirty skull than with your mates, so I won't keep you from it any longer. Remember, safe sex."

Jack paled. It was as if Joe had an uncanny ability to read his mind. *"Does this girl fuck on empty, or is my chamber loaded?"*

As soon as he had gone, Jack inserted the tape into the VHS player. He didn't know what to expect, but he guessed it would be unpleasant.

He was right. Again, while the box said *Eaten Alive,* the tape itself was something else. More dingy home-video footage, the hand axe chopping at a vague object, the sickening sound of flesh giving way to sharp steel. And then the candlelight was extinguished and a naked bulb flared on to take its place, and in the sudden brightness, Jack could see a small, bare room, and he could see what was being chopped. A hatchet blade lifted, sheathed in blood, and plunged down into a woman's naked chest. Up again. Down. Biting deep into the right breast. A spurt of blood covered it, but not before he saw the tattoo.

Jack threw himself backward, away from the television screen, as if he'd received an electric shock. He tumbled over one arm of the sofa and cracked his head on the wall as he fell. He sat there slumped for a minute. The aging punk in the flat upstairs was playing *Woman* by The Anti-Nowhere League. Rain spat on the windowpanes. Normal life settling around him. He tried to settle with it, squeezing his head with both hands. He tried to keep his eyes away from the mutilation on the television, but his head twisted around again as if turned by a vindictive, invisible hand.

The tattoo was unmistakably familiar. A crow resting on a skull. The last time he'd seen it, he'd been fondling and kissing it in Bane's bedroom.

On the screen, the carnage continued. Lila's face, almost bisected by the hatchet. He could almost admire the horrible special effects. Lunatic laughter swept up inside him. He shut it in with a hand over his mouth, screamed soundlessly into his clammy palm. He sat there until he heard the obscenity end, then he got up slowly and lurched to the window, pressed his forehead against cool glass.

Rain smeared his vision, but the chill pane calmed him. He shrugged into his jacket and jeans and pulled on his boots. Yes, he was calm now: an empty sort of calm, leaden with horror. He knew what he had to do. And he wasn't scared to do it. He left the flat and headed down Buckingham Road. To the Slaughter.

The pub was noticeably more packed than it had been the day he'd been there with Nigel, but Jack wasn't aware of it. He pushed through a throng of lads bellowing around a *Dracula* pinball machine and made for the bar. Bane was a monster. And what did you do with monsters? What did Beowulf do with Grendel?

But Jack was no Beowulf, was he?

The thought betrayed him, stealing a hefty slice of his bravado. He thought of Lila, of kissing her lips, her face. Of the hatchet, kissing her, too, in its own special way. Jack was a character in one of his own video nasties, and Bane was the director. This was too unreal. It was almost as if Bane had pushed Lila at him, like he was playing a game to make everyone as dirty and sick as him. Bane uses Lila, Lila uses Jack, Bane kills Lila, Jack kills...

Lila was dead. And no matter how defiled he'd felt lying with her, he couldn't let that pass. He broke through a gang of middle-aged punks and stood beside the Frankenstein Monster. Bane was there behind the bar, wiping a glass. He saw Jack and smiled.

Jack moved closer to the bar. A sense of the ridiculous almost swept away his resolve—The Man with No Name approaching a gunfight without a cool one-liner. Or an even cooler gun hand. But Bane's evil grin spurred him on.

He tossed the tape onto the bar top. Bane didn't even look at it. "You really did go too far this time." Revulsion exploded inside him. *"You sick bastard!"*

The punks swiveled to take him in, eager for a spot of the old ultra-violence. A young couple next to him at the bar backed away slowly. What a silly Clint. Bane put the glass down.

"Swing it," one of the punks urged Bane. "Slap the prick."

He saw Lila's bewitching, guileful features demolished by a hatchet blow, and all self-doubt vanished. He wanted to stuff that tape right down Bane's throat the way Bane had stuffed it into the jaws of the skull.

Skull? *Lila's?*

His hands shot out suddenly across the bar, and they were around Bane's wiry neck as if they were compelled by something greater than him, something he could no longer control. His breath sobbed out of him as he squeezed, *squeezed.*

And Bane just let him.

Of course, it wasn't Lila's skull. How could it be? He'd been with her just the day before. They'd made love, but it was more like making hate. He remembered his orgasm; it had been a moment of revelation, but a terrifying one, like he'd awoken in darkness, alone, and all he could hear was screaming. And then Lila had laughed at him, and he'd got up feeling like he'd just killed something and the stain would be with him forever, and—

And Bane just stood there and let him do it. His arms were folded, but his face was starting to purple. His eyes, fixed unflinchingly on Jack's, were getting larger, holes sucking Jack toward them, and all the time he kept right on smiling. And Jack began to smile, too. A mad joy powered his grip and danced in his heart because he knew he could kill Bane. He wanted to destroy him so much, wipe the stain away from his life. Throttle him like...

Like the squirrel in the woods.

He let go abruptly and fell forward across the bar top, gasping.

"Whassamatter wiv ya, ya fuckin'wimp!" a guy with a Mohawk snorted derisively.

Bane took his eyes off Jack, his face slowly regaining its normal color. He didn't even cough to show discomfort as he turned to Mohawk. "You're barred," he said in a low, deadly voice. The punk looked as though he wanted to argue. Bane's bottomless eyes warned him to think very carefully about that. He turned to his mates for support, but they didn't give him any, staying silent. Eventually, he gave up any pretense of defiance and jostled his way toward the door, lobbing an obscenity at Bane when he was at a safe distance.

Jack straightened up, breathing heavily. The spotlight had left him for the moment. He looked into Bane's eyes and saw himself reflected there, like a ghost of himself. He picked up the tape, clinging to it as if it were a life raft.

Bane watched him silently.

"You *killed* her!" He was still struggling to comprehend the craziness of what he had seen.

Bane picked up another glass and began polishing it with a dish-towel. "I enjoyed the film. Must pop round for another one sometime."

Jack stared at Bane's raw, dirty fingers as they held the glass: the same fingers that had wrapped around the hatchet handle. He felt sick, sick to death. Bane and Lila had changed him somehow, and he knew he would never be the same. *"To know life, first you have to rut with death."* Well, he had, and so had she.

He turned to go. It was over; let the police do the rest. The punks fell back, smirking at him as he passed. He was halfway to the door when Bane called to him.

"I take it you don't want a drink then." He was laughing. The punks were laughing.

Even Lila was laughing as she emerged from the room behind the bar and put an arm around Bane.

Jack groped his way out into the rain.

CHAPTER THIRTEEN

They were hanging around the phone box at the end of the street when Sam came out of the corner shop. Like overgrown teenagers, she thought, glad that they were on the opposite side of the road from her. She wondered what had brought them to this part of town, and the idea crossed her mind that they might be playing a gig in one of the nearby pubs. She just wished they'd stay away from her district as she hurried down Cotham Hill, clutching her shopping bag more tightly than she needed to.

She looked back once and was disconcerted to see they were watching her. It was nearly dusk, and their faces were lost to shadow, but she knew they were watching. Her shoulders drew together as she walked swiftly on, turning onto Ravenswood Road.

Seeing the band again reminded her of Jack, and that made her irritable, as if it was *his* fault they were lurking around. Her mood worsened when she saw someone had left the front door to the house ajar for about the third time that week. Jesus Christ, anyone would think burglars had gone out of fashion. She slammed the door behind her demonstratively and briefly considered posting a niggly note insisting on a proper door-closing procedure, then realized how pedantic she was becoming and almost blamed that on Jack, too.

Halfway up the stairs, she was met by Kirby, who nuzzled her tights and wound his ginger tail around her ankle as if trying to trip her up. The cat followed her up to Sam's flat, impatient for its dinner. Sam was rather less impatient for hers. She wanted a bath first to wash away the day's grime and hassles. She fed Kirby and trotted him back down the stairs again to let him out. The light timer clicked off as she was re-climbing the stairs, and darkness rushed for her. She stumbled over loose carpeting on the risers and banged her elbow painfully against the wall. She was in a foul mood by the time she reached her flat again.

She started running the tap immediately, the soothing sound of water gurgling in the bathtub offering her the first bit of comfort she'd had all day. She glanced at her telephone as she undressed in the bedroom, as if daring it to ring. *Wanting* it to ring. But she knew he wouldn't. Even Thomas hadn't bothered, which *was* surprising—he hadn't contacted her since the day of The Slaughter gig. It looked like he'd been frightened off for life. At least it saved her the hassle of finishing with him. But a girl likes to be wanted, for God's sake; it's nice to know someone out there still needs you. Right now, it looked like nobody gave a flying hoot. Certainly not Jack. She threw her shoe across the room in a burst of anger. But she wouldn't ring him. She *wouldn't*.

The bath received her with a gorgeous, steamy embrace, and she let out an elaborate sigh that carried with it all the frustrations of her life. She shut her eyes and sank her head back into the foam until the water closed over her ears. Music from the flat next door became muffled and hollow, and she smiled, retreating momentarily into childhood, imagining herself in a submarine, cruising beneath a warm, summer sea.

She'd been in a dream-like state for what must have been a quarter of an hour or so when the bathroom door, which had no lock (living alone, she'd never needed one), opened behind her.

A shadow impinged on her senses, and her eyes flew open. The woman from The Slaughter was staring down at her with a mocking smile. Sam sat bolt upright. She was awake—she could feel the foam squeaking in her ears and the lukewarm water around her waist—but this was a nightmare.

The nightmare spoke.

"Enjoying your bath?" She wore an immaculate leather jacket and a miniskirt revealing long, shapely legs sheathed in black stockings, but Sam only registered this dimly, without really taking it in. She was still struggling to swallow her shock. No words could get through.

She covered her breasts, and her mouth hung loosely as the barmaid advanced farther inside her bathroom. Her *bathroom!* Sam wasn't sure whether she was more scared or outraged. She found her voice.

"*Get the hell out!*" Her scream was high-pitched, uncontrolled. She gaped at the woman in gobsmacked horror.

"I let myself in," the barmaid said casually, as if they were friends chatting in a cafe. "I hope you don't mind. The locks these days!" She tutted and held up a credit card. "And you really shouldn't leave the front door open. You never know *who* might walk in."

Sam's brain was a pinball machine of frightened thoughts shooting off in different directions. What did the crazy bitch want? To hurt her? To *kill* her?

"I thought it was time I had a little chat with you." Her eyes were cruel and narrow in a cruel and narrow face. Her cheekbones sliced down to her lips, which were thin as blades.

Sam could hardly take in what she was saying. "I'm calling the police," she stammered, trying to affect a self-controlled confidence she was a million miles away from feeling. She groped for her towel, which was hanging over the small bathroom radiator. The barmaid beat her to it, holding it just out of reach.

"Are you *crazy?*" Sam didn't feel half as brave as she sounded. Her eyes darted around the bathroom, frantically searching for a weapon. A small pair of nail scissors beside the taps—they would do for starters. She began to gradually slide her buttocks across the surface of the bath to bring her nearer the scissors. She didn't know exactly what she could do with such a puny weapon, but it would make her feel safer to have them in her hands.

"I want to give you a little piece of advice," the barmaid said slowly, enjoying herself. "Woman to woman." Her lips twisted as she finished the sentence, and Sam stopped her slow progress toward the scissors, suddenly absolutely terrified. The barmaid's eyes were green and hard like the marble chips around a gravestone. She leaned on the radiator and watched Sam.

"You *are* pretty, aren't you?" She waited for an answer. Sam was shaking, but her eyes flicked toward the scissors again. "I can understand what he might see in you. But you're empty. Shallow. A brunette Barbie doll. All innocence and smooth cheeks. Better be careful no one snaps your head off." She reached out and touched Sam's chin, her hand ice-cold. Sam jerked away and felt the equally cold tiles of the bathroom wall behind her back.

She felt stunned and confused. Was the woman talking about *Jack*? She remembered her looking at him in the pub. The idea was ludicrous. Laughable. What was so special about *him* that he could cause all this? Was her tormentor just a jealous bitch in heat? A *psychotic*, jealous bitch in heat, she corrected herself—and that was a very dangerous cocktail. But the barmaid from Hell was also behind the times. Didn't she know Sam and Jack were history?

As if reading her mind, the barmaid said, "You don't want him now. He's found another way. A path through the dark, where Barbie dolls fear to tread. He's dead to you. Let him rest in peace."

Sam was sitting in a bath being harangued by a deranged barmaid, warning her off someone she'd already dropped. The insanity of it all suddenly overwhelmed her. Fury burst inside her, forcing the words out in an enraged rush. "You can keep him! I don't want him! Just get out of my flat! *Get out!*"

She snatched up the scissors defiantly; the idea was strong in her mind that she was going to ram the blades into the woman's pale neck. The triumph in the barmaid's eyes made Sam lower the weapon though, revolted. She caught the towel as her unwelcome visitor flung it at her and wrapped it around herself, trembling with anger and fear.

"I've upset you, haven't I? I've really crawled under your skin, I can see that. But don't worry, I'm leaving you now. Bye-bye, Barbie." The woman smirked and left the bathroom, closing the door gently behind her.

Sam waited a full minute. Then she lurched out of the bath, the towel tied around her, heart hard and painful in her chest, and yanked open the bathroom door, terrified that the woman would be waiting for her. She began checking all the rooms of her flat, still clutching the scissors tightly.

She went into the bedroom last and knew immediately something was wrong; the coverlet of her duvet had been disturbed near the headboard. Her stomach clenched tight as she stepped toward the bed. There was a lump under the material. She knew what was there before she pulled back the cover and saw it. She let out a cry of grief and impotent rage, her hands reaching out for the little body curled limply on the pillow, its glassy eyes fixed accusingly on her. She couldn't bring herself to touch it. She fell on the bed and wept while Kirby continued to watch her, mouth slightly parted in a frozen snarl.

Jack did this. It's all because of him.

That wasn't fair, and she knew it, but grief had pushed her beyond rationality. With a huge mental effort, she pulled herself together enough to get up. She carried the bin liner containing the little corpse out of the bedroom and into her lounge, hardly able to see where she was going through her tears. If it wasn't for him, Kirby would still be alive and this horror would never have happened. She believed she'd escaped Jack's dark world after returning from London, but she realized now she'd brought a bit of it back with her, and it was following her like a shadow on the wall.

She put the bag down carefully on the carpet and reached for the telephone. She managed to control her emotions long enough to call the police, and then crouched down beside the bundle, sobbing, until they arrived.

CHAPTER FOURTEEN

Anthony Butcher heaved himself out of his armchair, switched off the lamp and the television set, and left the living room. He paused in front of the full-length mirror in the hall and watched himself grow out of the darkness. His eyes held the dark, as did his beard and thick head of hair. He was thirty-two, unmarried, and still a virgin. He felt confined by his age, by his awkwardness, and, most of all, by his virginity. He stared into his own reflected eyes. A splinter of moonlight from beneath the kitchen blinds edged into them, an eager spark of freedom.

Freedom.

Freedom meant breaking bonds. Releasing the darkness within.

The house was quiet, as it should be. The kitchen clock was inaudible as the hands moved together to celebrate midnight. The grizzled, old border terrier raised a woozy head from his basket to follow Anthony as he opened the back door and stepped out into the night. The dog shook his head and tucked his muzzle beneath his forepaws. The cold air from the open doorway stroked his fur.

Anthony walked down the garden path, past the cabbages wrapped in moonlight, and stopped at the shed. He dragged the warped door open and reached inside. It took him a while to find what he was looking for in the blackness, but at last his hands closed around the wooden handle. He pushed the shed door shut behind him and re-entered the house. He stood for a moment in the kitchen, cradling the heavy object like a baby. And it *did* symbolize a birth of a kind, he thought as he watched the three-quarter moon paint oblongs of ghost light on the walls. The birth of his new self, the death of the old. The terrier lifted his head again, eyes blinking. Anthony looked at him fondly. "Go to sleep, small, old thing." But affection was a form of constraint, too. He moved into the hall.

The stairwell was black. Everything was black: the walls, the ceiling, his mind. But that was just the night, the shadows. The shadows had crept inside his head, and he welcomed them. He climbed the risers steadily.

Lizzie Borden took an axe ...

The stairs creaked under his weight. Around the bend in the stairwell. Up to the top, the landing lost in the dark. He could have been climbing into deep space had it not been for the absence of stars.

Into his parents' bedroom. Bedside clock ticking cozily next to his mother's head.

Anthony paused just inside the room. From between the heavy curtains, a thin strip of moonlight reached out to finger his father's old face, stroking the broad nose, the puckered mouth, cutting a silver path through his thick, white hair and up onto the headboard behind.

The enormity of what he was about to do touched briefly upon Anthony's soul. He felt it there like a silent child in a lonely room, its eyes turned toward him. He dismissed the child, bade it farewell forever, and lifted the axe above his father's head. He was a man now. He was free.

As it rose, the axe blade intercepted the finger of moonlight and his father's features receded momentarily into darkness. Anthony shifted his position slightly. The strip was back, lying across his father's left eye. Which was open.

Anthony Butcher became a stone man in the dark. A statue with an axe. His father's eye focused on him. There was no surprise or bewilderment there. The eye blinked.

...and gave her father forty whacks.

The axe fell. Anthony put all the strength and conviction that he'd never invested in anything else into the blow. The blade slammed through his father's face, along the line of moonlight. The crunch of bone and the shuddering of the bed made by both his father's death jerks and Anthony's efforts to free the axe caused his mother to stir. He couldn't see her; she was just a vague hump in the shadows.

"Anthony? Is that you?"

When she saw what she had done, she gave her mother forty-one.

"Go back to sleep, Mother." The axe head leaped at the mound. Again. Again.

He left the bedroom slowly. Descended the stairs. Into the kitchen, axe in hand. The border terrier was sitting up in his basket, head tilted uncomprehendingly. Anthony watched his dear legs jerking with age in a rectangle of moonlight. He put down the axe and hugged him fiercely.

CHAPTER FIFTEEN

Nigel was picking his nose.

Jack took his eyes off the road and wondered where Nigel would stick the results of his little archaeological dig. His irritation bloomed. It had been growing all morning. He could think of better ways to start the week than stuck on a motorway for two hours with this moron.

He tried to take his mind off his companion and wondered if Richard would give him the sack from the Video Vault for having too many sickies. It was a calculated risk, but Jack thought it was just about worth it. Eighty quid, cash in hand, was twice what he'd earn at the video store for a day's work. He glanced over at Nigel, finger still rooting around up his nose. *Just* about worth it. The bloke was a real social undesirable. He'd consumed a curry and a gallon of lager the previous night with his B&B mates and consequently thought it funny to keep releasing his internal pressure in the cramped confines of Jack's aging Fiat as they drove along. *Hey, Nige, not funny or clever, bud.* It was too cold to keep the window down for long.

Jack was not in the best of moods.

They turned off the M6 and took the A road into the heart of Birmingham. As Nigel began unreeling directions for the City Center. Jack's temper rapidly sharpened, although he didn't say anything. Nigel would tell him to hang a left or a right just a little too late, forcing Jack to swerve quickly to take the correct route, constantly cutting off oncoming vehicles in the process. Nigel would then criticize Jack's reckless driving. Jack simmered.

"Can't get a word in edgeways with you today," Nigel said after a while as they shunted in silence through the Center's traffic.

Jack continued to stare through the windscreen.

"You're supposed to keep me entertained with witty comments and stimulating conversation on these trips," Nigel added brightly. "That's why I got you the job."

"I'm driving."

"You're *boring*. Liven up a bit, mate. You're not usually this dull. Girlie problems, maybe? Sam still not turning up on time? Sam not turning up at *all*?"

Jack hadn't bothered telling Nigel about his doomed date with Sam at the horror festival. Nor about his entanglement with Lila, for that matter. Even if he had wanted to share his private life with someone as insensitive as Nigel, it would have all sounded a little too unlikely. Five years without so much as a kiss, and then two beautiful women fighting to get at him at the same time! Well, sort of, anyway. He still found it hard to believe himself. But that was all over.

He hadn't heard from Sam since dropping her off after the festival. He'd thought of phoning her, but something always stopped him. His pride? Maybe. Then there was Lila. She and Bane must have had a fine old time laughing at him after their little snuff video prank. He was surprised they hadn't sent him the latex dummy they'd obviously used to make it, just to rub salt in his wounds. He was still furious about being taken in so easily. Bane had presumably cut swiftly and neatly from Lila's real face to her prosthetic double without any noticeable sign of a join, but then Jack hadn't been looking for one; his horror had made the killing real.

Nigel was scrutinizing his photocopied list of Birmingham music shops. "Remember, leave fifteen minutes between each purchase, 'cause otherwise it shows up on their sales records."

Jack had heard it all before. It niggled him the way Nigel always assumed control of the operation, as if he were the organizational big noise. He couldn't organize his way to the toilet. "I'll do what I always do," he snapped, peering moodily through the windscreen at the gray city. "I've never had any problems."

"There's always a first time, though, eh? This is supposed to be a covert oppo, mate. You've got to concentrate on being subtle."

Oppo? For fuck's sake. "Nige, you just concentrate on picking your nose and everything will be fine."

Nigel looked at him. Jack could sense his companion was becoming annoyed and took perverse pleasure in the knowledge. He breathed deeply, like he'd achieved something, and aimed the Fiat at a blue NCP[9] parking sign.

"Not that one!" Nigel objected. "It's miles from the Center."

"Tough." Jack bucked the car up the entry ramp. "I'm sick of playing chariot races around the Bull Ring." Nigel's head bucked along with the car, and Jack smiled with satisfaction as it thumped the low roof. The music store list slid to the floor; Nigel bent down to pick it up. Jack hit the brakes a little too eagerly; Nigel's head connected sharply with the dashboard.

"Sorry, mate," Jack grinned.

He welcomed the opportunity to split up from Nigel for an hour and a half while he visited various record stores and bought the required but embarrassing CD singles—made by boy bands mostly. He felt a bit of a tosser buying the latest Westlife single ten times over, but what the fuck.

He zipped up his leather jacket against the cold Birmingham wind and plunged into Brash Sounds, a small independent store. He trawled along the singles rack, casually fishing out compact discs as if he were just another browser, before choosing the CD he was paid to buy.

In the album rack, he picked up a CD with the uncompromising title *Birkenau Babes* and nearly dropped it when he saw the four musicians posing on the cover against a fuzzy blow-up of the infamous Auschwitz gates. Grimy leathers, shades, and vicious smirks. Jack hadn't even considered the possibility that the inferno of mind-tearing sound they'd unleashed at The Slaughter Inn could be harnessed on record.

They were called Holocaust Freaks apparently, a name Jack couldn't remember seeing advertised at the gig. Perhaps such trivialities were unimportant to the band; all that really mattered was getting down to the serious business of disturbing people.

He studied the singer, standing slightly forward from the rest of the group, his body language all careless aggression and fuck-you nonchalance. *Stick you in the real world and tear away your shades, and what did we get?* He turned the CD over, scanning the track

---

[9] National Car Park

list, the titles as uncompromising as the name of the group suggested they would be.

The label was a small indie; Jack was amused to see it was based
in a small rural town not far from where he'd been born, twenty
miles from Bristol. On impulse, he carried the CD over to the counter
and paid for it along with the boy band single. If nothing else, he could
assault Nigel's eardrums with it on the way home.

Nigel was leaning against the Fiat in the multi-story car park
when Jack arrived. He winced when he noticed his companion had
decided to jam a baseball cap backward on his head. He unlocked
Nigel's door reluctantly and then opened his own, sliding behind
the wheel.

"Look, Nige," he said as he started the engine. "How about getting some shut-eye for a while, eh?" *How about all the way home?*
"At least until we get out of Birmingham so's I can concentrate on
where I'm going."

Nigel shifted in his seat, broke wind, chortled. "Wise up, mate.
I've got to give you directions."

Right. Plan B, then. Jack inserted *Birkenau Babes* into the dashboard CD player as the Fiat bounced out of the NCP. A hiss of low-fi
dead air. Nigel sniffed several times as if something was loose in his
nose and looked at Jack inquiringly. "What's this, then? Oasis? Blur?"

Jack smiled, and the holocaust began.

Jack nearly went into the back of a police van. Nigel's protests
were lost under the evil tumult. Screams, manic laughter, and dismemberment sound effects mingled with werewolf vocals. A guitar
chainsawed through the murky production, a visceral, blood-clogged
orgasm of fretted violence, while bass and drums burrowed inside
Jack's head and gave his brains a good kicking. It was like letting a
vanload of Millwall skinheads loose in his cortex while a murder of
serial killers hacked away at his synapses, sending him scrabbling
for the volume control. When Nigel said, "Thank fuck for that," he
turned it up again.

The Fiat mingled with the lunchtime traffic, plunged around the
Bull Ring several times before opting for a possible route. As they
flew down an exit road, Jack saw the sign for the M6 pointing the opposite way. He cursed silently. Nigel said nothing, frowning through the
windscreen. The Fiat battled on, jostling with traffic lights that lined
up like hurdles, tempting Jack to jump them. He searched for side exits
that would enable him to curve his way back toward the motorway

and found none, just a gauntlet of red lights. He ejected the audio nasty in an effort to get his head around the problem.

"Lost?" Nigel piped up immediately.

"Course not."

"This the scenic route, then?"

"Beautiful, isn't it?"

Nigel glanced around at the panorama of gray housing estates backed by cooling vats on one side and tower blocks on the other. There was a supercilious little smile on his lips. "Fancy stopping for a picnic? We could put up some deck chairs by that vat, take a shower in the acid rain."

"The trouble with you, Nige, is you always have to labor a joke."

"Did I say I was joking? See me laugh? I thought you knew where you were going, mate."

"I *do* know where I'm going. I'm just not telling you, that's all."

Childish maybe, but infinitely satisfying. He whacked the CD back on, and it screamed at him like a mutilated woman. He flipped it right back off again. The shriek had sounded too real, shivering with the genuine terror of a life forced to an unnatural end. He didn't want to hear it again.

Nigel contented himself with staring morosely out at the industrial estates, moored like islands in the surrounding sea of wasteground. Now and again, his finger sought the solace of his nostril. Jack concentrated on the road. The next time he looked around, Nigel was sleeping like a vulgar baby, head vibrating on the passenger window, mouth hanging open with innocent stupidity. Jack relaxed.

Rolling down from a flyover, the Fiat curved into a side road, escaping from the main northbound route. The road narrowed, nosed through a housing estate that gathered around them threateningly. Gray terraces bullied the car. Gangs of youths sat on splintered curbs, eyeing Jack bleakly as he drove through their silent neighborhood. He drove into a cul-de-sac, and reversing, saw his rearview mirror fill with a posse of lads with ugly haircuts and expressions to match. He considered waking Nigel, but the lads parted to let him out, saying nothing, staring.

He motored the Fiat down another road where the houses drooped against each other for comfort. Boards replaced windows. Chimneys lay ruptured on pavements. Doors were ripped away. The car humped and bumped over the ruts, and still, Nigel slept on.

Passing the shell of a small, dilapidated pub stranded on its own in a street of long-demolished houses, Jack slammed the car to a standstill. Nigel turned over in his sleep. Jack stepped out of the car, a hole opening in his gut.

He gazed at the empty window frames, the vacant doorway, the smears of graffiti spread across the gray concrete façade—at the vestigial black lettering above the shattered bow windows of the pub. THE SLAUGHT was all that remained.

Jack was pulled to the empty doorway like a fish being reeled in. The pub sign had gone; the hook dangled forlornly. The interior was a shambles of broken glass, broken brick, broken litter. What remained of the furniture was burned and smashed. Graffiti glinted obscenely on the once-white plaster. The bar had been trashed beyond repair. More spray paint crawled along the punctured woodwork:

JULIE GANNON IS A WHORE

Above the fireplace, something more ominous was inscribed in huge red letters:

THE SLAUGHTER OF THE INNOCENTS

and more succinctly, on the left-hand wall:

SICK BASTARDS

Beneath that, the simple legend,

R.I.P. MUM

Jack crunched over glass toward the center of the large lounge bar. Here, shadows festered like a black culture run wild, the daylight unable to reach this far. Jack tensed with shock when he realized he'd almost trodden on the corpse of a dog, its rotting head resting on a pillow of tin cans. What he took at first to be a large white eye patch was naked bone. The fur writhed with busy maggots.

"You'll die in here, Mister."

Jack spun at the voice, heart clubbing his chest.

A boy sat on a BMX bicycle in the doorway. He looked about nine or ten and was smoking a cigarette.

"You scared me," Jack said pathetically.

The boy shrugged. "What're you doin' in here?" His accent was perky Brummie, half inquisitive, half cocky.

Jack felt guilty, as if he'd been caught doing something bad. "Just looking around." He also felt foolish being quizzed by a snotty kid in a *Cat in the Hat* sweatshirt.

"You wanna die in 'ere, like the others?" The boy spoke matter of factly, as if it was no great deal, and pulled on his ciggy.

A sense of hopeless dread snatched at Jack. "What do you mean?"

The boy shrugged again.

"Was this pub called The Slaughter?"

The boy said nothing, watching Jack closely.

"*Who* died here?"

The boy smoked. It seemed he had said all he intended to.

Jack pushed on. "What does *that* mean?" He pointed at the ominous graffiti. He needed answers. This felt like a personal thing, like a private nightmare that someone else had started sharing with him. If he could find his way through it, all the disturbing things that had been done to him recently might take on some meaning.

His urgency evidently impressed the boy. "You're not from 'round 'ere." It was an accusation.

"No."

"That's why you don't know. Copper, are you? They don't know, either. They never know nuthin', Dad says. Even what's under their noses."

"Don't know what?" He was feeling increasingly anxious.

"People got lost."

"What d'you mean, lost?"

"Like stray cats." He grinned a bit at that, then his small face blanked again. "Never found." He nodded at the R.I.P. splatter on the wall.

Jack's chest tightened. He could taste blood in his throat. "How many?" It came out as a croak.

The boy shrugged, but this time it was more an involuntary twitch of his shoulders; he was bored of the conversation. He spun a pedal distractedly. Jack moved closer to him, and the boy looked suddenly nervous. He began backing his bicycle out of the doorway.

"Wait," Jack called after him. "What was the landlord's name? What did he look like?" Jack had left the shadows near the bar and entered the depressing pool of gray daylight near the windows. He must have looked pretty disturbing with his intense expression, wild hair, and leather jacket because the boy decided he had lingered long enough.

Jack followed him through the doorway. Nigel was relieving himself against the outside wall. The boy pedaled off down the road, staring back over his shoulder. Nigel smirked. "What have you been up to? Flashin' at a kid?"

Jack drove. Nigel talked. The empty houses fell behind them. The Fiat climbed above the decay, scaling the curving back of a flyover. Below them, Birmingham was a dirty gray swamp. Industrial smoke curdled the sky.

Jack drove.

CHAPTER SIXTEEN

She would never feel safe in the bath again.

The police had not helped her insecurity. A morose constable poked around her flat with a marked lack of enthusiasm. She'd shown him Kirby's body, and he stared at it thoughtfully as if wondering what breed it was. "There aren't any obvious marks of violence," his only comment.

"You think he just climbed in my bed and died in his sleep?!" She was aware that she was going to burst into tears again, but now more through frustration than grief. "She killed him! Aren't you going to do something about it?"

"Yes, of course." The constable squared his shoulders in what she was obviously supposed to take as a gesture of reassurance. "But I have to inform you there might not be much I *can* do."

"She broke into my *flat*! Are you telling me that's lawful activity?"

The policeman shrugged and took down the details, but it was obvious he was only going through the motions. "We'll speak to her, of course. But if she denies being here, I'm afraid there's nothing we can go on."

"What about fingerprints?" Sam felt silly as she made the suggestion but was too shattered to care.

The constable shook his head condescendingly, and Sam shut the door on his doleful impotence. She sat by the television, as if that might be able to tell her something helpful.

The officer was away for an hour and a half, and when he returned, his words were as unpromising as she'd known they would be. Lila Tarrow from The Slaughter Inn had been interviewed over the alleged incident but had insisted Samantha Giles was a complete stranger to her, and could she really be held accountable for the wild accusations of jealous girlfriends? She was used to this sort of paranoid and spiteful behavior from girls on the other side of the bar. Give a man a smile while serving him and some mad woman's trying to tear your eyes out. Girls tended to resent her because of her striking appearance, but she wasn't going to be held responsible because some men fancied her and their girlfriends didn't like it.

Sam had listened with growing fury. "She's twisted it around. It was *her* threatening *me*. She told me to stay away from Jack."

The constable had asked if she would like him to speak to Mr. Breen, but by then she had had enough. The constable apologized mournfully, gave Kirby one last, dubious glance, and left the flat. Early the next morning, Sam buried the cat in the back garden, blinded by tears, and then made a phone call to her landlord. She wanted him to install a better lock on her door and to fit one in the bathroom as well. She hadn't given him any explanations, nor had she needed to; he was always happy to oblige his pretty and reliable tenant.

Now she was sitting on her bed watching dusk crawling over the row of back gardens and wondering whether to ring Jack. She didn't know what she would say if she did. Bawl him out for involving her with such a mad bitch? Twenty-four hours after her horrible experience and she was beginning to realize she couldn't really blame him for it, no matter how tempting it was. But she couldn't imagine talking to him without some element of resentment creeping in either. Was that fair? What was *fair*? Her cat being killed wasn't *fair*, was it?

Had Jack been seeing Sam and the barmaid at the same time? But they'd only had one date, so even if he had, she was forced to concede, it was hardly a betrayal. So, if they had no real relationship, why had the bitch felt so threatened by her? Wherever the blame lay, Kirby was dead and her flat had been violated. And no matter what the constable said, she *knew* Lila had murdered her pet. She could imagine the barmaid strangling Kirby with her bare hands, maybe in the dark of the stairwell, while Sam sat blithely in her bathtub.

She shook her head to get rid of the image, but it stayed in her mind like a permanent stain. She'd never felt so vulnerable. At work earlier, she'd snapped at Sue and misfiled several claim forms. She'd almost told her boss *exactly* what she thought of him and his wandering hands, and she found herself breaking into tears when one of the salesmen told her a joke. That had been embarrassing. But she'd pulled through.

She decided she'd dithered enough, picked up the phone, and dialed. Dennis answered. "You want to speak to Jack?" he asked with an audible sneer.

"Only if that's okay with you, of course," she threw back at him.

"Perfectly. Absolutely no problem." She heard him stomp off toward the lounge, and then Jack was breathing down her earpiece.

"Hello?" He sounded cautious. She tried to detect some enthusiasm in the word, and then remembered she hadn't phoned him in the hope of rekindling their relationship, which only made her temper worsen.

"I don't care what you get up to in your private life, but when you start dragging me in, that's different." She was saying all the things she had intended *not* to say. But it was easy to blame him.

"Sam, you've lost me."

"I'm talking about your new girlfriend, Lucretia Borgia. She paid me a little visit yesterday. A very unpleasant visit." The thought of it made her feel sick all over again.

A brief silence along the line. Then, "Are you going to tell me what you're talking about, Sam?"

She thought of Kirby, stiffening on her pillow, and squeezed the receiver until the tears started again. She was losing it, and she had so much wanted to play it cool. "You bloody *know* what I'm talking about. That bitch from the pub. Perhaps you even sent her yourself; you're sick enough." Now she was being stupid. But now it was said, and there was another silence on the line. And maybe the silence *was* a form of guilt. He knew something. She sniffed back more angry tears and pressed her head against the wall to try and force herself together.

"What's she done to you, Sam?" He sounded genuinely worried. But she mustn't let that confuse her now.

She cleared her throat and said calmly, "She broke into my home and killed my cat. How's that for starters?"

"Lila?"

Was that all he could say? Was the concept of his precious slut being involved in something bad so hard for him to take? Poor Jack. Bitterness rose inside her.

"I called the police, but they weren't any help." *I need a different kind of help,* she thought desperately, closing her eyes, but there was no way she was going to ask for it. "What I want you to do," she said instead, determined to sound as though she was in control of every-thing, "is to tell that witch you're sleeping with that there's nothing for her to worry about."

"I don't understand any of this, Sam. I'm coming 'round."

"Don't even think about it! You've caused me enough grief. Please, stay away." She paused, breathing more calmly now. "I mean it, Jack. We just made a mistake, that's all. You can tell her that. And tell the psychotic bitch if she ever breaks into my flat again, I'll be bury-ing *her* in the back garden." That was a good point to hang up on, so she did.

She felt strangely better, as if she had achieved something. And she had: dignity. Let them have each other. It was a marriage made in Hell, really. Just the way they liked it.

She ignored the phone when it bleeped insistently at her and went to make herself a cup of tea. She had said all there was to say. When the doorbell rang a half hour later, she sat in front of the tele-vision and ignored that, too, feeling as if she really *had* achieved some-thing after all.

CHAPTER SEVENTEEN

It was with a helpless feeling of inevitability that he opened his eyes to see the shadow leaning over him, as if he'd been expecting it, and now it was here, he had to face up to whatever it might mean.

For a confused moment, he thought he was no longer in his bedroom, although he was still lying in his bed—he could see the footboard silhouetted against the darkness. He sensed a great coldness and a cluster of silent, indistinct shapes around him, creeping closer, while the shadow leaning over him reached out to touch him.

He stiffened under the duvet, his hair congealed and sweaty. Somewhere in the gloom, he heard the dripping of water, as if from a great distance. He remembered the pile of human pieces inside the barrow, and he remembered the shadow that had reached for him just as it was reaching for him now. But that hadn't been real. *This wasn't real...*

The huddled shapes slipped away into the dark. The brute remained, huge fingers now closing on Jack's throat. The dripping of water faded, to be replaced by the rasp of crows and the screaming of a girl. He couldn't see the girl, but the face of the brute was becoming clearer as it bent over him, hands pressing down on his windpipe, stealing his air away.

Going to die now. He's going to kill me because I touched her. And she's standing there in her bra and panties, and she doesn't know what to do because she's only fifteen years old and she's never seen the face of a maniac before.

Father.

He remembered the quiet. When the girl had stopped screaming, it had been so quiet. Just the bleak laughter of the crows outside and his own gasps for breath. The brute hadn't said a word as he slowly continued to strangle his son.

His father was gone.

Jack lay in bed and could breathe easily again. He could hear the dripping of water, the sound gradually changing, not so distant now as he forced himself toward wakefulness. The ticking of his bed-side clock.

Outside, he heard the hum of the first milk float[10] cruising the back-streets. Somewhere else, a car wouldn't start. He lay and watched the second hand tirelessly patrolling the small clock face. Soon, he heard Dennis stumble from his bedroom and head for the toilet, thumping the light switch bad-temperedly. Soon after that, he got himself up and stood peering out at the gray day developing beyond the curtains.

Dennis arrived with Joe just as Jack was settling down to watch the Six O'clock News. They entered in a burst of drunken sound, a wave of ebullient confusion that Jack really didn't need.

A cabinet member had been found hanging naked above a circle of child pornography magazines in the bedroom of his constituency home. Jack watched and listened. A three-year-old girl had been sex-ually abused and beheaded not far from her house in Hartlepool. Jack took it in. In America, a father of three had cut loose with a shotgun in his local Burger King, slaughtering eleven customers. Jack imagined him emptying both barrels, bodies falling, reloading, firing, reloading... Dennis and Joe burst in.

Dennis made straight for the VCR, clutching a tape in one hand and a bottle of Old Witch in the other. Joe trailed behind, hands in the pockets of his shabby overcoat. Before Jack had a chance to say anything, Alexei Sayle had replaced the fast-food massacre.

"How ya diddlin'?" the comedian asked an uninterested audience of pensioners, parodying a bad warm-up comic. "Bloody sod yer then," he griped, struggling to keep a ridiculous set of false teeth in his

---

[10] Milk truck

mouth. Dennis brayed. Joe stared like a pleased child.

"No." Jack was out of his chair and at the controls of the VCR while Dennis was still blundering around the room looking for a bottle opener. Alexei Sayle disappeared. A Wiltshire truck driver was making a court appearance, charged with strangling his girlfriend and hiding her body under the floorboards of his flat.

"What's up with you?" slurred Dennis. "Since when do you watch the news?"

Jack didn't answer. He stared at the screen as if it might hold a secret message for him. All at once, the world was weighing heavily on him; he felt responsible for the state of it, and he didn't know why. A sense of guilt and self-loathing had taken root in him some time ago now. *Ever since the gig at The Slaughter?*

Joe was watching him inscrutably. Judging him? Did he know Jack had killed, and could kill again? *A squirrel. It was just a squirrel!* No. There was no "just" about it. And it didn't matter so much *what* he'd killed; what was important was that he had done it. Without even being aware he was doing it.

Killed a squirrel, Joe. Ha ha. The pizza delivery man would probably laugh if he found out, it sounded so ridiculous. No. More likely he'd be revolted. Like Jack was revolted. And now another innocent animal was dead because of him; Sam threatened and terrorized.

You didn't do it, Jack, so cut this self-indulgent crap right now. Lila did it; she's the one. Lila and Bane. They're behind all this; they've been behind everything. But if Lila had killed Sam's pet because she was jealous of Jack, didn't that make him feel just a *little* bit excited? And didn't that make him loathe himself all the more?

"Nigel been giving you a hard time?" Dennis guessed. "Should've come down The Slaughter with us."

Jack looked at him sharply. "You've been there?"

Dennis had found the bottle opener. He hunched over his task. "Just for a couple of pints after work. That saucy gothic piece was there; Joe tells me she was feeling you up in the cafe the other day. Poor girl needs help."

Jack switched his attention back to the television.

"Your mate was asking after you," Joe piped up. "Mister Slaughter. A real head job, if you ask me."

Jack dared him to grin. He didn't. Jack's gut tightened, released a little gas of fear. "What did he want?"

"Said he'd be in touch."

A teenage boy had been tortured and set alight in Glasgow. Jack barely registered it.

"Probably wants to send you another skull in the mail," Joe deadpanned. "Next time, you might get the whole skeleton. Just don't expect me to sign for it."

"Cost an arm and a leg in postage," Dennis added.

A timid bachelor had been tied to a chair in Yorkshire, his teeth removed, and his head shattered with a baseball bat.

"Yeah, it's fuckin' hilarious, isn't it?" Jack snapped.

Dennis brayed with antagonistic mirth and lit a cigarette.

"If you're that freaked," Joe said, his eyes boring inside Jack's head, "why put the skull on top of the telly?"

Dennis moved over to stroke the bony crown with mock affection. "My flatmate's a potential serial killer. But at least you bothered to clean it first. What did you do with the maggots?"

"Remember that Mulligatawny soup you had last night?" Joe said without smiling. "That wasn't rice."

Jack stopped listening to his friends' inane babble. He stared at the television screen, hands clenched together as if in prayer. Why *had* he put the skull on prominent display?

In Norwich, a doctor and his wife had been brutally axed to death. There was no obvious motive behind the slaying, no obvious suspect. The neighbors recalled the gentleness of the old couple and drew attention to their insularity. Their thirty-two-year-old son, Anthony, who still lived with them, was being interviewed, explaining how he'd been away hiking Friday night and had returned Saturday morning to find their mutilated corpses in bed. Even the family pet had been mercilessly hacked to pieces. He put a hand to his head as he spoke, although his voice was steady. His eyes were as black as his beard. A solemn Chief Superintendent revealed to the press that there were no obvious signs of burglary, but they weren't ruling anything out in this savage and inexplicable case.

Dennis had nearly finished his Old Witch. "Come on, Jack, you morbid bastard," he bellowed, "Let's have a bloody laugh, for Christ's sake." He bent over the VCR machine.

The weatherman forecasted rain.

"How ya diddlin'?"

Sod you then. Jack left the room with rising irritation for his friends and so many unanswered questions, not least about himself, spiraling in his brain. Was he cracking up? *My flatmate's a potential serial killer.*

He needed to be alone. He wondered what Sam was doing, whether she hated him. He almost tried phoning her again, but at the last minute, something made him change his mind.

CHAPTER EIGHTEEN

Joe was thirty and had never had a girlfriend. He'd groped a sixteen-year-old when he was seventeen, but that didn't count. He'd molded her slight breasts with his hands as if he was trying to sculpt pottery. When he'd tried to plunge his hand beneath her skirt, she told him she didn't want to see him again. And that was quite funny because Charlotte the Harlot let *everyone* beneath her skirt. At least, all his schoolmates, especially Dennis, thought it was funny, even if Joe didn't particularly.

He took it in his usual stoical stride, however. There would always be other times, other women. But there weren't. His mother was beginning to realize the only way she'd ever get him off her hands was by dying on him. Nothing else would shift the bugger. He liked his home comforts too much. His bedroom had been transformed into a bedsit[11]: television, video, record player, wash basin. He only needed to leave it to take a dump. His mother even brought his meals up. Joe was cozy as a very strange bug in a rug, but he didn't have a girlfriend.

They didn't like his eyes. *Too weird,* one of Dennis's exes once said. *Gives me the willies,* another offered. But Joe was stuck with his eyes, and if they gave people the willies, well, that was just too bad. He didn't need to be loved to deliver pizzas.

----

[11] A one-room apartment typically consisting of a combined bedroom and sitting room with cooking facilities.

Lee snared him as soon as Joe trudged in through the door of Luigi's Pizza Parlor, empty delivery bags in hand. Lee was the manager and only a few years older than Joe, but stress had worn him down. That, and too many pizzas. He stank permanently of cheese and tomato sauce. He waved a doughy hand at Joe and thrust a piece of paper in front of his face.

"What's this?" Joe studied the address on the docket.

"Friend of yours. Said he wanted you to deliver it personally. I told him the pizza would be cold as a gravestone in fuckin' January by the time you snailed your way there, but he didn't seem to give a shit."

Cain. Joe frowned at the name. "Never heard of him. Don't know anyone at this address either."

Lee was already turning away as the evening's orders began to shrill through on the countertop telephones. He shouted at his staff to "grab those fuckin' phones" and waved Joe toward a bulging red pizza bag waiting on top of the oven.

"I don't fuckin' care. Just as long as it ain't one of your mates pissin' around. Now take that Pepperoni and fuck off. And hurry home. There's plenty more of the bastards lining up."

"And you ask so nicely, too." Joe hugged the hot, delicious-smelling pizza bag to his chest and left the shop. He slid it onto the roof of the Fiesta, right next to the large, plastic, yellow telephone receiver fixed there, and opened the driver's side door. He remembered to retrieve the bag before climbing inside and driving off (it wouldn't be the first time he'd driven off with it still sitting on the roof), and soon the perky, custard-yellow Fiesta was wending its way through the evening traffic.

He enjoyed his work, in a phlegmatic sort of way. He expected nothing of it, and it expected nothing of him, other than that he deliver a deep pan mushroom and anchovies to Mr. and Mrs. Punter before it was as stiff as tarmac. Joe could just about manage that most of the time. He even managed to avoid thinking about the ludicrous glowing phone perched above his head as he went about his deliveries. But people just had to keep on reminding him.

This time it was two teenage chavs.[12] They grinned at Joe from beneath their hoods as the Fiesta slid to a halt at a traffic light. Joe stared impassively through the windscreen, mind idling in neutral along with the engine.

---

[12] A young person of a type characterized by coarse and brash behavior.

"Give us a go on yer phone, mate."

Joe shook his head. No. He would not give them a go. The youth who had spoken, his baggy jeans drooping as if he'd loaded his pants, decided to try again. Just in case Joe hadn't heard how funny he was the first time.

"I said, give us a go on yer phone."

Joe wound down the driver's window. "Your spontaneous wit just staggers the hell out of me, boys. Let me ask you a simple question: Why?"

The chavs looked stumped, as if the question was anything but simple. Joe made it easy for them. "Why do you want a go on my phone?"

The other youth stepped forward, splaying his fingers in a gesture meticulously copied from a hundred rap videos. "I wants to call me mum; why the fuck d'you think?" He turned to his mate for support, a brainless grin on his face.

Joe stared him straight in the eye. "She wouldn't be able to hear you, mate. Not unless you can shout really loud and she's one of those old ladies waiting at that bus stop over there." He indicated a shelter across the road. Confused, the chavs followed his finger. "But a giant, plastic imitation phone wouldn't really be of much use to you, I'm afraid."

The youth who had spoken tried to follow Joe's reasoning. His wit began to desert him. He decided to make up for it by substituting a bit of abuse. That never failed. "You sayin' me mum's an old bitch? Fuckin' tosser."

"Not sure how to respond to your first question, not having had the pleasure of meeting her, but I certainly can't argue with your last statement."

"What's he fuckin' on about, Tone?" The other youth wanted to join in now. He had small eyes, and his chin receded into an acne battlefield. "He sounds like a kiddie fiddler to me."

"Wanker," the first youth offered up uncertainly.

"We've already ascertained that," agreed Joe, idly glancing over at the traffic lights, patiently waiting for them to change. "Though I'm not quite so flattered by your other allegation."

"Fuckin' Noddy," the first youth to speak blurted. He was short and fat, and in his bright green sweatshirt resembled an oversized tennis ball. Pleased with his imaginative insult, his confidence returned. "Fuck off back to toytown in yer Noddy car, ya prick. Give PC Plod one up the ass while yer at it."

Joe laughed delightedly. "That's a new one. 'Give PC Plod one up the ass.' Genius. I'll have to write that one down. Cheers for the life-changing chat, lads." Joe gave them an understanding, generous smile as the lights finally changed, and left them behind, their insults trailing around their ankles like their jeans.

The road opened up in front of him, the traffic clearing as the commuters arrived home for tea. He pushed the Fiesta up to fifty, slammed it down to thirty again when a police car hove into view around a corner.

He glanced down at the address docket tucked into a band on the pizza bag beside him. 47 Fernbank Road, Redland. He definitely didn't know anyone there. The Fiesta puffed up Church Hill, swept south along Horfield Common, past the new Tesco supermarket, which had just been built on a disused sports field, destroying thirty trees and a family of urban foxes in the process. The protestors' banners were still embedded in the bushes across the road. KILLERS.

Joe let the car run, content in his mission of hunger erasure.

He'd been the butt of many jokes since he'd taken on the job. He once delivered a prawn and pineapple thin crust to an address in Henleaze, which turned out to be the abode of an old school acquaintance. And hadn't he guffawed upon opening his front door and being confronted with Weird-Eye Joe, resplendent in glowing yellow shirt, orange trousers, and crimson baseball cap, all tagged with the "Luigi's Pizzas" label. He'd guffawed even more when he saw the cartoon car parked cheekily in the driveway.

Joe had been unabashed. "I really wouldn't laugh," he'd casually warned his ex-acquaintance. "You see, my pizza wagon can get real sensitive sometimes, and he might just get the crazy feeling you're laughing at *him*."

As he spoke, Joe took in the man's garden. The slob had done well for himself, it seemed. A driveway pushing between firs, expansive lawns, a large pond guarded by a couple of disinterested gnomes. Joe had parked near a washing line, from which dangled a Mr. Ben T-shirt and a pair of Y-Fronts bearing the legend EARLY RISER. Joe thought that let the illusion of respectability down somewhat, although he would never dream of being so elitist as to say so.

"My advice to you," Joe continued, "would be to apologize before he takes offense."

"Is that right?" The old school acquaintance squared his shoulders in anticipation, his features settling into the bully mode Joe remembered so well from school. "And my advice to *you,* ya loser, is to ram that giant phone right up your squeak hole and get back in your yellow kiddie cart before *I* take offense, pal. Fuck, you really should have paid more attention to the careers advisor at school, ya muppet!"

Joe had shrugged, handed the man his pizza, took the money, and climbed back in his wagon. The Fiesta managed to nudge one of the gnomes face forward into the pond and take the head off the other on its way out. The EARLY RISER Y-Fronts flew at full mast, pronged on the car's aerial, all the way through town. Joe felt *good* about his work.

Dusk was clustering around Fernbank Road as he pulled up alongside number 47. The thought crossed his mind that this might be another old "school chum" who wanted to crack a few funnies at Joe's expense. If so, Joe could take it.

He hefted the crimson bag out of the car and walked up the weed-grown path. When he saw the boarded-over windows, he paused gloomily. Forget it.

He was about to return to the car, convinced he'd been sent on a hoax call when he caught sight of a little white note pinned on the peeling front door. JOE. And beneath that, in smaller letters: *Please come in.*

Joe hesitated. His mind suggested plenty of possibilities, but he rejected most of them. It had to be someone who knew him. It could be Dennis, who might find it amusing to send him to an abandoned house. He could be waiting behind the door ready to jump on him and scare the shit out of him. Not very likely, though. Dennis never seemed to be in the mood for pranks these days. He was a shell of his former self. Jack, then? But he'd been acting weird lately, too. And it wasn't really his style anyway. Only one way to find out.

The door was slightly open, so he knocked once and pushed inward.

The hallway was dark. Dank. Mold splayed like dirty handprints across the curling wallpaper. A monk with a rotting face and habit sat in the shadows. Joe stared until his eyes came through for him, and he felt sure it was only a pile of old sacking. Then he moved forward, pausing by the staircase that stepped up into the blackness.

"Luigi's Pizzas," he shouted. His voice was hollow. He turned to a door on his left and rapped once. His fist was immediately seized by a clammy spider web. He pulled free with a grimace. Yeah, nice prank, this. Very chucklesome. The worst thing about hoax calls was Lee being too bloody tight to give Joe the wasted pizzas.

There was a light, very faint, creeping under another door at the end of the hall. So, someone *was* here. He sighed long-sufferingly, plodded down the hall, and stood before the door. "Hello?"

Silence.

"Anybody in?" He pushed the door open slowly.

A filthy table stood in the center of a large room. The windows were boarded over, the walls peeling and smattered with evil faces formed out of mold and damp. They scowled at Joe as he gaped at the naked, low-wattage light bulb that left much of the room in shadow: a dead rat hung by the neck from a fold in the light's flex,[13] hind legs dangling below the bulb. Joe took his eyes off that, put them instead on the skull set in the center of a table below the light.

"All right, Jack. Not funny. Lee's got the sense of humor of a pitbull with piles, and he'll make me pay for this pizza..."

His words sounded hollow and silly in the barely furnished room. He peered more closely at the skull. But it wasn't the same one Bane had sent to Jack, as he had first supposed. This one was larger, uglier. The bone was cracked and worn, like the surface of an ancient gravestone. The eye sockets were set abnormally far apart, fractured holes crawling with dark. Several teeth were missing, and those that remained snaggled out from dirty jaws. The skull glowed sickly in the dim light, like the cap of a giant toadstool, sweating evil.

"Nice one. Where did you dig up this gruesome bastard?"

The empty room swallowed his voice. He waited patiently. So, when was it jump-out-and-splatter-Joe's-boxers time? The joke was already wafer-thin, and Joe had deliveries to make. He shuffled over to the skull and unsheathed the pizza box from its warm bag, sliding it next to the ferocious relic on the tabletop. The grimy sockets watched him. The darkness seemed to move inside them.

"Enjoy your meal, sir," he said to the skull. He sighed extravagantly and walked toward the door again, waiting for his friends to make their move. Couldn't they get it into their heads that he was impossible to rattle? From a corner of the room the light couldn't reach, a movement. So, the room wasn't empty after all.

"Come on, then, let's do it. But you've still got to pay for the pizza." He addressed the dark corner, waiting for the punch line.

Silence. He peered into the shadows. Was someone there or was it just his imagination?

---

[13] Cable/wire

Joe shrugged. "As pranks go, I'll give it three out of ten..."

The light went out.

Joe heard the faint click of the switch from the corner of the room he'd been facing. He snorted in resignation, stranded in the dark, his eyes trying to dig out details. Nothing. He turned, took a few steps toward where he guessed the door should be, fumbling for the knob.

He heard his nails track along dust-rimed wood, and despite his determination not to be frightened, he felt panic edging under his skin. His fingers met something soft and warm.

A hand.

The hand clasped his gently, as if about to guide him out into the light. A whisper came from close beside him.

"We are for the Dark."

The shivery hiss touched Joe's soul with an even deeper shadow. He forgot all about Jack, Dennis, Lee, and a world where pizzas were going cold. He even forgot how to speak, how to reason. The terrifying whisper stole it all away from him.

"And you?" it whispered again. Joe didn't recognize the low voice, but he knew he didn't like it. *Didn't like it at all.*

"Are you for the Dark?"

The voice was a sigh of ecstasy and madness, and it speared Joe's heart with terror.

"Come join our family..." The whisper caught, as if reaching a peak of excitement. "Come play with us, in the dark."

Suddenly Joe felt very small and very alone. He thought of a seventeen-year-old boy caressing a young girl in a sunny field near Bristol. He thought of all the other girls he would never love. And suddenly, oh yes, he believed.

And the punch line came at last.

CHAPTER NINETEEN

"He left one of my bloody cars outside. Didn't find it 'til after midnight. Some kids had nearly ripped the phone off the roof, little bastards."

Lee was visibly more upset about almost losing his plastic display phone than actually losing Joe. It had been nearly a week, and still no trace of the delivery man. Joe's mother hadn't seen him either, and he never left home without telling her where he was going.

Joe's boss hadn't been very helpful when Dennis rang him, other than to reveal that Joe had failed to return to the pizza parlor after delivering to an abandoned house several days earlier. So, Jack and Dennis elected to pursue the matter on a more personal level. Lee hadn't been overly enthusiastic about receiving them in his busy little pizza kingdom either.

"You think it was a hoax call?" Jack asked the lugubrious manager.

"It was a bloody derelict house. Looks like it hasn't been lived in for years. What do *you* think, Sherlock."

"Could've been a tramp ordering a pizza," suggested Dennis feebly. "Or a squatter." His attention, never easily fixed on one subject for long, was already wandering toward the petite redhead single-handedly manning the parlor's phones. Jack was more interested in the plump, steaming pizzas as they rolled out of the oven. What was not so appetizing was the oil drum-shaped kitchen worker who was preparing them. Bedeviled with a cold, he was constantly wiping at his leaking nose with a hand daubed with a mixture of dough, sweetcorn chunks, and mucus. Jack watched him mold the mixture into the pizza pans arrayed on the shiny top before him and realized he didn't feel hungry anymore.

"Bloke who made the call said he was a friend of Joe's. Playing some kind of fuckin' prank at my expense, no doubt." Lee's patience was running on empty. "Maybe one of *you*. Maybe you're all just fuckin' me around while Joe makes off with my money."

"What money?" asked Jack, ignoring the accusation.

"Ten quid of my float money. He had it with him when he took off."

Dennis bristled. "He's not gonna get far on a tenner, is he? And Joe's no thief."

"He's gone. And so's my money. What the fuck am I supposed to think? And as far as I'm concerned, he can stay gone. Although if he does show his face again, you can tell him from me: if I don't get my tenner back—"

"What was the caller's name?" Jack interrupted him.

"How should I fuckin' know? It was nearly a week ago. Could have been Bruce fuckin' Forsyth for all I care."

Dennis smiled over at the redhead, who was following the conversation intently. She looked away immediately. Dennis's grin broadened. "We're wasting our time, Jack."

Jack agreed. On the way back to the flat, they decided to take a detour. Fernbank Road was quiet, but 47 was the only one boarded up and deserted. Dennis studied the rotting front door. "Even the tramps would think twice about kipping here."

Climbing out of Jack's Fiat, they tried the door. It gave a little, and when they shoved harder, it grated open. A black stink welcomed them. It rolled along the hall to breathe in their faces, settle on their clothing. Jack waited silently.

"Forget it, Jack. He's not here."

Jack looked at him, and then back at the shadows filling the hall. He stepped inside.

"Don't you think it's strange Joe was summoned here by someone calling themselves a friend?"

"Life's strange, Jack. *You're* strange. It's best just to get on with things."

Jack left him in the doorway and carried on down the hall, almost tripping over a pile of sacking. He tried a door on his left, cobwebs catching in his hair as he opened it and looked inside. A small room, empty but for a couple of shattered chairs and a rusted beer can. Daylight squeezed through cracks in the boards, showing him the wallpaper lolling out from the wall like pale, giant tongues.

He left the door open to give him some light and made his way to the end of the hall, where another door resisted his efforts to open it. He stepped back, frustrated, absent-mindedly reading the scrawled graffiti just about visible on the door in the gloom. Julie Someone was a whore, apparently. The message stirred a memory. He tried to focus on it.

"Jack! How long are you going to be in there?" He turned at Dennis's cry, the echo drifting around the old house like a grumpy ghost. To the right of the door, an uncarpeted staircase disappeared into thick shadow after five steps. Jack put a hand on the banister thoughtfully, then decided to go for it and started carefully upward.

The fifth step disintegrated under him, and he plunged downward, grabbing frantically for the banister. It came away in his hand. He fell to his waist through the hole, his legs dangling in space.

"What the hell are you playing at?" Dennis sounded annoyed now.

Jack pulled himself out with difficulty and gingerly made his way back down the ruptured staircase. Clouds of dust stirred in the darkness. He brushed himself off and re-joined his friend in the hall.

"He's taken off for a few days, that's all," Jack concluded as they drove home.

It was Dennis's turn to be dissatisfied. "Since when did Joe ever go anywhere without telling his mum?"

Jack cruised past The Slaughter. The day was slipping away from them. "Besides," Dennis continued, "you know he loved that job. He wouldn't just chuck it away."

"You heard Lee. A friend contacted him. He's taken a holiday."

"You've changed your tune. And you're forgetting one thing: Joe hasn't got any friends—apart from us."

"Perhaps he's just had enough. Wanted a change of scenery. We all feel like that sometimes."

"Yeah." Dennis was quiet until the Fiat pulled up alongside their house. Jack was just switching off the engine when Dennis whistled.

"What's that waiting for me on my doorstep? Looks like my lucky day."

Jack looked up. Lila was leaning beside their front door. He stiffened.

"This one's for me, I think you'll find."

Dennis grinned and shook his head. He was out of the Fiat and approaching Lila while Jack followed more slowly. She looked right through the electrician, her eyes fastening on Jack.

"Looking for me?" Dennis said.

"I don't think so." Her eyes remained on Jack.

Jack nodded at her, uncomfortable. Her gaze made him feel dirty, guilty. There was something in her eyes, possibly lust, certainly not affection. It made him feel ashamed and excited all at once.

"Take a walk, boy," she said to Dennis, and laid a pale hand on Jack's arm.

Dennis shrugged, grinned at Jack, then turned toward the house.

"It's been a while," she said, her cheekbones pushing at taut skin as she smiled. Dusk sneaked into her eyes.

He searched for something to say. "I haven't been avoiding you," he lied, thinking of Sam, of her angry phone call. Dennis was unlocking the main door with exaggerated slowness, a sly grin parting his stubble.

"Coming in?" The electrician paused in the doorway.

"No," Jack said quickly. He didn't like the thought of Lila in his flat, in his bedroom, touching his things. "Let's go for a stroll."

He led her away from the flat, away from his friend. Lila's face grew paler as they walked, as the evening began to paint shadows around them. His excitement escalated despite his misgivings, the dusk drawing it out of him. Lila stepped slowly beside him, close enough to kindle his anticipation. The rustle of her dark skirt sent fantasies skittering through his head like the bats flitting through the trees of nearby Victoria Square.

"Is this wise?" he asked. She turned to him, and twilight birds chorused plaintively from the bushes. Her eyebrows lifted. "Being with me," he prompted. "Waiting outside my house. If Bane finds out..."

"If Bane finds out, he might kill you," she said simply, and Jack iced over. Lila pulled him off the road between two pillars that marked the entry to the Lime Walk, a Victorian path cutting through an old graveyard.

They started along the cobbled walkway, bounded on both sides by iron rails and above by a latticed roof of intertwined branches. Suddenly she stopped, pushed herself on him, and fastened her mouth against his. He could feel the cold of the railing spikes digging into his back. A nibbled moon spied on them from between the wickerwork above, painting Lila's face a ghostly hue. Desire ripped through him, scattering guilt to the winds. Her lips were sweetly cruel. Her fingers laced around his nape as if she were trying to pull him inside her mouth, inside herself. He would have let her had it not been for a clacking of boots on the cobbles ahead of them.

A tall shadow approached. Bane. Jack was certain of it before the figure reached the old gas lamp suspended from the wickerwork and the man's features slid into view. A tall black man, a regular customer at the Video Vault, watching them with unguarded amusement. Jack's guilt increased, but he couldn't have stopped now even if he wanted to.

The man passed them, and Lila drew Jack farther up the Walk, pushed at the little gate that opened into the soft, moon-kissed lawns of the graveyard.

Beyond the bent, old yew trees and crumbling stone wall, the sounds of the city rumbled distantly. Unseen birds and squirrels stirred irritably. The moonlight picked out lichened inscriptions and flowers dying in cracked vases. Silhouettes of spectral angels watched over them as they moved between the tombs. Lila was kissing him again, unfastening his shirt to allow her hand and the cold to sneak in against his flesh.

He stopped her abruptly, unable to ignore thoughts of death any longer.

"Sam told me you killed her cat. Is that true?" The question sounded absurd, farcical in the weird hush of the graveyard. But he needed to know. He could still taste her lips, and he wanted to taste them some more, but the question remained. The doubt remained.

"Do you think I could kill?" she whispered, stroking his face.

"I don't know. You tell me."

"And what about you? Could *you* kill?"

He stiffened. The black gravestones seemed to shift closer, a silent jury. Yes, he could kill. He had taken a life in a fit of abdicated consciousness. His hands and mind stolen away and used as if by someone else. He looked away from her.

"Why did you break into Sam's flat?"

"Perhaps I wanted to see if she still wanted you."

Jack's guilt was hammering at him again. "And did she?"

Lila laughed coarsely. A startled bird twittered back angrily from a dark clump of bushes. "The cat was dead when I found it. Maybe it fell down the stairs." She chuckled softly again and pulled his face around toward her. "There. Feel better now?"

He fell on her, his lips mashing hers, his hands exploring her body in the darkness. He removed her wig as they lay down on the cool grass, the autumn chill forgotten. Her skull gleamed in the moonlight, splintered by the shadows of branches. Their tongues danced together. She loosened his belt, his fly. A night bird tutted them from the spiteful shadow of a yew. Jack let go. Wildness caught him, ran with him, into the dark.

Afterward, he lay back, sucking in the cold air. It wasn't enough to cleanse him. Lila lay silently beside him, her wig crouched amongst the dead leaves, a dead thing, too: a monstrous, dead spider.

"Bane sent me a skull."

He heard her breathing in the dark. He stared up at the moon, staked on the thrust of a bare branch.

"He sent me a skull covered with grave dirt and maggots." He waited for a response, and she let him wait. "Where did he get it? Here?"

Lila yawned extravagantly. "Does it matter?"

He couldn't see her features, just the bone-white glow of her head, hollowed by patches of dark where her mouth and eyes should be.

"Why send a skull? It's sick..."

"Perhaps he thought you'd like it." Her tone was mocking and accusatory, just as it always seemed to be.

"Why would he think that?"

She lay her head back on a pile of leaves. A couple passed by on the cobbled walk, and she laughed deeply, a treacly, winter sound, causing the couple to hesitate, scanning the darkness for the source of the laughter. Jack watched them hurry on.

"And why did you pretend to be dead in Bane's video? I suppose you both thought that was funny, too?"

"Death *can* be amusing."

"Is that why you called the pub The Slaughter? Because you thought it was *amusing*."

"Don't you like it?"

"No."

"Don't lie to me." She was playing with him; suddenly, he regretted the bitter ecstasy of their lovemaking.

"Bane likes the name, though, doesn't he? Maybe he's used it before."

He heard a dry crackle beside him. He thought for a minute she was laughing, and his scalp shrank, but it was only leaves beneath her hands. The cold crept in. He needed to know.

"I've been to Birmingham." He waited for a reaction, and when none came, he pushed on: "I found the ruins of a pub there." The rest came in a rush as his anxieties tumbled out into words. "People who went there—disappeared. Something happened to them... Are you going to tell me you don't know anything about it?"

"People always disappear. It's the way of things."

He sat up. The cold was getting to him now. He could feel it pressing up through the ground, like the bitter hands of the countless dead beneath the turf.

"What the fuck does Bane want from me?"

She could have been another corpse for all the answer she gave him. He tried a different tack. "Bane's obsessed with death, isn't he? He even welcomes murderers into his pub. And don't try and tell me he's unaware of their history."

"What do you think of the twins?" Lila's voice teased him from the shadows beside him. "Do you like them?"

"No. And I don't like Bane."

"Oh, *he* likes *you.*"

He ignored the mocking tone. "What makes them come to The Slaughter? And what about Bolton? I can't believe there's no connection to Bane. Does he invite them all?"

"Perhaps *they* like the name."

Frustration and anxiety stifled him. "What did you do in Birmingham?"

She paused. "What do you want me to tell you?"

He thought about it quickly. He didn't really want her to tell him anything. He didn't want to know, to get involved. So why couldn't he stop himself from groping in the dark to find out more? "Bane's sick. What's your excuse?"

"For what?"

"For getting your kicks from death."

"The way *you* do, you mean?"

He fell silent. He still couldn't see her eyes, just a pale moon face gouged with shadow.

"You thrive on death: in films, in books. Your imagination embraces it. Isn't that right?"

She and Bane knew so much about him. It was like they'd taken a look around inside his soul, sneered, and shut the door again.

"I don't make snuff films, even if they are fakes. I don't fraternize with psychopathic sadists."

"The twins were released because their doctors were confident they were safe for the general public. Would you have them locked up forever because they once went too far?"

"They're *not* safe. They're evil. I can *smell* it. I can smell it in Bane."

"Can you smell it in me? "

He had just made love to her. He stood up, shivering.

"Or perhaps in yourself?" She sat up, hugging her knees. "You're steeped in horror, too. Just like Bane, just like me."

"Not *your* kind of horror. Not *Bane's* kind. The films I watch— They're fantasy. Pretend blood and guts. Entertainment. There's nothing wrong with that. But Bane... Is he just waiting for the twins to start performing again or something? Does he want a replay of their greatest hits? I draw the line between imaginary horror and the real stuff, and no matter what you might think, the real stuff doesn't turn me on!" He realized he'd been shouting.

Lila was chuckling again.

"Safe horror. Swaddle yourself in anemic terrors. Don't you think you're hiding?"

"Why should I hide? What have I got to hide from?"

"Yourself."

"And what the hell is that supposed to mean?" he blustered, inexplicably frightened. "You've been living in the shadows so long, you tar everyone with your own sick brush."

"Oh no; not everyone. Just you."

"It's *you* who's hiding," he yelled. "Come out into the light, for Christ's sake!"

"What's Christ got to do with it? With anything?

He left her chill laughter behind him in the dark of the graveyard. It merged with the twitter of a night bird and faded as he strode between the pillars of the Walk, sweating despite the cold, and headed for the brightness of the streetlamps.

CHAPTER TWENTY

"You expect me to go in *there*?" Sue was gawping up at the sign-board, her face pinched with disbelief. She listened to the menacing thump of music from beyond the frosted windows, and Sam didn't have to work hard to guess what she was thinking.

"Just for one drink, Sue." Sam was wearing her chic leather jacket and tall boots. Her makeup was severe, her hair pulled back into an almost militant ponytail.

"But why here?"

"Come on. You'll love it." Sam led her unwilling friend through the door.

Music threatened them from the speakers. The dry ice was back, although not in such copious amounts as on opening night. Bikers, crusties,[14] rockers, and those floating somewhere in between filled the room. The students and casuals who had tried out the pub in its first couple of weeks were mostly conspicuous by their absence, the majority of them long since frightened away by the increasingly intimidating clientele that had adopted the place as its own. Sam didn't hesitate, moving straight up to the bar where the woman in black was serving a couple of rock chicks. Sue followed, bewildered and uneasy.

The barmaid looked up and saw Sam. She smiled coldly, passing

---

[14] A group of homeless or vagrant young people, generally characterized by rough clothes, matted, often dreadlocked hair, and an unkempt appearance

a handful of change to one of the biker girls without taking her eyes off Sam. Sam was determined to outstare her but couldn't help dropping her gaze to the plunging décolletage of Lila's black dress and the vile tattoo on her left breast. The tattoo defined the woman. Sam knew this creature was not worth all the anguish and hate, yet she had to prove to herself, if no one else, that she couldn't be subdued so easily. It had taken guts (and days of procrastination), but it was something that had to be done if she was ever to feel master of her own life again. The barmaid had done something no one had ever done to her before: damaged her sense of self, forced a hole in her security. Nobody should be allowed to do that. If she was to overcome the horror of it, the *guilt* it left her with, then she was going to have to make a stand and not shut herself away in her flat like a violated nun.

"A pint and a half of Butcher's Best," she ordered, her voice steady, her eyes hard, meeting Lila's again. She was surprising herself, and it felt good. The barmaid passed a pointed tongue over her lips lasciviously, and Sam's fingernails dug into the palms of her fists.

"You couldn't have found a more gruesome drinking hole if we'd gone on a pub crawl through Hell," Sue moaned, pulling her brightly hued jacket protectively around her skimpy top. She knew nothing about Lila's visit to Sam's flat; Sam hadn't exactly felt like chatting about it. Sue's eyes were darting nervously around the pub, from the noisy and disreputable drinkers to the wax monsters menacing the bar, and Sam felt guilty for involving her. *Using* her. Sue was middle class and middle brow; she liked Woody Allen and big, woolly sweaters. She stuck out in The Slaughter Inn like a virgin about to be draped across a stone altar.

Sam paid the barmaid without a single word, then passed the half to Sue, clasping her own pint firmly. She stayed by the bar, conscious of Lila's attention. She steeled herself and took a nonchalant sip, wondering what her next move should be.

Jack made it for her. He and Dennis threaded their way through the fog and the throng of drinkers, Jack pulling up in surprise when he saw Sam at the bar. She had hoped he might turn up. This way she could show them both exactly how she felt. There was a look of something almost like relief on his face (and longing?) She let the thought pass. *Too late for that, Sunshine; you blew it big time.*

Dennis scowled at her, but she had no time for his games now. Sam noticed Jack's eyes flick away from her to Lila, but she wasn't here to be jealous. That was over.

"Why wouldn't you let me speak to you, Sam?" Jack said, turning back to her while Dennis lumbered up to the bar. The electrician kept looking back over his shoulder, clearly reluctant to miss anything.

Sue was looking a little annoyed now. Sam knew what she was thinking, but her friend was wrong; she hadn't dragged Sue here to prop her up in her efforts to regain Jack's affections. Far from it.

"Hello, Jack," she said loudly enough for the barmaid to hear. She could see Lila out of the corner of her eye, serving Dennis while carefully watching Jack and Sam. Well, that was good. *Let's give her something to really watch,* she thought, and realized she was enjoying herself despite the tension.

"I really don't know what to say about Kirby," Jack began, looking harassed and uncertain. "I'm really sorr—"

Sam didn't let him finish. "I don't need your sympathy, Jack," she said and leaned forward to kiss him, long and deep. After a passive moment of bewilderment, she felt Jack respond, and that quickened her excitement, but *she* was playing this tune, and lest he forget it, she whispered softly as she broke the kiss: "Don't get any ideas; this isn't for your benefit." Then she turned, leaving him frowning, and faced Lila, who was frowning even more. She felt vibrant with strength as she reached over the bar, balanced the pint in her hand for a second, and then calmly tipped the contents into the barmaid's cleavage.

"The beer's off," she said and, gesturing for the astonished Sue to follow her, walked proudly toward the door. She didn't look back.

CHAPTER TWENTY-ONE

Sunday brought Nigel to the flat. To Jack's relief, it was only a flying visit; there was work on the next day, if he was interested. Well, he had a shift to do at the Video Vault, he began, but when Nigel told him they would be going to South Wales, cogs began to click and whir in his brain.

He managed to get rid of Nigel and then searched in his chest of drawers for a certain piece of paper. He found it and dialed the Pembroke number scribbled there. A sly voice answered, informing him this was Jerry's Garage. Jack hesitated, then plunged ahead. "I hear you might have some videos for sale."

A suspicious pause on the line, then: "I rent some new titles, pal, if that's what ya mean." There was an ugly edge to the Welsh accent that Jack didn't like at all.

"I was told you might have something special. I'm a bit of a collector."

"Oh yeah." Non-committal, wary.

"I was given your number and address."

"Yeah? Who gave you that then?" The sneer in the voice made Jack want to hold the receiver away from him, which was absurd.

"A friend of yours, " he continued. "Roderick Bolton."

A longer pause on the line. Then the voice returned with an added note of sly eagerness that Jack liked even less than the sneer. "So, are you going to tell me who *you* are?" It sounded almost as if the man already knew.

"Just someone who might be interested in your videos. Horror films. Bolton told me you might have some interesting ones."

"So what are you gonna do about it?"

Jack was a little thrown by that. "Well, I thought I'd come and have a look. I'm visiting South Wales tomorrow—Tenby, in fact—and I could easily make a little detour to Pembroke."

"Then do it," the man said and abruptly hung up. Jack almost changed his mind, but the memory of Bolton's enthusiasm at the film festival niggled at him. His curiosity settled the matter. His next call was not so simple: Richard at the Video Vault.

"You're probably not going to believe this one, Richard," he began, remembering all the excuses he'd unreeled lately, and then scolded himself for giving his boss ideas. "My grandmother's been rushed to hospital, and my mother wants me to drive her there. Tomorrow."

Richard was unsympathetic. Perhaps he suspected that the last time Jack's grandmother had been to a hospital had been in 1981, when she died. "I thought you didn't speak to your parents."

Jack hesitated. This was harder than he'd expected. "I don't, normally." He put on his dourest voice: "It doesn't look too good for the old stick, though. I felt I had to do something to help out." Then, all brightness: "I'll be in Tuesday, though."

"No. You won't." Richard was quite positive on that point.

"Why not?"

"Because I don't need you on Tuesday. Or Wednesday, come to that. Bugger me if I don't want you in Thursday or Friday, either. How's that?"

"What are you trying to say?" Jack felt a little hole open up in his gut. He hadn't seen this coming.

"I'm not trying; I've just said it. You've pissed me around one time too many. You're out." In the cold.

"Thanks for your sympathy and understanding, Richard. I'll be sure to pass on your heartfelt condolences to my granny— He was wisecracking to a dead line. He pushed the receiver onto its rest and sat for a minute contemplating this new twist. No job. How did that feel? Nigel had told him often enough. Okay, so there was still the occasional CD-buying nonsense, which could be very occasional indeed. He considered (very briefly) applying for Joe's now vacant position, but that didn't feel right for two reasons: one, Dennis would never forgive him for jumping into Joe's grave, so to speak, as the electrician still believed their friend would come running back with his tail between his legs any day now; and two, driving through the city in a custard-yellow car with a gigantic glowing phone on the roof wasn't his idea of cool. The Day-Glo uniform sealed it for him. No, for the time being, he was stuck with Nigel.

Monday found him stuck with Nigel in a traffic jam near the Severn Bridge: five inches an hour. Nigel seemed oblivious to the inconvenience, however, his neck craned permanently out of the passenger window as he ogled a gleaming red MG and its voluptuous blonde driver in the lane to their left.

His tireless leching irritated Jack. In fact, *everything* about Nigel irritated him, and that made the prospect of spending five or six hours on the road with him very daunting indeed. He shunted the Fiat forward another inch, his thoughts on dark things: sex, Lila, and video-tape. Not forgetting Sam, of course. He remembered her pouring her pint over Lila and his knuckles whitened around the steering wheel. He should have been defending Sam against the barmaid after what she'd done, yet he couldn't help feeling like a pawn in somebody else's game: everyone knew the moves but him. Sam's kiss had been a ma-neuver, too, no matter how justified she'd been in doing it; it also seemed pretty obvious to him that Lila's visit to Sam had not been motivated by so mundane and conventional an impulse as jealousy. He tried not to think about either of them and turned to Nigel.

"I've got to make a slight detour this afternoon, Nige. There's somebody I need to see in Pembroke."

"Yeah?" said Nigel, still gazing out the window.

"Yeah. Only be a short while." That had been easy enough, at least. He pushed down on the accelerator as a gap opened up between him and the Polo in front.

They slowly passed the cause of the hold-up: a sculpture of twisted metal on the right-hand lane in front of the bridge's toll booths. A Renault had concertinaed into the dented flank of a milk truck. Patches of milk mingled with a trickle of very dark blood running in a crooked line from under the Renault. An ambulance presided, two paramedics busy trying to ease something out of the metallic shambles. Jack found himself gawping.

"What the hell's going on here?" he remarked stupidly.

"Someone's dying, Jack," Nigel said with more than a hint of rebuke in his voice. He pointed to the road in front of them, which was now open.

Ashamed, Jack toed the pedal. A blush warmed his cheeks as he pursued the car in front toward the bridge. *Nigel ogles a beautiful, living woman, and you ogle a death scene*, he scolded himself. He shook his head, remembering Lila's words in the graveyard. No way. It didn't turn him on. But everyone got curious about death; it was only natural. As they sailed over the giant gray bridge, Jack glanced at the eddy of the tide swirling powerfully below, at the forlorn hunch of rock with its tiny lighthouse guardian stranded offshore, at the distant concrete bones of the second bridge under construction a mile downriver. He felt as dark and dirty as the water sluicing beneath him.

"I once had a job here," Nigel announced mournfully. "Counting the cars that cross the bridge."

"That must have been stimulating," Jack answered. They didn't say anything else for another sixty miles.

They hit Swansea, did the rounds, and then dragged on up to Tenby, Jack eager to reach Pembroke, Nigel subdued and quiet. The rain teased them, only deciding to play whenever they left the car in each town center. Meeting up with Nigel again in a Tenby NCP, Jack reminded him of his intended visit to Pembroke, but Nigel seemed uninterested in the proposal. As they set off along the winding coastal road, Jack's spirits lifted to such an extent that he even risked breaking the welcome silence from his colleague. "What's eating you, Nige?"

Nigel stared at the rain weeping against the windscreen. "Nothing."

"You're not your usual jaunty self." Paltry villages embraced them briefly, only to fall away again as the car sped on.

Nigel picked his nose glumly. "I was just brooding about where it'll all end."

"Don't go all philosophical on my arse, Nige. Don't think I could cope with that."

Nigel turned to look at him slowly. "Can I ask you a question?"

"I don't know. Depends what it is."

"What do you think of me? Honestly."

Jack groaned inwardly. "Let's stick to safe ground, eh, Nige?" Five more miles to Pembroke, and he'd never seen Nigel as morose as this. He drove faster, wishing he'd never broached the silence.

"Stick to safe ground. Hmmm. Cheers, mate." He paused, looked away. "You don't like me, do you? No, please: don't deny it. You don't have to. Be honest with me and admit it."

"Nige, for Christ's sake, what's got into you?"

"It's not compulsory, you know: To like me. Not many people do." He sighed.

"I like you, Nige," Jack insisted.

Nigel gave him a reproachful glance. "No, you don't." Before Jack could object further, he continued miserably: "Driving over the Severn Bridge got me thinking, you see. I used to do all right; I had a good job as Telesales team leader back in the eighties. Loads of mates. At least, I thought they were mates. Now I realize they just tolerated me—like you do. From Telesales to counting cars. And now this. Hardly a career progression, is it? It's like someone's trying to tell me something: no mates, no proper job, no girlfriend, no...fun. Yeah." He sniffed as if he'd just worked out something incredibly complex. "That's it. No *fun*. Like I've had my slice, and now it's all over."

"If you're expecting me to be able to cheer you up, Nige—" Jack began, but Nigel cut him off.

"No, Jack. You've got no worries there, mate."

The rain fizzled out, and the sun peeked shyly from its hidey-hole of clouds. As they crested a hill, Pembroke gleamed below them. Jack headed for the docks and then swung onto the road for St. David's. A side road lured him down into a quiet district on the edge of town. He followed the scribbled instructions on the paper Bolton had given him and was soon pulling up in the forecourt of a dusty-looking garage.

He was the only customer. The petrol pumps leaned in the frail sunlight, smeared with oil. Nigel looked at him inquiringly. "Ten minutes," Jack promised and ducked into the gloom of the garage office.

The room was tiny and filled with depressing afternoon light filtering through the single cobwebbed window. Recent video titles and spare motor parts stuffed in boxes lined the shelves. Dried engine oil patched the floor. A cash till perched on a small counter, shouldered in by all the part racks and crates. A stoat of a man with a D.A. and seagull eyes was sitting behind the counter, smoking.

Jack cautiously said, "All right?" to him and received no reply. The man studied him slyly.

"I phoned yesterday. About your videos," Jack reminded him.

The stoat nodded. "You want to see something nasty."

Jack felt unclean. He looked at his feet awkwardly. "I was promised something unusual. Different."

"Oh, I got that, all right." He didn't seem to be in a hurry to show it, however. He was enjoying Jack's discomfort.

Jack spread his hands in the air demonstratively. He didn't want to play. The stoat scratched at his dark, oily quiff and then slowly stood up, pushed at a door splattered with faded oil behind him, and called through into the back.

"Pop. Look after the pumps."

A figure shuffled into the office. It wore filthy overalls and a wrinkled bathing cap on its head. It took Jack a moment of peering in the dim light to realize that the bathing cap was actually the old man's bald pate, divided by a rim of grease from the rest of his head. His eyes twinkled dustily. He mumbled incoherently through a spongy, toothless mouth.

The stoat led Jack through into the back of the garage, where he found himself in a storeroom the dimensions of which he could only guess at; the dim bulb swathed in cobwebs shed only a dismal puddle of light over bulky engine parts and boxes of old video tapes.

The stoat took Jack through the gloom to the tiny oasis of orange illumination and with a gruff, "Fill yer fuckin' boots," left him there, like a guide abandoning his master in the midst of a desert. Jack paid him no further attention as he squatted on his haunches before the nearest crate, a child beneath the Christmas tree.

He pulled out video obscurities, video rarities, video collectibles, and quite a few nasties. He forgot all sense of time as he delved, sifting through the piles of antique esoterica, rooting like a happy pig. He was reaching down to pluck a VHS with a particularly repellent cover from the box of delights beneath him when the light went out.

Darkness threw itself at him.

He straightened up, dropping the video, feeling an irrational fist of fear tighten inside him. For a moment, he was back in the barrow—or was it a cave, like in his dream? But there was no sound of dripping water. There was nothing to be scared of. The shadow *wasn't* beside him.

Strong hands seized him from out of the dark. An involuntary shout of terror squeezed from him, and he twisted manically to free himself, but his arms were pulled harshly behind him. He felt himself dragged back and forced into a chair.

"What are you *doing?*" he croaked at his captor, his throat choked with dust and remorseless fear. His hands were bound by rope to the back of the chair, which seemed to be fastened to the floor judging by the failure of his attempts to rock it over. The darkness was absolute, as was the silence, apart from his own frantic breathing. *This had hap-*

pened before. This helpless terror, unable to move, unable to see, alone, so alone and left to die. Forgotten in the dark, calling out with no one to hear. This had happened to him before, and if he remembered when, he just might go mad. The child in him was crying endlessly, but he must not think of that now. Just a dislocated memory out of nowhere, and he must not—

The hands had released him, and his captor could have left the storeroom for all Jack knew. He shouted, yelled, cursed. And tried to calm himself by thinking rationally. Please let this be bloody Nigel, messing around and giving old Jack a little fright. It couldn't be the garage man, surely? People just didn't *do* this sort of thing to strangers for no reason. Did they?

He thought of the chair nailed to the floor as if it had been used often for some purpose, and his whole body broke out in a sweat.

Bane.

The thought stiffened him in the chair, made his eyes stare wider as if that way he might be able to see through the blackness. Of course... Bane had set this up with the help of Bolton. The stoat was obviously in league with them both. But why? There must be—and he sucked in a deep breath—a sane reason behind this persecution. Or was he to suffer constantly from these twisted games for no other reason than that Bane enjoyed them?

Games? A voice from the dark (from his own head) mocked him. *Who said anything about games?*

What could have been thirty minutes, but could just as easily have been an hour, passed, and Jack's cries had trailed away in silent, hopeless resignation. Surely Nigel would come to see what had happened to him soon? He could hear the distant sound of traffic murmuring on the main road that was only half a mile away but might just as well have been a hundred. The silence in the storeroom stretched into a thin wire of tension in his mind, his ears ringing with the tautness of it.

Then the noise began.

It was a noise familiar to him from a hundred cheesy horror videos, the wailing discord of countless cheap soundtracks, amplified and mixed together from invisible speakers all around him in the dark. Tinny howls rose and fell as tacky synthesizers squealed in a battle to outdo each other. Jack twisted his head around, feeling his mind begin to unreel as the pandemonium yanked at his reason. The storeroom was swelling with nightmarish possibilities, a playground of horrors.

With a gasp of relief, he noticed that the pitch dark was beginning to lift. He concentrated on the glow to his left, as if his salvation lay there. The glimmer became a square of crazy, sparking illumination, a television screen filled with snow. The TV set was sitting on the oil-stained concrete floor ten yards away, and now another set glared into life beyond the first. Squares of white noise winked on all around the storeroom, extension wires leading away from them into deeper pockets of gloom. Jack's head snapped from side to side, tracking each screen as it came alive.

Now the first screen held a picture. A huge, bearded man lifted a power drill to a pretty nurse's head. Jack watched as the drill bit was pushed very slowly into the girl's left temple. The scene punched Jack hard, although he had seen it on many occasions before. This time it seemed the bad actress was suddenly hitting upon real emotion in a moment of genuine terror. "Horrible," Jack whispered to himself, as if his disgust would somehow protect him. His wrists burned from his attempts at freeing himself.

To his right, an ape-like hand dragged an all-American teenager's throat across a jagged shard of glass spiking up from a window frame. Blood oozed, a cheap effect. But it was real to Jack.

There was more to see, no matter how he tried to crane his neck to escape the myriad images of death. A man castrated in a bathtub, blood staining the soap suds; a policeman's uniform and stomach undone by scrabbling undead hands in a peaceful churchyard, green grass splashed red; a fierce splinter puncturing a woman's eye in vivid close-up.

He tried shutting his eyes, but the images lurked behind his lids, the scenes coming alive for him in a way they never had in the cozy safety of his flat. Now they held *real* threat. Real horror. *So real it could happen to you*, a tagline on a cassette box had once screamed at him. Hate fused with his terror; a hate born there in the dark, nurtured by the shrieks of the video nasty scores, teased out of him by the seductive carnage on the screens.

"I hate it," he sobbed, while faces filled his mind. He saw his long-abandoned parents; his father's features black with anger and the urge to deal out violence; his mother, a ghost, fading into apathy. Bane.

A final television screen glowed into life directly in front of him as the others died. No image, just insane snow. And perched like an ossified creature on top of the set... A skull. A freak bone, a lunatic with a hatred left behind long after the flesh had gone. Then that too faded from view as the screen below it died, and Jack was alone in the dark again.

CHAPTER TWENTY-TWO

It was music from video hell, played by serial killers with blood-rusted instruments, and it sounded like it was never going to end.

Jack was panting heavily, and tears coursed down his cheeks, trickled into his mouth. It took him a full minute after his bonds had been cut for him to understand that he was free, but when he did, he leaped out of the chair, thrashing out in search of his tormentor.

He blundered into television sets, sending them crashing to the ground, tripped over boxes overflowing with videos, collided with crates of engine parts, his fury spurring him on.

He slashed at the dark with his hands hooked into talons, little guttural snarls issuing from his lips, a beast released. He embraced a stout television mounted on an old fridge and hefted it into the air before slamming it back down again, the roar of sundered glass infinitely satisfying.

His hands alighted on a smaller object, hard and smooth, and he realized exactly what he was holding just before the light bulb snapped on again over his head and the crescendo of discord was abruptly silenced.

He lowered the skull, brought it closer to his face, recognizing the expression of hate stamped on the bone as a mirror of his own. And there it was, just as he'd dreaded it would be—the echo that had haunted his dreams. Rocked by horror, Jack dropped the skull, the sense of familiarity so strong it felt like it was a part of himself he was dropping.

He backed into another TV, still intact after his burst of demolition fury. It felt moist through his sweater. He turned slowly; the blank screen, which should have been a metallic gray, was a moist, vibrant red. A freeze frame in scarlet. His hands were wet, too.

Not blood, he told himself. *Not blood.*

The floor was streaked with it; several other television sets were also daubed as if by a psychopathic painter. There was even blood on the light bulb, drip, drip dripping. The stink was hot and butcher fresh.

The storeroom began to revolve around him. He looked at his red hands and swayed. He shook his head and gulped down dusty air, left the circle of light, and began groping toward where he hoped the door was. He could just about see it, corrugated steel throwing out a faint reflection from the light bulb, but as he headed for it, he saw the door retreat down a tortured corridor of perspective, playing with him.

He scraped himself on a rusting engine, scattered a box of nails over the floor, but he kept going. The game was simple: could he reach the door and escape before the fine strings of his sanity finally snapped and left him groping around and around in this building forever?

Near the door, a stack of video recorders mocked him, their leads snaking across the concrete in a tangled spaghetti junction. Their significance eluded him; he could only think door. *Door.*

He was there. His fingers were on the handle. And it wouldn't move. He sobbed, wrestling with the metal, and the handle finally gave, rust dribbling from the door hinge. He left a print of blood on the corrugated steel and staggered along the dark passage to the office, where dusty daylight struggled to cheer the small room. Nobody there.

No Bane, no garage man. Not even the grotesque old Pop. Out into the forecourt, the autumn breeze stopping him dead, his shattered nerves overdosing on the cool, fresh sensation.

And no Nigel, either.

The Fiat was parked where he had left it in the forecourt. And scanning the roadside beyond, and the fields behind the grubby garage in his frantic search for his colleague, Jack was hit with the certainty that he wasn't ever going to find him. It was as if Nigel had stepped through a door and gone forever.

He looked back at the garage. Late afternoon sunlight played on the grubby window of the office, on the rusting corrugated roof of the storeroom. The office door hung open, inviting him to come back inside.

He fell into the car. Beyond all hope, the keys were where he had left them, in the ignition. All he had to do was turn them and drive.

CHAPTER TWENTY-THREE

Whoever said bus stops were magnets for lost souls wasn't exaggerating, Sam thought mournfully as she waited with the other human flotsam drooping in the wind.

She checked her watch. She had twenty minutes to get to her flat before *Neighbours* started. Then she'd tumble into a hot tub—albeit with not so much alacrity as she once would have done—and then, and *only* then, would she plan her evening. She looked forward to doing nothing: a glorious, lazy nothing of an evening eating chocolates in front of the box.

A pang of depression stabbed her; she'd been doing rather a lot of that lately, although it wasn't for the want of offers. She was an attractive girl, and upon hearing she was unattached again, many of the sales team at work had pressed to take her out. She was still waiting for the right offer from the right man. But Jack was a morbid loser, heading into the dark with all sails unfurled, and she had no desire to go with him. Besides, he already had a suitable companion for that particular journey.

She wished he'd call.

It was a forlorn, tiny voice, and she stamped it down immediately. Perhaps she could go out with Sue tonight. They could go to a nice pub, have a natter.[15] Then again, why bother? Perhaps she was getting old, but the thought of being chatted up all night by knuckleheads who assumed that two girls out on their own were naturally looking for a bed

---

[15] A casual and leisurely conversation.

to share didn't really appeal. There was always the cinema; she hadn't been there for ages.

There was always the telly.

She decided to buy an *Evening Post* just in case there was anything good on at the flicks. At least it was making an effort, she supposed.

Ten yards away, the vendor sat behind his yellow box beneath the awning of the Hippodrome playhouse. His washed-out eyes didn't focus on her as she took a folded paper. She was searching in her purse to dig out the correct change when a hand snaked past and paid for her.

"I reckon I owe you that for the way I've treated you in the past," Dennis said with a smile. His eyes held hers meaningfully. He was dressed in his scruffy work clothes, his van pulled up alongside the theater.

"And you think twenty-five pence is all I'm worth?"

"It's all you're getting. Climb in the van; I'll give you a lift home."

They nudged through the rush hour traffic, Dennis moody and quiet behind the wheel, Sam finding it strange to be sitting in his work van after so long. It brought back memories of conflict, which had epitomized their year together.

"Were you looking for me?"

He nodded. "I wanted to talk to you."

She stared straight ahead, avoiding his eyes. It was a bad idea accepting the lift. She should have guessed he'd try this on again, even after all this time. "There's really no point, Dennis."

"And what about Jack?"

She could see her reflection in the windscreen, pale and vulnerable. How she hated that. "What about him?"

"I still want you, Sam," he broke out suddenly. He turned to face her as the van idled before a red traffic light. The dark October evening was vivid with neon and the flurry of after-work people milling around the city center.

"You don't know *what* you want, Den. You never did."

"I want you."

She glanced at him and was unnerved by the naked pain in his face. He had never opened up to her like this before.

"No, you don't," she said, dismayed. "And I've only just finished with your best friend, remember?"

Dennis looked away, moved the van forward as the light flicked to green. "One date? That constitutes a relationship, does it? A few weeks ago, he was just another bum to you, and then suddenly you're slobbering all over him. Jack's a nobody, just like me, remember? A non-achiever. You shouldn't be lowering yourself to our level."

"You can't take it, can you?" she bit back. "Just can't take the fact I'd rather be with Jack than you."

"I thought so. You *didn't* want to finish with him, did you? As far as you're concerned, you're still together up here." He tapped his head with a forefinger. "And here was me thinking that kissy business in The Slaughter was just to get back at Morticia because of your cat. There was a lot more to it, wasn't there?"

She didn't answer. His bitterness was only too evident.

"He's in a bad way," Dennis said after a while.

She looked up sharply. "What do you mean?"

Dennis glanced at her, and she knew he could detect her genuine concern. She saw his own yearning twist in on itself, his face hardening into bitter resignation.

"He's losing it," he said after a while. "Ever since he came back from South Wales the other day, he's been spouting some really crazy shit. He's cracking up for sure."

"What sort of crazy shit?"

"*Really* crazy shit. One hundred-carat gold bollocks. He reckons that jughead Nigel's been killed. Butchered. Apparently, it wasn't the butler who did it, but the Landlord. Bane from The Slaughter Inn, would you believe? How does that sound to you?"

"It sounds like he's been watching too many horror videos." Sailing into the dark.

"That's how it sounded to me. Jack's convinced a horror writer mate of Bane's called Bolton lured him to Pembroke, of all places. Then someone tied him up and made him watch loads of nasty vids in the dark. I couldn't understand why he was complaining; he usually loves that sort of shit. Then he blurted out that Nigel Nosepicker had been snuffed. Blood all over the place, he reckoned."

Sam was becoming increasingly confused. "Pembroke? What the hell was he doing there in the first place?"

Dennis shrugged and turned the van along a residential road that led to Cotham, and Sam's flat. "His silly chart-rigging job. Personally, I reckon he's been dropping some dodgy acid and gone off on the Mother of All Bad Trips to places only folk who watch lots of video nasties ever get to see. A one-way ticket, it looks like."

"And what does Nigel say about it all?"

Dennis frowned. "I can't get hold of him. Never in when I ring. But that doesn't alter the fact that Jack's got these paranoid delusions about Bane. I mean, I don't exactly like the look of the bloke, but Jack *hates* him. Bane sent Jack a skull, you know, for a sort of prank, and I reckon that's what's behind all this Pembroke stuff: Bane pulling another stunt on Jack. Revenge, I suppose. You know what for, of course, don't you?"

She had a good idea. Dennis carried on, and Sam realized he was playing his best card: "They make a good couple, don't you think? Video Nasty Jack and Lila the pussy killer?"

"And I suppose you're hoping I'll come running back to you on the rebound?" He was bringing out the worst in her, just as he always did.

"I'm just telling you like it is. Jack thinks Bane snuffed Joe as well as Nigel, and all because Jack snaked his woman."

"You've got such a beautiful way with words, I really don't know how I ever brought myself to leave you."

"You're not listening." Dennis parked the van outside Sam's house and switched off the engine. He turned to her. "Jack reckons it's *his* turn next, and that so far Bane's just been messing with his mind. And I'll admit, his mind *is* pretty messed up, but then it was never in good shape to start with, was it?"

"Has he told all this to the police? I mean about Nigel and Joe?"

Dennis laughed mirthlessly. "Oh, he wanted to, at first. I had to stop him. I told him if he went to the law spouting that kind of acid babble that they'd lock *him* up and lose the key. Especially if they found his stash of dodgy horror vids. They'd fit him up with every missing child and unsolved murder case in the country. I told him the next time he'd see the light of day, there'd be eighteen to thirty holidays available to Pluto."

Sam was thinking hard. "You mentioned Joe."

"He's just rambled off on his own for a bit, that's all."

"And Jack thinks Bane killed him, too?" He must be really going off the deep end. Did she care anymore? Perhaps he was happier in the dark. Wasn't that witch there to hold his hand?

"He's fruiting out. Genuine acid casualty. He took off yesterday without a word. God knows where he's gone. He's lost his job at the Video Vault as well, and when he's in the flat, he just sort of sits around like a shadow."

"Don't look so happy about it."

Dennis glared at her. A flash of sudden hate creased his features. "I'm beginning to remember why we split up."

"Because I dumped you," Sam shot back at him. "Do *you* think something's happened to Nigel and Joe?" she added quickly, before he could turn nasty.

"Don't be bloody stupid."

"Then where are they?"

Dennis looked away. Sam had just echoed Jack's own words exactly. He didn't reply.

Sam opened the passenger door. "Thanks for the lift. And for your touching concern for Jack." She shut the door on his wince. It was obvious he was more concerned with getting back with her than helping out his friend. She was putting the key in the lock of her front door when something Dennis had said recurred to her. She turned, but the van was already squealing around the corner at the end of her street.

Bolton. Jack apparently said Bolton had something to do with Nigel's disappearance. She remembered the empty-eyed goth at the horror festival. She remembered Bolton. "*He has a feel for dark things...*" Sam shivered, glancing around the shadowy front garden. The bushes crawled in the wind. The lawn next door was a black square. A ghost was watching her over the wall.

She dropped her keys in fright, and the pale rag detached itself from a rose bush and drifted away on the evening breeze. Sam clutched at her walloping heart and retrieved her key.

She pushed open the door. The hall was bright and cheerful. She shut the door on the night and other dark things and headed up the staircase to her flat.

She woke much later from a dream in which she'd been in bed with Jack. She had reached out to caress him, her hand sliding across his slim chest, down over his belly, which wobbled beneath her touch— a gross, heaving mound. She had turned to him in horror, and Roderick Bolton had grinned up at her, his glasses filling with moonlight from the chink in the curtains, his face gleaming with secret sweat.

She got out of bed and poured herself a glass of water in the kitchen. "*He twisted my soul... Then he found others more like himself; sick, nasty...*"

She climbed back into bed and lay staring at the darkened ceiling. Several times she jerked around to confront the far wall, convinced the twins would be standing there, watching her.

CHAPTER TWENTY-FOUR

It was an evening visit. He felt it would be better that way. More fitting. Certainly more discreet.

He stood amongst the bushes in the back garden. Beside him, a dark pond rippled slightly as a sad old goldfish broke the surface. A garden gnome crouched nearby, studying the visitor with cheerful malignance. He stared back, then nudged the gnome over on its back with the toe of his boot. He flashed a grin in the dark.

The lonely house waited for him. It was a quiet, rural spot, the nearest neighbor half a mile down the lane. In front of the house, the country road tunneled through a dense copse before plunging merrily into the embrace of the small Cotswold town of Wellbury. Behind the house, the garden, and beyond that, a churned-up wasteland filled with the skeletons of half-built houses, bones of a new estate frozen in the difficult pangs of birth. A construction excavator parked near the garden fence clawed the red-brick house with its shadow. The visitor liked the image it conjured.

He crossed the lawn unhurriedly and moved up to the back door. A window to his right bloomed with subdued light behind drawn curtains. They were waiting for him, although they didn't know it.

His time for waiting was over. And it had been such a *long* time...

He tried the handle gently. Locked, as he had expected. No problem. He inserted a thin blade into the lock, manipulated it stealthily until the tumblers clicked sweetly. He straightened his coat, brushed a lock of hair from his face, and stepped into the kitchen.

The door into the hall was open, allowing some light from the lounge to filter through. He paused in the center of the kitchen, missing nothing; the curtains, patterned with orange owls in flight; the spice rack above the old oven; the linoleum-topped table and its small flock of worn wooden chairs; the clock above the sink, fashioned into the shape of a farmer pushing a wheelbarrow laden with happy fruit. He smiled at the clock and the table in turn. They were old friends. It was good to see them again.

He entered the hall, his boots soundless on the faded rug that covered the parquet flooring. The lounge door was before him, its four frosted panes suffused with light from the television and standard lamp within. He smiled one more time, a final smile—of readiness perhaps, certainly not of resignation. This was a pleasure long deferred. He put out a gloved hand and turned the doorknob.

And the sight he had been anticipating for so many years was revealed to him.

It wasn't so different from how he had expected it to be. There was the old woman, as skinny as she could be, twitching in an armchair, her eyes bugging in stupid surprise and stupider fear. There was the old man...

Old man.

The brute had gone. The giant with the pounding fists he remembered so well had himself been bullied by the years. Now he was just a gaunt shadow of his former self, his bent frame wrapped in a cardigan and worn trousers. He looked like a scarecrow stuffed in an armchair waiting for something to scare. Now it was *his* turn to be afraid. He looked up at the intruder with a fear that had always been alien to him. His face was the color of milk, folds of flesh hanging loosely around his features.

The visitor smiled at him.

There they were.

The lounge was small but cozy. His memory did not disappoint on that score. A traditional family lounge complete with a real-flame-effect gas fire sitting in the hearth like a pet; a small but comfortable settee, empty now of children or friends; vapid paintings of boats and forests; he remembered all these. The contemptible ornaments were mostly still there, too—mindless objects settled on top of the television and mantelpiece as if growing there. And the bookcase filled with books that nobody read.

Yes, apart from the brute, it matched the picture in his mind near enough.

"Hello," he said, entering breezily, "I've come for you at last."

PART III: BEAN

CHAPTER TWENTY-FIVE

They cruised slowly through the village. Drab houses and a couple of neglected-looking stores watched them pass without interest, their facades wind-scuffed and sad. The coastline behind the village was equally bleak: ghostly sand studded with rocks beyond the low sca wall.

The two students parked next to a housing estate that seemed to frown at them as they got out and climbed the wall. Jed filmed the thudding ocean enthusiastically, the Sony video camera tucked snugly against his right cheek. The wind tried to push him off the wall as he panned to take in the estate, the old disused church near the main road. Gravestones bent in woe beneath the wind and the afternoon drizzle.

"Perfect." Jed flicked a close-up of the church and its gathering of tombs.

Tim was not so sure. "Not much atmosphere. Just misery. Don't waste the batteries; save 'em for Bennane." He was a gawky pole of a lad, wire spectacles forever slipping forward on his beaky nose. His lids bulged over protuberant eyes; his teeth were crooked. Jed was athletic, muscular, huge. His features all held together well, *Boy's Own* handsome; his short hair neatly layered, his hero's chin without a trace of stubble. He lowered the camera.

"Misery's just what we're looking for, remember? Let's hit the town."

They tried the post office first. The bun-haired lady behind the counter greeted them with a gorgeous Galloway accent, but no, she was a relatively unadventurous soul and had no idea where to find the cave. She glanced over their shoulders as the door opened and directed them toward the man who stood there, a post bag strapped over his shoulder. He'd be able to tell them.

The apple-cheeked postman cheerily agreed to an interview. It would be his first, and he hoped it would be of great help to them in their video documentary thesis.

He wasn't of much help at all, as it turned out. Yes, he'd been in the cave as a lad, but it was a dangerous place if you didn't know about the tide and such; the sea came right up to the mouth, you understand. A grisly, horrible place, not much of a tourist attraction. Indeed, he could count on one hand the number of visitors who came to the village asking after the cave each year and still have fingers left to waggle, if they could forgive his levity. They filmed him anyway, standing outside the post office in the rain.

"Anyone else in the village that can tell us a little more?" Jed inquired robustly. The jovial postie thought about it. No, he shook his head at length, there weren't many folk around these days who could say much on the subject. "So long ago, y'see, and not much reference to it in the books, I'll bet."

They thanked him and walked on. At least he had given them an idea of how to find the cave. They turned past the church, heading for the car. Tim stopped and indicated a gnarled gnome of a man sitting on a tomb in the graveyard, oblivious to the drizzle.

"He looks cracked as an old jug. Why not try him out? Local color, if nothing else."

They stepped through the gate into the cemetery. The crumbling church hunched over the old man protectively. A gargoyle with an eroded face spat down on them with a pursed mouth of stone. The gnome watched them come, eyes squinting from under a wide brim. He wore time-gnawed slippers that revealed his wrinkled toes. His overcoat was a scarecrow's delight; Jed could imagine mice scurrying up the tattered sleeves.

"You're right," Jed hissed. "Crazy as a Clanger."

They were within two yards of the relic when his walking stick shot out, warding them off. The tip rested against Jed's formidable chest.

"What ye at?" a reedy voice piped at them. Jed lifted the camera. The man's yellow eyes shifted to take it in. "Bean," he shrilled.

Tim brightened. Jed, more obtuse, frowned. "I'm sorry?"

"An' ye will be. Ye're a'ter Bean, if I'm no mista'en." The relic sucked his gums lewdly. He lowered the cane, the knobbly hand holding it vibrating. Rain tapped on his hat.

"That's right," said Jed with a winning smile. "Can you tell us anything? A history, perhaps? The sort of things that might not have found their way into the books?" He hefted the camera to his shoulder and thumbed the Record button.

"I can tell aboot death," the gnome spat briskly, "if tha's what ye're wantin'?"

Tim swapped a smug glance with Jed. Bingo. Jed squared the gnome in his viewfinder eagerly.

"I culd tell ye bastards aboot death, aye. But thar's nae need. Ye fookers'll find oot soon enuff." He gobbed at their feet and his mouth slobbered in unappetizing glee. "Ye'll find what ye're lookin' fer!" He pounded the stick into the turf and wriggled his bare toes. His lizard eyes were shot with bloody relish. "Gae to't, an' thar'll be two less fookers wi' silly heeds on theer shoulders!"

Jed lowered the camera and shrugged. They left the foul-mouthed gnome on his tomb and stepped through the gate again.

"You wanted local color," Jed chuckled as they walked past the second, more-modern church, toward the housing estate and their car.

"All good material," Tim asserted. They climbed into the Mini, glad to be out of the depressing drizzle, and sat for a while, staring through the windscreen at the leaden sea sulking beyond the wall.

"Gets into your bones after a while, doesn't it?" Tim shivered and grimaced. "I knew we should have left it 'til spring."

Jed started up the engine. "What's the matter? Can't take the October sea breeze? Autumn is exactly the right backdrop for this little masterpiece of ours, believe me. Besides, we wouldn't have had time in the spring. Too many exams. No, like I said, this is the best time." He swung the Mini out of the car park and back onto the high street. No one turned out to see them off.

"Lively place," Tim grizzled as they left the last house behind them.

"A village of the damned," Jed pronounced grandly, "with the evil ghost of Sawney leering over them. You can feel his presence overshadowing the souls of the community."

Tim grunted. "Can you bollocks! Save the melodrama for when the camera's rolling."

"I'm serious," Jed retorted. "You can feel his influence everywhere."

The Mini climbed the coastal road that swept up toward the hills. Cliff faces cowled with netting to stop subsidence brooded over the road to the right of them. To their left, a truncated headland pushed bluntly out to sea. A set of temporary traffic lights stood on a bend in the road, powered by a generator that squatted like a strange pet beside its three-eyed master.

"This is it," Jed pointed out with mounting excitement. "The headland by the lights, Postman Jock said." He swung the Mini onto a gravelly verge beside the signals. They left the car and walked toward a wire fence that prevented entry onto the grassy headland. They hitched over it and advanced toward the cliff edge.

Bennane Head.

They stood, savoring the moment. The cliff face plunged sheer below their feet. To their left, the hillside collapsed into a deep gully stuffed with ferns, which led down to a curving beach. They could just make out a rusted pram that stood alone on the sand. Halfway down the slope, a fridge stood upright in the bracken, a seagull perched on top. The rain had just about stopped, but a cold wind swept up from the sea, numbing them.

"Not much of a beauty spot," said Tim.

"Did you expect it to be? It's a bitter place. Lonely... and bad." Jed's voice was laden with melodrama. Then he turned around, went back to the car to collect the video camera, tossing a large, powerful torch[16] to Tim when he returned.

They started down the slope of the gully, slipping on the wet grass, soaked by tall ferns. Reaching the fridge, they paused briefly, listening to the breathing of the sea, spiced with the wail of seabirds.

Jed was the first to hit the beach, running down through the last few yards of bracken and onto the sand. He surveyed the desolate beach with something approaching awe. Strands of belly-white seaweed were strewn over the rocks and along the shore. With his foot, he nudged a clump draped like intestines over a boulder. The stench dug into his nostrils.

"Let's find the cave." Jed set off north along the beach toward an outcrop of the craggy headland that thrust into the sea, its tip surrounded by a cluster of boulders. Waves slapped against the rocks, tossing spray at the two students as they pushed their way around the

---

[16] Flashlight

outcrop. Jed almost fell from his precarious perch when he saw the cave.

"Look!" His blood stalled. Tim drew himself up beside his friend.

A narrow inlet was revealed, more a passage than anything else, pushed in by mighty shoulders of rock. At the head of the inlet, a jagged wound was gouged into the cliff face, dribbling a spew of boulders and seaweed.

"It's not how I envisioned it," Tim said.

"It's worse," Jed answered quietly.

Tim looked at him. "It's just a hole, Jed. Don't let your imagination carry you away. You're not supposed to have one, remember? You're the macho jock with the lantern jaw and bulging pecs for brains."

Jed ignored him. "Careful with that torch, Timothy. Don't drop it in the sea." He clambered over the jumble of boulders toward the cave. A tidemark of weed and driftwood grew like a scruffy beard beneath the black mouth. Jed heaved his way up until he could see inside.

He swung the camera smoothly to his shoulder and thumbed record. Close-up into the orifice. Pause. "Come on, Spindly," he rapped at his companion. "I'm just itching to penetrate this unholy snatch." He couldn't wait any longer and pulled himself over a big rock wedged in the entrance and slipped into darkness.

Tim slid on a wet rock and grazed his knee. Luckily, he hadn't smashed the torch, but his temper was fraying. He pulled himself up again to find Jed had disappeared. The hole awaited him, silent, dark. The sea pushed from behind. Gulls pierced the air with unceasing noise.

Jed was standing in a large chamber, the slimy walls narrowing into pitch blackness after twenty yards or so. Water dripped from above. The stink of putrid weed and damp rock filled his head. He turned slowly and filmed the entrance of the cave, where a slice of pale sky was squeezed by the crack. Tim appeared, framed in the hole, petulant.

"Come on, you thin bastard, get that torch in here." Jed was brimming with impatience.

Together they explored the passage, Tim's torch casting a broad cone of light ahead, revealing cracks and crevices on either side and bulging walls covered with nitrous deposits. The roof was low over their heads, the tunnel twisting on into the dark. After a hundred yards or so, it ended in a blank wall, a buffer of rock. Here, the cave formed another chamber, smaller than the first. Jed filmed it all resolutely, Tim providing the lighting. Jed was babbling. He sat down cross-legged on the packed earth of the second chamber and placed the camera aside.

"We're in the brute's kitchen," he enthused. "Imagine it: three hundred years ago, Sawney sat right where I'm sitting, gorging on human flesh."

Tim shuddered. "At least he had a fire to keep him warm. It's well-freezing in here."

"A fire! Of course! We'll build a fire. Got to get into the spirit of things for the documentary, Stringman."

"Not on your fucking nelly." Tim decided to put his foot down. "All this talk of gorging's making me hungry. Let's go. Come on; it'll be dark soon."

Jed's eyes sparkled at the thought. "Okay. We'll come back later, build a fire, and spend the night in the cave."

Tim glanced at him, waiting for the punch line, and realized Jed was perfectly serious.

Jed clapped him on the shoulder as he followed his friend out again. "You'll see. It'll be an experience."

Ballantrae's foremost pub, although rather plain and basic, seemed like the coziest, most welcoming place on Earth after the dank grimness of the cave.

The landlady, a seamed crone of eighty upward, nodded tersely at them as they entered the small, empty lounge. She served them two mugs of ale and slid two plates of ham sandwiches and a couple of bags of salt 'n' vinegar crisps across the bar. It was all they were going to get at this hour. Her tiny eyes twinkled dustily at them as they sat near the cheery fire in the inglenook, the dampness of the cave seeping out of them.

Jed stared into the twisting flames and silently mulled over the night he had planned for himself while Tim warmed his bones and tipped ale down his throat gratefully.

"You absolutely serious about this?" Tim gasped after a mighty swig, smacking his lips with relish.

"Never more so. I'm sleeping in the cave tonight. You can stay here, or in the car, or wherever you want, if you haven't got the bottle to join me."

"We were going to share the price of a room, remember? I can't afford to stay here on my own. It'll have to be the car."

Jed nodded slowly. He looked tense and suddenly very tired. He noticed Tim watching him and made an effort to perk himself up. Taking their time, they finished their pints and sandwiches. Tim gazed at the fire, reluctant to leave it, aware that his friend was even more so, although he would never have admitted it.

Jed stood up at last with forced alacrity. "Ready?" He laid a meaty hand on Tim's shoulder.

Outside, Ballantrae was as empty of life as it had been during the day. They drove out of town, and the night was suddenly all around them, oppressive and foreboding. The Mini climbed the winding coastal road to Bennane Head, where the generator was waiting, throbbing monotonously in the dark.

They clambered over the fence and stood on the lip of the cliff for the second time that day. The wind was bitter, blasting up from the black gulf of the sea. The tall grass hissed around them. The stars looked scraped clean by the wind, sharp and bright. In the light of the half-moon, the crags falling away beneath them assumed ominous shapes. A bulge of rock to their right was the profile of a beetle-browed giant with a jutting nose and chin and a beard of moss. The craggy face dwarfed them, perched above the dark strip of the beach like a brutal god.

"I'm gonna *freeze* in the car," Tim whinged.

"So, sleep in the cave with me. There's plenty of driftwood around to make a fire."

"I can't do that, Jed. It's just too bloody horrible."

Jed chuckled. "Wimp. You haven't got enough iron in your soul."

"I'll help you build the fire," Tim compromised.

Jed stuffed the video camera and a sleeping bag into a haversack and slung it over his shoulder, and he and Tim stumbled down the slope to the beach, picking their way carefully in the dark. The ghostly shape of the fridge whistled uncannily at them as they passed it, the wind playing spiteful tunes through the slightly open door.

They reached the beach, the bulk of the ocean heaving listlessly. The cliffs reared above them, huge, black shapes hemming them in.

"Is the tide coming in or out?" Tim frowned at the dark expanse of the sea.

"Dunno." Jed was more interested in collecting the pieces of driftwood littering the beach. He shivered as he touched a length of pale weed; it was as cold and clammy as dead flesh. They scrambled around the outcrop to the cave, carrying armfuls of sticks. The moon was bright enough to make the torch redundant until they entered the utter blackness of the hole.

Jed tucked the sticks under one arm and led the way with the torch. The atmosphere of the cave had grown insidiously more awful with the lateness of the hour. A psychological thing, nothing to do with the cave itself, Jed mused, but his excitement was rapidly being replaced by a morbid insecurity. He felt a special, primitive fear reaching up inside him—as if it had always been there and only needed this terrible place to coax it forth. He cheered himself with the thought that if he could capture just a small part of the atmosphere on video, they would certainly have a winner.

They dumped the wood in the first chamber, and Jed examined his wristwatch in the torchlight. It was a quarter past eleven. A long way to go 'til dawn. Jed steeled himself to construct a fire while Tim aimed the camera at him, a smug grin on his face.

When Jed had finished and unrolled his sleeping bag with exaggerated movements, as if trying to prolong every action, Tim put down the camera and clapped his hands brusquely.

"I'll leave you to it then. Just shout *very* loudly if you get too scared."

Jed grinned up at him a little weakly. Now that he was on the verge of being left alone in this hellhole, his confidence was slipping away fast.

"Sure you won't change your mind?"

Tim recognized the poorly disguised plea in his friend's words and ignored it. Jed was a jock. At college, he predictably got all the women. He was good at sports, good at fighting, good at fucking; he was even better at drinking than Tim, and any idiot could do that. So, while he was fond of his butch mate, it pleased him to no end to see this so unusual thread of uncertainty appear in his normally solid veneer. Parasitically, it fed his own self-confidence.

"Hell no, large buddy," he mocked Jed in playful American jock speak, "you're batting in the Major League tonight. Score a home run, big guy." He turned to go, then came back with a little less cockiness. "Er, can you show me out with the torch?"

Jed guided him to the exit, standing on the boulders just outside and holding the beam on the rocks below until his friend disappeared around the headland.

He was alone.

The enormity of that fact slammed home. Across the smooth, dark wine of the sea, a darker stub protruded against the night. Ailsa Craig, the huge, gull-haunted rock that stood a few miles out from the shore. The island intensified his awe and sense of isolation. Sawney would have stood in this very position at the entrance of his lair, gazing out to sea at the same dome of rock. The centuries crumbled in the instant until he could almost hear the sound of stealthy movement from behind him as the cannibal brood stirred in the depths of the cave, preparing to creep out in search of victims.

He turned quickly, glancing back into the darkness. This whole thing had gone well beyond a dare. He didn't know if he could bear to go back into the cave alone.

He stood in the entrance and peered inside, his torch frightening shadows and picking out smears of white deposit on the walls that were like old, distended faces watching him eagerly.

After a while, he steeled himself, climbed back into the cave, and approached his sleeping bag, his scalp wriggling with atavistic dread. He desperately wished Tim were still with him.

He stood over the pile of sticks, wondering what to do with himself, oblivious to the cold. Every few seconds he swung the torch wildly around the cave to check nobody was hiding, waiting for him. Of course, there wasn't. Only ghosts.

He forced himself to concentrate on lighting the fire. Soon flames grew to warm him, sending shadows skipping over the bulging walls. The secret den at the rear of the cave was hidden by a wall of darkness that alternately retreated and then pushed back at him again as the flames waxed and waned. Jed crouched, picked up the camera, pressed Record.

Nerving himself, he stood again and began making his way slowly toward the blackness, lighting his way with the torch in one hand, clutching the camera to his eye with the other.

He knew he was pushing himself to the limits, and there was a certain morbid satisfaction in that. He stopped in the rear chamber, the heart of so much secret butchery, and realized he'd never felt so cut off from everything good and safe. He knew that after this he would never fear anything ever again.

He leaned his back against the damp rear wall, lowering the camcorder, and pushing his limits even further, he switched off the torch.

Darkness pounced at him.

It was like a tidal wave exploding down the length of the cave, drowning him in terror. The glow from the fire didn't reach this far back, hidden by all the twists and turns of the main passage. He put the camera to his eye again.

"This is Sawney's cave," he said, his voice an earthy croak. "This is the *real* heart of darkness. I've just switched off my torch to get a true taste of the atmosphere. I don't like it." He stopped, heart clamoring. His voice, although not much more than a whisper, sounded intrusively loud in the cavern. He thought for a truly mind-freezing moment that somebody answered him, a faint jumble of words that must have been his echoes chasing themselves out of the cave.

He couldn't take any more. He switched on the torch and stopped filming.

The fire was hissing comfortingly in the main chamber when he made his way back, although smoke roiled around in a frantic attempt to find some way out. The wind buffeted the entrance crack, like a giant blowing through a keyhole.

He looked at his watch, eyes smarting slightly from the lingering smoke. Half past midnight. Well into the witching hour, he thought as he crawled inside his sleeping bag. He lay prostrate, eyes fixed on the dark beyond the fire. It crawled toward him, retreated, advanced. He lay rigid, sweaty fear gluing him inside his bag. Water dripped slowly, mockingly. So much evil had squatted here in times gone by, so much horror. He could almost hear the distant shrieks of the mutilated drifting back to him through time.

He sat up in his sleeping bag, his throat like a dry gorge. He was sure he *could* hear voices. Shouts and awful cries snatched by the wind. A stamping of heavy feet thundered from the depths of the cave. He grabbed the torch and swung it frantically in that direction, then back to the entrance. The nitrous shapes on the walls leered at him. The voices were the wind itself, of course; the stamping just the muffled beat of the sea distorted by the weird acoustics of the cave.

He lay down, reluctantly let go of the torch, and put his arms inside the sleeping bag. He had to at least *try* to sleep.

The fire was burning low, the smoke beginning to clear as the wind sucked it out through the cave mouth. Jed resisted the urge to pull his arms out again for as long as he could, but in the end, the irrational fear of being confined and vulnerable forced him to withdraw them. He immediately groped for the torch again. It was obviously going to be quite a night.

Near the entrance, a particularly large pattern of white nitre on the wall looked uncannily like a figure with a stooped body and long face. A witch's face, with wild strings of hair and a grinning mouth. Black

Agnes, watching over the cave, Jed thought, and focused the torch on the shape, willing it to lose its human characteristics.

It was just a formation, a random pattern. It wasn't the imprint of Sawney's long-dead wife, stretching out spindly arms to snatch him while he slept.

But of course, he would never sleep...never slee...

He woke, staring into the most concentrated darkness he had ever experienced in his life. The memory of where he was came like a physical blow. Panic sent him scrabbling for his torch. The fire was dead; water dripped and echoed. His panting breath was hollow with unreasonable fright.

He couldn't find the torch.

He knew he had left it beside him, but his groping fingers could find nothing, only the loose dirt on the ground. He writhed in his sleeping bag like a terrified worm desperate to escape, and then froze.

The fire was not completely dead. A few embers still glowed fitfully, throwing off enough faint illumination, now that his eyes had adjusted, for Jed to be able to realize he was no longer alone in the cave.

"Tim?"

Tim had been trying to sleep for hours. His legs were cramped in front of him in his sleeping bag, jammed up against the dashboard, his head cold against the passenger window. The unceasing drone of the generator hunched in the dark outside wore away at his nerves. It was a horrible sound, irrational and meaningless. The headland was a nub of black projecting into the night beyond the Mini, the sea a distant pulse far below. In the rear-view mirror, he could see the red eye of the traffic light watching him. He felt surrounded by his own dread.

He didn't like to close his eyes. He imagined something swarming over the lip of the cliffs, creeping toward him, Jed's blood smeared on wicked fingers.

He chided himself for his timidity. Jed was down at the very root of the horror, sealed in with it. Alone. If he could endure it down there, Tim could certainly endure it locked safely up here in the car.

He couldn't.

He wriggled quickly out of his sleeping bag, started up the engine, fear prodding and picking at him. He wheeled the Mini around onto the road and sped away from Bennane Head and its sinister generator guard.

Panic herded him downhill, only gradually leaving him as he descended from the hills and the lights of Ballantrae appeared out of the plain of night. Tim released a sheepish chuckle of relief as he drove past the town sign. He would sleep in the car park by the sea wall and return for Jed early in the morning. Pretend he'd stayed above all night, watching faithfully over his friend.

Fifteen years of cultivating a macho image, fifteen years of football and rugby prowess, of impressing girls with butch swagger and inflated ego were all stripped away in a second. Jed was an infant again, frightened of the dark.

But there was something *in* the dark. His mother had lied, then, all those years ago. Perhaps there had always been something like this waiting for him when the lights were turned out. And, at last, he could see what it was.

Shadows, no more than shadows, sitting around the dying fire, part of the dark itself, slipping momentarily into separate forms only when the wind agitated the embers, and Jed could see the deeper black of their hunched shapes.

He knew they were all watching him. The silence was appalling. Just the occasional patter of water falling from the cave roof and the mumble of the wind and waves outside. He leaned helplessly on his elbows and tried to understand, his mind dragged past the thin line of reason.

The past had returned to the cave, regurgitating those it could no longer bear to hide.

He began to cry because that wasn't fair.

His mother had lied to him, and that wasn't fair.

A gray mist had erased the ocean. Tim jerked awake, his head numb, his back feeling as though Torquemada had been playing with it for a week or two. The grayness beyond the sea wall disorientated him for a few seconds as his mental faculties fought to reassert themselves.

The inside of his mouth felt like dirty wool. He rolled the window down for a gulp of fresh air, which revived him enough to make him think about food.

It was five to seven. Too early for the pub to be serving breakfast. He could go and collect Jed first, see how the big bastard had coped in the cave on his own. Probably slept about as well as *he* had, he thought ruefully. He swung the Mini out of the car park and drove along the high street. Mist curled around the houses, reaching for Tim, falling behind only when the car began to climb the coastal road.

The generator was still thudding, the traffic light stuck on red.

He left the car and started down the hillside, the bottoms of his jeans soon soaked from the early morning dew. The beach was a surreal strip of bone-colored sand floating before a bank of gray. The sea had disappeared, although Tim could still hear its hollow breathing.

Gulls sank into the fog, sobbing eerily. He paused before the rusted pram that was just beginning to slip into the encroaching mist. A baby's face, white and dead, was revealed within the hood. Horror pounded him.

He forced himself to take another look and chuckled in relief: a bunch of clammy weed stuffed inside the pram. This was all Jed's fault—he could have been back in Manchester, in his *bed*, for God's sake, oblivious to weird shit like this. He turned away and plodded toward the cave.

The natural porch of rock before the cave reverberated with the beat of all-but-invisible waves. They licked out of the mist, reaching for Tim's feet as he clambered gingerly over the boulders. At the lip of the hole, he paused. Jed had the torch. Oh well; he supposed he could manage that slight discomfort seeing as Big Jed had doubtlessly endured unrelieved horror all night.

He was grinning as he ventured inside. He reached the limit of daylight and stopped. Jed's fire was a pile of cold ash. Jed, his sleeping bag, torch, and camcorder were nowhere to be seen. Perhaps he had decided to sleep in the rear chamber to really freak himself out.

"Jed! Wake up, big man! Light me the way in." His voice bounded around in distorted echo. He waited for an answer.

"Jed! Wake up! Oh, sorry, I'm forgetting: you won't have had a wink of sleep in here, so don't pretend otherwise." Nothing. Echoes jeered.

Tim knew Jed's game; his friend would wait until Tim crept forward in the dark and then grab him and let him fill his boxers. What else could he expect? Jed had the imagination of a tortoise. Well, he wasn't playing.

He hovered on the brink of the dark, waiting.

Nobody emerged to jump him. Perhaps Jed *wasn't* in there. Perhaps he'd gone for a walk along the beach. Carrying his sleeping bag and torch? Nah. He could read Jed's mind; he was lurking all right. But Tim was becoming rapidly bored. And hungry.

All right, Jed; you get your scare, then I get my grub. Let's get this shit over with.

It was like walking into deep, starless space. On the edge of the infinite. His head collided with a bulge in the roof, not hard, but enough to startle him. And annoy him.

"Jed, my larger-than-life friend, you are very dead when I get my hands on you."

He followed the twists of the tunnel blindly, fingers sliding along the damp rock walls. When he came up against the dead end at the rear of the cave, he stopped, heart galloping, waiting for his friend to pounce. This was bloody agony. His breath was too loud in the hollow chamber.

"Jed?"

Tim was alone in the dark. Jed did not answer him.

A blur of faint noise reached his ears, a distorted echo. He listened intently. Faded screams, their source confused by distance? But they sounded to Tim as if they were emanating from within the cave, cries of violence buried by time.

His imagination was giving birth to monsters.

A burst of panic sent him cantering madly back down the passage, bashing his knees and arms in the process, but seeing him out of the hole in rapid time. Beyond the cave, the sea was pushing in, forcing Tim to move swiftly to escape the insistent waves slobbering over the rocks to get at him.

He didn't stop running until he was past the pram, still seething with the unique blend of fear the cave instilled in him. He let the panic fade in its own time, sucking in deep, salty breaths. The gulls swooped over his head, shrieking angrily at him.

Tim climbed the gully, tired and irritable. He must have missed Jed somehow. Of course, the bugger had walked into town, or gotten a lift. Wasting Tim's time again.

On the cliff top, the generator droned. He peered over the edge for one last look at the dragon's domain. The cave was not visible from this angle, but the beach was imbued with almost as much horror in its desolation, haunted by the lost wailing of the gulls.

The Mini slipped back into Ballantrae and trundled up the deserted

High Street. Tim pulled up outside the pub. It was open now, and Tim could hear eggs frying from inside. He entered the bar and lowered himself onto a stool. Eventually, the old lady appeared. She waited for him to say something, dusty eyes expressionless.

"Has my friend been in this morning?" he asked politely.

"I've no seen anyone but yerself, lad."

Tim sighed and ordered a full breakfast. The woman took his order and shuffled into the back parlor. The sizzling of eggs soon recommenced.

Tim took half an hour over his breakfast. The crone watched him constantly from the dim parlor. Eventually, he stood up to go, and the old hag emerged a little from the shadows.

"Folk disappear, lad."

He hesitated in the doorway. "Pardon?"

She said nothing more. He returned to the car, scanning the street for Jed, anxiety twisting his belly.

He stood aimlessly on the headland again. The tide heaved its way in across the shore like a gargantuan beast, the mist parting at last to let it come. Jed could not have gone back into the cave; Tim had had enough trouble leaving it an hour earlier with the sea stealing in. His calls were again answered by scornful gulls and nothing else. This was madness. Back to Ballantrae. Around and bloody around.

He parked beside the church, which was beginning to glow with mid-morning sunlight now that the mist had lifted. On his tombstone perch, the old man watched him. The weary student entered the cemetery. Gargoyles spat dryly. The old wreck puckered his mouth as if he were going to join in. To Tim's disgust, he did so, hocking a ball of phlegm into the grass at Tim's feet.

Tim looked down at the spittle glistening amongst the dew. "Morning," he said, undeterred by this show of contempt.

The old man trembled with age and venom. He clutched his stick as if it were Tim's neck. "Di' yer find what ye wer lookin' fer?" There was devilish gloating in the piping voice.

"I've lost my friend."

The ancient cackled obscenely. "An' I said ye wuld! Ye shake hands wi' Death an' Death'll gobble ye doon whole!"

Tim ignored his babbling. "Have you seen him? Please. I'm worried about him."

The old man twitched and rocked with glee. "I see no one. An' no one sees I."

The relic said nothing more, staring through Tim, out across town. Tim turned to follow his gaze. The village slept peacefully in the surprising warmth of the morning. The tide filling the tiny harbor was resplendent under a golden quilt of sunlight. But the old man was gazing beyond the houses, beyond the winding road that climbed into the hills. His eyes were fixed on distant Bennane Head, and on the fierce, craggy profile brooding above the waves.

CHAPTER TWENTY-SIX

Water dripping.

The man didn't move. He was crouching in the dark of the rear chamber, and he was listening.

The boy listened, too. The years between them fell away as if they'd never been.

The family holiday was over.

His first night in the cave. Sitting in the black chamber, listening to the bone whisper as the sea thundered around the mouth of the cave.

It told him of the secret that is inside every child, every man and woman. The secret of fear and how to reach it, set it free. How to use it. The boy could feel his own fear fluttering like a trapped moth inside his chest, but he wanted to know more. The skull whispered of strength and hate and the tyranny of dread, and the boy's fears eased a little. He would like that. To *cause* fright and never to feel it. That would be something.

And then a thought had come to him: he was sitting in the dark listening to a dead thing. That was crazy. People with weird heads did stuff like that. Perhaps *he* was going weird in the head. The idea frightened him more than the skull's words. Surrounded by darkness, he suddenly wondered if he would ever get out again. He would be lost in this cave forever. And ever, Amen.

There were figures in the dark with him. He could not see them, but he knew they were there. An awful coldness came off them. It chilled the little boy's mind, so he gasped and sobbed and almost didn't hear the skull as it whispered again.

Are you afraid?

The boy was *terrified,* but he forced himself to sit still, shivering in the cold. Night was out there somewhere. The gulls were silent now. Only the waves could be heard. Only the waves—and the hoarse whisper from the jaws of the bone.

Are you afraid of what you are?

The boy squeezed the skull, and tears of fright rolled down his cheeks and onto the dirty cranium.

"Who are you?" he shouted into the silence of the cave, echoes flinging his question back at him.

Who are you? Who are you? Who are—Darkness, the skull answered, the voice like a creak in the boy's head, a trickle of dust in the hole of his mind. *I walk in the black places, where nothing good passes. I am the wind that batters at your door. I am the dark shape at the foot of children's beds. Mine is the face in the moon, the scream that splits midnight into dawn, the soft tread on the stair. You've seen me, heard me, felt me. I am everywhere where fear is.*

"I know you! *I know you!*" the boy shouted. He knew all these things.

We are the same, you and I.

Show me!

Darkness. Waves, sobbing around the cave mouth.

Show me...

A fire spitting in the cavern. Stinking flesh skewered above greedy flames. Beyond the fire, a shadow cast on bulging rock. Hunched, massive. But just a shadow. A shadow on the wall.

"Father," the child breathed, sitting in the dark.

Old woman on the beach. Her body bent inside her cape like a coat hanger as she trawled the drab shore, filling her basket with seaweed and useful objects tossed in by the surf. She saw him sitting on a rock in the morning sun, gazing out to sea. She followed his gaze curiously, but there was nothing there. Nothing but iron-clad waves snatching at bobbing gulls, and Ailsa Craig humped out beyond.

He did not look at her as she approached, did not stir. She thought maybe he was dead there on the rock, his eyes so wide and lifeless. Not 'til she touched his cheek with a hand like old willow did he twitch and come to life with a twist of his face and a scream in his eyes that made her snatch back her fingers as if she had been burned.

"What ye doin' here, son?" Hate. Such hate in that face. She took a step backward, as if fearing he might bite her. But then the hate slipped away and weariness replaced it. Weariness and loneliness, and more than a touch of sorrow. It brought the old woman closer again.

"Ye're the one, int ye?" She poked his shoulder. "The one the police bin lookin' fer all this week? What ye doin' here?"

At her words, the boy got to his feet, alarm and desperation replacing the other emotions. He was going to take to his heels, she realized.

"Wait. There's nae need tae be fearin' me, lad. I'm no one o' them."

He relaxed a little, and she could see just how tired and dirty he was. His trainers, jeans, and pullover were encrusted with grime, his face, too. He stared at her, and for a moment, his eyes made her balk. So black and deep, they were, like that hole in the rocks beyond the headland. And now she understood.

"Bin in the cave, haven't ye? Bin in there, where there's only darkness and grim ghosts. Ye shuldnae've gone in there, lad."

All week, and they hadn't found him. Now they were widening their search to the surrounding countryside, and he had been here all the time, in that dark place. She shuddered at the thought, shuddered even more at the lost spaces in his eyes, at the deadness, like something childish had rolled over and given up the ghost. Suddenly she knew what she must do. No matter why he was hiding, no matter what he had seen, she would save him from seeing any more.

"Ye'll come wi' me, though, won't ye?"

And he did.

She lived in a hut, a hovel, that peeped through a comb of dead conifers beneath the crest of the ridge on the far side of the road from Bennane. An avenue of nettles ran up to the door, which hung crookedly, as if weighed down by its coating of fungus. Inside, everything seemed crooked to the boy; the chairs, the wooden table caught mid-hobble in the center of the tiny kitchen, where a crooked stove leaned beside a crooked window throwing a bent pattern of light over wobbly stone flags. Even the short hall seemed to tilt slightly, leading to a bed chamber and a living room hidden away at the back of the hut. Here, the ragged curtains hung askew on the rails, and two armchairs bulging with stuffing like cancerous lumps waited before the dirty hearth. A dead cat sat there, too, staring at the boy with glass eyes. Birds hung above the cat, suspended from the low roof. They eyed him wickedly, as if blaming him for their resurrection through taxidermy. His new home.

She was good to him after a fashion. Whether he was good to her was something he couldn't have said. It wasn't something he really thought about. But she did okay by him, hid him when the police came searching for the last time. He lay in the loft space above the living room and stared through a crack in the wood, watching the officer ask his questions and thinking, *This is my last chance to go home. I could come down now, and everything would go back to how it was.* Back to the beatings, the blasts of fury, the nervy betrayal of his mother as she pretended that nothing was wrong and failed, yet again, to defend him. Go back to living with an ogre. No. He had found another ogre. A truer father. It had come alive in the cave to be with him, and there was no turning back.

Ever.

He watched the policeman go. Together they stood at the grimy window as the officer climbed down the slope to the road where his shiny car waited to take him away to civilization. Away for good.

"That's it, I reckon," the old woman told him. "Ye're mine now. Ye can stay as long as ye like. It's bin years since I've had a soul to talk tae, unless ye're countin' wee Smokey here." The boy looked at Smokey perched permanently beside the fire. The old woman was weird in the head. But that was okay.

While he lived at the hut, he was close to the cave. That was the best thing about his new home. He went there every day. The skull was there, where he hid it. It told him many things, things that made his head swell in the dark, filling with tides of blood, making his eyes wide as lakes. In the dark, that's where he felt truly alive.

He didn't think much about his parents anymore. They were gone. Past. It didn't hurt to think that way. Why should it? It had hurt more living with them. Now he was away, free as the gulls that sifted through the clouds and toyed with the waves. No school for him, no lessons— except the ones he learned in the blackness of the cave and the things the old woman told him.

He didn't think about his parents, but one day he saw his mother. She was standing on the beach, and even from his position behind a rock fifty yards away, he could tell she was crying. He waited until she climbed back to her car before returning to the hut. He didn't see her again. Not for many years.

Years. Years that once meant moving from one class to another, swapping old books for new, now meant something more vital: the growing and dying of seasons. Summers, winters, the brief ones in between. He watched them come and go, and nobody was counting anymore. Certainly not the old woman. They lived their secluded lives, and neither was discontented. The old woman kept him away from the village, but he didn't want to go anyway. He had his cave—that was the only world he needed. A world of dreams he knew would be clammy nightmares to others. A secret world. A world where he was king of the castle.

Often, he would spy on the old woman bending over the well out back and wonder what would happen if she fell down it, swallowed by the black pit. He wondered about it so much, it was like he'd actually seen it happen. She'd stay down there forever and a day, he reckoned, her coat-hanger body wedged at the bottom in six feet of dark water. Her head would bloat up like a wrinkled puffball, and bits of skin would come off like soggy cornflakes. He would pull up the water, and there'd be swollen parts of her in the bucket. Maybe a bone clacking around, or a tooth. Or wisps of her dirty white hair. He wouldn't like that. But there was no other water.

It was a week after he came up behind the old woman at the well that he found the intruder near his cave. A man standing outside and staring in. The boy's world shook. The cave was *his*. Nobody else was allowed near it. He slipped behind a boulder and waited, wondering what the man intended. If the man went in, the boy didn't know what he would do. Perhaps the intruder would find— The boy stood up at the thought, and the dark rushed into his mind.

The man went into the cave. He was like many the boy had seen around the hills over the last few months, with his silly woolen hat and thick woolen socks pulled over his jeans. Hikers, with their big boots, cagoules[17], and backpacks, as if they had to wear a special uniform when they dared to explore the wild countryside. They were frightened of dying, or injury. Frightened. *He* didn't have to wear silly clothes when he sprang amongst the rocks and roved over the hills and crags. But then, he was different. Special, the old woman had called him.

When the hiker entered the cave, the boy knew he must do some-

---

[17] Windbreaker

thing. The man was defiling his secret place, and he couldn't let that happen.

But what could he do?

He followed the man inside, creeping behind him like the hiker's own shadow, listening to him huffing as he progressed slowly inward, his torch beam raping the sanctity of the cave. The boy saw the man's breath spilling out inside the tunnel, funneling down the torch beam like poisonous smoke.

The hiker was halfway down the passage, and soon he would be near the skull. The boy could hear it seething in his mind, like the hiss of a wild beast. His own breathing began to increase until it was almost as agitated as the hiker's.

The hiker wasn't long in the cave, but the damage had been done nevertheless. The boy watched him reach the end chamber and sway his torch around while his breath stained the air and his eyes betrayed his uneasiness. The man was afraid. Afraid of the dark. Afraid of the cave. Perhaps he knew about the one who once occupied it. Perhaps he just sensed the atmosphere, and it turned him cold. The boy wondered if the hiker could sense his hate.

Always unseen, a part of the dark, a part of the cave, the boy followed the hiker back out of the tunnel. The man had found nothing, heard nothing. He watched the bearded man clamber stiffly over the arm of rocks and onto the beach. The boy pursued him stealthily, hiding whenever he seemed about to look around, behind boulders on the beach, in the tall grass of the hillside.

The hiker reached the summit and moved toward the cliff edge, trying vainly to look down upon the cave from above, his vision restricted by the bulge of the overhang. The boy moved without thinking, blurring over the grass, hands outstretched. The man's head whipped around at the impact, and the boy saw surprise there, then horror as his body lurched off the cliff edge and into space. Cartoon time, thought the boy as the hiker tried to run on air like the coyote out of *Road Runner*. Funny. But he'd never seen *that* expression on any cartoon character: true terror. He felt strange, like he had created something new.

The hiker got to see the cave again. The boy climbed down to look at him. His head had snapped around to face the hole, his body sprawled across the rocks near the entrance. His staring eyes seemed to be searching for something, and the boy didn't like that, so he kicked the head until it was facing the sea instead. He bent to examine the man's face, thrilling at the tableau of horror he had created, frozen there forever, or at least until it rotted away.

Or until he kicked it away. What he had created, he could also destroy. He kicked the face. His head bulged with the skull's stories, the old woman's stories. Stories of blood, always of blood. There was blood around the squashed man, around his mouth, bubbling from the side of his broken head. But it wasn't enough.

He scooped up a boulder and positioned it carefully above the hiker's face. About to let it fall, he stopped himself. That wouldn't do. Not enough force. Instead, he smashed it down with both hands, using all his strength. Lifting it away, he examined the damage and, still dissatisfied, pounded again, reveling in the sound of bones crunching, like when he'd once pulverized a crab on Borth-Y-Gest beach. Blood stained the pebbles, the sand, his legs, his shirt. The man's head looked like a wonderfully strange thing, hair growing from a mess of red and ruin, beard a gorgeous crimson, too. The boy hadn't finished. One eye still peered up at him, white amongst so much red. The boy pounced on a sharp stick of driftwood and returned eagerly to his piece of art.

You looked inside my cave...

He rammed the shattered end of the stick into the offending eye as if he were planting a flag.

It's MY cave! Mine!

He fell down, slipping on the bloody rocks, and the gulls laughed at him.

CHAPTER TWENTY-SEVEN

They said he pushed the old woman, too, like he pushed the hiker, but the boy said nothing. Others said she could have fallen. Down a well? How did you just fall down a well? Even the boy thought that was stupid, but he wasn't going to say anything. He kept quiet. About the cave, about the— *What if they found the skull?* The thought terrified him, shook him until he wanted to scream. Shock, they said.

They'd caught him in the hut as they searched for the old woman, who hadn't collected her week's supplies from the village like she always did. He was sitting in the hut, dried blood all over his clothes, all over his face. He hadn't liked to wash it off. He'd come quietly enough, though. Shock.

"Why did you do it, son?"

"Did he frighten you?"

"What made you mess him up like that?"

They thought he was sick. He could see it in their eyes. Depraved. And so what if he was? At least it made him special.

They wanted to know how old he was, how long he'd been living with the old woman, where he came from, why he pushed her. They wanted to know so many things, the police, the social workers, the nurses, the magistrate.

The boy said nothing.

What was there to say?

So they—the social workers—spoke for him. They created a story for him, and it was as good as any, so he let them, saying nothing.

He was about thirteen, fourteen, they guessed. The old woman must have looked after him, giving him what little food she could afford on her pension. She'd fallen into the well, and he'd found her there when he went to draw up water. The shock had left him like this, without words, without reason. He must have wandered the hillside around the hut until the hiker found him. Maybe the man frightened the lad, and in his disturbed state he felt he was being attacked. So, the boy defended himself, maybe pushed him off the cliff.

But why did he make such a mess of him, both the police and the magistrate wanted to know. Why make such a mess? What sort of child would do that?

Who are you? It always came back to that.

Who are you, and how did you come to live with old Mary Tayin? Of course, it had been several years since his disappearance, and nobody connected him with the missing boy, lost one endless summer holiday. Why should they? He was a different person in every way. *Who are you, son?*

But the boy wouldn't say a word. So, they put him away. They didn't know what else to do with him.

Two years in an institution for disturbed children on the outskirts of Ayr. He endured it because he knew they would let him out eventually. He endured it because he knew the skull would be waiting for him when they did. He could hear it often in his bed in the dormitory lying next to twenty other children, the whispering reaching him across the miles of night. And in the dark, silent amongst the breathing of twenty troubled souls, he smiled.

He never spoke. Soon they gave up trying to make him, thinking he was no longer capable, if he had ever been. They thought he was abnormal, but really, he was just biding his time. They tried to teach him things, to explain about the world, but he just stared. Stared with his bottomless, coal-chute eyes that could see into their futile souls and gloat on the weakness he found there. They were so spineless; they wouldn't even beat him. So, he invented a game to test their limits of restraint.

He almost drowned Phil Constable in the kitchen sink he'd filled especially for that purpose, forcing his head under the water 'til his eyes bulged like the dead hiker's and his struggles were as wild as a slaughtered bullock... But they still didn't beat him. So, one night he set fire to arrogant Jim Robson, who always said he'd be a pilot one day. He chose to teach Jim about the fable of Icarus and burned his wings. While all the other children stood around speechless, Jim Robson burned. Rolling around the floor, screaming, his pajamas bursting into flame. If one of the instructors had not entered at that moment, it might have been better still. And instead of punishment, they dished out words. *Words.* They were supposed to inspire him with understanding for his fellow "students." They only inspired him with contempt.

Students? That was the most pathetic thing of all. They weren't there to learn, but to be forgotten. He understood that much about his fellow inmates: they were all unwanted. Rejected. They didn't belong in society's pretty picture; they were jigsaw pieces that would never fit right. Bloody nature's orphans, and the only place where they *could* fit was on the edge of this frightened world. And when they were old enough to be kicked out, that's exactly where they'd stay.

Apart from *him,* of course.

They released him eventually. He walked out of the institute one spring morning, and everyone was glad to see him go.

He set off for Edinburgh. It had to be Edinburgh. Glasgow was closest, but he wanted to get back to his roots. Before he went, he collected the skull.

The gulls welcomed him back. The cave was as dark as it should be, and the skull was where he had left it, wedged in a cleft in the chamber wall. Two and a half years bridged in an instant. He held it in his hands, and the words were still there, creeping through the darkness as the wind fastened itself against the cave mouth like a wild kiss.

The words were still there, yes, and they slipped through the tissue of his brain like fingers easing into a glove, and the fit was perfect. Electric hate blasted through the youth and his smile was a snarl, and the cave celebrated his coming into manhood.

To Edinburgh then, to seek his fortune. *Ha!* Where to begin? Almost seventeen, and no money, no possessions—just his wits and dark purpose. He hitched a lift from a gregarious truck driver who soon gave up entreating his passenger to talk and left him to his livewire thoughts. Edinburgh.

Somewhere to live. Food. The first found in an all-but-abandoned allotment potting shed, the second easy. Stealing was something he took to very well. Hanging around a cemetery in one of the eastern districts of the city, he came to the attention of the grounds foreman. The youth, gangly and ill-kempt, with pockets of shadow lurking beneath his brows, was nevertheless capable of wielding a shovel, and if he wanted work, there it was. And for the first time in many years, he spoke. Just once, when his workmates asked him who he was and where he came from. "Bennane," he said, as if that explained everything.

The work appealed to him. Digging amongst the dirt, sifting through bones, watching the fresh dead tucked away into their beds of soil, sealed in pine or teak, the caresses of their loved ones replaced by the caresses of the worms. It gave him a feeling of accomplishment; he was helping to put them there. In this way, he felt close to something he understood. Rotting shrouds, crumbling bones, and worms. He was close to death.

Then one sunny day in May, the carrion crows called to him as they hopped amongst the graves. *Idling in a field of corpses*, they rasped, *wasting your time*. And, of course, he *was*. Here he was, just an observer. A tidier. There was so much more he could be doing.

That night, in his tiny flat with walls purpled by spreading damp, the skull whispered to him again, and he began to understand what that "so much more" might be.

A year after starting work at the cemetery, he knew it was time to move on. He needed to discover more about himself. He remembered the ridiculous look of horror on the hiker's face, the odd croak of the old woman as she tumbled into wet darkness. He needed more of that.

He left Edinburgh and headed south. History hung over him, strode along the dusty road with him. Three hundred years before, the East Lothians had harbored a hedger and his family, the son about his own age. Lazy, work-shy, brutal—he remembered the old woman's words as if she had only just recited them to him. Maybe on a day such as this, the hedger's son had stepped out, dragging with him a woman of the vilest appetites, off to seek their bloody fortunes.

On a day like this.

Who are you?

The question an echo from the past, never answered. The police, nurses, social workers.

Who are you?

The old woman had known. She'd told him often enough as they sat before the fire and the dead cat. She'd recognized him almost immediately. Perhaps she'd smelled it in him, the way the hiker had smelled the terror of the cave. She showed him old books, nurtured the darkness within. *Ye carry it inside, lad,* she'd said, her eyes eaten away by the reflection of flames. *What shuld I do wi' ye? What in the name o' the De'il shuld I do? Ye've bin in the cave, and ye know, too, what ye are...*

The well swallowed her fear forever.

"Who the bloody hell are *you*, breaking into our house?"

The old man started to rise from his armchair, face purpling with indignant rage.

"Get out now, before I call the police!"

The intruder laughed lightly, as if he were enjoying the company of good friends, where the joke didn't have to be particularly funny to be appreciated.

"They didn't find me before. Why should they now?" he said. "But I can see time hasn't mellowed your foul temper. And it has been a *long* time, hasn't it? All the same, I was hoping you might remember me."

The old woman knew, even if her husband hadn't cottoned on yet. She half rose from her chair. A dreadful recognition blanched her wrinkled face. Her eyes misted with long-suppressed grief.

He advanced on her. "Stop that!" he ordered sharply. "I don't want tears. It's far, *far* too late for that." He grinned at her with hollow eyes.

The old man lurched after him, seized the arm of his coat.

"Out of my house," he spat, his thin chest heaving, his throat knotted like old rope. "Out! Get out!"

He shook the grip off his arm and leaned closer to the old man, like a doctor about to examine a patient. "You *know* who I am, don't you?" He heard the old woman sobbing behind him as she wavered beside her chair. He stepped toward the television and switched it off, killing the BBC newsreader in mid-sentence. He turned to see the old man bending over the telephone, corded hands shaking.

"Do you really want to do that?" their visitor asked with mock hurt. "Are you *really* that frightened of me?" The old man looked at him with shocked, hooded eyes, glanced down at the receiver shaking in his hands, and dropped it back on the rest.

"There. That's better. After all, why should you be frightened of *me*? It always used to be the other way around. But I'm forgetting: you've changed, haven't you? Not the man you used to be. That's a saying, isn't it? Not the man you used to be... How true. You're a shadow of your-self—all skin and bones." He smiled expansively. "But surely, instead of calling for help, you should be welcoming me with open arms?"

The old woman looked as though she was considering whether to do just that, only her sense of something terrible about this man pre-venting her. He read the confusion in her face and spread his arms wide with heavy irony.

"We waited for you for years! We never gave up hope," she stammered, hands trembling like a bunch of twigs beneath her chin.

He glared at the boniness of her, the frailty, and dropped his arms by his sides. His laugh was the sound of a cockroach cracking under a boot heel. "You never gave up hope," he copied her mockingly. He turned his grin on the old man. "That's really very touching."

"The police searched for you for three months," the old man said quietly, his eyes lowered.

"Hmm. Yes, I remember." A brief image of blue-clad figures scouring the hillside and the beach. A small boy watching them with intense, excited eyes, playing a game of Hide 'n' Seek for real. And it had been a *long* game.

"Perhaps they didn't try hard enough." He held the memory, relished it, let it go. "That's the trouble with the police today: no fucking dedication." He addressed the last remark to the old woman, enjoying seeing her wince at his obscenity.

"No," said the old man with sudden grim satisfaction, raising his eyes steadily and drawing himself up to his full height. "You can't blame the police. Perhaps I didn't tell them where to look properly. Perhaps I didn't *want* you found."

"Derek," the old woman broke in, staring in disbelief at her husband. "What are you saying?" She turned her watery eyes to the stranger in her household, the cuckoo who'd decided to fly back to the nest after so many years. "I always clung to the hope that one day you *would* be found, that you would come back to us. You *do* believe that, don't you? You have to believe that."

He studied her closely. She had changed. Perhaps she no longer cringed in her husband's shadow now that he was a mere shadow himself. There seemed to be a stubborn resolution to her features that was new to her. He could almost believe she meant what she said. It was so hard to tell after so long. Perhaps she did. But what did tears and regret mean to him?

He smiled one final time. "Well, here I am."

Father's shout.

Mother's scream.

Water dripping.

CHAPTER TWENTY-EIGHT

He sat in the darkness because it reminded him of something bad. He wanted to remember what it was because it seemed important now. There was an image just out of reach in his mind, a dream that was more than that.

Perhaps it was not dark enough in the room because the memory stubbornly refused to form. In this other place, it had been so *very* dark. No glow from any streetlamp. Certainly no sound of traffic.

Perhaps, if the memory was *so* bad, he shouldn't search for it. He should get up and turn on the lights. But he knew that would make no difference in the end. It was waiting for him in his dreams, and since he'd returned from Pembroke, those dreams were every night.

The dark. The *dark*. It had something to do with—

I'm alive! Not dead!

Then why are you here? Why can't you see, why can't you hear, why can't you move?

He almost cried out as the memory jolted through him like a spear rammed through his soul. Sweat squeezed from his forehead, and he let out a long sigh of horror. It was gone. He'd caught just the briefest glimpse of a child mad with terror, and now it was gone.

Outside, a car horn sounded angrily. Night had settled thickly against the windowpanes, but he hadn't bothered to draw the curtains. He could hear Dennis moving around in his bedroom.

Someone was ringing the doorbell. Maybe it was the girl. But which one? The good or the bad? Should he let either of them in?

Dennis decided for him. He was at the entry phone and pushing the button to open the main door for Sam before Jack had a chance to hide.

"You better sort yourself out, mate," his only comment before shouldering through the door of the flat to meet her on the stairs.

Sam stood in the doorway of the living room, her eyes smudged by the twilight filling the room. The streetlamp picked out the soft coils of her hair and her bright winter coat; the rest was darkness. He hunched in his plastic armchair and wondered what she would do.

"Jack?" She moved forward, and the streetlight found her face. Her eyes were full of astonishment, and—

"What do you want? I don't need your pity."

"Who said I was here to pity you? It looks like you're doing a good enough job on your own."

She sat down in the dark, moving Dennis's overflowing ashtray that was perched on one arm of the sofa.

"He's got a problem," Jack croaked, indicating the cigarette butts, and Sam let out a snort of disbelief.

"He's not alone."

She wouldn't take her eyes off him. Accusing eyes. But... Beautiful. He was glad, after all, that she had come.

"Dennis tells me you've been acting strangely."

Jack laughed, but there was no amusement in the sound.

"He says you've been away."

"Been talking about me, have you?"

She leaned forward on the sofa, and passing headlights illuminated her elfin beauty. She made him feel warm, just for a second. And safe. How he longed to feel safe.

"He was worried about you. I can see why now. Have you seen yourself?" She was trying not to show her sympathy, her voice neutral. He knew what he looked like. It didn't matter anymore. What did?

"Where've you been, Jack?"

Where *had* he been? Into the darkness. *Beyond* the darkness.

Dennis stumped down the stairs and let himself out. The night was cold, but he was colder inside. She had come, like he knew she would. Then it wasn't over.

But it was for him.

He strode down Buckingham Road, headlights celebrating him, then abandoning him. He wished he'd died in the desert. The Gulf had been one moment of glory in his soulless life, and that had turned bad, too. Just like his relationship with Sam. He was out in the cold. Jack had lost it, yet, she still wanted him. Dennis had left them together, perhaps the first decent thing he'd done in his life. It was a start. But it was too late.

He remembered the face in the burned-out tank. The driver's head framed in a shell hole in the steel. He hadn't looked real, like a charred Action Man® toy, gray, melted plastic for flesh, lips and eyes stolen by the heat of the blast. His teeth had been bared, grinning at this silly game of soldiers. They'd progressed along the Highway of Death, and the bodies had piled up. Corpses of boys falling to ash, bits snatched away by the wind and the slipstream of passing allied vehicles.

This is what you did, he kept repeating to himself. *This is what you did.* Republican Guard: that sounded impressive, didn't it? That sounded like an enemy you could respectfully fire big shells at. They didn't tell you about the shards of burned-up boys, barely old enough to shave, that they'd find on the other side.

This is what *you* did.

And they gave him a medal for it. Gave him a medal and took away his right to live. Took away his soul.

He wished he'd died in the Gulf.

She had been expecting him to look a mess. But not like this. It made her feel empty, like she was letting something important slip away. She stood up to switch on a lamp, and his urgent croak stayed her.

"I want it dark," he said.

"Why? Come out into the light, for God's sake." She turned it on anyway, and he recoiled.

"What are you hiding from, Jack?"

He looked at her sharply. His eyes had fallen in, pouched by ridges of skin blackened from lack of sleep. His hair was a dark shambles, and stubble climbed his face. A stale smell of old sweat came off him, and it looked like he hadn't changed his clothes in a long while. She wanted to shake him, but something made her keep her distance.

"Dennis tells me you only got back tonight. So, are you going to tell me where you've been?" She had noticed something different about the room as soon as she'd entered it. Now she realized what it was and felt a little chill zip through her. She was thinking of Bolton and the twins. She pushed them out of her mind again hurriedly.

"What have you done with all your videos?"

His head snapped around. "Burned them, of course. Isn't that what you're supposed to do with video nasties?"

"Well, I'm glad." She paused, collecting herself before pushing on with what was really on her mind. "What have they done to you, Jack?"

He gazed at her blankly.

"You know who I mean. She's evil; I've learned that from experience. And he's probably just as twisted. What did they do?"

He shook his head, his eyes searching the wall ahead of him as if for an answer. Alex the Droog smirked back coldly from a poster.

"I don't know."

She was becoming impatient now. She still wanted to be with him despite all he'd put her through (and how crazy was that?). But he was so bloody strange. He could be on the verge of a breakdown. The idea made her feel cold inside. Perhaps she ought to back off, leave him in more capable hands. But whose? Dennis hardly fit the bill. And Jack had disowned his parents years ago. *He's got no one. No one but you.*

"I don't think it was anything to do with them," he said suddenly, quietly, staring through her. "You see, I've been back. And... I don't know anymore."

"Been back? Back where?"

His eyes were so dark; she felt herself falling toward them. She didn't *need* this. She really didn't. But...

"To the garage, of course. To Pembroke, where it happened. Where Nigel..." He tailed off.

"What about Nigel?"

He wiped his hands down his face, stretching it like elastic, stretching his eyes, too, until he looked like a cartoon of himself.

"There was nothing there." He hadn't even heard her question. "All boarded up. Like it never happened."

She shifted nervously. She could see their reflections thrown against the windowpane, and hers looked as lost as his.

"All boarded up," he repeated, as if struggling to understand. "With a sign outside. And dust."

"What sign?" She was struggling to keep up with his aimless thoughts and finding it far from easy.

He laughed strangely. "An old 'For Sale' sign, what else? I broke in through some loose boards over the window to have a look. But there was nothing. The place hadn't been used for years. Dust everywhere, like it never happened. So, tell me, Sam," he leaned forward and rested his elbows on his knees, his head cupped in his hands. "Am I going mad?"

Am I going mad?

It wouldn't be the first time. Jack, ten years old, lying in bed and wondering what it would be like to kill his parents. He would lie stiff as a marble knight in a church nave, the sweat rolling off him. In his head, he could see himself stealing down the short landing—it was such a *short* landing. They would be in there, sleeping the sleep of the unjust, and he would simply creep in and...

And?

That was the darkest, most shattering moment. He tried not to let his mind push him beyond that point, beyond that "and," but it always disobeyed him, dragging him screaming soundlessly into doing the unthinkable. And locked in his rigid, waking nightmare, the ten-year-old boy had realized that insanity would be the most terrifying thing in the world.

His father had killed Puff. Puff, his little terrier with eyes like trusting brown buttons and a sweet little tail that beat against the boiler next to his basket in the mornings when Jack came down for breakfast. His father had done it. Taken Puff and twisted the life out of him, like he would try to do to Jack a few years later. He imagined those big hands around the throat of his only childhood friend, those brown buttons losing all their trust and love, going dark and empty.

Coming home from school—he remembered it so clearly; the moment framed in early summer. Walking around the house into the back garden, looking for Puff. Puff would be waiting to play ball like he always did, but sometimes Jack wouldn't feel like it; Puff would stand over the ball, watching him enter the house, and his little tail would droop, and Jack would have to come out again to kick the ball a few times for him because he couldn't bear to see Puff unhappy.

Only this time, when Jack came home from school, flinging his rucksack over a tree branch as he always did, Puff didn't bound toward him from his kennel, didn't pounce on the waiting ball and guard it eagerly, daring Jack to try and take it away from him.

Jack stood in the center of the lawn, and the ball was there, a bright blue and red plastic football shining in the sunlight. Jack waited for a moment, and he could hear his father shouting at his mother from inside, roaring like an ogre, and his mother's querulous response. And then he could see Puff. Part of Puff. Puff's fluffy right paw sticking up from the soil near the rose bed.

It made him cry sometimes. What was inside him scared him so much. At nights he lay in bed, stiff as one of those church knights with the marble eyes and petrified hands, and the sweat and tears would roll out of him as he imagined what it would be like to walk down that short, dark landing.

CHAPTER TWENTY-NINE

Lila was wearing her black cloak, the one she always wore when she went picking mushrooms in the woods. It was threadbare and tattered, a present from Bane, who said it once belonged to a Pendle witch. It made her feel steeped in Olde Worlde wickedness, a throwback to a darker, purer age, when fear stalked the land and women burned.

She'd worn it for years, picking mushrooms. She'd worn it when she gathered the hallucinogenic fungi for Bane, the ones he gave to Jack. She wished she could have watched the results. That would have been fascinating: to see him trip on his own darkness.

Today, she was wearing it to pick something with a little more potency. And that made her feel like a real witch. Black Lila.

She'd only been living in the area for a few weeks when she'd found the secret glade in the woods. It was near the old burial mound and hidden away from all the well-trodden paths. It was as if she'd been drawn there, beckoned to the darkest part of the woods, where the trees were older than any she'd ever seen and the undergrowth formed a wall of bramble to keep out all but the most tenacious.

In the glade, the trees rotted and the blades of grass were white as shards of bone. The branches, crooked overhead, joined like the interlacing fingers of a giant. It was a sunless, evil place. Lila had smelled the decay and the thick odor of fear that lingered around the spot and forced her way through the brambles and nettles, squeezing between tree trunks that grew into each other like dancers around a circle fused together by some old Halloween spell.

The first time she had broken through, she had fallen to her knees in awe.

They grew thickly at the center of the glade, toadstools, dark and swollen as the Devil's penis. She put out a hand, tentative, breath sucked in. The smell of them almost blinded her. It was a morgue stink, and she had never expected to find it exuded by any natural, living thing. Natural? There was nothing natural about these satanic roots. She touched the nearest, and it was clammy: a black candle of corpse flesh. The veil hung from it like a shroud.

She had carefully picked two of the toadstools and returned to The Slaughter with them. She felt an overwhelming urge to eat them herself but managed to resist. Instead, she had waylaid a small boy on a side street as he stepped off a bus, a nothing lad with no promise, no need for life in his dull eyes, and taken him to a deserted playground. It wasn't hard to take him. She had the charm and beauty of true evil. She sat him on the roundabout, all trembling and pale, and forced half a stem down his throat. Then she watched as the roundabout swung around, around, around.

She had taken several books out of the library, scanning the pages eagerly in search of her coveted discovery, but found nothing. Destroying Angels approximated the shape and appearance, but the color was wrong. The Angels were the purest white, and though fatally poisonous, their effect took many hours, even days, to become apparent. Lila's toadstools were a lot more efficient than that.

Now she knelt beside the ghost of an oak and picked them quietly, oblivious to the chill, the approaching dusk. Jerry Owen sat at the base of the dead tree, head slumped on his chest. He'd stopped talking an hour ago, which was a blessed relief. But his excitement had made her smile as he followed her through the woods.

"You sure Bane won't find out about this? I mean, I wouldn't want to tread on anyone's toes, you know?" He kept looking at her legs, bound in fishnet tights beneath the long cape. He was struggling to keep his hands off her, and his lust was clouding his judgment. It had been ridiculously easy to lure him from his flat in Pembroke, and his gullibility had only confirmed her suspicions that he was a weak link, a loose end that needed tidying.

She told him she needed his help to pick her special toadstools, and how would he like to be alone with her in the woods? Of course, he understood what that meant. He thought it was gratitude for helping set things up for Bane in Pembroke. It would have been silly to dis-enchant him.

"But why in the woods, Lila? Why not in your bedroom, now that Bane's gone?" He had slipped his hand beneath the cape as they entered the woods, cradled her buttocks.

She let him. "You haven't been listening, have you, Jerry? I need your help here."

And that was true. She sat him down against the base of an oak, looped a rope around it, and tied an end to each of his outstretched wrists. He was so hot with his own carnal desires that bondage was perfectly fine by him. Jerry was stupid, but even Lila had been surprised by just how stupid. She'd helped him comply by undoing his fly first, just so he knew she wasn't simply leading him on. He'd done as he was told, face flushed, tongue licking his lips.

Then she'd smiled, turned her back on him, and picked one of the toadstools. He hadn't been able to see what she was doing as she crushed the growth in her hands, allowing the black juices to run like sweat into the goblet she'd brought with her. But his annoying Welsh whine had prodded her from behind.

"Can't you pick those later? My bum's getting cold."

She pretended to swig from the goblet, smacked her mouth. Then she advanced on him, letting the cape slide from her shoulders.

His eyes had bulged like a frog's when he saw the basque she was wearing underneath.

"Take a drink," she told him, and he reluctantly dragged his eyes away from her breasts.

"You sure these work?" She'd told him the toadstools were hallu-cinogens, and aphrodisiacs to boot.

"They'll give you an erection like a rhino's horn, Jerry."

That had been enough for the Welshman. He opened his mouth eagerly as she tilted the goblet to his lips.

He started to go green after the first hour. He stopped squealing and wriggling well before the end of the second. By the third, his face was the color of royal blue mold, his hair withering like dried grass. He'd lasted much longer than the child, telling her what she had needed to know.

She gathered her cloak more tightly around her as she continued to fill her basket with the fungus. It was very cold here at the heart of the wood. A creeping cold that seemed to emanate from the pale oaks encircling the glade and its deadly secret. The trees were like gnarled mothers, bending over their toadstool children with outflung protective arms.

Beyond the ring of fungi, there was a pool, small and fringed with purple weeds. Lila stopped picking and went over to kneel beside the pool, drawn by its loneliness. Her reflection appeared in the water, a floating ghost face. Only her eyes were dark, holes in chalk flesh, their color leached by the pool. She smiled, admiring the lascivious curl of strawberry lips, teeth cold and white. A hungry face, a cruel face... A sad face?

Her smile disappeared, that too sucked away by the pool. She leaned closer, disturbed now by what she saw. Sad? Why sad? She was beyond frailties such as melancholy. She'd walked where devils feared to tread. Sadness was long since dead and gone, along with her innocence and youth. There was nothing to mourn.

No eyes.

She felt gripped by bone-cold terror for an instant. The pond had taken them, and the dusk, too, as it settled on the water, obscuring her face; it was as if she were being eaten by the darkness.

Why sad? Why scared? I have Bane. I have *everything.*

The shrill cry of a rising wind keened through the tightly packed trees. Lila started, and utter sorrow edged her heart. Just the wind. Not...

I have Bane, and Bane loves me beyond all else. We have each other.

The cry came again. A bitter, lonely sound, spearing her heart and sealing the breath in her lungs. She darted a glance at Jerry Owen, but his mouth was locked by death. It had been a hollow wail, horrible and lost. Just like the cry of...

A baby?

She met him in a pub in Winchcombe, a quiet North Gloucestershire haven of conservative rural values. She was in the sixth form[18] and was already tired of leading a privileged, predictable life.

He stepped out into the beer garden as dusk began to gather in the apple trees, sweet with the high summer scent of blossom. She watched him sit on the vacant bench nearest her table. She was with a group of

---

[18] Junior year of high school

school friends who were affecting a sort of mannered rowdiness while they swilled, and suddenly she felt ashamed of their callow respectability. Even then, he looked old beyond his years. It was the eyes, she supposed; black eyes that had looked into things, into so many scary things. She tingled madly as she watched him. His hair was jet black and long. He wore an old-fashioned, baggy, white shirt and dark jeans, and his face was strange, wild, maybe a little vicious.

He'd noticed her looking at him. Their eyes locked. Twisted fate did its work.

He told her later he'd sensed her frustration, her burgeoning, unsatisfied need. Her eager green eyes were bursting with stifled desires and undeveloped appetites. He could help her out.

They sat together long after the others had gone inside, chased away by the increasing coolness of the evening. They sat oblivious to the chill, communicating more with their expressions than with words. He was twenty-one, and the Devil lurked in his eyes. She was sixteen and had never been keen on God anyway. Still a virgin, hungry for danger she'd always dreamed of and never found. Her hair was almost as dark as his, her long face still fresh with strange sensuality. Dusk sat with them, whispering with the voice of bats.

She asked him why his eyes were so black. He told her he would show her one day. She asked him his name, and he said people just called him Bane. She liked that. He stood up after a while and looked at her, waiting silently. She turned and glanced back at the cozy pub behind them, buzzing with contented chatter, bustling with safe, unthreatening conformity. He waited. She turned back to him, and she knew what she wanted.

Lila's father was a headmaster, and he didn't take too well to the idea of some young devil absconding with his little darling.

For years, Lila had been telling her school friends that her father molested her when she was a child. He never did, of course. Maybe some twisted part of her wished he had. He was so distant, always had been, ever since her mother died. But he'd always looked after her, always loved her. She knew that much.

So, when Bane came to collect her a few days after they met, Daddy, quite understandably, didn't want her to go. She watched as Bane killed him in the hall. It was quick and painless enough, she thought, but his eyes had been fixed on her as he died. She had been flushed with excitement as Bane lowered the body. She seized him and they'd made love on the hall carpet, next to Daddy. He'd never been able to understand that she was all grown up now.

May Eve. In her arms, a child. She was standing in a stone circle in Oxfordshire while the moon peeped between branches so still they could have been painted against the night. Beside her, Bane was watching the cowled figures hunched around the circle, and she could see the naked contempt on his face.

"Is this the best you can do?"

The fat man wearing a hooded cowl and thick spectacles shrugged. "It's a start."

"Not a very good one." Blood on an altar stone. A pile of headless chickens, wings still fluttering. *Even the standing stones look embarrassed,* Lila thought; *if they had feet, they'd be shuffling them by now.*

"And the Devil's supposed to be impressed by this fiasco, is he? So where is the Horned One, anyway? Perhaps he doesn't watch the same films as you do."

The fat man looked away, humiliated. Lila knew he'd been trying his best to impress Bane. It wasn't working. But the fat man continued to stand and watch. And wait, as if he thought something amazing was going to happen.

"Waiting for Godot," she said.

"I'm sorry?" The fat man swung his thick lenses toward her. This was the first time she'd met him, and she was surprised at Bane's choice of disciple.

"He never appears," she told him.

"Send them home, for fuck's sake," Bane sighed. "I've seen more sinister gatherings at a W.I.[19] coffee morning. Send them home."

The fat man moved to obey. He'd learned quickly that this was a wise thing to do.

"So, what do we do now?" Bane spread his hands with mock resignation. "I don't like to waste a good occasion."

"Why don't we show them something more interesting?" She was in a long, black dress. The soft evening breeze nuzzled her hair. Her baby mewled in her embrace, pale as the Beltane moon.

Bane looked at her carefully. "Why don't *you* show them?"

She glanced at him. His tone frightened her. Oh yes, she could still be frightened, and he knew it. He hadn't killed everything in her.

He reached for her child. Instinctively, she pulled away, causing him to laugh softly.

---

[19] Women's Institute

"Are you feeling like a mother tonight? A *real* mother, my Lila?"

Her eyes regarded him steadily, but she could not answer.

"If you want me to show you true darkness," he continued, "you have to understand it first. And to do that, you have to renounce everything you were brought up to believe. You know what I am: so, what do I deserve?"

He tapped the baby's bald head. It wriggled more snugly against its mother's breast. "Do I deserve this?"

She said nothing. He stooped to uncover an object from a sack as the last of the sheepish coven disappeared amongst the trees. Bolton returned a little out of breath, as if from shooing a herd of geese. His tiny eyes dilated when he saw what was in the sack.

Bane carried the skull toward the moist altar stone. He set it down in a pool of blood and stared at Lila.

"Mother and child. Isn't that beautiful? Don't you think that's beautiful, Mister Bolton?"

The fat man sweated. He looked at Lila hungrily, anticipating Bane's next move.

"It has to be real, Lila," Bane said and beckoned her toward him.

She'd let him kill her innocence, let him kill her youth, even let him kill her father. Hadn't she given enough? She looked into his eyes.

"We're not like others, Lila. It has to be different for us. It has to be *real*."

She was looking at an empty, haunted face in the water, fading fast, like a ghost.

The blackbirds sounded anxious as night closed in on the glade. Lila knelt and gazed at the darkness between the trees. Jerry sat where she left him, crucified in a sitting position, arms dangling from the rope, fly still open. She got to her feet and collected her basket.

CHAPTER THIRTY

He wasn't listening to the service. He wasn't looking at the two coffins lined up, ready for their glide into burning glory. He was lost somewhere in childhood, remembering things long buried and labeled DO NOT OPEN.

Puff.

It could just as easily have been you lying there.

Dead and buried.

No, not dead. But...

He was trembling. Sam probably thought it was with grief for his parents, but even now, he couldn't spare them that. He was grieving for the little boy.

Tears. Bloody tears. It was far too late for that boy, the vicar said, staring right at him. Only his dubbing was bloody awful because the words didn't match his lip movements. Jack glanced at Sam, so elegant in black, her face cut from exquisite porcelain. Coils of hair tousled neatly under a black hat, her lips pouting sexily, even here. They would have crawled away from her teeth in loathing if she suspected what he was thinking.

He leaned his forehead against the back of the pew in front of him and squeezed his eyes shut. He hadn't done it. He *couldn't* have.

Just as he couldn't have strangled a squirrel in Leigh Woods. But that was different, surely, to God? He'd been out of his head, then. He couldn't have killed Joe or Nigel because... *He wasn't insane!* Couldn't have killed...

A little boy lying in bed, stiff as a marble knight.

Perhaps Bane's mushrooms released something. It had been dead and buried like Puff, and now it had stretched and awoken like a hungry beast. Had this beast been let out to play with his friends, and Jack hadn't even been aware of it? He raised his head and looked again at the coffins on the conveyor bier.

No...

A sob broke out of him, and Sam turned and pressed his hand in hers. For what must have been the first time in a month, she smiled at him. She pitied him, a monster. Then he saw her eyes widen, go hard with hate. She knew then: she'd seen through the skin to his soul.

He realized she wasn't even looking at him. He turned, and Lila was leaning forward from the pew behind. Bolton and the twins were beside her, and one other man Jack didn't recognize, or maybe he did; the black eyes and beard reminded him of something bad.

They were all watching him carefully, just like that night at The Slaughter. They must have arrived late and slipped in after the service had started, and their presence had suddenly tilted the occasion from the solemn to the horrible. Lila was dressed in black, as usual, but her expression showed no sign of mourning. Her eyes gleamed with excitement, and for a moment, Jack thought she was going to lean further forward to kiss him.

He drew back in disgust, which only made her smile more. She had something in her hand, and now she passed it over the back of the pew and dropped it in his lap. An envelope. Then she was getting up, along with her four sinister companions, heading past the rows of mourners and out of the chapel. The vicar halted his sermon for a moment, looking flustered, then resumed a trifle nervously, blurting out grandiose platitudes.

Jack stared at the envelope in his lap.

"Don't open it," Sam whispered. "It'll only be something nasty."

Don't open it. That was good advice. He tore one end of the slim package and pulled out the black-and-white photograph inside. There was something else in there, but he ignored it for the moment, all his attention on the old, crinkled snap.

It showed two boys sitting in a garden. One was maybe six or seven. Jack recognized him immediately. The other was older, staring into the camera with open disdain, eyes hooded and cruel, even at that age. Jack recognized him, too. His big brother.

His big brother, Bane.

CHAPTER THIRTY-ONE

He leaned against the wall outside the chapel, still holding the old photograph, gasping for air as if he were drowning.

A hand on his arm, and Sam was beside him, smiling a sad, reassuring little smile. "She's gone, Jack. They've all gone."

"I didn't kill any of them, Sam," he whispered, focusing on her with difficulty.

She looked at him like he was mad, and that was only fair after all, wasn't it? But she also looked at him like she cared, and that meant everything right now.

"Of course, you didn't." Her eyes filled with repugnance at the idea, and a little fear, too. Well, he had plenty of that for the both of them, thank you.

"He's back," he said simply. He scraped at his face with his hands, and the photograph slipped to the grass. Sam picked it up.

"Jack?" She was staring at it, and when he took his hands away, he could see only confusion in her expression.

"He's back," he repeated, as if that made everything clear. He was going to be sick. He bent over sideways and retched, forcing out a bellyful of dry heaves and nothing else. He flopped back against the wall, and the sky spun.

"Who is this?" Sam held the photograph in front of him. For the first time, he noticed the spots of dried blood crusted on one corner.

He closed his eyes, let the memories swim around his head.

"I think I'm..." He paused, sucked more breath. "Having a flash-back. To the worst time in my whole life." He was trembling uncontrollably, feverishly. "I just…blotted it out. Rubbed my childhood out, like it was a bad drawing, and I—I wanted to start again. Up here." He tapped his forehead. But, of course, you never could start again, could you? The past *always* found you out. Nothing stayed dead and buried for long.

Sam was becoming a little impatient. She grasped his face in both hands and turned it toward her. "What are you talking about, Jack? Try to get a grip."

He laughed weakly. A crazy laugh. "Get a grip! Yeah. You think I've got problems now? You should have seen me when I was a kid." His laugh was a choke now, a sob, and it came all the way from his childhood.

"Don't you recognize the face? Oh, it's changed. Of course, it has. But the eyes are the same. Now I know why he freaked me out so much that first time in the Video Vault. Fascinated me, too, like I felt some sort of bond with him. Perhaps a part of me realized all this time and just couldn't face up to it. I wiped him out, you know, Sam, along with everything else. Back when I was seven. I thought I'd forgotten him for good. What he did to me."

"Forgotten who?"

"The killer. Yeah, *he's* the one of course, not me. Killed them all: Joe, Nigel, my parents. My brother, the psychopath. My brother, Bane."

But he hadn't always been called Bane, had he?

Sam was incredulous. "Bane's your *brother?*" She peered at the photograph again, a disbelieving frown on her face. But now he knew she could see it, too. He watched a couple of crows hopping across the bright grass toward the crematorium plaques as if they wanted to read the names, examine the bright-as-blood wreaths.

"As in, long-lost. I mean, who else would turn up like a *really* bad penny, start slaughtering my friends, and twist my mind until it felt like I did it? Shit, I'm so blind! Now I see that photograph, it's so bloody obvious. I just got too used to pretending he no longer existed, I suppose. Until he no longer *did* exist."

"Your own brother? And you didn't recognize him? This is all—" She groped for words, and there weren't any.

"Yeah. Isn't it, though?" His eyes shone. "Me and my mad brother. But which one's the real psycho? Maybe we both are. Maybe we're the same."

"Stop it!" She wandered away from him, and for a sickening moment, he thought she was going to leave him. Again. He reached out a hand, but she was just pacing, trying to fit it all together.

"I was only seven when he left. All I've been able to remember for years, for over twenty years, is just a vague shadow of something from my childhood. Something nasty I shut away. And now he's got out again, and he's out there." He gestured vaguely beyond the crematorium grounds.

"But the trick is, he's still in here, too." Again, he touched his head, and now the tears were rolling down his cheeks unashamedly. "Can you understand, Sam? He ruined my life with the things he did. *God.* The things he *did...*"

The door was open now, and the memories were rushing through, eager to take center stage in his mind after twenty-three years of exile. There was no shutting this door.

Beetles, worms, and spiders in a jar, and Jack tied down in the school playing field. Slugs pressed like greasy lips to the sides of the glass. The crows had hopped toward him then, too, as he lay staked beneath the impassive oak tree. They hadn't helped him, enjoying his terror. He'd never forgiven them since, and only now remembered why. The other children hadn't helped him either. Too scared. Everyone was scared of Jack's brother. Choking on worms forced down his throat, coiling moistly, gritty on his gagging tongue, beetles scuttling over his teeth. The stink of his own fear and vomit. Tears running, snot running, joining the slime and filth between his lips. Closing his eyes. Let me die now. Please.

Endless nights kept awake by the things his brother had done.

Gagged, petrified, helpless. Knives probing, matches burning. Drowning in a bowl of his brother's vomit, in his urine, in his...

"Let me up! Can't breathe anymore! CAN'T BREATHE! NO MORE! Pleeease...

The bird caught in the garden. Tied to a chair while big brother held it in front of him, a sewing needle in his hands. "Out vile jelly," *he said. The needle went in, out. In, out.*

Drinking his own blood. "D'you like that, Jack? What does it taste like, Jack?"

Or there was ...

The one he'd been dreading, holding back until he could hide it no longer. The one that had been torturing his memory with brief snatches for the last few days. Here it is, at last, Jack: the complete, uncut version. Does the memory cheat? Does it, Jack? Does it?

Dead and buried. He'd preceded Puff by three years. That was the best, though, eh, Jack? Buried in the woods. When I took you amongst the trees, holding your hand like a big brother should, and showed you the hole I dug. Tied you up and buried you there for the day, and most of the night too, with just a long, thin pipe to breathe through, and sometimes—just for fun—I'd block that pipe up, wouldn't I, Jack? Just for a few seconds, just to get you a little frantic down there. And then when I stopped playing with the pipe and you heard nothing for three hours, maybe four, and you thought I was never coming back... Four feet down and sweating in the dark, with worms wriggling against your cheeks and the soil pressing into your nostrils and your eyelids fluttering like trapped moths. Just you and the dark, eh, Jack? You and your screams that no one heard; thin wails coming out of that old pipe, and you thought I'd leave you there forever...

Endless nights, kept awake by the things he did.

And he was still doing them.

Sam was talking, and all Jack could hear was *his* voice. "How could you forget," she was saying. "How could you forget him and everything he did?"

Quite easily, Sam. If you really wanted to. Very easily, if the alternative was a rubber room for the rest of your life. Go ask a psychiatrist; he'll tell you about suppressed trauma. Better still, just ask me.

She was talking, her gorgeous face close to him, so close he could have kissed her.

"You once told me it was your father who made your childhood a nightmare."

He was silent, dizzy with reawakened memories. More horrors than he could stand. He lurched to his feet, shaking, panic jogging around his system.

Sam hugged him suddenly, and he grabbed onto her like she was a lifebelt[20] and he was going under for the fifth time.

She led him to a bench beside the memorial plaques. He stared at the crows until they wobbled away disdainfully. The sun might have been a child's crayon sketch in the sky for all the warmth it gave him. He breathed deeply; let it out. Let it all out.

"My father?" He remembered she'd asked him a question. "He was a

----

[20] Life preserver

psychopath, too." Suddenly, he was laughing because it was bloody funny really. "Must run in the family, eh? But he wasn't as bad as Bane. He never terrified me as much as Bane did. Oh, he murdered my dog, and almost murdered me once. But he stopped, as if he didn't quite have the guts to finish the job. Bane always had the guts. He always carried it through to the end. Dad got worse after *he* left, though. Like he no longer had any competition, or because I reminded him of my brother, I don't know. The beatings got worse. And my mother, she never stopped him. Never. She always had this disapproving air, and I thought she disapproved of me. Thinking about it, perhaps that was all she could do against my Dad—disapprove. Anything stronger and she got beaten, too. But the shadow my 'father' cast over my childhood was really just hiding something worse. I remembered what was easier to bear."

"Didn't your parents know what Bane was doing to you?"

"Of course, they knew! They just let him." He banged his fist lightly on one knee. "They let him, that's all." He grunted. "He could only have been about ten or eleven, but they were scared of him, too. Isn't that funny? No, it's not so funny if you knew what he was like. It's not funny at all."

She held his fist, opened it out. He turned to look at her, and over her shoulder, he could see the crematorium chimney looming above the chapel. Smoke. Gray smoke, issuing out of the chimney, hanging in the air.

He laughed harshly. "Adios."

She turned to follow his gaze, and he squeezed her hand. He needed her now more than ever. And to think he'd once turned away from her, wanted Lila instead. Lila, his brother's woman. As twisted as he was. And Jack had been attracted to her. What did that say about him?

"Jack?"

He looked at her guiltily.

"Do you still hate them?"

"There's nothing left to hate, is there? Just ashes. And Bane, of course. D'you know, they never talked about him after he left. Just like he was dead."

She was looking at him with horror and pity. He could handle the horror, but not the pity.

"But why would he want to kill your parents? Why is he still tormenting *you* after all these years?"

"Because he's a monster. And as I said, he always carries things through to the end."

"What about Joe and Nigel?"

"We were in a car," he said as if he hadn't heard her. He was staring into the past again, grasping at all the bits and pieces, all the driftwood. "That's when he left. We were on holiday. I can't remember where. Just the car and Dad shouting. The car swerving..."

Mind the road, for God's sake.

The hate on his brother's face. And the hate inside himself. He could feel it, even after all this time. His father pounding his eldest son, and the car veering dangerously—

Hit him! Hurt him! Kill him...

His brother opening the car door.

Yes! Go on! Jump!

"I wanted him to die. To break his neck when he jumped."

"Slow down, Jack. You're losing me."

A red Sierra was pulling into the crematorium car park. It drew Jack back into the present; he recognized the two occupants immediately.

"They think I did it."

Sam had noticed the Sierra, too. "They don't know about Bane, do they?"

"And they're not going to." It was an impulsive decision, but it felt right.

"Why not? If you think he killed your parents?"

"Do *you* think he killed them?"

"I..." She avoided his eyes for a second, then looked up again, her gaze resolute with her own decision made. "Yes. If you're certain, then I'm behind you."

"Well, that's good. But you *know* me, and you're still not really sure. *They* want to believe I'm the killer because that'll make life easier for them."

The occupants of the Sierra were still watching him, making no move to leave the car. The one with the mustache—Jack couldn't remember his name or rank now—had been polite and reasonable as he asked his questions. It was a couple of days after Sam visited him at the flat. The two policemen told him about his parents, how they'd been found, and in what state, and waited for his reaction. Jack didn't have one. They'd put the same question to him two or three times, slyly dropping it into the conversation. Where was he on the night they died? That was a good one. Pity he didn't have a good answer.

He could have lied, but he didn't see the point. So, he told them the truth. Sort of. He was in South Wales, Pembroke. Just…getting away from it all for a day or two. *Searching for his dead friend.* The policemen waited for him to add more. He didn't; just watched them watching him. It wasn't until they'd gone that he let himself react to the news.

His parents had got their just desserts at last. And he'd started thinking that maybe the police were right. Maybe he *had* killed them. He supposed that was how it felt to be mad: not knowing what you had done, what you might do next. He was glad Dennis had kept out of his way—he hadn't wanted to hurt anyone else.

But… He hadn't killed *anyone.* That was all down to his long-lost brother. The dried blood on the photograph told him that much. So, he wasn't mad. He could thank Bane for making him realize that, at least.

Sam was watching the Sierra uncertainly.

"The police wouldn't be able to help, Sam. It's too personal for that."

"Just you and him, right? Cut the *High Noon* crap, Jack; people are dying. Look what he did to your parents. It might be you next."

Or you. He mustn't even *think* that. "And you reckon they'll believe in the tale of the prodigal psychopath?"

"They will if I tell them."

"No! It's none of their business, Sam. He's *my* brother. He's *mine.*"

His voice must have sounded odd because she glanced at him nervously. From behind them, a subdued murmur of voices streamed out into the grounds. The mourners were leaving the chapel. The funeral was over.

Jack drove through Wellbury in silence. He'd refused to go in the funeral limousine—he seemed to want to distance himself from the event as much as possible. His eyes were firmly on the road ahead, just as they had been on the way to the chapel that morning when Jack had driven through the small Cotswold town for the first time in God knew how many years.

Sam understood he was unwilling to let any memories reach out for him. He'd spent sixteen years of his life here, and it was obvious from his strained expression that even another minute really was too much to bear. She wondered where, exactly, his parents' house was, or if they had already passed it. She gazed at the brown stone cottages and peaceful village green, amazed that such a pretty town could hide the memory of so much sorrow.

It wasn't until Wellbury was five miles behind them and the Fiat was happily ensconced on the A38 that he visibly relaxed a little. Without warning, he pulled over into a lay-by and stopped the engine. Sam looked at him expectantly. From his leather jacket pocket, he pulled out the envelope Lila had given him and slipped his fingers inside. He removed the photograph again, gazed at it inscrutably for a second, and then made to tear it in two.

"Don't," said Sam, restraining him gently. It seemed a futile piece of destruction. He couldn't eradicate Bane that easily. And it might prove helpful.

Jack shrugged and handed the photo to her. Then he reached into the envelope again and pulled out the other item he still hadn't looked at. It was a flyleaf torn from a book, a reproduction of an old illustration. Jack held it tightly, examining every detail, his expression unreadable. Sam leaned over to get a closer look.

The simple, crudely drawn sketch depicted a man in seventeenth-century attire: tattered hose and jerkin with buckled shoes and an enormous cutlass in his right hand. His hair was long and lank. His face leered with an insatiable malevolence that was incongruous with the rest of the conservatively restrained artwork. The man was standing in front of a cave mouth while a woman, her back turned, was dragging a severed limb inside. A corpse was folded over a rock beside the man, waves lapping at its feet. In the background, a troop of soldiers with pikes and swords were galloping on horseback along the beach toward the cave. Below the sketch, there was a caption:

SAWNEY BEAN AT THE ENTRANCE OF HIS CAVE

"What the hell is that supposed to mean?" Sam was gaping at the picture, clearly mystified.

Jack pushed the illustration back inside the envelope. "Have you ever heard of him before?"

"Sawney Bean? No. Should I have done?"

He didn't answer as he started the engine again. He drove Sam home in silence.

CHAPTER THIRTY-TWO

It was the first time he'd been to The Slaughter since Nigel disappeared. Since Bane made him disappear. And now that he'd faced up to that and the other atrocities his dear brother had committed, it was time to stop hiding from everything else, too.

Oh yes, he was all done with hiding.

It was Friday night. He hadn't seen Sam since the funeral the day before. He hadn't told her where he was going tonight because she would have gone crazy. And that was nice to know because it showed she cared. For the first time, somebody actually cared. But she had nothing to worry about, really, because he felt certain Bane wouldn't be in the pub.

And how had he worked that one out? Instinct. You see, it was Bane's turn to go into hiding now that Jack had emerged from the shadows. All Jack had to do now was hunt him down. The illustration Lila gave him was obviously a clue of some sort, in this game of hide and seek. The place to find out more would be in Bane's lair. Former lair, he reminded himself as he walked toward the pub. He was sure the beast had fled.

Perhaps he was walking into a trap right now. Perhaps Bane's freaky disciples were waiting for him in the pub. And perhaps he should have brought Dennis with him. Absolutely not; this was down to Jack alone. He'd lost enough friends. Besides, Dennis didn't have too much to say to him these days. Maybe he blamed Jack for Nigel and Joe, or maybe he just resented him still for making a go of it with Sam. Either way, Jack would let him brood.

Sawney Bean...

He was near the pub now. The bloody glow from the windows, the burst of spiteful music as a punter pushed his way inside. The sign above the door, the gathering of painted freaks seemed to leer at him as he approached. He paused for a second or two outside the door. So much had changed since he first saw that sign.

...at the entrance of his cave.

He hated that flyleaf. And the name, too. Sawney Bean. Loathed it. Just the sound of it made him...angry.

Joe's face flashed before him as he pushed at the door.

What did they do to you, Joe? Where did they put you after they'd done it? If it's any consolation, I'm sorry. And Nige... It was all down to me. Because he's my brother. I'm so bloody sorry. Is that okay? Is that good enough? Of course it bloody wasn't. But there was something he COULD do, wasn't there?

He entered the pub.

On my way, Bane. And I'm different now. I'm no longer scared. You changed me again, just like you did before when we were kids and you made me a screwed-up shadow of a child. Well, this time you've made me something else. You see, I'm ready for you now.

I'm going to find you.

And I'm going to kill you.

There's a little boy, and he's been waiting for this for a long time. I owe that little boy; I owe you, Bane.

He walked through the crowd and the dry ice, past Red Jack and his waxen misogyny, past the tables filled with tribes of youth and the wistful not-so-young, past the Frankenstein monster, who welcomed him back with open arms, and stopped at the bar.

The nearest table was being used by the band, Holocaust Freaks, and they were all studying him with interest. He let them know he wasn't scared. They let him know they didn't give a shit, grinning at him as they sipped their pints, leathers glowing in the lurid spotlights. Jack swiveled back to face the bar.

No Bane.

No Lila.

Just the man with the ponytail, a nobody, an innocent in this little game, thought Jack. *But was anybody truly innocent? Everyone was hiding something.*

On a pillar beside the Wolfman, he saw the poster. Huge, red letters. He read it slowly, and there it was: clue number two. Or should that be *lure* number two? Instead of ordering a pint, he asked for Bane.

"Gone away, mate."

Just confirming what he already knew. "Gone away where?"

Shrug. Honest ignorance. "Gone away, mate. That's all I know."

"Lila?" he said with more of a snarl than he had intended.

The bartender looked as though he wasn't going to reply, then shrugged again. "Upstairs."

Jack was already moving around behind the bar.

"Hey, you can't..."

Jack didn't stop. "Oh, I think I can."

He knew where to go. Up the curving stairway, along the black-carpeted hallway to the door. No sound from behind the thick oak. He didn't knock.

She was lying on the bed, smoking a joint and wearing a black silk dressing gown with nothing beneath, but Jack hardly even noticed. He shut the door behind him and leaned against it, eyes searching the room. Red wallpaper, lurid as blood and sex. Goya, Bosch.

"He's not here." She was watching him without surprise, her bare legs crossed, one arm behind her head, smoking lazily. Her lipstick blazed. Her eyes were narrowed, just slits of green beneath each lid.

Jack crossed to the bookcase beneath the single window. Big, black, hardback tomes with obscure titles written by obscure writers leaned against each other, as if seeking dismal solidarity. One larger than the rest, bound in thick, greasy, brown material. Jack pulled this one out, held it up for Lila to see. No title.

"Human skin? Not very original, I'm afraid." He flicked open the cover and gazed at the title page. It was in Germanic gothic script, a swastika printed beneath the lettering, spread across the page like a large crushed spider. He tossed it at her and turned back to the book-case.

"You know, I'm really disappointed in his reading matter. Or is it yours? I suppose it makes no difference; you like everything he likes, don't you? Poor little Lila, the girl with no mind of her own. I wonder, did you have a *real* personality, once upon a time, before Bane came along? Are you just another of his victims, someone else he's fucked up along the way?"

He flung another tome at her, beetle-dark and crumbling with age. She caught it like the one before, putting them both down beside the bed, the joint still inserted between her lips.

"Aleister Crowley? Oh, *pleeease! Demonology and Arcane Wisdom.*

Hmmm. Yes, I really thought he had more to him than this. A sick shit, yes, but at least an unconventional one. I'm sorely disillusioned. This is just sad."

He let the top row of books tumble to the red carpet. "Sorry. Getting careless... Where is he?"

Lila chuckled with genuine pleasure. "You're starting to sound just like him. You're obviously more impressed than you let on."

He opened the dark wardrobe looming against one wall. Clothes hanging from a rack above, boots standing in a row beneath. The chest of drawers revealed nothing but Lila's cosmetics, undergarments, and belts.

"You won't find him amongst my panties, dear."

"I'm sorry for you, really, of course," Jack said after a while, facing her again.

She grinned and held the joint out toward him. He ignored the gesture.

She giggled. "I'm supposed to ask why, I think. No, I can probably guess: Bane corrupted me, left me a ruined woman. How am I doing?"

"How are you *doing*?" It was his turn to laugh, a sardonic chuckle that didn't sound like him at all. "You're already dead, Lila. You've got a graveyard where your soul should be. Bane ran away from home before he could damage me too much, but it doesn't look like you were so lucky."

"And you're sure *you* were? Maybe Bane didn't have to do that much. Maybe all he had to do was encourage what was already there."

Jack moved closer to the bed. "Just tell me where he is."

"Why don't you beat it out of me?"

"I don't want to give you any unnecessary pleasure. But I can wait. I imagine the poster downstairs will lead me to him."

"So, you've read about our forthcoming attraction? Exciting, isn't it?"

He wandered over to the window without answering, lifted the curtain to examine the ledge behind.

"Cold."

He ignored her, let the curtain drop, and opened a small cupboard beside the bed.

"Even colder."

He controlled a leap of rage. Let the bitch play her games. He was about to leave, but her next words stopped him.

"Is this what you're looking for?" She slipped a book from beneath the bed and held it out toward him. He took it without a word, examined the artwork on the hardback cover.

"It's a bit more disturbing than the other picture, don't you think?"

A huge shadow at the entrance of a cave. Only one gnarled hand could be seen extending from the darkness, clutching raw and bloody things. The figure seemed to Jack to be threatening to emerge into the light at any moment, and he squeezed the book until his hands were bloodless, waiting for his giddy terror to relent.

It was just a grisly piece of suggestive art, but Lila was right: the tasteful and stylized caricature in the sketch she'd given him at the funeral, and obviously torn from the same book, had been so far off the mark that he'd only felt a vague ghost of foreboding. The picture he was looking at now—this wasn't good. Not at all. It hinted at unreasoning slaughter and horror waiting in the dark; it put Jack right back inside the barrow of his mushroom trip, stalked by a shadow just like the one on the cover of this book. It was as if the artist had peeked inside Jack's head for inspiration.

"You recognize him, don't you?"

How could she know...? "He's real," Jack stammered. Not just a nightmare shadow inspired by memories of his father.

"Of course, he's real. That's a reference book, not a fucking novel."

Her mocking spite pulled him out of himself. He shoved the book into his leather jacket. "If you wanted me to have it, why not just give it to me at the funeral?"

"This way's much more fun, don't you think? Let you join the puzzle together piece by piece. But you haven't done very well so far, have you? You still don't know."

He was going to let that pass. He just wanted to get out of this red room, away from her cloying presence, but she seemed intent on keeping him. "Remember what I told you in the graveyard?"

He had his hand on the doorknob but couldn't stop himself from turning around again. She was sitting up on the bed and undoing her dressing gown. She let the silk slide from her shoulders to puddle around her waist, gazing at him alluringly, eyelashes lifting to uncover the startling green of her eyes. Her burning red lips parted sensuously.

He strode over to the bed, yanked the long raven wig from her head, stepped back, and flung it in her face.

"Sorry, Lila. You're just not my type."

Spurned fury lashed her features. Her bald head was sweating like the cap of a toadstool. "Oh, I think you are. In the graveyard, I said you were just as steeped in horror as Bane and me. I think you're *exactly* my type."

He slammed the door on her vicious snarl.

Down in the bar, the band was still sprawled around their table. Jack grinned wildly at them and deliberately ripped the poster from the pillar, folded it up, and thrust it inside his jacket pocket alongside the book. He gave them a final dazzling smile, then pushed his way through the crowd.

CHAPTER THIRTY-THREE

Golden days. When happiness was never something you thought about, just took for granted, grabbed it, and ran, never expecting it to disappear.

Dennis gazed at himself in the window of Burger King, the reflection dark and insubstantial, happy eaters at their tables visible through his fragile image. A ghost. A ghost of the youth he used to be.

Cut the crap. Less of the self-indulgent whinging. He'd been saying that to himself a lot lately, but it didn't seem to help. No matter how much he rebuked himself for his bouts of self-pity, it was so easy to let himself go. He *was* a ghost. You see, a part of him had died in the searing blasts of the desert when he realized there was no sanity, no order to anything. And part of him had died even before then, when someone he'd cherished more than he could ever have told her walked out and left him with meaningless years to wade through. Alone.

Let's face it; he was as dead as they come.

He turned his back on the ghost and wandered on through the lunchtime crowds. Inside the Galleries shopping mall, he rode the escalator to the third floor, feeling like a package on a conveyor belt. Hopelessness crushed him. He wanted to shout, to rage and scream, but only tears of sickening self-pity emerged, and that just made him hate himself all the more.

Couldn't she see what she was doing?

Agreeing to meet him like this, their first assignation since...since they were together. And why did she want to talk to him? To discuss Jack, of course. That was all she could think of. And all he could think of was...

Seventeen. Eyes vulnerable yet sexually knowing, too. Her face baby-smooth, exquisitely sculpted, the playful girl and the burgeoning woman emerging together in her coy, sensual smile. She'd been standing with a boy her own age in the dark nightclub while swirling gothic rhythms lashed the dancers into self-conscious abandon. She was under the plastic oak tree that reared up in the middle of the room—and from which the club took its name—and Dennis froze in mid-joke. He let Jack wait for the punch line, concentration snatched away by this gorgeous, exotic creature, slender and lissom as an elf, smiling at him across the club while her male companion babbled unheeded into her ear.

Of course, he'd gone straight over to her; he'd never been shy of chatting up the maids. But as he approached, he felt suddenly robbed of self-assurance. The closer he got, the more stunned he felt. The facile line he'd intended to use curdled on his lips, and he brought himself up short, the pint in his right hand sloshing beer onto the floor. He hoped Jack wasn't seeing any of this; he had an image to keep up. So, he pulled himself together, remembered he was a cocky, go-for-it adventurer, and steamed in.

"I've been coming to this club for months now, and I was beginning to get a bit jaded," he said as the music paused for breath, and her pompous companion—a sixth former, no doubt—electing to accompany her to the club "as a friend" but obviously with delusions of progressing beyond that limitation, gaped at Dennis with all the indignation and hostility he could muster without getting himself into a fight.

"But when I saw you," Dennis continued, "it was like waking up to a fresh new dawn." Okay, so he'd used the line anyway, and admittedly it was appalling, but for once, he'd meant it.

She looked him over. Summing up his shock-rock hair, purple shirt, and red jeans with amusement in her eyes. And perhaps a little interest.

That first line had been the only corny thing he'd said to her all evening—it became something of a running joke between them in the months to come. The hanger-on had done just that—kept hanging—but he soon realized he'd been relegated to a division somewhere below even "friend," right down there with acquaintances and lesser mortals. He didn't get a bloody word in. And Dennis, twenty years old and flying.

Flying high.

And Jack...

Jack had been there. Over at the bar of the dodgy Bristol Goth club, waiting for his mate to return. Dennis had left him there, oblivious to everything as he talked to her, excitement swooping in him with each sentence he spoke and each response she gave.

Jack...

At the end of the night, walking with her to the exit, he met up with Jack again. And now he remembered something he hadn't thought of in the nine years separating that night from this day.

She was leaving the club with her hanger-on, and she paused to stand at the foot of the steps. The hanger-on was getting into a taxi, and Dennis was leaning forward to give her a goodnight kiss, not too eager, not too casual, and then she was walking toward the taxi and turning. She'd looked back, not at Dennis, but at Jack. A strange expression appeared on her face that Dennis hadn't given much thought to at the time, but nevertheless, the memory of it must have been stored away somewhere, ready to surprise him at an unguarded moment like this, and that expression said—

What had it said? She'd shown no overt signs of interest in Jack for nine years, either during the twelve months Dennis had been with her or the long period of yearning afterward. Not until...

Until when exactly?

He stepped off the escalator as it sank into the concrete of the third floor and walked toward the Food Court.

Until the gig at The Slaughter.

But she had made it more obvious a couple of days afterward when she came around to see Jack, and Dennis had thought, hoped, she'd been coming to see *him*.

And just why the hell would she do that, you sad, old sap?

Something happened that night, that Opening Night, that made her see Jack in a wholly different light.

Sam wasn't anywhere to be seen as he ordered his coffee and sat down near the ice cream bar to wait. He was early.

What had she seen in Jack that night? He'd changed; that had been evident over the last month or so, even before his parents had been murdered. Something to do with Bane. The landlord had twisted Jack inside out, left him brooding, aggressive, strange. Hell, he'd been driven half out of his mind. That might make Sam feel maternal toward Jack. Or perhaps it had even turned her on. Maybe she fancied a bit of the dark and dangerous.

And that other woman... Lila. She'd been after him, too. What the fuck did Jack have that *he* didn't?

What made him so fucking special?

Golden days. With Sam, feeling like summer would never, *ever* die, even when it was autumn, winter. Always so alive, so fresh and young and...

Golden days. Dead and buried.

Sam wasn't looking forward to meeting Dennis, even though it had been her idea.

She entered the Galleries, glancing at her watch. She was five minutes late. And she shouldn't be. She should never put herself in a position where she felt beholden to Dennis. For anything. Not ever again.

But this... Yes, this had been her idea.

She wanted to know what to do about Jack. She sensed a cold, frightening rage in him that was steadily building. A destructive thing that needed an outlet. But what would Jack do? What the hell was he going to do?

There was a look in his eyes that said he was going to kill. She had to find a way to stop the calamity that was set on course, speeding toward them. Jack's parents horribly murdered, Joe and Nigel missing. Dead, Jack said, and he seemed to know. So many horrible things, and Sam playing piggy in the middle...and she didn't know what to *do*.

There was always the police, but Jack was so adamant they shouldn't be involved. But perhaps just a little phone call hinting at Bane's possible involvement with the murders. Surely Jack couldn't blame her for that?

She needed to seek Dennis's advice, as hard as deferring to him was. Perhaps, for once, Mr. Arrogant could actually do something helpful.

She passed the second floor on the escalator. Meeting Dennis still felt wrong. She prayed he would manage to restrain himself and not try bringing up the old days again like there was a bond between them, an obligation that committed her in some nebulous way to him. If he tried any of that "it was good between us once" crap, she'd just—

She'd have to bloody hit him.

She was here for Jack's sake, and only Jack's sake. She hoped this wasn't a really bad idea.

When she saw him sitting at the table staring miserably into his coffee, she was sure it was.

But it was too late to back off now. He'd seen her, and her heart sank at the desperate look of need that sprang up in his eyes. She clenched her jaw and sat down opposite him.

"Can I get you a coffee?"

She shook her head. "I need your help, Dennis. Like I said on the phone, we need to talk about Jack."

She saw the resentment replace the yearning and felt her own barriers rise up, the irritation he always stirred in her, ever since their disastrous relationship. It had been a year of discomfort and spite, like dating a grumpy scorpion. How did she ever put up with him for so long? Because, her conscience reminded her, he could be good, too. Funny, kind, reckless, which made him exciting—to a seventeen-year-old. At twenty-seven, she could see the charm peeling like old paint.

"He doesn't want me to go to the police," she said with a shrug. "About Bane, I mean. But I feel I should. He's just not himself, you see; he could get hurt."

"He won't thank you for calling the coppers." He slurped at his coffee moodily.

"Then what do I do? He's looking for Bane, and when he finds him, he— He'll do something stupid."

"He thinks Bane killed his folks, doesn't he? Well, perhaps he did. But can the police prove that? I doubt it."

"So...what? You're telling me to do nothing, just sit back and let him and Bane kill each other?"

Dennis didn't say anything, staring into his cup.

"You know Bane's his brother, don't you?"

That made him look up. "What?"

"Jack's older brother. Hated each other as kids. Bane used to torture Jack, apparently. He wouldn't go into details."

Dennis whistled softly. "That would explain a hell of a lot. But why didn't Jack tell me? I mean... How long have you known?"

"About as long as Jack."

Dennis frowned. She sighed in empathy. This still sounded unreal to her. "Bane ran away from home, it seems, when Jack was only seven, and Jack shut him out like he didn't exist. It all came back to him at the funeral—Bane's girlfriend turned up with a photograph of them as kids."

"Christ on a fuckin' spacehopper! That's fucked up. What's he trying to do to Jack?"

"I don't know. Perhaps he's just sick, full of hate or something. Wants to kill or torment his family because he felt, I don't know, unwanted, rejected? Who the hell knows, Dennis? It's frightening. I don't know if Jack can cope with it. I certainly can't. I don't know what's going to happen next. Remember Joe and Nigel? If Bane *did* kill them..."

"What's to stop him killing me or...*you* next? Is that it, Sam?"

Sam looked down at her hands, twisted together on the tabletop. "I just want to help Jack."

"Yeah..."

She had been right. Definitely a bad idea. He was twisting everything she said, like he always did. Making her feel guilty for things she hadn't meant.

"So, tell the police. Tell them all about mad, bad brother Bane. If Jack can't take that, well..."

You'd like that, wouldn't you, Dennis? To see us split up. Jack would never forgive her for getting in the way of what he saw as a personal vendetta. He wanted Bane all to himself. He *wanted* to kill his own brother, just like Bane had killed his own parents.

Crazy. Frightening. Why was she mixed up in all this? Why, in her turn, did she *want* to be mixed up in it? Did she crave the drama, the excitement, to take her out of her own dull existence? She looked at Dennis and could see the same question in his eyes, now slightly mocking and scornful.

"What did you see in Jack that opening night at The Slaughter, Sam? What was it that made you suddenly need him so much?"

She stiffened. "I don't know what you mean." It was like he was peering deep inside her, poking about amongst her confused emotions.

"You saw something, didn't you? What changed good, old, dependable, dull-as-ditchwater Jack into Sam's wonderful Mister Right?"

"Just do something for me, will you, Dennis?" She tried to keep the anger out of her voice and didn't do a very good job.

Dennis opened his arms magnanimously.

"Just keep an eye on him. Make sure he doesn't do anything stupid."

"You want me to follow him around like a faithful old dog? It's not really my style."

"You're his friend, aren't you? Start acting like one."

She got up and left the table, let the escalator bear her away from him, both furious and anxious.

What *had* she seen that night? She recalled the repulsive band, the way they'd somehow spoiled the air she was breathing, made Thomas green as a rotten turnip, made them all feel sordid, violent, edgy. And she remembered Jack beside her. He was trembling like a scared horse, eyes wide and blasted like he was mainlining on black terror. Something had stirred in him that she'd never seen before, like it had been hidden away in a box somewhere deep down in the dark of him, and now it was starting ever so slowly to lift the lid and peer out. It had frightened her, and it had exhilarated her. She'd reached out to him instinctively.

Sam had grown used to Jack and his friends. She'd hung out with them on a fairly regular basis for nine years, ever since meeting Dennis at the Burned Oak Club, almost, but not quite, one of the little group. After the shambles that was her relationship with Dennis ended, she hadn't abandoned them. She enjoyed their company: Joe, Jack, hell, even Dennis sometimes. Nine years, in which time she'd felt cozy with them. They were fun; interesting and amusing in equal measures, although she knew not many of her other friends understood the appeal. Most importantly, they were dependable and supportive. Like a second family she could trust (yes, even Dennis). She could say things to them she'd never been able to reveal to her staid adoptive parents.

Then, on that wild night, shaken to the core by the subversive, disturbing nature of the band's music, and everything she'd ever believed to be secure turned suddenly on its head without her understanding why; the sanctity of self, the privacy of inner phobias popped inside out for everyone to see—just like it had later, when Lila broke into her flat. She'd experienced a loneliness of the spirit that was unbearable.

And desperate to regain her composure, yet *excited* by her own fear, too, she turned to Jack...

Jack, a dependable, well-liked friend, suddenly transformed into something more.

Yes, she'd seen something that night, all right. She'd seen a thrilling, unfamiliar wildness in Jack's eyes that intensified her own terror, yet deliciously reassured her, too. Terror and safety. Fear and need.

You couldn't have one without the other. Whatever it was that had awoken deep inside him, she had stretched out to grab it, too. It was dangerous and dark, but so very *vital.*

Love could be a terrifying thing.

And she'd *never* understand it.

Dennis felt like throwing his empty cup at her receding form, but a passing waitress took it out of his raised hand with a mollifying smile. Fuck Jack. Fuck Jack! *Fuck him!*

He took the bus home, wedged in next to a smelly man with a cold, who sneezed every few minutes as if on cue. Dennis looked out of the window and considered turning up for work, late as he was. Sod that. He'd better telephone his Dad and make out he was on death's door before the old bastard fired him. And he would, too. Then again, why bloody bother.

He leaped off the bus outside the student union and strode over the zebra crossing, hands in pockets. He wondered what Jack would be doing up in the flat. He'd spoken hardly a word to his flatmate all weekend. Jack had stayed in, preoccupied as ever, reading some stupid book like it was important. He opened the main door and thumped up the stairs, hoping Jack was out so he wouldn't have to talk. He didn't feel like talking.

Jack was in, sitting in his plastic armchair, reading the book. Irritation pricked Dennis.

"Why're you always reading that?" He didn't care about the answer; he was just expressing his vexation. It made him feel better.

Jack lowered the book and stared at him as if he didn't know who the hell Dennis was.

Oh, for fuck's sake! Living in a sodding madhouse. Dennis strode to the window, glowered at the ugly bulk of the union for a moment, then swung around on Jack, who was reading again. Something caught his eye as he turned. A bright red poster stuck to the wall with blue tack where Jack's *Clockwork Orange* quad used to be.

"What the hell's this?" He read it twice, as if looking for a catch.

**THE SLAUGHTER INN PRESENTS:
THE SAWNEY BEAN TOUR,
THE ULTIMATE IN THRILLING HORROR.
THE TRIP TO END ALL TRIPS.**

**SATURDAY, NOVEMBER 16TH, COACH LEAVES PUB 10 AM.
TICKETS AVAILABLE BEHIND THE BAR, £20 (INCLUDES
WEEKEND ACCOMMODATION)**

"Well?" He turned to see Jack watching him closely.

"Something important, Dennis. A challenge."

"Who from? Bane, I suppose. Your psychotic big bruv."

Jack looked surprised.

"Yeah, I heard all about it from Sam. We've just had lunch together." He smirked complacently. Stir the bastard up a bit. Jack returned to his book, showing no reaction whatsoever.

Dennis felt lost in his own bitterness and confusion. An overwhelming emptiness threatened him. When he spoke again, his voice was almost cowed. "Are they really dead, Jack?" His flatmate frowned up at him. "I mean Joe and Nigel. That's what you keep saying, but no bodies have ever turned up."

Jack sighed. "Leave it, Dennis. Please."

"I just want to know where my friend is." And just lately, he really *did* miss the pizza man. All this strangeness would have slid off Joe like water off a duck. Joe could cope with anything. He really missed the bastard.

Jack had nothing further to say on the matter. He simply gave Dennis a sort of sad, resigned look, then lowered his eyes. That wasn't good enough. Dennis's anger returned. He tapped the book Jack was holding almost hard enough to knock it from his hands.

"Reading that isn't gonna solve your problem, is it?" He read the cover scornfully: *Blood Clan: The Grisly Life of Sawney Bean.*

"Sawney *What*?" Dennis laughed. "Something to do with this trip, right?" He jerked a thumb at the poster. "Bane's laying on a little Maniacal Mystery Tour, and I suppose you're going."

Jack put the book down. "Like I said, it's a challenge."

"If you're right about Bane—him being a rubber-room job and all that—then this jolly little outing might very well live up to the poster blurb. D'you want to end up like your folks?"

"Don't worry about me, Dennis."

"Oh, but I *do*. I do. So, who the fuck is Sawney Bean, and what's he got to do with Bane?"

Jack stood up. There was a dangerous glint in his eye that Dennis was becoming used to seeing lately. "Perhaps I'll find out, eh, Dennis?"

"On 'the trip to end all trips'? Your funeral, buddy."

Jack didn't reply, already burying himself in his book again.

Your funeral.

Great choice of words, Dennis, ol' chap.

Sensitive to the end.

He left Jack to his book and went to fetch a beer from the fridge.

CHAPTER THIRTY-FOUR

If you look at the rocky cliffs that overhang the beach at Bennane Head today, you might see a face. The profile of a beetle-browed man, perhaps, with shaggy hair of moss and grass, jutting nose, and brutal chin formed from stone and used as perches by seagulls. Is this purely imagination on the part of the perceiver? Maybe... Landscapes assuming human characteristics, nature affected by evil events—these are romantic notions from weird tales and ghost stories. Yet the tale of Sawney Bean and his hellish brood that once dwelled beneath these crags is no ghost story. It happens to be true. Every gory word of it.

And the strangest thing of all is that Sawney's deeds have been all but forgotten by modern man, relegated to the status of an atavistic fireside myth. But Sawney Bean lived and breathed and butchered in his cave, and the atrocities committed by icons such as Jack the Ripper and his Yorkshire namesake pale into insignificance in comparison. Perhaps the mind of civilized man is capable only of assimilating horror in moderation, as if too much will addle the spirit, shrink the soul. The exploits of Red Jack are shuddered at gleefully today, widely and extravagantly celebrated in film and book; the Whitechapel murderer was elevated more to the position of anti-hero than psychopath as the years passed. But Sawney Bean? Perhaps sometimes, we'd rather forget. Perhaps Sawney and his family were just too horrible for mass public consumption.

Born the son of an East Lothian hedger and ditcher eight miles east of Edinburgh in the early 17th century, Alexander "Sawney" Bean was a surly youth with a prodigious idleness, totally averse to the demanding and arduous work required by his father's occupation. Sawney favored lying on his back in the meadows and frowning at the sun, sowing bloodcurdling oaths and cultivating dreadful fancies. His father had beaten him as a lad to drive the devilish laziness from his bones, but this had served only to transform his sloth to truculence; as Sawney broke into adolescence, his sinewy form stretched to a fearsome height, and the beatings ceased.

Sawney would not work, and no man could force him to. But a life of discontented boredom sat ill with his developing flagitious appetites. Although the corpses of babies were found sunken in wells and livestock was slaughtered in the fields, he still remained unsatisfied, craving something more as he idled away the days.

He found it in a young maiden, Agnes Douglas, daughter of a reputed witch, and accused by many of having inherited her mother's arts. Whether this was the case or no, her nature was ideally suited to Sawney's needs. A pliable, sordid girl of depraved inclinations, she was the perfect companion to the brute Sawney. Alone he was a brooding sadist; coupled with his heartless concubine, he truly became a monster.

Their deeds increased in grossness and frequency with the result that, reveling in their new-found infamy, they soon found themselves hounded by an outraged community. Whether Sawney had, at this point, already indulged his taste for human flesh is not known. However, there seem to have been many recorded instances of children and wayfarers, left homeless by plague and war, who disappeared around this period in the counties and burgs, which lay in Sawney's wake as he and his unwholesome companion made their way across the country. They went in search of a life of bale coupled with impunity. A life apart from their fellow man.

They found themselves in Galloway, and arriving at the coast near the small community of Ballantrae, they decided to cease their meanderings and settle permanently. A cave below brooding Bennane Head was to be their bolt hole, and no darker, more noisome place could they have chosen. In this unhallowed cave, feats that stagger the timid imaginings of man were performed. Men, women, children in their hundreds were seized from the road above, disemboweled and dismembered, their limbs and torsos roasted over a crackling fire around which Sawney and Black Agnes would squat, drooling over their feast. For nigh on twenty-five years, the Beans lived here, raising a family of cannibalistic murderers, the children inheriting Sawney's monstrous desires, adopting his depraved tastes as naturally as any offspring emulates the habits of its parents. Breeding incestuously amongst themselves, the family swelled into a score or so of degenerate freaks: the Bean clan.

The cave was secured from prying eyes by the sea, which laps around the mouth at high tide. No wonder, then, that despite over twenty years of reported disappearances of travelers from the coastal roads of Galloway, it took so long to find the cannibals' lair.

The carriageway on the headland above the cave was a fairly well-used route to the market at Stranraer, and thus provided the ravenous family with plenty of victims. At times up to five or six footmen would be waylaid, although never more than two on horseback. These victims were mutilated or battered to death, then dragged down the grassy slope to the lair of the damned, and there…

Bodies were dismembered in the cave, the heads pickled. Often there would be a superfluity of corpses due to the unbridled barbarity of the clan. Limbs and torsos were then tossed into the sea at a distance from the cave, only to be pushed back in by the tide, to the horror of all who lived along the Galloway coastline.

Was Sawney Bean a pathological misanthrope? A sadistic psychopath? Whatever the correct psychological term, Sawney was, by any definition, a monster. But in his tide-hidden lair, invisible from the road above, he remained a thriving one. To satisfy the outrage of the county folk, several innocent travelers, strangers to the region, were wrongfully accused and hanged, along with several local innkeepers, the last to see the victims of Bennane Head alive. The number of missing persons lost along the Galloway coastline was becoming too obvious to ignore, and word soon reached the ears of James VI of Scotland himself.

Yet it was not until one extraordinary day, when a victim actually survived the onslaught of the clan for the first time, that Sawney's fate was sealed.

Jack put the book down in his lap and let his gaze wander. It settled on the poster. He closed his eyes. He had developed a fierce headache that prodded against the bone of his skull, and not just because of the writer's fetid prose.

He felt sick and drained and had no idea what to make of the book.

The writer had dragged the legend screaming into the light of the 20th century. It belonged skulking in the dark of the 17th.

The sound of a piano tinkled softly through the walls from the flat next door. It should have soothed him, but he felt beyond soothing. He wiped a hand across his tired eyes, closed the book to look at the cover for the hundredth time. The shadow from the burial mound, from the cave of his dreams, thrusting gore at Jack as it inched slowly out of the dark, held back just in time by the inflexibility of the artist's paint, by the fact that it was just a picture.

He wiped his hand over the picture as if hoping to smear it away. It was simply a pulp artist's impression of a dubious legend, he told himself. If Jack had dreamed of a similar brutish silhouette, it was because some fears are universal: he didn't have a monopoly on bogeymen. Perhaps he'd once heard the tale and subconsciously buried it; perhaps he'd seen this book before.

You recognize him, don't you?

Lila knew. She knew this was his own, very private, little nightmare. It wasn't something he could ease by sharing. The book was for him, even if he didn't understand its implications.

He felt an urge to throw the book against the wall. Burn it, even. The book shook in his hands. There was a collar of sweat around his neck. Burn it. Forget the whole morbid deal. Forget Nigel and Joe. Forget your parents.

Forget Bane.

He opened the book again. He still had a chapter or two to read.

A man and his wife were returning from a fair at Stranraer. The Bean clan seemed to appear from nowhere, swarming over the edge of the cliffs, filthy demons with mad eyes and blood-rusted blades. The man fought with pistol and sword, riding over some of his attackers with his horse. The woman was dragged from her saddle and mutilated in front of her horrified husband. Her throat was opened by the loathsome females of the clan, who set about gulping the jetting blood, their frightful faces running with gore. Then they unfastened the woman's abdomen with their knives, yanking glee-fully at the entrails inside.

The husband, in the meantime, discharged his pistol wildly into the horde and sliced around him with his cutlass. He was to be lucky this day, for a group of stout-hearted travelers returning from the fair came upon the horrible scene and put the cannibals to flight. With their leader Sawney slumbering in the cave below, the clan lacked the courage to fight on against such a body of men and withdrew, issuing foul imprecations.

The husband, the first ever to see the clan and live, collapsed in tears and relayed to the travelers his awful story, whereupon they set off for Glasgow to inform the magistrates, who in turn passed word to the king. Three or four days after the ambush, a hundred of the king's troops, together with a couple of bloodhounds, descended to the beach below Bennane.

At first, they took no notice of the cave with its almost imperceptible opening as they moved along the seashore, despite the baying of the hounds. As they retraced their steps past the hole, however, the dogs insisted on entering, disappearing inside while the soldiers hesitated, not really believing anything human could live in such a horribly dark and unwholesome place.

Finally, some of the soldiers ventured inside. They found Sawney Bean waiting for them.

He heard them come.

The head of a young lad crackled on a spit over the fire. The skin popped and blistered, coddled by flames. Black Agnes poked the scrawny limbs that hung beside the spit, dangling from hooks driven into the roof of the cave. Already they were turning a handsome brown. Fat spat on the fire, loud as a musket shot. The hag watched the head cook until the eyes burst like grapes, flames steaming as they devoured the tissue. The remains of hair glowed and fell into red ash.

Sawney heard them coming and turned his back on the fire, on his brood that squatted beside their nightmarish mother. They were subdued and sulky, beaten down by their father's ire. Sparks, caught on the wind creeping through the entrance, scattered amongst them.

Sawney crept to the mouth of the cave, nostrils flaring. He tensed, a bludgeon of oak clasped in his right fist. The lad's brains still adorned the wood. Beyond the cave, Sawney heard the baying of hounds, the scuffle and jingle of boots and buckles slipping over rocks uncovered by the receding tide. Many boots…

What was fear to Sawney? It was something outside of him. He generated it in others; he ate it along with the bodies and heads that housed the alien emotion. He certainly could not feel it himself, not even now, as his domain came under threat for the first time since he had dragged his crooked stick of a whore here to copulate in the dark many bloody years before.

No. No fear. But rage. Oh, yes, there was rage… A gargantuan fury that would paint the walls of the cave red, incarnadine the sea that frothed outside in an orgy of bestiality.

Two hounds bounded into the cave, baying like devils. The passage reverberated with their tortured howls as Sawney slammed the life out of them with his bludgeon. Soon the howls stopped, and the beasts ceased twitching.

The first soldier to appear in the entrance, framed against the noonday sky, Sawney took with simple violence. The trooper's neck cracked like rotten driftwood as the cannibal squeezed him into hell with his giant hands, the corpse tossed back out of the cave as if it were a broken moth. The soldier's musket rolled on the ground. Sawney ignored it, preferring his own tools of butchery.

The second gaily-colored intruder had time to lift his musket to his shoulder, his face a pale thing of terror as he caught sight of the monster in the cave. He didn't have time to fire it. Sawney's bludgeon exploded through tricorner hat and skull beneath, mashing felt material into shattered bone.

Two more troopers burst in together, and three more. Sawney's club was a blur, staving in a face here, collapsing a head there, splintering ribs, rupturing organs. The floor of the cave became a stream of gore beneath his naked feet. Troopers were filling the gaps left by their slaughtered comrades, an unstoppable tide.

A musket coughed in the confined space. A bayonet lunged. Sawney dropped the club as a musket ball punched through his right forearm. The bayonet ground against his thigh bone. His fingers clamped around the teeth of the man who had shot him, widening his mouth unnaturally, rending until the lower jaw flapped loosely against his throat. The soldier with the bayonet backed away, the will to fight leaving him in an instant. Sawney's left hand took him by the neck, launched him off his feet, made a smashed, bloody eggshell of his head against the cave roof.

But there were always more. Muskets leveled, faces terrified but determined. Sawney backed off slowly, facing them with a malefic, lopsided sneer. His tangled beard was red and slick with blood, his ragged jerkin dripping. Pain fired his illimitable rage.

Sawney will gnaw yer heads open, spit out yer dreams.

A musket exploded. Shards of rock spouted from the wall beside the cannibal's head. He scooped up a corpse from a pile at his feet and hurled it at the soldiers as the eldest of his sons crept from the dark to assist him.

Hang yer shanks fer the flies tae feast upon. Scarf yer souls, drink the gore from yer sundered skulls. Eat yer fear, eat the bloody world...

The soldiers hesitated before the sheer horror of the butcher.

Sawney shrieked. And all went red.

All red.

Bane was sitting in the darkness, the familiar, absolute darkness that merged with his body and mind, all one now. His breath, the stink of the cave; his heart, its pulse. The cave was alive.

Red thoughts, bloody pictures from the past. Centuries crumbling to dust in the cave. Sawney had stepped between the years: he was then, and he was now. The cave was always.

The intruder had seen him, too. After fifteen years, Bane had returned the skull to the cave and found the lad curled in his sleeping bag beside a dying fire. Bane's outrage had been overwhelming. The sanctity of his cave violated, mocked by someone daring to sleep there, as if it were a hostel. Bane had waited silently in the dark, watching the intruder, and the youth had woken, staring into the blackness as if instinctively knowing he was not alone. But his terror had not been caused by Bane's presence. He'd been totally unaware of Bane crouching in a hollow of the chamber like a spider in a crack. The youth's fear had been intoxicating.

The lad had seen what remained in the cave, of course, what time could not erode. The horror festering perpetually in the dark, a bloody stain on the fabric of reality.

A rip in nature.

The youth's terror had reached an unbearable peak, and Bane had answered it.

As the bones jumped and splintered beneath the rock in his hands, it had no longer been a stocky lad he was destroying, but a bearded hiker with no face, a stick jutting from his eye. And a boy, reveling in the red mess he had made, on the brink of something wonderful.

After, Bane sat and cradled the skull, although he could not see it. Light was an intrusion here. Like the lad in the bag by the dying fire. Like the one who had come after, seeking his friend.

He'd found him eventually. The first time he'd eluded Bane's clutches by a hair's breadth, scampering from the cave like a frightened cat, although the youth had not even seen him. The second time he returned, for one last search, Bane was happy to show him the bits and pieces of his friend.

The thin youth put up more of a fight than his larger companion. But the result was the same.

Red.

Red things, soon turning brown on the fire he'd made.

What does that make you, Bane?

The voice came out of nowhere, a worm burrowing into his brain. A wriggling worm of—fear?—gnawing through tissue and synapse. He hugged the skull closer and let the darkness fill his lungs.

It makes me strong, that's what it makes me. It makes me like Him. I ate the lad, and the cave was satisfied. I ate his fear.

Bane was in control of fear. He'd used it all his life, a weapon, a friend—the only friend he'd ever known.

Remember when we were young, Jack? Before I accepted what I was, I could never understand the rage, the blackness in me. All I knew was that it had to be let out to play. Play with you, Jack. I had to do those things, you see, or… And I enjoyed them too much to stop.

After twenty years, he got to play with his parents, too. But their hearts just weren't in it. He'd thanked them for bringing him up in the only way he understood. But the experience hadn't proved to be as satisfying as he had anticipated. Sitting amongst their corpses, surrounded by memories of a feral childhood, he'd felt curiously let down. Empty. Perhaps the anticipation had been too strong. Nothing can live up to twenty years of expectation.

Now he was back at the cave again. Home.

He was waiting for brother Jack to come and play… Bane had spent a long time showing him how.

He had a feeling Jack wouldn't disappoint him.

On an impulse, he got up and reverently slipped the skull into its secret niche, finding it easily in the dark. He moved along the twisting passage, every angle familiar to him as if he'd spent all his life in the cave.

He stood at the entrance, and it was a fine, bitter morning. The sea was sluggish and grumpy, as if finding it hard to wake up for the day. Ailsa Craig shone like a holy isle, bits of seagulls falling around the crest like ash from a volcano. He made his way over the arm of rock and along the beach, his boots sinking into pale sand, the stink of the weed filling him with well-being. It was time to survey all that was his. The boundaries of his kingdom.

It took him half an hour to walk to Ballantrae, the wind picking at his face, prying under his long coat. He hardly noticed it. He liked to walk into the village, sniffing out the fear that resided behind facades of complacency. He would step into the post office and buy nothing, just there to watch the postmistress's reaction. He would see the unease flare up in her eyes, and it made him feel special. That was better than anything. It always had been. He never spoke to her, nor she to him. But he was sure she knew. She recognized the darkness in him, and the ghosts stood by her shoulder; the ghosts of her ancestors, back with their three-hundred-year-old dread to haunt her. Oh, he was certain she knew.

They all knew, though they might pretend they didn't, going about their everyday lives as normal. Only the old man who sat perpetually in the cemetery refused to pretend, relishing the darkness that had returned to his community.

He stopped outside the post office. Through the window, he watched the face of the bun-haired woman behind the counter twitch as she noticed him. He smiled. She turned away—he wasn't there, you see. That amused him greatly. He was tempted to walk in and cup her chin in his hand, as if to say: Oh, but I am here. This town's worst nightmare is back, and you know it. You all know it. You all know me.

Of course, that wasn't quite true. Inevitably, there were those ignorant of the village's ancient little secret. He crossed to the small newsagents and stepped up to the newspaper rack. The balding Englishman behind the counter eyed him warily, but without the fear Bane was sure he drew from the locals, those whose families had lived here for generation after generation. This man merely disliked the look of him. Bane smiled a rictus smile at the shopkeeper, like a scary actor in a museum of horror.

"Can I help you?" The man clearly hoped not.

"One day, maybe," Bane told him. But not now. Not yet. There was plenty of time for that. Leaving the newsagents, he strode on, bootheels clicking on the stone of the road. At the far end of the street, he could see the old church and the diminutive figure of the pensioner trembling on his tombstone bench. He considered approaching him to jitter his old bones with dread. But Bane didn't want to confer any favors today.

He stood in the center of the quiet road, the sun cold, the wind harsh, spread his arms like Jesus on the cross, tilted back his head, and grinned at the sky.

The real Master of Ballantrae had returned.

The cannibal fought like something spat from the bowels of hell, casting men down like shattered toys, splitting spines and bursting skulls until the sheer weight of numbers drove him and his evil sons ever farther back into the depths of the cave. The soldiers lit torches and pursued him, and so came to the rear chamber of the twisting tunnel, to where the mother and her cursing, stinking pack had retreated. And it is said they were confronted with a sight full of the utmost horrors of which man can conceive: shanks, genitals, torsos, and the heads of men, women, and children hanging from hooks in the stone roof while numerous limbs lay in piles on the floor, soaked in pickle. Money, too, gold pieces in great heaps, trinkets, clothes, jewels scattered in the gloom of the chamber. And Sawney defending his treasure to the end.

But the end it was. Even he could not overcome an army bearing muskets, bayonets, and swords. Five men held him down while another lopped off his fierce head. Where this grisly trophy rolled to, none could say; it was lost beneath the frantic feet of the monster's kin as they struggled to escape the soldiers. None did; all were taken.

The remains of the clan's victims were buried in the sand outside the cave. The score or so members of the wicked family, including Black Agnes, were chained and taken alive to Edinburgh. Sawney's headless corpse was dragged behind the captain's horse until the flesh was all but scraped away.

After parading their ghastly prisoners for the citizens to vent their spleen, the troops committed the clan to the Tollbooth, there to languish while their fate was determined. Sawney's bloody cadaver was furnished with special treatment, impaled on a large spike on top of the Tollbooth gate. Here it became an object of much abuse and loathing until, along with the rest of the clan, it was taken to Leith, the final stage in the journey of royal retribution.

There then followed punishment of the most horrific nature, as the King's magistrates ordered the mass execution, without trial, of every member of the clan. In the main square, a vociferous crowd gathered to watch the cannibals' fate. A platform had been erected, and upon this, the men and boys were quartered, their privy members first to be hacked away, the torsos piled atop each other in a bloody heap while the females of the clan were forced to watch.

The massacre was almost absolute, the soldiers performing the mutilations zealously, if not, it appears, with total precision.

One child, it was reported, so silent and still as he awaited his turn beneath the axe, prevailed upon the pity of a guard to such a degree that his bonds were loosened to afford him some respite from pain. The boy seized his chance and made off through the crowd.

Although hotly pursued, the urchin made good his escape, whether through the aid of some compassionate member of the crowd or solely through his own frantic efforts. In the event, the child fled and was not discovered. The escape of one small boy was a blunder that was readily overlooked in the face of such wholesale righteous slaughter.

The womenfolk, having endured the spectacle of butchery with much flinging of the grisliest of curses that paled the hearts of those unlucky enough to hear them, were next to suffer the King's retribution. They were hauled to three great pyres and there manacled to oak posts. The faggots were lit, and the women roasted like the countless victims they themselves had cooked in their stinking lair. The sight was gruesome in the extreme. Never before or since had Scotland given witness to such ferocity and horror. The unnatural wenches twisted, searing on the pyres, flesh dripping, fat hissing, their faces steaming and cracking into ash. And as they burned, Black Agnes, her daughters, and granddaughters continued to hurl forth, mingled with the most abominable shrieks, curses of the most loathsome nature that would ring in the ears of those who heard them to their dying day.

Jack closed the book, threw back his head, and laughed. Laughed raucously until his throat burned, long after the pulpy zeal of the writer had ceased to amuse him. Then he leaped out of the chair as if it, too, was on fire and crossed to the window. Outside, a fine, bitter morning. The sun struggled to warm the busy road below and the hulking union opposite, but the wind dissipated its rays. Jack could feel draughty fingers poking through the cracks around the old Georgian window frame. Nothing out there he hadn't seen a thousand times before, but the view reassured him with its banality. Everything was as it should be.

In the bathroom, he studied his face in the mirror. It was the same, but it was different; as long and gaunt and pale as ever, his nose slightly hooked, his hair uncontrolled and wild. But his eyes—they'd always been cautious of life, dreamy and touched by a hint of unease. Now they were shocking holes. Black holes. His Leigh Woods trip had become a permanent one. Lines had sprung up like spider-web scribbles around his eyes and mouth. His eyes were brown, not black. Not black, like...

Panic seized him, only fading slightly when he realized his irises hadn't changed color; they had simply been eclipsed by his pupils, which were the size of pennies. He hadn't studied himself so intensely in months, and now, as he futilely waited for his pupils to shrink back to normal, he could, at last, see the likeness that had eluded him for so long. Just a twist of his features, just a slight rearrangement...

And he would be looking at Bane.

CHAPTER THIRTY-FIVE

"I'm sorry, Sam. I just don't feel like laughing."

A bald head turned around from the row of seats in front, features vague in the semi-darkness. Sam glared until it swiveled back to face the cinema screen.

"I know. I *know*. But you've got to try, Jack."

"Have I?"

"If not for your sake, how about mine?"

The head gave a warning quarter turn. Sam frowned at it with sudden, irrational hate.

"I love you, Sam. How's that? Now then, do I still have to laugh?"

She searched his face, splashed with light from the film, hoping to find a sign of genuine emotion. It was impossible; lately, his features had assumed a stony inscrutability that would have done Joe proud. It gave the impression that even possibly heartfelt sentiment might be sleeved in irony. Was he being ironic now?

"Yes, you *do* have to laugh. It's a very funny film."

A voice came from the row in front—the bald man, although this time he didn't turn around. "How do you know? You're not bloody listening to it."

Sam leaned forward and prodded him just below the neck. "Excuse me; this is a private conversation."

"Could've fooled me." The head remained resolutely facing forward. Specks of dust freefalling from the silver projection shaft settled onto his hairless crown.

"Sam, it's *not* funny. But I appreciate what you're trying to do."

Frustration bunched inside her. The bald man had interrupted at the crucial moment, and now it was gone. She felt like prodding the man again, harder this time, right in the back of his head. Instead, she stretched out a hand, searching for Jack's.

"What you said a moment ago: did you mean it?" She spoke very quietly so the bald man would not hear the insecurity in her voice.

"Of course." He squeezed her hand reassuringly, and she was left without words, happiness despite everything pushing them all out of tongue's reach.

"Of course, I meant it," Jack carried on, "It's not remotely funny, is it?"

John Candy was a computer-generated ghost on the screen. Sam could have died with him.

"Sorry," he added after a moment, as she removed her hand from his.

"What for?" Her voice was flat and empty.

He couldn't look at her. Both of them stared at poor, funny, long-dead John Candy, and there was a mourning between them. Jack's thin pretense at levity all evening had been a mask for her benefit; it was like taking a corpse with the decaying memory of a smile on its face out for a date.

"It's just not the right time. For anything...right now."

A funny moment must have arrived on the screen because the audience rippled with shallow laughter. Sam waited for it to subside.

"I know you've been through a lot, Jack—"

"No. No, you don't, Sam."

"—but feeling sorry for yourself isn't going to help." She was being nasty now. And that was his fault. "You've got to try and forget. Just carry on with things."

"I'm not feeling sorry for myself, Sam. Like I said: you don't understand."

She could barely hear him now as the light-hearted soundtrack chased John and his co-actors through a rip-roaring, slapstick routine. She waited for a quieter scene.

"I understand your parents are dead—"

Again, he wouldn't let her finish. "I don't care about my parents!" His voice boomed across a lull in the soundtrack. The bald man swiveled on cue. Jack leaned forward, shoved his face close to the middle-aged man's.

"Anything I can do for you?" It came out in a warning growl. The man took in Jack's dark eyes and feral expression and instantly and very obligingly showed them the back of his head again.

Jack sat back. Other faces, both in front and beside them, were turned in their direction now. Sam felt Jack tense and wondered crazily if he was going to stand up and launch into a Basil Fawlty from hell impersonation. She realized bringing him here had not been the smartest move she'd ever made.

She pulled his hand. "Come on." She led him along the aisle of disgruntled viewers and up the ramp toward the glowing exit sign.

Out in the foyer, she dragged him toward the small bar, almost deserted now. "You were right," she said as they stood at the bar, "It wasn't funny." She bought the drinks, waving away his protestations. "I'm working; you're not," she told him as they carried their drinks to a table and sat down.

"Thanks for reminding me."

"That's okay." She sipped her pint of bitter. Not her usual style, but what the hell. Watching her figure seemed a pretty petty occupation right now.

"You're still thinking about Bane, aren't you?"

He smiled grimly. "Only all the time."

"Look, Jack..." She hesitated, guessing his reaction, but going ahead anyway. "I'm sure the police will soon take care of him."

He looked at her sharply. "Take care of Bane? Now why would they want to do that?"

"Because he's a murderer. That's what the police are for: to protect innocent people like you and me from monsters like him."

He laughed bitterly. "Innocent? In a way, I'm just as guilty as Bane."

"Don't be stupid. You didn't kill your own parents."

"No. But only because I'm not as brave as Bane. I wanted to often enough when I was a kid."

"Bane's not brave. He's evil. He needs to be put away."

"So, when did you tell them?" he asked coldly after a moment of silence in which he studied his pint without drinking it.

"What?" She looked away. She'd made an anonymous call to the local police station, got through to the desk sergeant, and faltered. She had no proof, no idea what the hell she was mixing herself up in, knowing only that she wanted to help Jack. She'd replaced the receiver on the sergeant's repeated request for her name.

"You know what I said, Sam: I don't want them involved." His voice was a low warning.

"I haven't told a soul." *Yet,* she thought defiantly. There was no way she was going to let Jack handle this on his own.

He watched her carefully for a moment. She stared back, confused and uneasy.

"Please leave it, Sam. It's a family matter."

"Why don't we go just away for a while?" she suggested. "We certainly deserve a holiday."

He looked down, swished beer around in his glass. She felt a little punch of dread. "What's the matter?"

He wouldn't look at her as he spoke. "I *am* going away. But not for a holiday. And not with you."

She didn't like his solemn tone. Nor the grim determination on his face.

"So...where *are* you going?" she asked slowly.

He shrugged evasively. "Just on a little trip."

She waited for him to elaborate. "We're not leaving here 'til you tell me. Or would you rather I do the talking—to the police."

He looked up at last. And she knew it was going to be bad news.

"Let me buy you a drink, dear."

"I'll buy my own."

Lila smiled graciously. "Of course." She was wearing a lacy black shawl over a revealing basque. The crow tattoo peeked through the sworls of lace, eyeing Sam as she ordered a pint of Butcher's Best.

Lunchtime in The Slaughter and Lila didn't look surprised to see her. Her black leather gloves caressed the hand pull saucily as she poured the beer, one for Sam, one for herself. The pub was fairly full for a Wednesday, and Sam, gazing at the tour poster taped to the Wolfman's outstretched paws, wondered if curiosity over the forthcoming attraction might account for the increase in business. Foreboding was a barbed wire knot in her belly. The crowds didn't ease it at all.

"What shall we drink to?" Lila asked, pushing a pint toward Sam and holding her own aloft. "How about parents and absent friends?" Her grin was obscene.

Sam was unphased. "How about psychopaths?" She lifted her own glass. *I'm braver than I was. You made me this way. And Jack, too. I've got to fight for both of us now.* "You don't scare me," she added aloud. Was she trying to convince Lila or herself?

Lila was chuckling indifferently, so Sam carried on the attack. "Your Lord and Master snaps his fingers, and you jump to the tune. You haven't even got the imagination to think for yourself. How does that feel?"

Lila drank her beer down calmly, her eyes smirking. She smacked a dainty glove across her mouth with slovenly relish.

"How about another one? I'm paying this time." She refilled her glass and got a fresh one for Sam. "Now then, where were we?"

Sam took a large gulp of ale. It made her feel stronger. "I want you to leave Jack alone. I want you to tell Bane that he and Jack aren't children anymore. It's time the games stopped."

"The protective female, standing by her man. Where is he today, by the way? Afraid to stand by *you*?"

"Bane's going to be put away for a very long time. And if you had anything to do with the murders, so will you."

"Then I should be very worried, shouldn't I?" Lila ignored a fat biker who was nudging an empty pint glass across the bar toward her. She leaned forward and fixed Sam with a vulture stare. "But then, if what you say is true, and I *am* involved, so should you."

"Didn't you hear what I said? You don't scare me."

The biker was witnessing the conversation with great interest.

"Oh, but I do," Lila said slowly. She let her gloved fingers scuttle up Sam's arm like a spider. "I *do.*"

Sam finished her pint. Rushing it made her feel slightly sick. Or was that the unrestrained spite pouring out of the barmaid? She understood at last that this woman would never let *anything* stop her from doing exactly what she wanted, or rather what Bane wanted. Reason, morality, fear: she was beyond them. And Lila was right: Sam *was* still scared. She'd always been scared. Now, she was more scared than ever before because, for the first time, she accepted they really were intending something bad for Jack, and she had no idea what that might be. Why had she imagined they were only playing twisted little games with him? Nobody was playing. She reached for her second pint and drank deeply.

"Why Jack?" she heard herself muttering through the haze of alcohol settling on her brain. "What does Bane want from him after all these years? What do *you* want from him?"

"The same as you, Samantha."

Sam forced nonchalance. "And what's that exactly?"

"Do you really need to be told?"

Everything was being pulled from under her again. Lila made her relationship with Jack sound sordid, unhealthy, and it hadn't been like that; it wasn't like that. She'd needed him; she...loved him. She had sensed his fear and vulnerability and been drawn to him, moth-to-flame style. Bane and Lila had played on those qualities, twisted them, appealing to his dark side in a way Sam couldn't understand. She suddenly wished she'd told him where she was going, wished he was here now.

"You never wanted him at all," she accused Lila, her voice slurring a little. "You were just toying with him."

"Educating might be a better term. You were such a bad influence on him, you see. You're too bland, too sweet, too innocent." She made it sound like a vile pox. "We wanted to guide his interests in other directions, but...well, he's stubborn, isn't he?"

"'Scuse me, girls," the biker butted in, bored of waiting. "How about a pint of Cannibal's Sup?"

"How about you go fuck yourself, fat boy?" Lila told him, not even looking his way. The biker held up his hands in a placatory gesture and moved farther along the bar to where the ponytailed barman was serving.

"Jack, Jack, Jack." Lila sighed theatrically. "He's been a real trial. But I'm sure he'll come around in the end. He's got so much in common with his brother." She flashed a snaky smile. "Oh, and before you think about throwing beer down my cleavage again, I'd better warn you—this time, I'll snap your pretty little neck."

Sam flinched. She was in too deep. She just wasn't used to the full-on vileness of people like Lila. She *was* too sweet and bloody innocent. God, she needed Jack.

"You should pop in to see me more often, Samantha, dear. I've enjoyed our little chat, and we girls ought to stick together. Just like brothers should. Wouldn't it be nice to see Jack and Bane become a real family again?"

Sam put out a hand to steady herself against the bar. What the hell had she hoped to achieve coming here, like an overprotective girl fighting over her man in a nightclub?

Her head was beginning to spin. She focused on the poster clutched by the Wolfman and sucked in a deep breath. She'd wanted to find out exactly what sort of trap Jack was walking into. Only she wasn't doing a very good job.

Lila followed her gaze. "Sounds good, doesn't it? I do hope you'll be coming, too. Sorry we couldn't send you a free ticket as well as Jack, but, well, he *is* the honorary guest. Twenty pounds isn't much for a wonderful weekend of mystery and... Well, you'll just have to wait and see. But do hurry up and decide because the tickets are going fast."

Sam slammed her half-empty glass down. "What do you *want?*" It came out more like a scream. She sucked in more smoky air and tried to calm herself. "What's Jack ever done to you? To Bane?"

Lila tilted her head in mock contemplation. "Hmmm. It's more what he *hasn't* done, dear. He hasn't lived up to our expectations. But he will."

Sam turned away and cursed herself when she realized she was stumbling. She headed for the door, and it was like walking along the deck of a cross-channel ferry. She was going to be sick. Dimly, she heard Lila calling after her.

"By the way, we're having a little bash here Friday night. A celebration, and a farewell. Be sure to tell Jack; I'm sure he wouldn't want to miss it for the world."

Sam just managed to make it through the door before the nausea finally won.

CHAPTER THIRTY-SIX

To Marion, with cruelest wishes. The best things in life are dark.

He signed his name in a broad, elaborate squiggle below the dedication and handed the book back to the attractive girl standing before him. He held her eyes for a moment as she thanked him, then held onto the book for a lingering moment, too, as she tried to take it from him. She smiled shyly at him, and he let her go, a little sadly. Another lost opportunity. The things he could have done with such a girl, such pouting innocence to be disfigured in the dark. It had been a while, and the yearnings were returning more frequently. He'd once believed that writing about his desires would be enough, would purge him of the cravings. But it wasn't enough. It wasn't enough.

The next punter in line slid a copy of Bolton's latest hardback across the desk for him to sign, and he frowned impatiently. The redhead had re-awoken his frustrations. He thought of the twins, wondering whether they'd be able to relieve him when he got back, and squeezed the pen in his hand until it cracked. He always got the feeling they were using him with contempt and not the other way around. Bolton didn't like to be used. And he knew they couldn't satisfy him anymore. He'd grown bored of their pointless, synchronized sadism. Cruelty without intelligence, viciousness without ingenuity was meaningless. They were like beasts of the field. He could understand why Bane had wanted them along for the ride, but surely they'd outlived their usefulness. They'd done their bit. He wished Bane would get rid of them.

Anthony had done his bit, too, although whether he had been sufficiently effective wasn't yet clear. Still, the axe murderer had been on television a few times; he'd got exposure. It was up to Jack to put two and two together and come up with patricide, even if the police hadn't been up to the job. That was what had attracted Bane to the nervous bearded man in the first place—Bane saw him on the news and had identified with the act of parent murder, recognized it as part of his own destiny. He'd wondered whether Anthony would strike a similar chord in Jack.

But in reality, the twins, Anthony, and—yes, he had to admit it—even himself were just trappings, on hand simply to add that little extra frisson. They were nothing more than scary tools a film director might use to tease fear out of the audience with gradually accumulative skill, or plot devices Bolton might include in one of his own books to heighten the suspense. But in the end, that's all they were. He wasn't self-deluding enough to believe he, or any of the other disciples, would be in on the final act. Bane would want to keep it all in the family. However, he was satisfied that Bane wasn't using him in quite the same way he was using the others. Indeed, in his own fashion, Bolton was using Bane. For inspiration, for experience. Documenting Bane's progress would give him enough material to write a whole series of novels. The man was a veritable muse. After that May Eve in the stone circle at Chipping Norton, Bolton was certain of that.

He scribbled an inane dedication on the flyleaf of Down in the Dark and passed it to the callow youth whose acne spots reddened more intensely as he thanked Bolton. The writer looked up at the next punter, but his thoughts were far from the Bristol bookshop in which he was sitting, condescending to his fans.

It was about two years after his first novel had been published and proved to be something of a success. His third book was out and not performing as well as he had hoped. In fact, it was failing badly, mauled by the critics, virtually ignored by the public. He'd been desperate for some new inspiration. Bane provided it.

Bane forced him to open his eyes and peer beyond the veil of banality around him. Seeing this dark man rip his own child away from the stiff embrace of its mother and carry it to the stone altar, already sodden with the ineffectual blood of fowls, had been a turning point for the jaded writer.

Soon, his work throbbed with a new vitality, screamed with a fresh urgency. It was as if he'd found a new religion. He dedicated his next book to Bane. It was a harrowing celebration of intellectual horror and physical carnage combined, and it was a monster hit. By then, Bolton knew how to describe horrific events effectively. He'd bloody well lived them, thanks to Bane.

When Bane first showed him the skull, he didn't believe it. He'd known the dark man two days, and the story was just too preposterous to be true. Like Jack the Ripper's diary. But the more he stared at the abnormal relic, the more he realized just how wrong he was.

Bane kept it in a little shrine at the back of the seedy Birmingham pub he'd virtually taken over. He listened to Bane's story, and he listened to Bane's philosophy. But it wasn't until he saw the skull sitting on that stone in Oxfordshire, drenched in baby's blood, grinning at the moon with lopsided teeth, that Bolton really believed. It was authentic, all right. It was just too bloody horrible to be anything else.

Bolton had struggled to articulate his own concept of evil for so long, and here it was, encapsulated in bone.

A man who looked like a bank manager was mumbling sycophantic drivel at him. Bolton paused, annoyed at being forced into making a response of some sort. He'd prepared a few morbid catchphrases beforehand and used one of them now. It seemed to work. The man laughed ingratiatingly and took his treasured purchase.

Sometimes, only sometimes, when the old depression returned to bite deep into Bolton's mind with its gray jaws, he wondered if Bane was merely mad and the skull just an ugly bone, the cave simply an ordinary hole in rock. But if he thought that... If he believed that, everything was lost and he just couldn't go on. His writing would fail again, like it used to in the days when there was no one to ignite his dark fancies. No, there was too much at stake; he had to believe, and Bane was always there to help him, the calm, dark beauty of his eyes filled with the promise of things to come. Bolton believed.

He remembered the old Slaughter Inn, where he first met the dark man. It hadn't always been called that; Bane insisted on the change, and the licensee did as he was instructed. Bane could make people do whatever he wanted, if he tried hard enough. The pub owner became a disciple, one of the very first, and The Slaughter Inn became Bane's sinister little den. A quiet, down-at-heel boozer on the outskirts of Birmingham, filled with losers, winos, and other human driftwood. Bane believed pubs were wildernesses for lost souls, forgetting their identities along with their woes as they drank, dying a little more with each gulp, thirsty for self-obliteration. Bane just hurried them along a little, that was all. He called the pub a lethal dress rehearsal for the main performance. The old Slaughter was Bane honing his skills, perfecting his talents for the big show. He was getting into the feel of things, he said.

The pub was also a beacon for kindred souls who'd slipped down a strange path in life. It lured Bolton, just as it lured Jerry Owen and the twins. They were "people looking for something different to believe in," Bane had explained. "People who nurture the dark in themselves." The garrulous Welshman had been drawn to the pub when Bane held a sick, little horror convention there for the sole purpose of attracting deviant psychopaths, as Bolton saw them. Some of the people lured by the advertisement never left the building again; they were still buried beneath the ruin. They were the fakers, innocents seeking vicarious thrills instead of real ones. Jerry, however, had obviously impressed Bane. Bane said he could tell from a man's eyes what he believed in, and Owen believed in torture. He'd taken them to see his treasure trove of video depravity in Pembroke, and Bolton had been forced to admit the collection had its corruptive charms. It had certainly proved useful since. It wasn't enough to save him in the end, though.

Bolton smiled a little worriedly at a lithe brunette waiting for her dedication. He remembered how easily Bane had disposed of the original pub owner, too. Once he had outlived his purpose and signed the pub over to Bane, he'd joined some of his former customers under the weeds in the beer garden. It was fine if Bane wanted to shed some of his less-useful hangers-on, but...maybe the readiness with which he did so alarmed the writer somewhat. But dangerous as he undoubtedly was, Bane was also material, pure material.

He'd thought the twins might inspire him, too, at first. He'd been quite excited when Bane invited them to Birmingham upon their release from the psychiatric hospital. That initial enthusiasm had long since faded. He realized now that the twins should never have been let out. They'd fooled their doctors into believing they were sane and safe, just like they'd fooled Bane into believing they were worthy of his faith. Once a lunatic, always a lunatic. You couldn't expect anything constructive from them.

Bane, however, insisted the twins remain in his little fold of hair-raisers, and when he remembered Jack's anxiety at the festival, Bolton was grudgingly forced to admit they weren't entirely useless. They still had the power to scare, Bane said. They all had the power to scare. Bringing the disciples out on show together at the funeral had been the culmination of Bane's torture technique, surrounding his brother with icons of death and horror. The photograph was the coup de grace. Bolton could certainly appreciate the subtlety of the act, the beauty of it. Even if it had involved the twins.

Shortly after the sisters arrived on the scene, they left the old Slaughter. It was virtually falling down about their ears anyway. The new pub, bought with the proceeds from Bolton's novels, was far grander, altogether a rather wickedly extravagant interpretation of a spider web. Jack had flown right in and, in a sense, never left again. Part of him—his innocence, his naiveté—stuck forever, quivering in the sticky strands.

"I think I can show you something you need."

Bolton had been sitting on his own in the dingy bar, glumly staring at the peeling red walls and wondering what the hell he was doing in this depressing hole on the fringes of Birmingham. He'd heard strange rumors about the place, enough hints of dark and dubious undertakings performed here to lure him from his usual haunts. Upon arriving, he felt like he'd been cheated. This was just another dump. The pub name lied: there was no excitement here.

When the quiet voice came from behind his shoulder, he looked around irritably, ready to refuse any offer of drugs that must inevitably follow the statement. But the man standing over him didn't look like your average dealer weasel. Bolton's fingers twitched, and a queer sensation had pitched through his gut, like he was falling down inside himself.

The man's hair was longer then, unkempt, deepest raven. He wore a knee-length black jacket that looked like it might have been worn by a gravedigger in some Hammer film. Dark jeans and square-toed biker boots completed the image. But it was the eyes that made Bolton look down suddenly into his glass, almost frightened to reply. They were naked things, shining with violent truth. There was no pretend in their Satan-skin depths.

The stranger sat down at the table with Bolton. His eyes fixed the writer in his chair, and for a moment, nothing was said.

"I've been watching you," the stranger said at last. "I watched you come in, watched you look around with a nervous...distaste...on your face. I watched you order your drink and take your seat, resigning yourself to disappointment, and I thought: this man needs something real."

Bolton shot a glance toward the door. A group of filthy bikers was standing near it, observing him silently, and he wondered if they might impede his efforts to get out. Suddenly, he seemed to be the focus of the whole shabby pub. Outside the window, the day was turning ghost gray, dusk already on its murderous course. What did this man want with him?

The stranger was continuing to talk: "I did some more thinking, and my conclusion was that here was a man lured by a pub name and a sinister reputation he's beginning to think might be just so much hyperbole. Maybe this man came looking for some genuine inspiration. Material for a book, perhaps." He grinned wolfishly at Bolton's start of surprise. "Oh yes, I know you; I know what you are, what you need. If ever there was a man looking for demons, it's you, Roderick Bolton."

Bolton clasped his sleever of ale until his podgy fingers were white as grubs. "What do you mean?" He couldn't look at the stranger's eyes for too long, just a quick dart of a glance and away. It hurt to look for any more than that. Too much in there. Too bloody much. He felt a touch of hope, and a lot of fear. But he didn't want to be disappointed again. He was so tired of searching amongst the sham for something meaningful in his life.

"I think you know what I mean." The stranger leaned forward, resting his slightly pointed chin on the back of his left hand in an almost feminine pose. "Have you ever taken a walk into the dark, my friend?"

Looking for demons. Bane had been right about that. And he'd found one. Now he could fill a hundred books with what that demon showed him.

He was smiling at the memory, staring vacantly at the desktop in front of him, oblivious to the dwindling queue of punters waiting for their autographed copies. He was snatched back to the present when a book was taken from the pile beside him and thrust rudely under his nose.

"Dedicate it to Breen: Alexander Breen." The voice was quiet, just like Bane's had been that first night he met him.

"Oh, of course, he likes to be called Bane these days, doesn't he? How could I forget?"

Bolton raised his head, put down his pen, and smiled slowly at

Jack. "Quite easily, it seems. You forget rather a lot, I'm thinking."

Jack swept the pile of books to the floor. The last few punters in the queue behind him backed away a little nervously. A store security guard, alerted by the noise, appeared behind Bolton's shoulder.

"Do you want me to handle this, sir?" the guard asked.

"No, no; I can take a critic."

The guard wandered off, but didn't go far, continuing to glance at Jack. Jack leaned forward over the desk, and Bolton was startled by the darkness in his eyes.

"I want to know where my friends are, Bolton. Bane's not here to tell me, and Lila won't. But you will. I'm sure you realize by now that I'm no longer scared to do anything to find out, don't you?"

"I'm impressed. Yes, I do realize that. Bane's taught you well. But you sound as though you almost think your friends are still alive."

"Where are they?" The violence was evident in his growl. Bolton sighed and picked up his pen again.

"You really need to know, don't you?"

Jack waited. Bolton stooped and gathered up the fallen books. "Then let's go."

Jack followed Bolton in his own car. The writer's Datsun left the Galleries car park and headed out of the city center. The afternoon was darkening. When they pulled up at traffic signals, he could see Bolton's face in the writer's rearview mirror, lit up by his dashboard lights, smirking back at Jack.

He'd left this a long time. But now things were coming to a head, and before he went for Bane, he wanted a few other things tidied away first. He winced. Joe and Nigel were not "things to be tidied away." They were his friends. He was sure they were dead, but that didn't stop him from needing to know how they had died and what had happened to the bodies.

Bolton was the obvious one to tell him; he knew he would get nothing further out of Lila. He could have threatened to kill her, but he had a feeling that even then she would just smile her cruel smile and get herself comfortable for the big event.

When he saw the poster advertising Bolton's signing session, he remembered the weak link in Bane's pantheon of monsters. He didn't even need to waste time searching for the writer's house. Just confront the bastard in Waterstones as he signed the atrocities he called books.

In a couple of days, he would find Bane. He knew where to look now. So, Bolton's job was simply to tell him some things he didn't know and maybe to pay for causing them to happen.

The Datsun was on the Bath Road, heading for Totterdown. Jack tailed him patiently. Bolton turned right off the main road, climbed a steep hill with sagging houses sliding down on either side. Reaching the crest, he headed for the Arnos Vale crematorium, finally pulling into a quiet terraced street alongside the overgrown cemetery.

The house the Datsun stopped outside was, from the outside at least, no different from any of its neighbors. Not exactly homely, not exactly seedy either. Jack guessed it was just a temporary abode, and the relevance of its proximity to so much death didn't escape him at all.

Bolton was walking up the short path to the front door. Jack parked his Fiat behind the Datsun, climbed out, and paused at the gate.

Bolton turned around, the door open. "Surely not hesitating now, my friend? I thought you wanted to know?"

Jack followed him into the hall. The wallpaper was gray and smeared. He could hear strident classical music blasting from upstairs. To the right of the hall, an open door spilled light onto the humped carpet.

"Not exactly a Des Res, but it suits our purpose." Bolton pushed his way through the door and led Jack into the living room. The black-bearded, nervous-looking man Jack had seen at his parents' funeral was sitting on a plain sofa, eating a bag of crisps and watching the ITV news. He looked up in twitchy alarm when Bolton entered, saw Jack, and gaped.

"I'm sure you recognize my housemate, Anthony? He's always watching the news; never misses a bulletin. He's afraid they're going to eventually realize what he did. But I keep telling him the police will grab him long before the media."

Jack stared at the man, and the sense of familiarity he'd felt upon seeing him at the chapel returned, more strongly this time. He gazed into those frightened but dark eyes and remembered at last. It was the man he'd seen on the television, mourning his butchered parents. Even from the objective distance of the TV screen, his eyes had told Jack what had really occurred. Only Jack hadn't thought about it until now.

Bolton ushered him to sit down next to Anthony. Jack stayed where he was, taking it all in. The television was large, dwarfing the small, untidy room. There were no ornaments or pictures on the walls. Boxes and crates were piled in corners. Everything had a temporary, makeshift air. Bolton was rummaging through a cardboard box next to the TV. He pulled out a small video camera and put it to his eye, aiming it at Jack.

The music from upstairs seeped through the ceiling, making the room seem even more confined and stuffy. There was a lingering reek of B.O. and something else more unpleasant hanging in the air. Jack realized it was emanating from the man called Anthony, and it was the rancid sweat of fear. Anthony was trying to watch Jack without being seen, twitching his head back to the TV when he thought Jack had noticed him. Jack waited.

Bolton lowered the camera as if it had proved an empty threat. He looked eager, his little eyes glinting behind the thick lenses. He was enjoying himself.

Jack crossed to stand in front of the television, blocking Anthony's view. The bearded man looked at him anxiously, then his eyes fled to a safe corner of the room.

"What was it like, Anthony?" Jack said, his own eyes grim and unfaltering.

Bolton raised the camera again. Anthony tried to rise from the sofa, white-faced. Jack pushed him back down.

"W-what?" The man was having difficulty talking. His eyes were dark with terror, not menace.

"Killing your parents. What was that like for you?"

Bolton moved in for a close-up. He spoke for the bearded man, never moving the camera from his eye. "You'll never know now, will you, Jack? Bane beat you to it. How does that feel? Do you feel robbed? Of your parents...or of the opportunity to kill them yourself?"

Jack turned slowly to face Bolton, reached out, and pushed the camera down. Bolton was all smirks as he placed it aside and crossed to another box against one wall. Debussy boomed from above, and the writer straightened up, a videotape in a plain cardboard sleeve in his right hand.

"I'm sorry I've kept you waiting. This is what you came for, I believe." He handed it to Jack. Jack stared at the fat man, then down at the slipcase in his hands. The white cardboard was crusted with dried blood. He threw it back at Bolton.

"You wanted to know," the writer said, kneeling before the small

VCR tucked beneath the television. "You needed to know."

Jack watched video snow fill the screen.

When it cleared, Jack was looking at Joe. Joe was standing in a semi-dark room, clutching a pizza box and peering toward the camera. "Come on then; let's do it," Joe said, the poor sound pickup making his voice thin and weak. "But you've still got to pay for the pizza." His expression was implacable as ever, but waiting there in the gloom in his Day-Glo uniform, he appeared to Jack suddenly, unbearably, vulnerable.

"As pranks go, I'll give it three out of ten..."

The screen went dark. Completely dark. Behind Jack, Bolton chuckled like a proud father viewing his child's first walk on tape.

Jack tensed. Although the screen was pitch-black, he could still hear the sound of Joe's breathing, or someone's breathing. There was a rustle and the sound of footsteps. Joe's?

The footsteps stopped. The breathing was louder, ragged. He thought he heard a whisper, but it could have been just another rustle of movement. Silence. Then a violent scuffle, followed by a sigh, then nothing else.

The hiss of the tape filled the room.

"Not very spectacular, is it?" Bolton said. "I apologize for the poor lighting, but you know how it is. Never mind, the next scene's a lot clearer."

The television screen filled with bright daylight. A garage forecourt, a Fiat parked next to the pumps. The camera wobbled toward the car, and Nigel was sitting patiently in the passenger seat, staring into space. The camera tracked around the Fiat, filming Nigel from different angles, although never from directly ahead of him. Nigel was oblivious to his video debut. He was doing things people do when they don't realize they're being scrutinized, and Jack forgave him everything. A close-up of Nigel's odd profile filled the screen. His head began to turn as he noticed someone out of the corner of his eye.

"Jack?" Nigel was squinting against the bright sunlight splintering through the passenger window.

Jack's right hand closed around the video camera Bolton had put aside and swung it in an arc. Bolton was still fawning over the tape and didn't see the blow coming until the last moment. The compact equipment slammed off the side of his skull, knocking his spectacles into an open cardboard box. Bolton fell, plaster coughing from the wall as he crumpled against it in a sitting position. Blood bubbled from the wound on his left temple. His eyes lost their focus for a second, then dilated as Jack stepped up to him, still holding the camera.

"You wouldn't be so stupid," the writer gasped, putting a podgy hand up to his head. "You've too much to lose."

Jack could hear screams coming from behind him. From the television. Whirling, he kicked the screen with his right boot. The tube exploded with a hollow pop. Glass sprinkled onto the rug. Anthony was cringing on the sofa, terror squeezing his eyes shut. Jack turned back to Bolton.

"If you kill me, the trip will be canceled; you'll never find Bane." His eyes lifted briefly to the ceiling. "Besides, you'd have to kill the twins, too, and you might not find that so easy." His unbearable smugness was back, ghastly under a runny makeup of blood.

"Did I ever tell you I'm going to make you famous?" The writer was gabbling now, as if slightly concussed. "I'm going to write a best-seller, all about you and Bane."

His voice was loud in the room; the classical music from upstairs had been switched off. Jack knelt in front of the fat writer, staring into his squirming eyes.

"You want to know where they are, don't you? I thought I'd made it rather obvious. You've been to the old Slaughter, according to Lila. She was going to tell you about it, so you could visit the place and thereby add to your paranoia. But you found it first—what gorgeous synchronicity." He touched a hand to the wound on his temple, winced. "No, they're not there. But if you'd looked carefully enough amongst the shambles, you would have noticed a clue as to their whereabouts."

He sniggered, wiping at the blood running down his face. "My idea, but then I always had a penchant for the cryptic. It was just an extra little bonus, really; you might pick up on it, or you might not. You see, the folk who lived near the old pub never had anything nice to say about a local girl, once a dear friend of mine. Julie, her name was. Julie Gannon. You obviously didn't notice my ironic little tribute when you went searching for your Joe."

His sniggers dried up. He must have noticed something in Jack's eyes because his smile became a wooden, cracked thing. "You can't hurt me, and you know it. I'm going to make you famous, I'm going—"

Jack rammed the elongated barrel lens of the camcorder into his mouth, forcing his head back against the leaking plaster. He continued shoving the narrow lens down the writer's throat, Bolton's teeth scraping on the hard plastic casing, his body bucking wildly. He held the fat man still with the weight of his own body, ignoring Bolton's snorts and frantic muffled cries. The writer had been wrong: there was nothing to stop him from killing Bolton.

Behind him, the door opened quietly. Jack glanced back over his shoulder, took in the twins watching him inscrutably, wearing nothing but identical purple culottes.

He went back to work on Bolton. One of the writer's front teeth slid down the casing and dropped to the carpet. The fat man's body thrashed beneath Jack's weight, but his awkward position in a corner of the room prevented him from gaining good leverage to wriggle free. Jack forced the long camcorder lens further down his throat and felt... nothing. No triumph, no satisfaction.

Nothing.

The twins made no move to stop him.

Julie Gannon is a whore.

Jack shone the torch on the spray painted message and swayed as a dizzy spin of hate and grief took hold of him. He put out a hand against the rotting door to support himself.

Just a game to them; people's lives reduced to a cryptic clue in a monstrous crossword. As soon as Bolton mentioned the name, he knew he'd heard it somewhere before. No, not heard it. Read it. Jagged graffiti on an old pub wall, spray paint on a locked door inside a dilapidated house in Fernbank Road, Joe's last pizza call.

Julie Gannon is a whore.

He tilted his head back, sucking at musty air. The blackness of the hallway pressed in, cobwebs groping for him like the fingers of ghosts. Something crept through his hair, inched down his neck, and was gone. He put out a hand, traced the grain of the wooden door, almost caressing it. Touched the knob, turned it slowly, like it was a door he was trying to open in a dream.

Locked.

The house creaked around him. It sounded like stifled midnight giggles to Jack. The house had been turned into an evil thing.

He leaned his face against the wood as if hoping to hear someone on the other side. But he wasn't listening.

He was crying.

CHAPTER THIRTY-SEVEN

Wellbury was dead.

Thursday was half-closing day in the small Cotswold town, and the long main street was deserted but for a knot of youths lurking outside the chemists. They glared at Jack as he drove past, exuding as much menace as they could, trying to make up for the fact that they were small-town yobbos and would never make it to the big city leagues. Jack ignored them, carried on around the bend that swept out past the church and the fire station and on toward an avenue of trees that marked the town's exit.

This time he wasn't fast enough to elude the memories. They grabbed at him as he passed the church. Bane had dragged him through the secret door behind the bell ropes and up the winding tower stairs, shut him in the bell chamber with the cobwebs and the skeletons of crows and the scurryings in dark corners. "Rats," Bane told him with a smile too old for his age. That smile had always seemed to the boy Jack to be a dead thing rotting away on his brother's face. It always signaled pain and terror to come.

Bane locked him in for the afternoon and part of the evening. Threw the key into a field of nettles. Jack had sat very still and listened to the scuttlings. He began to think they were coming from inside his own head after a while because he never saw anything. It hadn't been that dark at first. A forgotten dusty cobweb of a room, the great bells hanging solemnly, stained with what looked like blood but must have been rust. Then, as evening fell, it got very dark. He'd curled up in a ball, the scrabblings surrounding him, tears soaking into the dust.

By the time the vicar rescued him, armed with a spare key, he'd almost forgotten where he was, *who* he was. He'd never trusted churches since.

Jack grinned at the tower as he drove past. *That had been a good one, hadn't it, Bane?* His sobs had echoed in the stairwell as the vicar carried him away to safety. Perhaps they echoed still, trapped in the stone chimney forever.

Beyond the church, the bleak fields, gray rather than green in the heavy November light. And beyond them, the woods. He laughed again. That was your best effort, wasn't it, Bane? Remember that one? Of course, you do. That's why you tied me up in the dark in Pembroke: to remind me of when you played Let's Bury Jack Alive. Hours of fun for all the family.

Now Bane was playing Hide 'n' Seek. *I've nearly finished counting, big brother, and then I'm coming for you. Ready or fucking not.*

He pulled up alongside the small front garden. He sat for a while in the car, staring ahead at the road that wound its way through a copse and disappeared. He hadn't been here since he was...what? Sixteen? Slowly, he turned his head. Looked at the house.

A yellow police tape stretched across the gate. He read the notice asking for information from potential witnesses to the murders, and it felt like nothing to do with him. Just like the house itself.

He felt *nothing*. There'd been no need to run away from this for fifteen years. There was nothing here to scare him. Just a detached house built from Cotswold stone. Four windows facing him, a chimney, a garden path cutting between herbaceous borders toward the front gate. Just like a child's happy drawing of a house. Although definitely not one that Jack had ever drawn. His classroom sketches had always been skewed, crazy, the house lopsided, the windows red crayon wounds, the door a screaming mouth. He smiled at the memory of his primary school teacher looking at one picture, then looking at Jack. Her dismay was as fresh in Jack's mind now as if... Childhood *had* just happened yesterday; he could practically reach out and touch it. Like reaching out and touching the front gate.

He ducked under the police tape and walked up the path, and the house leaned over toward him like it was about to fall on him. He scratched at the lock with the key given to him by a hearty solicitor. All this was his now. This house of discarded memories, this house of tortured childhood.

He was being melodramatic now. He smiled again, wolfishly, and pushed the front door open.

Ghosts scurried away up the stairs, lost themselves in dusty gloom. The hall was still and quiet, a patch of daylight sneaking around the kitchen door the only break from shadow.

He glanced up the stairwell. He saw himself scampering up there as a child, terror ripe in his throat. Behind him, big brother. Or was it his father? Weren't they the same in many respects? And Jack, too, becoming more like them every day. He could taste the salt of the boy's tears.

A vase stood on a small table next to the coat rack. He gave it a grin that was more a snarl and reached out to turn it slightly on its pedestal. There was the crack, glued together, still holding after all these years. He'd been about eleven, hadn't he? He chuckled bitterly and remembered it falling, his father apoplectic with rage, his fist pounding, pounding. Pausing only to grab a walking stick from beside the coat rack, bringing it down on Jack like he was a mad dog.

I couldn't help it, Dad. It was an accident. Didn't mean to... Just brushed against it. Couldn't HELP it!

Jack, thirty years old, pushed the vase off the pedestal.

It exploded on the faded carpet. Jack stepped past, heading for the lounge, nudged his way through the door on the left of the hall, and there it was. Nothing to see. He could sense memories lifting like dust off a chair that's just been sat on and let them drift away. Not interested.

He looked at the furniture, the ornaments, the television, the paintings, the bookcase. He was wasting his time. There weren't even any outlines on the carpet to show where they'd died. The police had finished in here for now. Been over the place with every forensic instrument known today. Nothing. Jack could have told them whodunit, of course. *Oh, by the way... Let me tell you about my big brother, Bane.* But his brother had long since ceased to be, officially. Missing, presumed dead more than twenty years ago. And there were no such things as ghosts.

Coming for you, Bane... Coming soon.

He paused in the kitchen, tapping his fingers on the linoleum table. The farmer's clock ticked happily on the wall, a cozy family thing. Jack lifted it from its hook with his forefinger, let it tumble and crack in the sink below.

He looked through the window at the back garden. Puff's yellow and blue plastic ball was over by the rose beds, right next to the stiff paw rising from the soil.

He unbolted the back door and walked across the lawn toward the rose bushes, deadheaded by winter. The earth was smooth and undisturbed.

The growls of a digger came from over the garden fence, the yellow monster churning through the mud at the far edge of the building site. A builder wearing a protective helmet leaned out of a window in the nearest unfinished building, flicked cigarette ash down below, watched him curiously for a moment, then withdrew.

Jack stared at the rose bed, empty but for the dry bones of shrubs. He had a sense that the house was creeping up behind him, dragging itself forward on its concrete haunches, not prepared to let him escape again.

He could picture his father doing it, almost as if he'd seen it happen. Squeezing the dog's throat out here in the garden, his face bland as his big hands did their work. The little terrier's hind legs scrabbling against his killer's jeans. He imagined the floppy body dropped at his father's feet like an old rug no longer required.

Jack had learned a lot from his old man, hadn't he?

And from Bane, of course.

The builder was watching him again, leaning on the window ledge. Time to go, Jack.

If the house will let you.

He walked determinedly back toward the kitchen, and the past was just that, and the house was just a house.

CHAPTER THIRTY-EIGHT

She was dreaming of sex and death.

Sex and death and symmetry.

When she woke, she couldn't remember the details, and frustration pumped through her. She was stimulated, horny, aching for the things she'd been dreaming of, and they'd been taken away.

She lay on her side and stared into the darkness. Her skin was slimed with sweat, the thin sheet beneath the blankets fastened to her naked body like cellophane.

She peeled it off her and wiped a hand over her body, enjoying the sensual moistness of her sweat. The bedside clock beat out the hollow moments of the night, the hands pointing at ten past five. Morning, then, but you'd never have guessed it, it was so dark. Her hair felt like the wet end of a mop, the inside of her mouth hot and crusty.

Exasperated, she turned on her back, yanking the blankets in a deliberate attempt to wake her sister, whose soft breathing floated in the shadows beside her. The sound altered key slightly, became shallower, then trawled deeper waters again. She was alone with her itch. No one to scratch it.

Was that Bolton's snore she could hear from the room next door? She giggled. She didn't think ghosts could snore. She listened again, and there was nothing. Just the wind grumbling around the loose drainpipe outside.

She imagined herself squatting naked on the writer's face, making a shambles out of his throat with a pair of scissors. Pressing tighter with her thighs around his ears, the sweetness of approaching orgasm, one of the blades easing his windpipe away from his neck like a moist cable.

She would never sleep now.

She'd often thought about killing Bolton. Usually after screwing him, revulsion replacing undiscerning lust. She was sure her sister had contemplated the deed, too; they often shared the same fantasies. Of course, they did: they were twins. More than twins, some said— Bane said. More like two parts of the same person, split in two, living as two, but really only one. Did she believe that? Of course, she didn't. Her sister was different in many ways. Bane wasn't *always* right.

Bane.

The only man ever to reject their seductions. As if they weren't good enough for him. That only made the twins want him even more. But all *he* wanted was Lila. What did she have that they didn't? She wasn't so special. Looked like a carthorse, with her long face and coarse black mane. She thought she was above the twins, too. She wondered what Bane would do if they did things to his Lila... What would Bane *do?* Would he turn to them instead if they made a mess of his Lila? She grew hot at the thought. To fuck Bane would be like fucking the night, rutting with the dark itself. Shagging death. Bane was the *face* of death: gorgeous, living death. She would kill her own sister for the chance to sleep with Bane.

Bane.

He led them. They were his black flock; he was their shepherd, guiding them toward an orgy of murder and sex—total satiation. She knew he would relent to their charms only when they joined him in the darkness.

It felt like the end.

The thought was a sharp needle in her soul. It came out of nowhere, a scare in the dark, an insecurity born in the small hours. It left her feeling suddenly terrified and, despite her sister's presence next to her, very alone.

It felt like the end of everything.

She was sure her rapid breathing would wake her sister, but the dark hunch remained still, silhouetted against the slightly paler patch of the window.

She squinted her eyes at the curtains. There was something odd about that pale square. Shadows against the material, where shadows shouldn't be. Dawn coming behind them, making them slightly more solid. Chairs? There weren't any chairs near the window. The shadows were too tall anyway. Two shapes. She strained her eyes. They felt gummy with dried jam. Her heart paused for a rest behind the sweat now chilling her breasts. Beat again.

"I know you," she whispered at the two shadows.

They'd come again. *She* hadn't let them in, that was for sure. Her sister, then? They hadn't visited her for a long, long time. When *had* she last seen them? That first night in the psychiatric hospital, the twins had been placed in separate cells, pulled apart for the very first time in their lives. She'd been scared. Didn't know what the future held. And they'd come into her hospital cell. No, not *come* in; they'd just sort of appeared against the wall. She'd been locked in with them for the night.

She wasn't scared now. Perhaps she should wake her sister. But her sister hadn't seen them that other time. Another thought that *did* scare her: perhaps her sister might not see them now.

They were becoming clearer.

She thought she could see the color of his hair now. Peroxide blond? Couldn't see his eyes, though. No, of course, she couldn't; they'd taken them out, hadn't they? With a chisel. She tittered, held her hand up to her mouth to stop the noise. She could see the other shape—what was her name?

"Sally," she whispered, and a snigger rose again, heavy in her throat. "Sally's still a young girl. Never grew up."

Neither of the shapes moved, black against the dawn. The birds would be up soon, she thought, and they'd have to go then, wouldn't they? They'd look pretty silly hanging around in the daylight. See, I'm not scared, so why are you here?

Just shadows against the curtain, as dark as the wardrobe against the far wall, still holding onto the night.

But could she see little Sally's eyes? Were they watching her?

"Do you think I should feel sorry for you?" She was still whispering, not wanting to wake her sister. "I don't. You were just the first, and that doesn't make you special, does it? I don't feel *sorry* for you. We enjoyed what we did. We'd do it again too." Her voice was husky, dragged out of her throat.

You're not really there, are you? Fading. Dawn coming. She couldn't see Sally's mouth, what she'd done to Sally's mouth, to her teeth. *Poor* Sally.

"Why don't you say something...do something? You can't, can you? Just shadows. I fuck shadows, too, you know. Would you like that? Would you *fucking* like that?" She wasn't whispering anymore. Her titters broke out unrestrained. The two shapes were just stains on the curtain now, gray dawn light easing into the room. She could see the dressing table piled with clothes; she could see the wardrobe stepping out of the dark, could see her sister's naked back turned toward her. Just stains on the curtain, then. Goodbye. Come again any time.

Because I'm not scared.

Never was.

When the other sister awoke, she found her twin sitting up in the semi-darkness, her eyes turned toward the curtains.

Giggling.

CHAPTER THIRTY-NINE

"You are both completely... You're out of your minds. Stop this. Now. Before someone else gets hurt, or dead."

Sam was wasting her time. They were going; they were both going all right, and the fact that she knew—and *they* knew—there was something very bad about this trip didn't make the slightest bit of difference. They were going.

They were immovable on that point. It was like trying to budge a Sherman tank all on her own. She felt like crying from frustration and anger. They were not going to listen to her.

Behind the bar, she saw Lila. Watching them through the crowd of punters, when the drifts of dry ice allowed her to. Sam glared back but knew there was nothing to be gained from that particular game anymore. Lila was deadly serious. The emphasis being on deadly.

Dry ice shrouded the bar, and Sam turned back to her two friends. They shouldn't even be here. But Jack was determined to play this Bane's way for the moment, and Sam and Dennis had no choice but to tag along. At least this way they could watch over him.

"I'm going to do something now that's going to embarrass me, and it's going to embarrass you, so if you don't want me to do it, just tell me you've changed your minds and you're not going after all."

Jack looked at her with solemn, determined eyes; eyes that had looked into...what? Destiny? Whatever it was, it couldn't be good. There was tragedy there, and the darkness she'd become so familiar with recently. But Jack also looked prepared, and almost self-assured. He'd changed so much since she first knew him. She loved him desperately at that moment.

"You're going to your deaths."

Dennis laughed hoarsely. "Leave it out, Sam."

A roadie was speaking into the microphones on the stage behind them. One, two. One, two, two.

"We're going for a weekend break, that's all," he continued. "Don't get all melodramatic on us."

Jack held her hand under the table, squeezed it gently. Sadly. Dennis grinned and tipped his pack of Benson & Hedges upside down to shake a cigarette free. His grin looked shallow. Jack hadn't smiled all evening.

"Then you don't leave me any choice," she told them, fingering her glass of wine and turning slowly from Jack, quiet and grave, to Dennis, with his cocksure nonchalance. "*Please* don't go. I'm begging you now. I can go down on my knees if that's what it'll take."

Dennis looked away, uncomfortable. Jack met her imploring gaze, however, and held it, and somehow that was worse. Everything felt so final.

"Oh, fuck this!" Dennis stood up abruptly, suddenly angry. Sam looked at him and saw the fear smarting in the electrician's eyes.

"What d'you think you're trying on here, Sam? Just leave it, will you? You're talking a load of bollocks!"

"I'm telling you what you don't want to hear, Dennis. But I'm also telling you the truth. Bane and Lila have got something very nasty in store for Jack, and probably anyone who's with him. Don't go."

"I said *leave it!*" Dennis stomped off toward the bar, clutching his empty pint glass.

Jack squeezed her hand harder. "You're freaking him out, Sam. I've never seen him look so insecure."

Sam stared at the pack of Bensons left on the table. Even though she'd given up five years before, she desperately needed a smoke. "But I'm still not getting through, am I?"

"You've scared him. That means you are."

"But he's still going."

"That's Dennis. He can't turn away from a challenge. He's been looking for somewhere to run away to all his life. Always looking out for the big adventure: Dennis's Great Escape from Reality. Now he thinks he's found it, and the more you go on, the more determined he'll become."

"And you, Jack? What would it take to make you stay behind?"

He looked at her, and she didn't need an answer.

"Just macho bullshit!" she exclaimed, angry herself now. "It always comes down to the same thing, doesn't it? Why are men such wankers?"

He smiled faintly, finished his drink, and said, "It's not macho bullshit, Sam. This is something I've been heading for all my life."

"Now who's being melodramatic?"

One, two. One, one. Two.

The pub was bursting. Sam hadn't seen it as full as this since Opening Night. Apparently, all thirty tickets for the mystery tour had rapidly sold out. Dennis was lucky to get one. Sam didn't get it: where was the appeal? The unknown, she supposed.

The pub was full, that much was undeniable. Ticket holders celebrating the eve of the "trip to end all trips," their friends along to see them off in style. She caught Jack the Ripper looking at her, a glint in his eye, as well as on his knife. He was stalking a table of Rastas openly smoking joints the size of cannons. Were they going on the tour? How many in this spirited pub were looking forward to a weekend of near-the-knuckle thrills and a good laugh? They didn't know what to expect. Nor did Sam. It *was* a mystery tour, after all. But at least she had an idea. Should she warn them all? And have them laugh at her, call her a nut job?

How many laughing, cheerful people…?

One, one. Two.

More than that, anyway. But there were only two she cared about.

She saw Dennis returning through the crowds, carrying three drinks balanced in his hands. She hoped desperately that the electrician wasn't going because of her. Was she being vain, or was he going just to spite her, full of his own resentment—*Look what you made me do, Sam; it's all your fault if I don't come back.* That wasn't fair, though, was it?

He avoided her eyes as he sat down and handed them their drinks.

"So, is someone ever going to fill me in on this Sawney Bean shit?" he said, pretending to be cheery.

"You'll find out all you need to know tomorrow," Jack said darkly.

"But *I* won't," Sam said.

"You don't want to know."

"You think it'll scare me? You two scare me enough already."

"Then you don't want to hear anymore, do you?"

"I think you should tell Dennis what he's letting himself in for." Sam shot Jack a dangerous look: *It's up to you to stop him.* He gave her a firm look back: *It's too late for that.*

"I know who he was actually," Dennis grunted. He'd almost finished his pint already. "That Bean geezer. Some crazy bastard from Scotland. What's frightening about that? No shortage of them up there."

"Bane's obsessed with him," Sam said. "Why? You're the one with all the secrets, Jack. Let us in on it."

Jack waited a moment before answering. "Just because Bane's my brother doesn't mean I can see inside his skull. All I *can* say is that I'm pretty certain where we'll find him."

They waited for him to elaborate.

"Bennane Head," he said eventually. It was about as ominous a name as any Sam could think of. It sounded old and horrible. It sounded like Bane. It sounded right.

Dennis sniffed. "And where's that?"

"The Galloway coast, Scotland."

Sam said, "How do you know he'll be there? Something to do with Sawney Bean, right?"

Jack shrugged. "Put it this way: this magical mystery tour is no mystery to me. I know exactly where we're going."

"And now you've ruined the surprise for me as well," Dennis grumbled.

"Then there's no point in you going, is there?" Sam told him. "No point in either of you going."

"There's every point." Jack raised his glass. If it was at all possible, his eyes looked darker than ever. "Here's to Joe." Sam and Dennis hesitated. Jack waited until they raised their glasses uncertainly, then drank deeply. "And to Nigel." He raised his glass again.

Sam took a sip, and the finality of Jack's toast filled her with dread. Dennis had fallen silent. It was clear he still wasn't sure what to believe about his friends, nor was Sam, for that matter.

She raised her glass one more time. "And here's to you, Jack." She looked him straight in the eye, and there was no mistaking her meaning. She turned to Dennis, repeated the gesture.

Dennis laughed, but the laugh sort of trailed away. "I came out for a good time," he said. "Didn't think I was going to a wake."

They left their table and moved to stand beside a wooden pillar as the canned music faded and a crowd of expectant punters gathered before the small stage. The lights dimmed. A purple spotlight showed them the gruesome backdrop: a heap of bloody human torsos inside a cave, severed arms and legs hanging from hooks overhead, decapitated heads stacked against a wall like a display of gory pumpkins.

"Tasteful stuff," said a heavy metal warrior with a wide bald spot standing next to Dennis. Dennis grunted. It didn't impress him. Next to him, Jack had become tense and hunched, his face haunted. Dennis tried not to let it freak him. He waited for the band to appear, and the familiar foreboding snuggled down in his gut anyway, like a big worm curling up to sleep.

He'd been feeling it on and off for the last few days. Jack and Sam getting to him, he supposed, with all their morbid claptrap. But... Well, he had to admit this trip didn't feel good. That crazy Lila bitch was out there where the sun didn't shine. Proper under-the-stone job. She spooked him.

He could see her now, still sitting behind the bar, and was she looking at him? In his direction, anyway. Probably watching Jack. They had something between them for a while, of course, something strange and unhealthy. His own brother's girlfriend. Dennis watched her for a minute and decided sleeping with her would be like sleeping with a nasty, rotting corpse.

He was clearly mad to go on this trip because he was beginning to believe Jack was right: according to him, Bane was a psycho killer, maybe Lila, too, and psychos didn't usually make for the best tour guides. Bane was obviously waiting for them at the other end, and then what? A sick family reunion? It was all too bizarre and twisted for him. He couldn't get his head around it. Not at all.

He gazed at the painted backdrop on the stage. This was Jack's territory, all this horror and death malarkey; human corpse piles, bloody thighs hanging in the dark. So why *was* he tagging along? Looking out for Jack, to stop him from ending up a nasty corpse, too? Looking out for Jack 'cause Jack was his friend? Yeah, *right.*

Nobody was going to die. Sam was exaggerating. Maybe Bane *did* kill Joe and Nigel, Jack's parents, too, and maybe he didn't. What proof was there, for Christ's sake? They just had Jack's say so, and Jack wasn't all there these days.

The worm turned over heavily, queasily. It was simply a weekend break, that was all; a big adventure to take him away, out of it all, even if it was only for a couple of days. Something to do, wasn't it? God knew, there was little enough excitement to be found in his life lately. You had to grab what you could.

Even if it killed you.

Was that why he was going?

Did he want to die?

Let's face it; he had nothing to live for.

The worm was big and fat and snug down there next to his vitals. Now and again, it shifted, getting comfortable for the night, there to stay. He looked at Sam. She was watching Jack closely, worriedly. Dennis had been forgotten again. He turned back toward the empty stage, lit another cigarette.

I'm ready.

Let's go.

Sam put her right arm around Jack's waist as they waited. Her hand rested there innocently as she leaned in to kiss him. He responded reluctantly, his mind far away. She hated to do this in front of Dennis, but it couldn't be helped. As they kissed, her hand sneaked inside his right pocket, closed around the car keys she knew were there, and eased them out. Jack didn't notice a thing. She broke the kiss and, dropping the keys surreptitiously inside her jacket pocket, slipped her hand into his.

A nerve-shattering female scream broke out from the stack of speakers, then cut off just as abruptly. Something was going to happen. An expectant hush settled over the crowd, an uncomfortable, expectant hush.

Sam shared the general presentiment. It worsened when, glancing to her right, she saw two familiar faces mingled in amongst the crowd. She squeezed Jack's hand on impulse, and he tried to look reassuringly at her, believing her concern was caused by the imminent arrival of the repulsive band. She didn't disillusion him. No doubt he would be seeing more than enough of the twins over the weekend.

"Here they come," someone nearby said.

Beast, one hand gripping the microphone, the other loose at his side. Beside him, Bad Eddie, angular skull glowing in the red spotlight like a skin-headed demon. Bal, hunched away at the back, tickling cymbals with his drumsticks, ready for blast off. Tramp, dangling his guitar like he'd forgotten what it was for, to the singer's right. Beast waited. The crowd was silent now.

"Wanna hear a joke?" he grizzled into the mike. "What's got no brains, no hope, thirty tickets, and screams a lot?"

Tramp let a cheeky jingle escape his guitar. Beast turned to him with exaggerated remonstrance, left the punchline undelivered. He cocked his head theatrically. "Hark..."

Cue a sinister drum roll from Bal.

"...I hear the sound of *bad* things." No sooner had he finished the sentence than the band exploded into action and noise, a wild grenade lobbed willy-nilly, impacting on stage.

This was it; what made it all worthwhile. He took his stance, legs wide apart, clenching the mic like it was a woman's throat, and screamed his rage. *Let it all go.* The Beast was out and running, snarling, tearing, loping across the moors, the moon a silver spotlight picking him out, all fur and blood and fucking great claws, red-eyed wolfman bastard ripping through the flock. Come to old Beast, you fuckin' sheep. He felt his eyes behind the wraparounds popping, knew his pupils would be transformed into little hate holes, letting it all gush out from the burning brain behind. A bad man, a vile singer in a hate band, he chuckled inwardly as he roared—that's what he was. Playing to a crowd of punters, and were they enjoying this? Respectable and well-adjusted by day, they came here tonight to pretend they were really rock 'n' roll. He scanned them, the upturned, noise-blasted faces, white and pure, so fuckin' white, bleached by fright and shock. Is this what they fuckin' wanted? The thrill of hearing the soundtrack to their own base desires relayed back to 'em at five-hundred fuckin' miles an hour by a bunch of monsters tossed out of hell—that was how Bane described it, anyhow. Beast preferred to put his own slant on it: they was just fuckin' the twats up, and that was all he ever wanted to do. Just wanted to fuck 'em all up. Had to do it with hate riffs for now. Yeah, that would have to do for now.

This was ultimate fuckin' rock 'n' roll. It was what happened to rock if you dragged it down, put the bite on it, gave it a good fuckin' kickin'. Lost all the pretension, all the pose, all the *shit!* They weren't just bad to the bone; they was fuckin' the most evil bastards ever lived, ever played. In a minute, they would play *Dancin' with Mr. D*, and it would sound *nothin'* like the Stones' version. Jagger would fuckin' load his pants if he ever heard the Holocaust Freaks' cut. Fuckin' Richards, too. What had they ever done? Thought they was so bad back in the sixties, seventies, fuckin' with drugs an' sex and booze. *What did they fuckin' know?* They was choir boys. They'd fuckin' cry their eyes out if they ever met the Freaks.

Tramp swaggered to the lip of the stage, cut loose a razor-to-the-throat riff that brought Beast's grin out to play some more. Sympathy for the Devil? Old Nick sucked *their* dicks and *begged* 'em to use His tunes. And Bane should be paying 'em three times what they got already for treating these pukeheads to the real stuff.

He rocked back on his heels and let out a bellow of tonsil-torturing ferocity, a disemboweled grizzly howling out its death rage at the world. Then he hunched forward like Quasimodo, began throwing twisted, fucked-up fairy tale lyrics at the crowd, all intimate-like, tellin' 'em a little story with grumbling vocals kept low and ugly, crawling like hairy fingers right down their throats.

Bad Eddie rumbled out bass thunder, Bal gave a slow Gallows beat, and Tramp was prowling, chucking sharp, vicious riffs here and there into the audience. Beast could see Bane's brother and his friends down there in the audience pit, and he shuffled closer, still all crouched up like a troll, and told the fairy tales to *him*, stories of terror and people-eating and things that fucked you up in the night. He could see 'em working away at the bastard's mind, playing games with his head, and *he* could see he was being singled out and not likin' it at all, and he shouldn't let the Beast know that, 'cos now he wouldn't give him a moment's peace; just keep diggin', diggin', pickin' at the fucker like he was an itchy scab that he wanted to peel away, see what was underneath...

Tramp finished the song with a wail of feedback. Beast straightened to his full six-four, shrugged, and turned his back on the audience. Strolled off into the shadows like the Man with No Name after slaughtering a bunch of assholes with a brisk hand-fan across the hammer of his .45 Colt.

The Beast had peeled that scab, all right. He'd seen what was underneath, just a fleeting glimpse, but he'd seen.

The music opened Jack up, and the Beast had seen Bane in his brother's eyes.

He'd seen Hell, too. And that was only right, wasn't it?

Because that's exactly where they were all going.

PART IV: SLAUGHTERING TIME

CHAPTER FORTY

There were six vehicles between herself and the coach, one of them the band's scruffy van, and Sam tried to keep it that way, drifting along at just below seventy miles an hour, the needle rising and falling as the demands of the motorway traffic caused her to overtake or slow to compensate, always watching the coach.

By the time they passed the Manchester exit, her ankle was aching from the constant strain of keeping her foot on the pedal, and her neck was aching in sympathy. Her arms felt like plastic robot limbs attached to the steering wheel of the Fiat, divorced from her. She wanted to go to the toilet, and she was hungry. The coach, however, hadn't stopped once since leaving Bristol two and a half hours earlier. With each service station that hove into view, she hoped the coach would indicate a turn and roll up the exit, but it never did, heaving on its predetermined course, never deviating.

The M6 was a gray metal arrow pointing to Scotland. Her eyes were like hot little chunks of stone as she followed it. The dashboard CD player threw Bauhaus back at her as she drove, one of Jack's old discs, the music harsh and skeletal, prising through her ears, picking around in her brain. She would have turned it off, listened to a chat station, but at least it kept her awake, chiseling away at her drowsiness.

She wondered what Jack was doing right now as he sat on the coach. She pictured him all silent and moody, trying to switch himself off from Dennis's cynical banter, and a grim smile came to her lips, then died just as quickly. Maybe Dennis was quiet, too, contemplating everything she and Jack had told him. She'd seen his eyes at The Slaughter the previous night. She couldn't remember ever seeing Dennis spooked before. Surly, spiteful, aggressive, yes. But never spooked. She suddenly, desperately, wished the coach would break down, veer off the road onto the hard shoulder so she could pick up her friends and whisk them off back to Bristol, have a drink in a *normal* pub, have a laugh about it all.

She knew that wasn't going to happen, though.

She felt very cold inside thinking about it, as if a ghost were cupping her heart in a chilly fist. Why was she doing this? Chasing a coach from one end of the country to the other? That was a good question, and considering it, she realized that out of all three of them, she was the only one who had a decent reason for going on this trip. She wasn't doing it for revenge like Jack, or for thrills like Dennis. She was doing it because she cared. She didn't want Jack to die—the ghost fist crushed tighter at the thought—and she didn't want Dennis to die. She loved them both, albeit in very different ways. This was the most important thing she'd ever done in her life, and it made her feel alive, filled with vital purpose. She *cared.* She was going to save them. Replacing the butch hero in all the romances, she was going to sweep in at the last moment and rescue Jack and Dennis from the claws of the evil villains.

Real fear gripped her, hard. Wake up, girl. This ain't no story; you're screwing around with something very, very serious here. She felt the pull of normality, safety, everything she'd ever known and trusted back south. *All right, you had your moment of reckless bravery; you can pat yourself on the back and say you did your little bit. Now cut the crap and go on home. Ring Sue and go out for a drink, have that laugh you promised yourself. You really don't need this. Jack and Dennis got themselves into it, despite all your begging; now they can bloody well get themselves out.*

She carried on driving, the miles rolling up the dash counter in front of her, because she cared.

Eventually, the coach did pull in. They'd left the purple-brown ramparts of the Lake District behind, the motorway churning upward past magnificent thrusting peaks that filled her with thrilled sadness as she remembered holidays past; Sam, smiling, innocent, ten years old and blissfully content with her family, not a worry in the world beyond blisters on her feet from too much fell walking and wondering whether she would get to see any telly in the hotel each evening.

The coach had muscled on, and she imagined Jack blind to the sweeping splendor, his mind focused on one single purpose, three hundred miles of tunnel vision.

When the motorway leveled out again, and the blue sign ticked off the half mile to the next services stop, the left-hand indicators began flashing on both the coach and its obedient pet van, now four vehicles ahead of her.

Sam eased up on the accelerator, slid off the M6, and glided along some distance behind the two vehicles as they nosed toward the coach bay. She turned into the car parking area and pulled into a space, sitting for a while with her hands still on the steering wheel, engine droning, watching the coach rumble to a halt in the next bay. She wondered, not for the first time, if Jack and Dennis had spotted her following them. It didn't really matter. If Jack came over now and demanded she turn back, she would simply tell him where to go. But then, she reflected, he was going there already. He would have to knock her out and tie her up to stop her.

She waited. The band was the first to emerge, dropping out of the van like dirty fleas shaken off by a grumpy animal. The singer joined them from the coach, having been elected to drive the tourists. People began jumping off the vehicle: bright and breezy students; a group of punks, their early-80s worldview firmly nailed to their crusty masts; nonchalant heavy metal lads, guffawing as they swaggered away from the coach; a gaggle of casually dressed curiosity seekers. A bit of everything, really, Sam reflected. She'd watched them boarding the coach that morning while waiting for Jack and Dennis to join the tour before sneaking back to the flat and discreetly borrowing his Fiat—she had no car of her own.

Sam counted them as they peeled away from the vehicle, fifteen, twenty, twenty-eight. There'd been thirty tickets in all. She waited, and there was still no sign of Jack or Dennis, and she began to feel helpless and suddenly very frightened—which was ridiculous because nothing was going to happen to them here, in the busy rest area.

Then Dennis appeared, leaping out of the coach, stretching his back and arms, and looking around dazedly. Jack was not behind him.

Sam switched off the engine, fighting an urge to get out of the car and run over to Dennis and ask him what was going on. Jack would be staying on board, of course, playing this strictly by his own rules, and they didn't include allowing himself even the luxury of grabbing a coffee and a bite to eat at the service station. She felt a flush of irritation. Silly bastard!

She tensed as she noticed more signs of movement at the coach door. The twins. They followed the rest toward the refreshment area.

She'd noticed earlier that Bolton wasn't on the coach. She couldn't remember seeing him at the pub the night before either. That left only Lila on board, alone with Jack. Irrational jealousy spiked within her, and she flushed it away, angry and tired. Then Jack appeared in the doorway and she relaxed her grip on the steering wheel. She watched him saunter toward the building, stopping once to look back. At her? No, at the coach. Lila was standing on the step, following him with her gaze, a cruel smile as ever on her lips.

Sam reached for her thermos flask, pulled the cup off the top, unscrewed the cap, and poured herself a steaming mug of coffee. Her hurriedly made sandwiches were in the dashboard compartment, sweaty and curly in their cellophane wrapping. She sipped her coffee and nibbled the cheese and chutney sandwiches without tasting either, watching the coach long after Lila had disappeared back inside.

Twenty minutes later, the trippers began returning to the vehicle. Jack with Dennis, walking stiffly, warily, his poise that of an antelope sniffing the wind. Dennis looked grumpy and on edge. It didn't exactly look like they were having a ball.

She watched them board the coach and wished she could join them. But that would be stupid; someone had to keep a safe distance. She forced all conjecture out of her mind because she didn't know what would happen when the coach reached its destination. She didn't know what the hell she was going to do if anything *did* happen, but at least she would be able to watch everything, hopefully without being seen, and go for help if need be. That was the plan, anyway. It wasn't much of one.

The coach and its attendant van trundled out of the parking bay. Sam gunned the engine, waited until the vehicles were rolling down the exit ramp, and then moved slowly to follow, allowing four cars in between herself and the van. The journey continued.

The baleful, continuous note of a horn plucked her head up, slamming her eyes open. She was veering over the hard shoulder, mere yards from the guardrail. She corrected her course frantically, heart out of control. Cars passed her, drivers' faces turned toward her scornfully. She shook her head to clear it, thumbed the music up louder, rolled the window down a bit more despite the cold.

She searched for the coach and saw it topping a rise, now at least ten vehicles ahead. She ought to stop for more coffee but couldn't afford to get farther behind. She studied the next blue sign as it whisked past: Carlisle 27 miles. She glanced at her watch: 2:21. God, she'd been on the road for nearly four and a half hours.

Shortly after a sign informed her there were only nine miles to Carlisle, she had her next episode of fun. The car bucked madly to the right, lurching over as if preparing to sink. She fought the wheel gamely and dragged the car onto the hard shoulder, panic squeezing her. Blow out. She leaned her head on the steering wheel and wanted to cry from sheer frustration. Instead, she banged the wheel, twice, bruising her hand and doing absolutely nothing to help her situation. God, God, *God!*

She climbed out, the cold seizing her through her overcoat, and looked at the deflated front offside[21] tire. Stared at the rip for a dejected moment before coming to the conclusion that it certainly wasn't going to mend itself. Her gaze followed the motorway upriver. The coach had disappeared into the hazy perspective of the M6. The draught from passing cars buffeted her, throwing her hair around, adding to her frustration.

Sighing, she crossed to the boot hatch and yanked it open, shoving old shoes, ripped jeans, and plastic bags filled with battered CDs out of the way so she could lift the rubber sheeting and get at the spare wheel. She'd helped Sue do this once a couple of years ago. She undid the center nut holding the spare in its well and tugged the wheel free, bouncing it down on the road beside her. She paused for a rest, hoping no gallant passerby would come charging to her rescue; she might just tell them where to stick their gallantry the way she was feeling right now. She was quite competent herself, thank you very much.

It was as she was jacking up the car that a knight in shining armor did indeed appear, pulling up behind her, his charger a gleaming red Porsche. This particular knight was a smug and carefully good-looking salesman type watching her with a superior smile from behind the windscreen. Sam cursed and waved him on, grasping for the wheel brace. She heard the driver's door snap open and groaned, feeling all vestiges of patience draining rapidly.

---

[21] Driver's side

"No!" she barked as the man strolled up to her, the complacent air of one who has just arrived in the nick of time to put the world to rights breezing off him along with his potent aftershave. He halted in his tracks, anchored by the anger in her voice. Sam sighed and said, "Sorry, I didn't mean to bite your head off, but I can manage, thank you."

The man studied the torn wheel, the spare she was spinning into place, and lastly, Sam herself, before smirking patronizingly and returning to his car. She heard him mutter something as he climbed in and was sure she caught the words "ungrateful bitch" before the door slammed and he started up the engine. She flipped him two fingers just in case and continued tightening the nuts.

It was 3:16 before she reached Carlisle, the coach nowhere in sight. She pulled up on a double yellow line outside the Nat West bank and reached into the back seat for the road map. She felt drained of life, arms, neck, buttocks, and legs aching with strain. At least the cold air squeezing through her slightly open window kept her awake. She had a feeling of having traveled beyond her limits, of being on the brink of something she couldn't handle—pushing past the threshold of the unknown. It was far from comforting. She had no idea where she'd be sleeping that night. No idea of anything beyond chasing after Jack. Crazy, crazy. She felt so very far from home and so very alone in that moment. The Saturday afternoon bustle of Carlisle's picturesque city center only intensified her sense of isolation. But she was also wasting time, indulging in these apprehensions. The coach already had a good half-hour lead on her.

She checked the index at the back of the road atlas, forefinger gliding down the columns of names until it rested on Bennane Head. She found the appropriate page and studied the coastline as if it might tell her something beyond merely locating the coach's destination for her. It reassured her to see how far off she still was, but that attitude was futile because Jack, of course, would be closer. Bennane Head, despite its baleful name, looked harmless and distant on the map, a tiny headland near the small town of Ballantrae. Maybe two to three hours' drive.

She traced the route and flung the atlas onto the back seat, switched the engine on, rammed the gear stick into first, and pulled out into the whirl of traffic. She sailed around a roundabout twice before taking the correct exit for Dumfries, and then set her sights on eliminating the miles between herself and her goal, mind bent on one purpose, trying to shut out all other concerns.

She pulled over once, at a BP station to fill up, thanking the cashier tersely and walking back to the Fiat, grim-faced and bone-weary. She wondered what they were doing on the coach, what Jack was thinking. She wondered if the trippers were bored yet of the seemingly endless mystery tour.

Dumfries came and went, a river sliding sad and gray in the last hour of daylight beneath majestic bridge arches. The road went on, heading for Ayr by what she hoped was the more direct route, even if it wasn't the major one. She finally ejected the Bauhaus CD and flung it into the back, groping for a fresh source of music. Her left hand netted The Damned in the little pocket between the front seats. She fitted it into the player. *The Black Album.*

Four-fifteen and still driving, dusk creeping around the car, erasing the voluptuous countryside. Cows blended into the background, hedges dimmed against the darkening sky, copses became spreading patches of shadow beyond the roadside. Something began to rise in her with the coming of twilight.

Dread.

Pure and simple.

Night coming.

CHAPTER FORTY-ONE

Shortly after leaving Dumfries, Lila started handing out skulls.

The passengers had been becoming increasingly restless, weary of the journey. Most of them hadn't expected it to go on this long. Some were pissed on cans of booze and boisterous with it. Others had fallen asleep while the rest grumbled amongst themselves or suffered in silence. Lila had used the coach microphone only twice during the tour so far: once, to archly welcome them on board, and secondly, to announce the services break. This time she promised them in dark, theatrical tones that their journey was entering its final stage. Putting the mic down, she brought out the skulls, and the grumblings promptly and dramatically ceased.

Jack watched her move down the aisle, the twins helping her, passing dirty clumps of human bone with earthy teeth and cracked eye sockets to the passengers, one per pair of seats. The trippers received their gifts with dubious revulsion for the main part, although some were clearly intrigued. Lila caught Jack's eye as she advanced with her box of skulls like an usherette clutching a tray of ice cream treats and smiled enigmatically. She was wearing an old-fashioned black dress complete with ruffles and frilled cuffs, girdled by a belt of antique brass. Her raven wig curled beneath her pointed chin, and her green eyes glimmered. She looked stunning. Before she reached Jack's position halfway down the coach, she had to return to the front for another box. Jack heard a mixture of uncertain laughter and disgusted sound effects from the trippers as they examined their grisly souvenirs.

"I'd have settled for a brochure and a free mug myself," Dennis said, then lapsed into silence. There was a nervous grin on his face, disturbingly redolent of the grins on the skulls being handed out around them.

Lila was approaching them. She gave a skull to a couple of students on her way. One of them turned the relic over curiously, then asked Lila, "Are these real?"

Lila looked down the aisle, searching for Jack before replying. "They're old friends of ours. We thought we'd bring them along for the trip."

"That's well-sick!" came a voice from farther up the coach. The student who'd asked wanted to know more, his face pinched with bewilderment and fascination.

"Where did you get them?"

"Bane collects them. It's a little hobby of his. Quite harmless, I assure you." She moved on, still watching Jack, handing out skulls to the delightedly disgusted passengers.

Jack had a vision of a broken pub puddled with darkness. SLAUGHTER OF THE INNOCENTS, blood-red graffiti on stained, peeling walls, and R.I.P MUM. *People die in here, mister.*

Julie Gannon is...

He could have smashed the door down, entered the room, and found out the truth. But he could already see them in there in his imagination, and that was enough. He didn't want to see them in the flesh, didn't want to be manipulated like a pawn into observing his dead friends, wouldn't give them the satisfaction of hurting him even more. If he *had* gone inside, he would have known, wouldn't he? He would have his proof. Would he have been able to control himself? Would he have been able to stop himself from killing them all—Bolton, Lila, the twins? And what then? The tour would be off, the game over. It would be Jack who was arrested. And he wouldn't be able to go after Bane.

He realized Lila was standing over him, grinning like she could read his mind.

She showed him the empty cardboard box in her hands. "Oh, look, I'm all out of skulls. Not enough dead people around, I suppose. Don't worry; we can always change that." She rested one hand on Jack's knee. He picked it up slowly and let it go again, expressionless. Her grin widened.

"By the way, you might have noticed Roderick and Anthony are missing out on the trip. Really, if you're going to start something, Jack, you have to see it through. Didn't you ever learn that at school? The twins had to finish the job, clear up your mess. But all's well that ends well. Bolton won't be writing any more shit books." She lifted her hand to stroke his chin with her forefinger, and he shook his head away, refusing to be baited.

"Pity. That you didn't have the guts to finish it, I mean. The twins told me you started off so well. They told me how he tormented you, so I didn't mind them indulging themselves afterwards. I'm sure Bane won't miss Bolton now." She turned her back with a swish of her hips and returned to the front of the coach. Dennis stared at her backside as she went, then turned to Jack with a troubled expression.

"What did she mean, finish the job you started? Is Bolton...?"

Jack remembered what it had felt like. It would have been so *easy*. It had felt right; God, it *was* right to do it. For a moment, he'd been someone, *something* else that knew no control or order. If killing a small animal in the woods had been good, killing Bolton would be so much better, robbing him of his sordid, pointless life, watching the cruel intelligence slip away from his eyes.

Jack had stared into those eyes, wide with real fear for the first time in the writer's life. And let him go.

"Forget it," he told Dennis, staring out the window as the spread of green fields gradually became draped with dusk.

"I'd like to, my old mate. But the problem is, I'm beginning to believe all this loony stuff you've been spouting."

Jack looked at him and didn't know what to say. His friend's hardened cynicism was fracturing. The insecure teenager he used to be was showing through the cracks.

"You shouldn't have come, Dennis," he said simply.

The twins had finished dishing out skulls and were now distributing A3-sized photocopied booklets to each passenger. They, too, were dressed for the occasion in matching short crimson dresses revealing long, slender legs and sleek thighs. Their expressions, gestures, even their positions in the aisle in relation to each other, were purely symmetrical as they doled out the booklets to opposite sides of the coach. It was as if a long mirror were stretched down the aisle, reflecting one image exactly. It was a choreography they'd obviously spent years perfecting. Jack wanted to throw a spanner in their clockworks, throw them out of sync, make them human instead of wind-up dolls. Instead, he accepted the booklet handed to him without looking up at all.

Dennis seized his almost gratefully, as if it might add some sanity and sense of proportion to this trip into the unknown.

"No expense spared, I see," he quipped with false jollity, flicking through the smudged booklet. Jack glanced at the cover of his. *The Horrible Tale of Sawney Bean.* A poorly photocopied image of the flyleaf Lila had given him at the funeral accompanied the title. A greaser with a belly like a petrol tanker barged past him after returning from the toilet at the rear of the coach, causing Jack to drop the booklet. It slid under the seat in front of him, and he left it there.

Darkness had spread outside the coach like a widening ink stain, blotting out everything. The coach lights flicked on for the trippers to read their booklets, and Dennis chuckled sourly over his. Jack felt tied up inside, like Houdini meeting his match: he couldn't escape from himself—Bolton had proved that.

"So, *this* is what it's all about," said Dennis.

Jack looked at him, and then at the booklet in his hands.

"Apparently."

"We've all paid twenty quid to go on a six-hour coach journey— just to see some smelly cave that once belonged to a dodgy geezer who ate people?"

A young man with long, dyed-black hair sitting with his girlfriend in seats across the aisle grinned at Dennis and Jack. "Great, innit?"

Dennis groped for the cigarette packet in his denim jacket and lit one, turning to Jack. "Did you notice he said that without the slightest trace of irony?" His hands were a little shaky as he held the Marlboro to his lips.

Jack watched the goth couple. They looked as though they were genuinely enjoying themselves. The young man's face was crisp and youthful. His eyes were wide and unclouded by cynicism, looking forward to Hammer Horror jinks and larks, and maybe a good piss-up, too. His girlfriend was small, cuddly-plump, with a cheerful prettiness and trusting blue eyes that clashed startlingly with her dark, spiky coiffure. Jack suddenly, painfully, envied them their hope and innocence. Then he remembered where they were going and what might be waiting for them.

He should be warning them. Warning everyone.

Warn them of what? They wouldn't listen. He had no idea what to expect himself—apart from Bane. Did Bane and Lila want everyone's blood or just his? But then, if they simply wanted Jack dead, why hadn't they killed him before? In the garage at Pembroke? Upstairs in The Slaughter? They'd had plenty of opportunities.

They wanted to do it in style, of course. Bane wanted to rid himself of his hated kid brother in a grand gesture with thirty innocent tourists thrown in for seasoning.

He shook the thoughts away; they were fruitless and well-worn. He'd been thinking them for over four hundred miles, and they always led to a dead end—and Bane's gloating face.

Warn them of what?

There was the rub.

Dennis had finished the potted history booklet and looked unimpressed. He crumpled it into a ball and lobbed it toward the front of the coach, aiming at the biker driver but missing him by a good few feet. He nudged Jack. "Hey, isn't it me who's always supposed to be the mean and moody one? Speak to me, for God's sake! Remind me I'm alive!"

Jack didn't respond.

The road was serpentine, looping through steep countryside, the coach laboring up inclines and around sharp bends. Jack could make out the silhouetted hunched backs of domed hills out there in the night, as well as the occasional isolated specks of light from lonely houses. Now and then, the coach would grumble through small towns and villages, deserted in the November chill, cozy glows filtering through closed curtains as families settled down to watch Saturday evening television. They made him feel lonelier than he'd ever felt in his life, even though he was sitting next to his best friend in a coach filled with people. They made him wonder about Sam, back at her flat, and wondering if he would ever—

Forget it. Just don't think about it, or you mightn't be able to get through this. Might want to jump off the coach and run, just like...

Something hit him, a memory like a punch in the gut—*or a punch in the arm.* His father's fist swinging, striking his elder brother on the shoulder as the two children sat in the back of a car on a curve of road just like this one, above a hillside just like the one he could vaguely make out beyond the window.

And his brother opening the car door... *Yes! Go on! Jump!*

They had arrived. He knew that beyond doubt.

And like Bane, he'd been here before.

CHAPTER FORTY-TWO

During the coach journey, Dennis had taken a couple of sly slugs from his hip flask when Jack wasn't watching. He didn't want his friend to think he was anything less than the fearless, cynical ex-Legionnaire, did he? Only a couple of swigs, mind you: two or three, just to stoke his courage, keep him confident and in control. Jack hadn't noticed; probably thought the stink of whiskey was alcoholic halitosis from the night before. But as the coach slowed after taking a sharp turn and lumbered off the road onto a gravel lay-by, Dennis suddenly felt the urge to hit the flask hard and sod what Jack thought.

The fact was, Dennis felt anything but confident and in control. Yeah, he was scared. *Okay, Jack? It worked: you freaked me out.* He glanced at his friend, who was peering fiercely through the window at the night. He looked like a rabbit nailed to the road, eyes wide and dark, body tensed. Dennis nudged him, and he whipped around, a dangerous look on his face, lips drawn back from his teeth.

"Take a slug of this; it looks like I'm not the only one who needs it, after all."

Jack took the flask and tilted it against his lips, a long gulp. His expulsion of breath came with a defiant grin, though his eyes looked like...like weird, dead things. *Freaking me, Jack!* Dennis took the flask back and treated himself to another fortifying slurp.

"I've been here before, Dennis."

The trippers were all staring through the windows, vainly trying to make something out of the darkness. Apart from a chattering generator and a set of traffic lights glued on green, there wasn't a lot to be seen. Lila was climbing out of her seat at the head of the coach and fiddling with the microphone. Dennis lowered the flask, looked at Jack.

"Why didn't you say?"

"Because I didn't know until now." Dennis could see Jack's ghostly reflection as his friend strained his eyes to see out. He suddenly felt terribly afraid he was going to lose him. He took another hit of whiskey.

"We were on holiday...a summer holiday in Scotland. Dad's idea. I was only seven." He cleared his throat, which was dissolving into silt.

"And?"

Jack turned around to face him. "We drove past here. I remember it very clearly now. This is where big brother said goodbye to his family."

Dennis peered beyond his own pale reflection but couldn't see past the night.

"I remember praying he'd bust his neck as he fell," Jack continued, reaching for the flask and then changing his mind. Resolution replaced the weirdness in his eyes, and he faced the front of the coach, where Lila was preparing to address the passengers. "They never found him."

"*He* found *you*, Jack, me old mate."

"Welcome to Bennane Head," said Lila, evil unchained in her smile.

As the trippers began to assemble on the gravel outside the coach, a fresh wave of grumbling began to make itself heard. Jack and Dennis walked past Lila and the twins without looking at them and stepped down onto the grit. They waited, stiff in the chill wind gusting over the cliff tops that reared darkly against a starless sky. It was ferociously cold here, and as dismal and unwelcoming a spot as any Dennis could think of. The trippers were watching the four bikers lugging their equipment from the van toward the edge of the headland, and Dennis could tell they were beginning to feel cheated.

"You mean we came all this way just to see the band play another gig?" grumped a skinhead with bright blue jeans. "Coulda fuckin' done that back at The Slaughter. Where's the nearest boozer, for fuck's sake?"

"Jesus pissin' Christ," a heavy metal girl near Dennis whispered. "This 'as gotta be the coldest place on Earth." She was hugging herself, as were most of the trippers, and looking more than a little miserable. Welcome to Bennane Head...

Dennis watched the drummer uncoil a length of cable and attach one end to the generator, muttering away to itself near the traffic lights. He returned after a while to drag the rest of the cable toward the bulky amplifiers being arranged by his mates in the grass beyond the torn fence.

"So, what happens now?" Dennis's breath was a phantom swiftly ripped apart by the wind.

Jack didn't respond. He was watching the grassy line of the headland and the plunge of blackness to their left where the hillside fell away into a gully. The headlights of the coach and the green glow from the traffic signals were the only relief from the dark. But as they waited, the guitarist began carrying armfuls of logs and branches from the luggage compartment at the side of the coach, erecting a bonfire near the huddle of amplifiers and musical instruments. The drum kit clattered and chimed as the drummer swiftly assembled it. Lila appeared in the coach doorway, surveying the proceedings with regal interest.

"Is this where we're spending the night?" called out a horrified tripper with sideburns stretching toward his lips. He squeezed his pinched-looking girlfriend to him for warmth. "Because if it is, I want my money back. Promptimondo."

A rocker joined in the protest, "It ain't exactly 'weekend accommodation' like it says on the ticket."

Lila smiled, her hair windblown tendrils. "You didn't think you were coming here to *enjoy* yourselves, did you? Oh, dear. No, that wasn't the idea at all."

The crowd obviously thought she was being her usual ironic self, and there were a few tired laughs. Dennis watched her pale face, whipped by hair as she outstared the crowd, and had to admit she was fascinating. He found himself envying Jack his more intimate knowledge of this horrendous, sexy creature, then realized what he was thinking and self-disgust flushed the fantasy.

As if to mollify the crowd, the twins emerged from the coach carrying trays of glasses filled with what looked like dark wine. The trippers reached for the offerings, anxious to get their money's worth out of the tour. Dennis realized they would grab anything that was going.

The bonfire was lit behind them, and with the flames came the first guitar pluckings and microphone testing as Holocaust Freaks prepared themselves for their impromptu gig. The bonfire was about five feet high and sparsely sprinkled with petrol. Flame bloomed up in a curling streamer as the wind caught it, hurled it into the night. The shivering crowd moved closer gratefully, Dennis and Jack with them, eager to banish the chill from their bones. Above the rumble of the crowd and the noises from the sound check, Dennis heard the distant swell and boom of a restless sea from way down below them in the darkness. The wind blustered over the edge of the cliffs thirty feet from the bonfire and charged the crowd, spraying sparks like clouds of fireflies.

Dennis was feeling better as the fire restored warmth to his numbed hands and face. He finished the whisky flask, and his earlier fears seemed childish and unwarranted; the sinister conclusion of the tour they'd been so worked up about was just another gig. The alcohol in his system made him light-headed and almost cheerful. He watched the twins making their way through the crowd with the drinks and wished they would hurry up and get to him.

"So, where's Big Bad Brother?" he asked Jack, clapping his hands together melodramatically.

Wind calling mournfully from the cliff tops was his only reply.

Jack said nothing. He sensed his friend was becoming more than a little tipsy and knew he'd have to keep a closer eye on him.

He was back at Bennane Head after over twenty years. The cave would be somewhere below his feet. Waiting for him. A doom chord from the guitarist vibrated through his bones, startling shadows of fear inside him. Jesus, he hadn't even brought any weapons. Not so much as a pen knife. Going to fight them with spiteful words, are you, Jack?

"At last!" said Dennis with alacrity. The twins were beside the electrician, one of them holding a tray with two drinks left on it: a clear glass and a black goblet.

The twin without the tray handed the clear glass to Dennis. She picked up the black goblet and offered it to Jack.

"Don't drink it, Dennis!" Jack said sharply.

"Hey, how come he gets the special treatment?" Dennis hadn't heard his friend; he was too preoccupied with the black goblet in Jack's hand. The twins watched them silently. Jack slowly tilted the goblet, let the black liquid inside pour onto the grass at his feet.

"Behave, Jack! I would have drunk that!" Dennis swayed a little. To make up for his friend's wastefulness, he tipped his own glass to his lips and gulped.

"*Dennis!*" Jack slapped the glass away from his mouth. It rolled at the twins' feet.

"What the *fuck?!*"

"I told you not to drink it!" Jack waited for some reaction from the sisters, but their expressions were bland and inscrutable as ever. They turned and headed off toward the bonfire.

Dennis was about to protest further, the whiskey slowing his re-actions. Then he stopped and put a hand to his throat. "It tastes weird," he spluttered. "Like..." He looked up at Jack and fear cleared away the alcoholic glaze from his eyes. He doubled over, forced a finger down his throat, but succeeded only in releasing a few dry heaves and a string of spittle. He straightened up, face pale, eyes fraught with doubt. "Bane gave you mushrooms, didn't he?"

"Did you swallow any?" Jack asked, already knowing the answer.

Dennis was groping at his throat, looking like he was expecting a heart attack any moment. "Jesus wept. The last thing I need right now is a trip!"

"You'll be all right," Jack said, hoping he sounded more reassur-ing than he felt. "You didn't swallow much." He searched for Lila, spotted her talking to the band, the twins at her side, their stewardess work all done. "It's okay," he told Dennis. "It looks like the band's drinking it, too." As he watched, the twins reached for their own glasses and sipped. Only Lila abstained, gazing out toward the dark sea beyond the cliffs, oblivious to the singer rumbling in her ear.

Jack patted his friend's shoulder and left him for a moment, making his way through the throng of tourists who were sipping their strange wine, not unappreciatively, and approached Lila.

She turned, sensing his presence, and took his left hand in both of hers. Her skin felt sickly smooth and clammy, like a python's hide.

"You needn't have worried about your drink," she told him. "The others might find theirs a little odd, but why would I want to do any-thing to you?"

He pulled his hand free of hers, and she let it slowly slip from her grasp. He glanced at the singer, gulping at his glass enthusiasti-cally. The twins sipped daintily beside him.

The singer raised his glass to Jack. "We got to *see* hell if we're to fuckin' raise it."

Jack noticed Lila's enigmatic smile and a shiver of fear rippled through him. He got the feeling she knew something the singer didn't.

"Is he waiting in the cave?" Jack asked, his voice low, almost nonchalant.

Lila's smile dropped away. She looked at him for a moment, and he sensed a cold excitement bubbling beneath her surface calm. She strode slowly away, toward the clutter of instruments waiting before the bonfire. Jack watched her move: sinuous, measured steps, her left leg ghost pale beneath the slit in her dress. He felt a pang of the old desire, like the memory of a cobra's bite, and quickly buried it away inside himself.

The band had taken up their positions, standing ready, clockwork figures waiting to be wound up. The singer's hand rested on the shaft of his microphone stand. Lila raised her right arm in front of them, let it drop.

The band began to play.

The trippers were already clustered around the fire seeking warmth, a captive audience. Jack rejoined Dennis as the first thunderous chords were thrown out into the night. The flames coiled up and whipped around like a blazing twister, spurting embers as if agitated by the music, not the wind. Everybody had resigned themselves to listening to the band one more time; there was a look of trepidation in their flame-tinged profiles. Reluctant fascination, too. They *needed* this. It made them feel special. It made them feel alive.

Jack had seen it all before, and familiarity bred contempt. The band was just a bunch of thugs with a nasty talent for twisting contagious tunes into their audience like skillfully but viciously wielded knives. Mental butchery with chord changes, nothing more.

But it always worked.

He closed his eyes as vile melody hooks snagged his gut, and he was thinking of Bane.

Oh yes, it always worked.

Hate growing, an ugly tree in his mind, twisted roots sinking down through twenty years of suppression. His breathing fell into rhythm with the band.

Lila in her bedroom, a gloating mockery on her face as he tried to leave. *Maybe Bane didn't have to do that much. Maybe just encourage what was already there.*

The cave was near, and it was beckoning. Calling to that part of him that wouldn't stay buried. He felt himself answering the pull.

You're steeped in horror, too. Just like Bane.

The shadow was in the cave; it was stirring eagerly. It began to move slowly out of the darkness to greet him.

Jack's lips were dragged back in a rictus, his hair electric. He could feel his fingernails gouging the palms of his clenched hands.

He opened his eyes.

The shadow man was still there, emerging from the dark. Soon he would see its face.

The music stopped.

"Are you all right, Jack?"

Dennis's words came from miles away, from another lifetime, drifting through the blackness, fading before they reached him.

Lila had taken over the microphone from the singer. Jack blinked at her, clearing some of the fog from his brain. Grasped at her words for meaning and sanity.

"It's time", she said, and Jack nodded although he wasn't sure why. The cave was waiting.

Lila turned to the band. "Play for your lives, boys..." The noise began again, and Lila was moving, pushing through the throng, followed by the twins. The crowd parted for her, then began to file after her curiously as she made her way toward the edge of the hillside, where it led down to the gulley below. She held a powerful torch in one hand, and without hesitating, she stepped over the edge and was gone.

Dennis said, "In for a penny?"

The wind shot a cascade of sparks into the air, surrogate stars quickly dying. Above the smoke and push of flame, the night sky was black as the inside of a cave.

Jack followed the crowd, Dennis with him. Behind them, the band finished their number, the guitarist strumming aimlessly at his instrument, looking indecisively at the singer. Jack turned around once before setting off down the path, and the skinhead bassist was rumbling away, eyes staring at nothing, while the drummer shifted his sticks like a discredited witch doctor fumbling with bones. The singer's voice sounded suddenly mournful and lost as the band started another song, playing on with nobody left to listen. The noise washed over the lip of the slope and followed Jack and Dennis down the steep hillside, drowning out the heave of invisible waves below them.

CHAPTER FORTY-THREE

Midges splattered against her windscreen and dived into the twin cones thrown from the Fiat's headlights, and Sam had never felt so tired in her life.

She knew she was close now, and she also knew she was late. *You'll be late for your own funeral, girl,* her adoptive mother always used to tell her. *Or if not hers... (Stop that!)*

She was late, and anything could have happened by now. The coach had at least an hour's lead on her—probably more. Her misfortunes hadn't been confined to falling asleep and nearly killing herself and swapping a ruined tire. Half an hour out of Dumfries, a high-pitched insect whine had startled her out of her forebodings. She'd pulled over to the side of the road, engine idling, and stared in despair at the oil indicator light that was winking a mystifying red light at her.

She got out of the car, lifted the bonnet, and checked the oil, gazing at the little dab of fluid left on the dipstick with something approaching cold fury. Of course, Jack would have some spare oil in the car somewhere, wouldn't he? She'd spent ten fruitless minutes searching through the back of the car and under the seats before coming to the inevitable conclusion that she should have realized Jack, of course, would have no such thing. There had been nothing for it but to drive on regardless, the whine seeming to become more urgent with each mile of lightless countryside she passed through.

At last, a town, Newton Stewart, streets deserted, population diminutive, and yes, a garage. She swung into the forecourt and had actually turned off the engine before noticing the padlocks on the pumps and that the glow from inside the office was illuminating an empty cash desk and rows of multigrade oil tantalizingly just beyond her grasp.

Starting the engine, the whine came out to play again. Sam turned up the volume of The Small Faces CD she'd found in the glove compartment and let Steve Marriot's soulful ebullience drown the noise; it almost succeeded in putting terrifying images of the engine seizing up out of her mind.

Ogden's Nut Gone Flake had decided to only emerge from one speaker, the whine resurfaced every time a song finished, like an insistent rebuke, and her neck felt like a rusted metal hinge by the time a fully illuminated petrol station appeared on the horizon like a tarmacked oasis equipped with petrol pumps rather than palm trees.

Lazy Sunday afternoon, aah! Sam couldn't think of anything more inappropriate to the way she felt now, but she welcomed Marriot's prepunk wailing. She welcomed the sight of the grizzled, middle-aged station cashier, too, as Sam got out of the car and walked creakily toward the office.

She bought her oil and met the man's sorrowful gaze. *You're miserable because you've got the evening shift, stuck out here on your little island of neon, surrounded by darkness and petrol pumps, cut off from the telly or the pub, or whatever turns you on of a Saturday night. But I'd swap lives with you in an instant if I could.*

Clutching a bottle of oil, she left the office reluctantly, and looking over her shoulder, saw the man watching her through the window with his drooping eyes and sad, gray mustache. Then again...

Midges blasting against her windscreen.

Quarter to seven now, and she was close. Her headlights pointed out a dark expanse that she realized with a jolt was the sea as she swept around a corner. And those black bulks rearing up to her right were foothills. When the sign declaring Ballantrae glimmered beneath her lights, she felt a stone drop down deep inside her, and her fingers clenched and released the steering wheel convulsively.

She swept through the village at forty miles an hour, the open road atlas on the passenger seat beside her. But she knew by now where she was going without having to look at it. Past the sign at the other end of town, out into the night again. Hills that were more like mountains, rising black against black, no stars or moon to show her the sights. Just the road and thirty feet of headlight cones.

The CD player hissed from one speaker. Sam hadn't noticed the music had died.

The chickens have come home to roost.

They'd barely been able to see their way on the rough path twisting down through the gully. People had stumbled and fallen into the ferns, emitting oddly subdued curses.

Jack was silent as they followed the weird procession along the dark beach.

Inside, he was screaming.

The cave.

He could feel it, smell it. Closer.

"I feel...strange, Jack," Dennis said as they trooped over the sand. Jack didn't even hear him. He was oblivious to the sluggish behavior of the group, too, as they followed in Lila's wake. Their conversation had dropped from an excited chorus when they first set off down the slope to a low murmur, and now virtual silence. They stumbled along like zombies, understanding only that they should keep walking, as if no longer remembering why.

They came to the arm of rocks at the end of the beach. Lila was already climbing nimbly over it, then disappeared around the headland. A couple of people tripped and dropped into the waves lapping around the rocks. They seemed to take a very long time finding their way to their feet again. Jack watched without seeing them.

He was up and around the outcrop, following the rest, while Dennis was still struggling to climb the first rock. Jack froze, gazing at what lay beyond.

Waves prowled around the mouth of an inlet like hungry, wet monsters. The crowd was huddled on the slight incline, shivering in the biting sea breeze. They were all staring up at the darkness at the head of the inlet, at a bulging cliff face shouldered in by walls of granite. Lila's torch beam stroked the rock face, found what it was looking for, and slipped inside.

The trippers began to follow like subdued sheep.

They were disappearing into the dark.

Jack put out a hand as if to restrain Dennis as his friend jumped down onto the rocks beside him.

He let it fall by his side.

Sam saw the low-burning bonfire first as she swept around a bend, then spied the coach parked up beside the traffic lights. Caution urged her to drive right on by, and she did so, scanning the coach apprehensively as the Fiat droned past. The vehicle was all dark. Empty. She let the Fiat take her around another bend and then pulled onto a grass verge. She got out stiffly, thinking: *This is it.* She closed the car door and walked slowly back around the corner. *Please be all right, Jack. Please let this all be one big wind-up, just a game of Let's Scare Jack. We'll laugh about it, and Jack will shake hands with Bane, and I might even lower myself to shake hands with Lila, and then...*

Then we can all go home.

The dark coach filled her with dread. But that was silly because it *would* be dark if there were no one in it, wouldn't it? It didn't mean...

She could see the shapes near the fire, and for a horrible moment, she thought one of the huddled bodies lying there was Jack. Then she saw the guitar still clasped in one hand and another figure slumped behind the gleaming drum kit and realized she was looking at the band.

One of them was still sitting up, head hanging low. Drunk, probably. But where was everybody else?

She scanned the headland, or what she could see of it in the glow from the fire. Nothing. She stepped through the ruined wire fence and hesitantly approached the fire. And stopped short.

A hoarse, goatish cackle brought her head around. The singer of the band was still sitting, head hanging, shades covering his eyes. She could see his face quite clearly now; it was as blue as a mold-furred loaf. His mouth was crooked in an agony-wracked grin, and ever so slowly, he lifted his right hand, cupped, like a beggar asking for spare change. A thick clump of greasy hair slid over his forehead, dropped into his lap. He was croaking something, his lips writhing.

"Sympathy...for...the Devil?"

His lips locked around the last word and didn't move again. Sam was rooted in shock, staring at a dead man.

And through it all, there was pain. Pain grinding, paralyzing, suffocating. Beyond the pain, something small, moving closer. A spark, like a cigarette glow. A flame. Growing. A desert lit by flame.

How did they feel? *How did they feel?* Did they feel like *this?* In the moment of death, had they suffered as badly as he was suffering now? He had to know. *Had* to.

Their agony would have been condensed into an instant, encapsulated in the heartbeat of an explosion. His would never end.

Well. Didn't amount to much.

Dying now.

He'd helped nobody. Saved…nobody. Not his friend, his best friend, not those boys in the desert.

Another image, a freeze frame: a girl laughing soundlessly in a nightclub. Hair long, curls like leaves around a hauntingly beautiful face. He could still lift his hand toward her (or was he dreaming that, too?) and say,

I'm sorry…

Flames of the desert, burning low. Now just a glow. An ember, telescoping away. A cigarette spark in the night.

They couldn't get away with killing everybody, could they? *Please, God, not Jack! Not Jack.* She slipped on the path and almost fell into the dark ferns surrounding her. She was near the bottom of the slope now, although the weak beam of her torch was unable to reach as far as the beach. The sea rumbled below.

They *couldn't* kill everybody. What would they do with all the bodies? Throw them in the sea? And the bus? *They could drive that into the sea, too. Or over the cliff.* Nobody even knew where the tour was going. So, if she died too, nobody would know anything. *And how she wished she'd informed the police earlier, when she had the chance.* But people back in Bristol would still miss their friends and relatives, wouldn't they, when they failed to appear? The Slaughter Inn would be the first place the police would search and—

Unless Bane and his evil crew had no intention of going back to the pub.

It was all insane.

No sense to it. No reason.

Hadn't she realized by now that they were beyond reason?

The slope evened out, the ferns began to thin. She stumbled forward onto the sand. Breakers were pale before her. She scanned the desolate beach with her torch, but there was nobody around. But footprints, plenty of footprints in the sand. Like a school trip had passed this way, heading toward the north end of the beach.

She headed for the arm of rocks, black against the night. Where was she going? What was she doing? *Don't think about it; just keep going.* She should drive back to Ballantrae, call the police, get help. Of course, she should. But she also knew she really couldn't waste another minute. Not if she wanted to save Jack.

The waves tumbled onto the sand to her left, the sea so huge and powerful and dispassionate. The mournful hiss of the surf urged her on, filling her with dread at the same time.

The footprints ended at the outcrop. Then they must have climbed over it. Was there another beach beyond? She hauled herself up the damp rock, struggling to keep the torch shining ahead of her so she didn't misplace her feet and plunge into the sea as it crept in. It wasn't as hard as it looked. She was around the outcrop and looking down on a dark inlet without even getting wet from the spray.

She lowered herself down on the other side and threw her torch's beam around the inlet. The beam found something pale wedged between two boulders. Wind pushed her on. Sam followed the line of the beam until she came upon the object. A woman's face, staring up at her with skin like bad cheese, half of her scalp bald and slimy. Her body was stuck between the rocks where she'd fallen.

Sam staggered back, a scream loosening inside her, coming up for air. She squeezed it back down, not daring to move. An incoming wave trickled over her shoes and on up to the woman's head, played with the long hanks of hair still remaining, withdrew with a sigh.

Her hand shaking badly, Sam forced herself to move the torch upward slightly, the weak cone finding two more corpses strewn over the rocks farther up the incline. She whipped around in terror at a movement behind her. The sea, filling a hollow, swirling out again. The tide could be coming in. She would be trapped.

Whose were those bodies ahead? Were they—?

Fighting off her panic, she stumbled toward them, slipping over rocks and weeds.

Not Jack. Not Dennis.

Thank God.

She'd never seen them before. Both men. One wore denims, lying on his belly. The other a leather jacket, his face turned toward her, mouth locked open in a permanent scream. His cream-white face oozed with sweat and corruption.

She swung the torch around her frantically. The tall shoulders of rock pushed her in. The sea crept behind her.

She found the hole.

The ghostly beam picked out two identical bodies in the narrow entrance, sitting in slumped positions opposite each other, as if on guard. Their blonde hair was all but gone. The face of the one on the left was turned toward Sam, the blandly pretty features convulsed in agony.

Sam would have to step between them to enter the cave.

Go in there! It was more than her life's worth to go in there.

More than Jack's?

She wasn't a bimbo in a bad thriller. She wasn't going to walk into the dark, where she knew something horrible was going to happen.

It's already happened. They're all dead. Jack, Dennis. They're dead.

Go home.

Apart from the churning sea, an ominous silence pressed on her. She heaved herself over the boulder partially blocking the entrance and stepped into the crevice.

She was a bimbo, and she was going into the dark.

You see, Jack wasn't dead. He was in here. She would take him out, and they would go home. Together.

She stopped. She was standing between the two dead guards. One twin had her hands locked around a punk's throat. The rest of the victim's body was hidden by shadow inside the cave. The other twin was smiling at Sam, her last giggle trapped on her waxwork lips.

There were more bodies near the twins. Those who had tried to crawl back out of the cave and not quite made it. Sam's torch picked them out one by one, the beam wavering crazily with each new terror found.

The cave echoed with the dripping of water. It stank of horror, and it stank of death. The large chamber was choked with corpses. Sam stood amongst them like the last person on Earth.

Small, alone.

There had never been anyone so scared. She would never be able to move again. She was passing beyond fear now; madness beckoned.

She would slip into its arms, and everything would be all right.

She was going to die in here with all the rest.

Her torch found Dennis.

A cacophony of screams erupted out of silence.

The chamber exploded with shriek after shriek. The 17th-century death agonies of butchered victims—men, women and children—echoing once more as if a horrific music box had been opened, then just as swiftly closed. The screaming faded into the walls.

Deafening silence again.

Sam's torch lay on the floor where she'd dropped it. Its beam played across the far wall of the chamber. It gleamed on the maggot-white people watching Sam with hellish leers, blood drying on their rags and buckles and butcher hands.

The torch beam illuminated only nitre deposits and graffiti splashed against the wall, and her own shadow stretched and spidery.

She was alone with the dead.

Her fingers were thrust so far into her mouth, she would choke if she didn't move them. But if she moved, she would be seen.

A tapping came from the darkness. Not water dripping—a hollow, measured rapping as of bone on rock. The sound drifted toward her from the tunnel leading to the rear of the cave.

Tap, tap, tap.

A ragged sound joined the tapping.

Breathing.

Someone breathing in the cave.

The tapping stopped. The ragged gasps of breath came closer.

Sam was slick with sweat and colder than she'd ever been. Her mind told her to *move*, but her body was beyond action.

A shadow was emerging from the tunnel.

Sam moved. It was just a step back, but it was a start. Her mind screamed: *Again, move again! Get out, for GOD'S SAKE, GET OUT!!*

Her feet slowed, as if dragged at by many hands; the dead wanted her to stay with them. Darkness embraced her body, and it was reluctant to let her go.

GET OUTTT!!!!!!

She swung her back on the shadow, lunged for the narrow entrance slit. One of the twins snatched at her—the grinning one. *Her coat was caught on the corpse's stiffening hands, that was all—the twin wasn't still alive!*

Sam yanked herself free and sprawled through the entrance, rolling on her back, gasping, eyes huge as she stared up at the shadow figure slowly emerging from the dark after her.

A hand showed first, pale as it quested from the cave, as if reaching for her. The moon was buried by cloud, but a faint illumination showed her the caked blood gluing the fingers together. The figure shuffled farther out, and a face came into view.

Blood had made a ferocious mask of the features. The hair was stringy and crusted with gore. Eyes gazed at her with the lust of insanity. The figure swung its other hand out of the cave as it lurched toward Sam, and she saw the monstrous cracked skull gripped by its lower jaw, splashed with crimson, several teeth smashed away. The skull dangled, drip, drip, dripping with blood.

The figure reached down for Sam where she lay, its free hand closing around her throat.

Bean.

Bean.

Breen.

The one that got away.

The child that got away.

Horror and Fury would breed again, spilling from this hole, ripping out the guts of the world.

Eat 'em all.

Eat.

Sawney's here with us now. Can you see him, Jack? With his bloody grin? Agnes, too, with dead spiders in her hair, she nods. We've brought you to join them, brother, a family reunion in hell.

Remember I once told you it wasn't me you should fear: it was you. You're ready to accept yourself as you really are, indulge those appetites you've always repressed. You're home. Me and you, Jack: Sawney's children have come home.

Breathe the cave's breath, smell its smell. Once you've been inside, you won't be able to leave. It'll never let you go. You see our forefathers sitting in the dark? They're all still here; they've waited so long for the score to be settled. That's why there's so much death, Jack. Blood for blood. For all Sawney's butchered children.

Come and join the family, Jack.

Breen, Bean, Bane.

You speak to a bone, and it answers, Bane. Does it speak to me? In you, in me, Sawney... I hear him rage across the centuries.

And Lila...Agnes...do I love you, too, here, in the dark?

This bone, here, in my hand now. This is for you, Lila, for you, Bane. With love. With Sawney's special love, screaming down the years. Kiss its old lips, Lila, kiss the bone with your blood, your brains. Sawney's hungry. You cry, Bane? You feel? Blood for blood, you said. And now Sawney wants yours. Now he's all red, and you're all red. Red ruin. Red Sawney, red Bane, red Jack.

Sam had both her hands around the grip that was choking her. She couldn't move it. Her breath was a thin thing. She was sucking in life through a reed.

The hand eased its pressure, fell away from her throat.

Her head sank back against a boulder. She retched, gasping for air. Above her, the dim figure dropped the skull. It clattered beside Sam's head, rolled to face her with its splintered bloody grin. The figure reached down with both hands, lifted a jagged rock high in the air. It paused, the rock hanging over Sam's face.

Love kills, she thought, and closed her eyes.

Beyond the girl, the tide was seething.

Weeds lifting lazily, tossed by the surf. Not just weeds. He looked again, saw nightmare infest the breakers..

Obscene things reaching from the slobbering waves. Flesh gleamed sickly in the water as a corner of the moon edged past cloud, showed it to him. Flesh rotten, clinging to a severed arm, stripped partly to the bone, where his teeth had gnawed, his knife pared. Remains floating in on the tide. Look—a sea-bloated hand clutching for him...a knife-hacked leg revolving in a rock pool...and there, guts looped around boulders, twitching with unnatural life. I see you, see you all: filthy torso festooned with spectral weeds, cresting a breaker; gnawed heads bobbing on the mid-

night tide. Ha! Bits and pieces, centuries old, flung to the sea. I carved you; I made you meat. I'll fish yon head from the waves by its dripping hair, pulp it with a rock.

But this head beneath the raised rock...not rotting, not dead. Alive. Beautiful...

But there, there next to it...grinning horror. Rictus smirk. Bone. Bane.

"Bean..."

The rock came down on the skull, cracking it apart. It lifted again, came down. Bone fractured, skittered across the pebbles.

Sam.

Sam!

Jack dropped the rock, fell down beside her. He hugged her until he felt her gasp, then pushed her away from him slightly, looked at her tear-lined face. She stared back at him with eyes locked in horror. He stood up slowly, pulled her gently to her feet. She swayed, clung to a rock for support.

Jack turned his back on her, stumbled down the slope, toward the sea.

Killed them.

Bane. Lila.

Smashing, pulping, my arm strong and deadly as any butcher's, blood a filthy tide. With HIS skull, I killed them.

If I stay near Sam, I might kill her, too.

Once you've been in the cave, you won't be able to leave.

It'll never let you go.

He clambered over the rocky outcrop, down onto the beach on the other side. Behind him, Sam followed slowly, carefully. He dared not even look at her.

Walk.

Just walk.

Walk up to the road, leave the cave behind.

It's that easy.

It's that easy.

He turned his back on the cave and walked. And if there was a whisper in his ear, it was just the sigh of the wind; and if he heard his name, it was just the sobbing of the waves.

ABOUT THE AUTHOR

Leo Darke's first novel, *Mr. Nasty*, was a surreal, uncompromising debut, paving the way for the mayhem to follow. The supernatural punk carnage of *Lucifer Sam* and the folk horror *Pandemonium* cemented his reputation as a no-holds-barred purveyor of unconventional terror. *Sawney Bone* completes Darke's quartet of ferocious outrage.

Leo Darke lives in deepest Somerset. He is the proud owner of a ceremonial skull and bone knife he was given in the cannibal-infested jungles of West Papua, and once witnessed the appearance of terrifying demons in Java. He lived to tell the tale, but nobody ever believed it…

LUCIFER
SAM

Chapter One

1989

Barra boy no more, my son…

Ray was staring at 15,000 upturned faces. And they were all staring at *him*.

The realization didn't hit him at first. He stood on the lip of the stage, struggling to take it all in. Proper head-fucked, as Barney, the drummer, would have put it. He was half naked, his slim torso slick with sweat. Two songs in and he still couldn't accept the enormity of it all. He stood still in the few moments grace between songs, hand unconsciously brushing at his spiky mop as he tried to get his head around it. Jezza, the guitarist, was busy tuning, head down as he concentrated so Ray couldn't see his expression. Probably thinking about playing *Dungeons and Dragons* with his Tolkien-obsessed mates, the nerdy twat. He only got hard for prog rock solos. Ray was sure his guitar mags were all very sticky. Phil, the bass player and band leader, was staring at the audience, too, a dumb grin on his square face, long, curly hair matted with sweat. Ray beamed over at him, shaking his head numbly, sharing a WTF moment. They had never been close, but this was a moment even enemies could share. This was momentous. The crowd was roaring for more, and distinct above the colossal noise, Ray could hear his name in a rising chant. He felt electrified. The vestiges of coke left in his system buzzed through his veins, boosted by his euphoria.

Then the truth of it smashed him like a hammer. This was it. He had made it. No more getting up at 5:00 a.m. to look after his old man's fruit and veg stall on Portobello Road. No more skimping on beer money to feed the electricity meter in his dingy flat off Brick Lane. No more borrowing a sub off his surly old man to take a bird to the flicks. No more scrapping outside the Ten Bells on a Friday, Saturday night cos some bastard looked at him wrong. There was gonna be no more of that shit! From now on there would be chauffeurs to every venue, drinking champers like water at top London clubs with big-breasted tarts falling all over him. He was *big time, baby!* He sucked it all in, standing on the lip of the stage. This was a fuckin' epiphany! He felt joy orgasm through his body. He spread his arms, tilted his head to one side to take in the adoration of the crowd. His name was a massive chant that would shame the rest of the band: "Starling, Starling… STARLING!!!"

Ray Starling, twenty-one years old and at the top of the world. Headlining the Frankfurt Rock Festival to 15,000 punters all screaming his name was his Mount Everest scaled. He had the voice, he had the look. He certainly had the attitude to achieve—he took no bullshit, and the desire to make it had driven him through a poverty-stricken childhood and teenage years that had seen him punch and struggle every step of the way to this moment. But it wasn't just his sheer brute willpower. His voice was unforgettable. It could chisel stars and make the Gods roar. Ray had a vocal range that allowed him pinnacle-ascending falsettos one minute and punky, thunderous growls the next. His voice had a quality that transcended the puerile subject matter Phil insisted the band concentrate on: all fantasy imagery, torture implements, and dodgy war films. It reached your soul and your gut at the same time. And not only was Ray's voice pretty damn unique, but he was also young and eminently shaggable. The first album had gone platinum across the globe, and things really couldn't get better than this.

Within two months he would lose it all.

Chapter Two

2014

The punch took Ray in his left eye, and for a moment he could only see in mono.

The blow took him clean off his bar stool, dumped him on the floor of the boozer like the sack of shit the geezer who hit him obviously thought he was.

"Fuckin' rock star? More like a used-up tissue that everyone's spunked in, mate. Ain't nuffin' sadder than a pathetic Has Been who still thinks he's got what it takes. Fuckin' loser." The big man took a step back as if to deliver a kick to the fallen idol. Ray saw it coming but was too pissed to dodge it. The toe of the geezer's boot caught him on his left cheekbone, just below his foggy eye. The pain was sickening. He rolled over on his back, and the dingy pub revolved around him, darkening.

He could see a couple of faces hanging over him, repeating his name in anxious tones—certainly not the 15,000 that once roared it in exuberance. Michelle's face was tear-streaked as she knelt down next to him, her sister, Bella, turning away to scream at the man who had kicked him.

He peered up at Michelle as if wondering who she was. Was she still his bird? The last in a looooong fuckin' line of 'em. But this one had been a keeper. Before Michelle, none of 'em had meant much to him. Not really. Apart from Michelle, *nothing* meant much to him anymore.

He stared up at the cracked ceiling of the Victorian-era boozer and wondered where it had all gone wrong.

Now it was Phil Carter's face looming into vision. But Cat O' Nine Tails' bass player certainly wasn't in this back-street boozer. Nah, he'd be drinking champers on a jet somewhere on the latest leg of a world fuckin' tour no doubt…

It was just a memory. Just the same old memory that had rolled through his mind throughout the last twenty-five years like a mossy stone that could not be stopped. Phil's face was young again, just a couple years older than Ray's had been on that fateful day in October 1989 when Phil finally called time on Ray's Cat O' Nine career.

He was sitting in the EMI office again, the shades partly pulled down over the gorgeous autumn day that filled the Kensington street outside. He'd been summoned to the meeting the day before, his manager sounding curt and evasive on the blower. "Tell ya what it's all about when we see ya, Ray, old son. Gotta go."

But his manager was late. Ray had always been punctual. That was something you learned in the East End. Certainly on the fruit market. Be on time or lose your fuckin' place. Well, here he was on time…

Doug, the manager, finally showed his face, ten minutes late, and Phil was with him. They entered the office quietly, shook his hand formally, and Ray knew why he had been called before they even opened their mouths.

"Sit down, Ray, son." Doug was a tough, no-shit businessman from Essex. The band looked up to him like a father figure. He was tight as a hamster's ass with their money, but he always looked out for them and had got them where they were today. Phil might have written most of the songs, and Ray sung the fuck out of 'em, but it was Doug who had the unerring business sense to broker the deals that had sent them into metal orbit. Ray had always respected him. Which was why looking at him now and reading his fate in that boxer's mug of a manager's expression, Ray felt even more betrayed. Doug was avoiding his gaze. Something he'd never done before.

Ray dropped into a leather swing seat like he'd been felled. He stared at Doug and knew his mouth was opening to say something, but there was no breath. He coughed violently, clearing his throat, but Doug was already speaking as Phil and the manager took seats across the oval table from him.

"Ray…" Doug began, flicking a quick look at the singer, then directing his gaze to a pen he'd fished from his pocket. "I think you know why we've called you."

Ray swung his gaze to the bass player. Phil was studying the blind over the window, his stolid face expressionless.

"No," Ray said. He stood up slowly. The world had suddenly grown very small in his head. "No," he said again. "You ain't gonna—"

"Mate, you've really left us no choice!" Phil had his hands wide, and his eyes were all wide, too, in "I'm the real victim here" innocence.

Ray started to shake. He felt sicker than ever before in his life, the evilest hangover was nothing on it. His mouth wouldn't let any more words out.

Doug took over, rising from his chair to grab Ray's arm in a consoling fashion, trying to ease him back into his seat. "Ray, you know I love you like a son. You know how much it fuckin' hurts to do this to you?"

Ray looked into his eyes, and at last Doug met his gaze. The forty-one-year-old looked genuinely sad. Was that a glint of a tear in his eyes? Crocodiles cried, too… Ray began to feel the familiar anger building, replacing the shock, the hurt, the desolation. The anger that had carried him through childhood and beyond, made him the tough fucker he was today. He shook Doug's grip away and rounded on Phil.

"You cunt," he said slowly, his voice trembling with rage. "You never fuckin' liked me. I *made* this band. Without me, you're fuckin' nothin'!"

Phil sighed heavily, studied his fingers for a minute—the stubby fingers that Ray had always thought too short for a bass player—and then sat back in the swivel seat. "You did it to yourself, mate. We can't control you. We can't take it anymore. We have to look to the future and take this seriously. Me an' Jez are always experimenting with the music. We want to push it further, but you don't give a fuck. You're just here for a ride, not to take it to the next step. And you're ruining your voice. You're always fucked out of your nut on coke or speed. And that's when you're not pouring Jack Daniels down your throat like there's no tomorrow."

Ray took that in. That was a major speech for the usually laconic band leader. He sat down again. His anger, tipped nearly to the boiling point, curdled, miraculously stalled. Phil was right; he was diametrically opposed to the bass player in literally everything. Phil very rarely drank, certainly never took drugs. He was a family man, with two babies—twins—to look after, and even when he was on tour, he would stay in his hotel room reading a Sven Hassell novel rather than boozing and shagging like Ray and whoever was brave enough to accompany him on one of his blitzes. And Phil was right about the other thing as well: they thought he didn't know about their stupid experimental sessions, but he did, and it wasn't for him—the three of them jamming together secretly without Ray, fixated on Jimmy Page, Aleister Crowley bollocks, tryin' to add some quasi-mystical, arcane nonsense to the music. He'd always just let 'em get on with it. His job was to sing, not fuck around pretendin' to be into Black Magic when they was just four ordinary blokes from the East End. To Ray, it was only Rock 'n' Roll, and he liked it. He should've seen this coming. He really should.

"But there is no tomorrow," he finally answered Phil, his voice slow and empty.

Phil looked at Doug, and then both of them looked at the table.

"We're offering you a deal, son." Doug said eventually. "Sixty grand for signing off rights to the songs you wrote for the album. It's a good deal, son. You should take it."

Ray took it.

He walked out of the office on shaky legs, but he took it. Suddenly the future didn't seem so bright, the birds wouldn't be so fit or so numerous, and the champers and the clubs would be a lot cheaper.

But there is no tomorrow…

The haze began to clear, the dingy décor of the back-street boozer swam back into focus. Michelle was still bending over him, tears streaking her pretty face. Ray shook his head to clear it. The five-inch metal sword on a chain around his neck jangled. He remembered the fans who'd forged it for him, gave it to him after he'd been fired, when they told him he was the best singer the band would ever have. He saw their faces now. He began to push himself up from the grubby floorboards.

"Comin' back for more, old timer?" The muscle-bound bastard who'd slugged him was grinning from ear to ear.

Ray had always been a scrapper. Outside his local down Canning Town, impressing the birds by being the hardest, the mouthiest, the meanest. Top Dog. Leader of the pack. He'd filled many a chick's panties on that rep. You had to fight to prove who you were, and Ray had instinctively understood that. He understood it now, twenty-five years older than that slim, sexy Rock God who had stood on the stage at Frankfurt and surveyed all that he owned. Except he was a bit slower now, a lot fatter, and that punky barnet had fallen to the winds. But he was still Ray Fuckin' Starling, and he'd been proving that just about every night he hit the boozers. Been fighting that memory of the office in Kensington for twenty-five long years, fighting anyone who got mouthy and called him out. Because people *always* wanted to take him on so they could tell their mates they put one over on the ex-Cat O' Nine singer. And now here was another one itching to get his bedpost notch. Ray's head began to buzz the way it always did when the Beast was coming out. Couldn't they ever let it lie…? *Couldn't HE ever let it lie?*

No. If he had to prove he was still Ray Starling, badass lead singer of the biggest rock band in the world, then a twenty-five-year-old Best Before Date wasn't gonna stall him. Ray had always been the mad one in the band. The others were boring pussies. But did he really have to point that out to every cunt in a bar who wanted some of him?

So be it.

Ray blinked to clear the haze in his left eye. He felt the rage surge through his veins, the way euphoria had done once upon a long time ago in Frankfurt.

He focused on the big man who'd started on him for no reason other than he'd once been famous. The big lug was still grinning, still waiting for Ray to get up. *Latest in a long line, son.* All the years of regret, despair, smashed dreams, oceans of booze, and mountains of drugs had led to this. Had led to every other night just like it.

Ray was on one knee now. The pain in his head was like a pile driver battering away at his skull. His left eye was half closed.

He faced the big man, swaying slightly. Then he let the anger take him.

When Ray got really mad, wise men knew to duck for cover. All hell was there, all ready for the breaking. Unfortunately, tonight's assailant wasn't too wise. "Reckon I got one more Comeback in me…" Ray said.

And suddenly everything got *very* messy.

Ray Starling had always been a scrapper.

Chapter Three

Rose said, "I don't believe it."

Kirk said, "Fuck-ing *hell*!"

They were both watching the news in Kirk's ropey Stoke Newington flat. The TV screen showed stills of four long-haired musicians, then a video clip from one of their colossal stadium gigs. The caption beneath rolled across in the Breaking News red banner:

PRIVATE JET CARRYING FAMOUS ROCK BAND DISAPPEARS OVER INDIAN OCEAN

Kirk started to speak again, but Rose shushed him urgently. Cat O' Nine Tails had always been her favorite band.

The newsreader was short on facts. Kirk and Rose watched breathlessly as he delivered all he had, then Rose flicked to another news channel with the same headline news and tried to pick scraps from the slight variation of detail. But there was nothing more. The facts were very minimal: the band was on the last leg of their world tour, taking them to Asia with dates in Jakarta and Japan before finally climaxing the tour in Sydney. Somewhere high above the Indian Ocean at approximately midnight GMT, Air Control had lost contact with the private jet. It had simply and inexplicably disappeared from airspace. Australian and Indonesian maritime rescue patrols were already covering the area where contact had been lost, expanding to allow for wreckage drift patterns. So far, absolutely nothing had been discovered, although, as all newscasters on all channels kept repeating, it was a vast area of empty ocean to cover. A spokesperson from EMI, the band's record label, was rolled out to completely insipid effect—Kirk wondered if he'd ever even met the band. One channel scooped Phil Carter's distraught wife and his teenage son (a younger copy of his Dad), red-eyed and devastated, trying not to fear the worst despite the words the news anchor seemed determined to put in their mouths. Baz Cropper's wife, a still-glamorous blonde with a sensitive face in her early forties, looked broken as she eulogized on how attentive and kind her husband was. And there was Jez Tweed's girlfriend, who looked remarkably like the guitarist, equally as sensible and thoughtful in appearance as her missing lover. She looked a little shell-shocked but was keeping it real. She dismissed the anchor's suggestion of terrorist hijacking as absurd. It was a private jet with the same pilot and aircrew they always used. There was no question of anybody suspicious being on board. Besides the pilot, co-pilot, and two air stewards who had been flying with the band for the last ten years, the only other occupants of the jet were the manager, Doug Roscoe, the four members of the band themselves, and a handful of road crew who, again, were loyal and trusted members of the band's entourage. Besides, she pointed out patiently, rebuffing the anchor's interruptions, Air Traffic Control had reported conversations with the pilot for the first two hours of the flight since leaving Kuala Lumpur, and there had been nothing out of order reported.

Speculation continued to fly on all the channels. Had the jet crashed, or had it indeed been hijacked, despite protestations from family members of the band? Engine failure or terrorist activity? More experts and spokespersons were rolled out. Aircraft engineers who had checked over the jet before the flight and found absolutely nothing amiss. "This craft was exhaustively and extensively serviced since the last flight," one engineer stressed somewhat defensively as the headlines unspooled on a strip beneath his strained expression. "And the service records speak for themselves. This jet was good to go." But where *did* it go, that was the question that was on all news anchors' lips.

In between footage of Cat playing Wembley Arena and happy, smiley interviews with the four musicians that constituted the band (Barney cracking fart jokes, Baz beaming in his Sherlock Holmes titfer), there were more family members dredged up. Rose was close to tears when Barney's parents appeared, looking fragile and utterly overcome with grief. The old couple clung to the hope that their drummer son would be returned safely to them at any minute. Kirk had his doubts but said nothing; he could see how increasingly upset Rose was becoming with each revelation.

Finally, the news channels appeared to have exhausted all avenues, exploited all potential resources. When they had seen the same clips of the band laughing and joking on a previous jet tour and touching down in Japan the year before three times in a row, even Rose was tiring of the repetition. Kirk took the remote from her and switched off the TV. He pulled her against him on the sofa, stroking her long brown hair, saying nothing for a while, and if he felt she was maybe wallowing, being a little *too* melodramatic in her grief (after all, it wasn't as if she knew any of the band personally), he certainly wasn't going to mention it. She was a sensitive soul, which is why he loved her.

She had dragged him to see them twice on the European leg of the tour. Once at the London O2, and again at the not-so-accessible Birmingham Arena. She had all their albums—all fifteen of them!—and while Kirk liked the band's first album well enough, the rest left him cold. While Cat O' Nine's music was undeniably appealing in a mass-market fashion with riffs and melodies as catchy as a docker's billhook, Kirk had always found their lyrics a little naff and the subject matter a trifle undergrad. Hell, that was being polite; sixth form nerd metal would be more accurate. Cat O' Nine had made themselves accessible on such a huge scale by ostensibly not being offensive to anyone, something Kirk had always struggled with. Surely, the true appeal of a band lay in their ability to challenge. To outrage as well as excite. And in his opinion, Cat O' Nine Tails (again, with the honorable exception of their first album, which, grounded by the ferocious vocal abilities and punk-rock attitude of their original singer, Ray Starling, had been vital and blistering) was anything but exciting. They had forged a career in safe, melodic metal. Pleasing to the ear, easy on the mind. Nothing wrong with that, of course, but metal had never really been Kirk's cup of tea. The genre was way too conservative despite its obsession with imagery the practitioners obviously deemed shocking. No offense, Cat O' Nine, but horror movie covers and references to stranglers and gibbets steeped in chiming guitars and twinkling solos was as far removed from shocking as you could get.

Crypt Metal was how he'd described them to Rose once, and it seemed accurate enough. The band floundered in adolescent obsessions with fantasy gore and Hammer Horror chic while lyrical howlers decimated grammar left, right, and all over the show.

It had always struck Kirk that Cat O' Nine had dabbled in pretend Crowley Satanism and dark imagery, but in a comic book fashion without ever seeming to really believe in it. He was pretty sure they didn't subscribe to the Black Arts. He'd once attended a Cat O' Nine signing with Rose, and Phil Carter had chuckled dismissively when Kirk asked him if they really believed in the Horned One as the guitarist signed a copy of *Fear Stalkers* for Rose. "Nah, mate. The missus would kill me. She banks with the other side, know what I mean?" Jez Twist had confirmed the bass player's statement in a couple of subsequent interviews, and the band's jolly drummer, Barney Smolt, had once joked on a chat show a few years back about "riding bronco with the Devil, just for a laugh like" in a mock oafish accent. It was all a piss take, window dressing. Cat O' Nine Tails were four down-to-earth geezers, cheery, a little middle-of-the-road, not to mention middle-aged; a little *conservative* with the collective imaginative powers of a squad of road menders. Long-haired, good-natured Brit rockers up for a hearty chuckle, but as boring as accountants in their private lives. In fact, Baz had been an accountant when he first left university, a fact that didn't go unnoticed by the music press eager to spotlight the new guy in town who had replaced the infamous headline bagger, Ray Starling. They wouldn't get any booze and whore stories out of Baz; no threesomes in a Premier Inn coffee lounge there. Baz was a fine vocalist, but he was dull as Dutch cheese. Then there was Barney Smolt, who had retained a hobby most boys grew out of when they were fourteen—he spent a lot of his adult pocket money buying and assembling model airplane kits. Jez Twist did role playing! Phil Carter played golf. R.I.P. rock 'n' roll. Sid and Elvis died for *this*?

But for all that, Kirk didn't exactly hate them; he'd listen to them if he had to, say on long drives with Rose or while doing the gardening at his Mum's little bungalow. Mostly only if Rose asked him to, though.

But it hadn't always been that way. He would never forget the first time he saw Cat O' Nine Tails when he was barely ten years old and visiting his big brother who lived in Germany. He had never heard of most of the bands, but his bruv was a metal fan and dragged him along to the open-air festival at Frankfurt.

What was more eye-opening than any of the raucous and wild hair bands was the sight of his brother smoking a joint with his mates as they sat in the sun watching the festival. He appreciated the way his bruv had trusted Kirk enough not to say anything to his parents. That had been mutually understood. He'd even offered Kirk a toke for a joke. And then Cat O' Nine Tails had come on stage…

It had only been about one man for Kirk; the others were just background to Ray Starling's barnstorming performance. Kirk would never forget one moment that had burned itself into his mind and chased him through childhood to the present day—an instant influence: Ray, standing on stage between songs, legs slightly apart, his shirt stripped away, chest heaving from his exertions, hair bushy and semi spiked. He was surveying the audience as if he wasn't quite sure he was really there, a "This is It" moment unlike any other Kirk had witnessed before or since (Kirk had certainly not experienced it with his own band up to this point). Then Ray had flung out his arms, head tilted to one side, Jesus on the Rock Cross, and the chanting had lifted into the sunny skies, rising, deafening: "Cat O' Nine, Cat O' Nine… CAT O' NINE!!!"

The first album was an indispensable rock classic, burning with Starling's barely contained fury and a handful of compositions that blew away Carter's songs in terms of intensity and unleashed craziness. But it had been evident then that Ray was too much of a loose cannon for his more staid fellow band members, and the signs were there that he wouldn't last if you really looked for them. After Starling's departure, the band racked up a truly impressive amount of albums and went interstellar in terms of sales. The music became less fierce, less punky and in your face. A thoughtfulness and lyricism replaced the fury (at least in the music, the lyrics themselves remained as dodgy and English teacher-baiting as ever). Cat O' Nine settled themselves into almost cozy respectability to accompany their newfound massive wealth, despite the playful gore of their cover imagery and bellicose pretense of their song titles.

As for Ray Starling…?

He had dropped out of the public arena completely. He had taken the sixty thousand pounds for the rights to the songs he had written for the band and disappeared for all intents and purposes. Although "disappeared" was not entirely true. Kirk was vaguely aware he had started up a couple of bands, attempted a solo career, and attempted comeback after comeback over the years. But all this was just stuff he'd heard down the pub; Kirk had never heard any examples of Ray's non-Cat stuff, and there was probably a good reason for that. As one of his mates had told him, "It sounds like his heart wasn't in it." And that made sense to Kirk. After seeing Ray live when he was ten and witnessing the absolute euphoria burning out from him, how could he ever truly replicate that in any other band? Cat O' Nine had been his life, even if it had only been for a short moment in time…

"I don't want to hear any more, Kirk…" Rose said, turning away from the TV.

Kirk switched off the news and pulled Rose against him.

"You don't have to, Rosie," he said and kissed her cheek fondly.

She turned to him, her dark brown eyes troubled. "Do you think they're really dead?" She sucked in a breath, and when it came out again, it trembled. "Baz is one of the nicest musicians ever. He kissed my cheek last time we saw them, remember? Such a true, kind gentleman… This just isn't right. It isn't *fair*…"

He stroked the red stripe that grew from her crown and snaked through her thick brown hair. He loved that stripe; his very own Bride of Frankenstein dipped in blood. Kirk shrugged, then leaned in to kiss her, and knowing she was sorrowful, he felt a little ashamed of his instant arousal. She always did that to him, though, and he hoped she would continue to turn him on for a long time to come. Her face was a sexy contrast of strength and vulnerability; her finely chiseled cheekbones guarded eyes that were sensual and soft, yet her lips were stubbornly firm, her nose curved, forceful. She had a temper you wouldn't want to unleash (and Kirk had set it free a few more times than he would have liked), and she was tall and imposing, maybe with half an inch on Kirk. But right now, she was bare, confused, and had never looked sexier.

So Kirk forgave himself and kissed her again, pushing her gently back on the sofa and getting to work caressing her right breast through the material of her tee. He was pulling her shirt up over her head to get at her purple bra when she stopped him.

"What the fuck!?" She pushed his hands away and sat up. "I don't fucking believe you…"

Kirk sat back against the sofa cushions, his mouth dropping, hands wide and adopting what he hoped was his best look of bewildered innocence. "What?"

"You can really be an unfeeling bastard, d'you know that?"

He shrugged again. "Thought you wanted consoling, hun."

"Do you normally console people with a hard-on? Hate to see you at a funeral."

He smirked at that, which didn't help his case. But that was another thing he really liked about Rose; she could always make him laugh.

"Sorry, Rosie." He gave her a quick kiss on the forehead. "Forgiven?"

"No. Fuck off and make me a cup of tea."

He did as he was told. He was no fool.

As he bustled around in the kitchen of the small flat, he heard the first bars of "The Stranger" start up from the living room. She'd slipped on Cat O' Nine's second album. She had always preferred the band post Starling, something Kirk could never quite understand. The volume rose as she adjusted the remote on the stereo, and he smiled. *Rosie's little tribute*, he thought fondly and put the kettle on.

"Best rock band on the planet, my arse! A fuckin' metal Genesis is all they are. *Were*. Tweed jackets and plus fours be more suitable for 'em than leathers, the phony bastards. 'Bout fuckin' time they took their last encore, if you ask me." Davey Crooked finished his tirade and took a hefty gulp of lager.

"Well, I'm not asking you. Show some fucking respect, they're dead," Kirk told the bassist before Rose could rise from the pub table and lamp him one. She could take him, too; Kirk was sure of that. Davey was a lanky streak of piss, and all the leathers in the world couldn't make him any good in a scrap. Kirk had seen him go down too many times in rucks both before and after gigs. He remembered one particularly funny moment when Davey had decided to get involved in a post-gig punch-up in a dodgy pub they'd just been playing in Cardiff. The brawl between two huge Welsh women was getting increasingly nearer the table where the members of Lucifer Sam were sitting. Davey had no idea what they were fighting about, and Kirk had no idea what made him stand up and get involved. Maybe he fancied one of the big tattooed lasses—Davey was never renowned for his refined taste in females. But there he was anyway, jumping up to part them, and he succeeded in doing so, even if only for the second it took for one of them to turn around and chin him with one meaty fist. The time between Davey rising from his feet and landing on his ass couldn't have been more than five seconds. The two Welsh gals ignored him as soon as he hit the deck and turned back to slapping the hell out of each other. Kirk and the rest left him underneath the table where he'd landed, stunned as a felled calf. Let him rot, was their motto.

"Why the fuck should I show respect? We're better off without 'em. They'd become an embarrassment. Silly old bastards pretending to worship the Devil while playing golf and selling afternoon teas to the middle class." Davey pointed a long finger at Kirk. "You do know Baz Cropper bought a cream tea shop for his Missus to run down in Devon during the Summer Season, don't ya? They're about as rock 'n' roll as my old Nan. Fuck no, she's got way more attitude and rhythm in her mobility scooter than those twats ever showed. They've been pedaling the same cartoon shit for way too long."

Even if Kirk agreed with him, he wasn't going to say so for fear of upsetting Rose again. But Rose didn't need Kirk to protect her—not when she had her own Sir Galahad in the form of Johnny Diesel (nee John Dover). The slick-haired guitarist had always been a little too quick to step in on Rose's behalf for Kirk's liking. It was probably his paranoia, but were the little conversations and smiles they seemed to be sharing all the more frequently of late entirely as innocent as Rose would have him believe? She had been furious with him the one time he'd broached it, but the paranoia remained, the little pricks of jealousy kept coming, and here was one now.

"Because they're Rose's favorite band, you dick. And if you don't respect your mates' feelings, what kind of twat does that make you?" The guitarist glared at Davey with his blue eyes (dreamy blue? Is that what Rose thought of them?), and the bass player dropped his gaze and took another gulp of lager.

Rose didn't need a knight with a gleaming Gibson right now, however. "I'll tell you why you should show respect," she said, eyes flashing with real anger. "Because not only were they a great band—yes, a *great* band, not everyone thinks *Sid Sings* is the best album ever recorded you twat—but also because they've left loved ones behind who will be in a very bad place right now. Loved ones, Davey. I know you're not familiar with the term. But you mentioned Baz's wife. Do you think she gives a shit about how musically diverse or challenging they are? She just wants her kind, lovely husband back, her childhood sweetheart who stuck by her all these years. These are *real* people who lived *real* lives. *Moron!*" She took a furious sip of her vodka, and Kirk felt his love for her swell more than ever. He put his arm around her (before Johnny could?), but she was too angry and prickly now and shrugged it off.

"Bollocks to it," Crooked muttered. "Just sharing my opinion around. No need to climb on my ass for that."

"Your ass is the last anyone would wanna climb on, cabbage head," Ned assured him. The drummer emphasized the statement with a minor twitch. His arm rose half-heartedly, as if his Tourette's couldn't really be bothered to play with him today.

"Fuck you, Brain Crack," Davey responded defensively. He never knew quite how far he could go with insulting Ned on account of his disability, no matter how minimal it was. But today he was feeling the pressure and would take on any comer. "Gonna take my head off with that tic in a minute, retard. Get your straitjacket on."

"Doesn't take a guy with Tourette's to take your head off, not when we can find any five-year-old girl to do the job."

"Fuck you all. I got better things to do than chat to a bunch of wank-cocks like you lot. Stickin' my prick in a mouse hole would be more productive."

"Way too roomy for you, mate." Ned was straight in.

Kirk could tell the bassist was feeling outnumbered, and tiring of the banter, he shut them all up with a slam of his pint glass on the table. He hadn't failed to notice the grateful smile Rose had flashed at Johnny either.

"We're not here to talk about how Davey achieves his pleasure. Or even to discuss Cat O' Nine Tails…"

"R.I.P. Rockin' in the Pacific."

"Shut the fuck up, Davey. And it was the Indian Ocean, you moron. This is supposed to be a band meeting. We need to discuss what we're actually working toward because it seems to me one or two of you seem to be losing interest." That was aimed at Diesel, though it could equally apply to Ned. Both of them had missed the last rehearsal, and Diesel had missed the one before that as well. He could feel the entire band beginning to crack at the seams, and he wasn't sure how he could reverse the situation, especially with everyone seemingly at each other's throats. Still, maybe it would be a good thing if Johnny decided to quit…

Kirk glanced at the handsome guitarist and felt guilty for even wishing it. He couldn't let himself give in to his own insecurities. Diesel was a good guitarist. Johnny blinked back at him over his beer. Even so, the man was just *way* too good looking. The bastard.

Johnny tipped him a little grin. Had he read Kirk's mind?

"Lucifer Fuckin' Sham, faggots…" Davey brought everyone's attention right back to him. Did it make him happy irritating them all the time? It seemed like it.

Kirk sighed. "Got something useful to say, Davey?"

"Yeah. Just this: you're all a bunch of pussy wipes, and I'm not sure I can be arsed pluckin' my strings for you anymore. And why the fuck does the Bride have to be at every band meeting anyway? She don't fuckin' contribute musically." He sat back in his chair, folding his arms, screwing Rose with his narrow eyes. His hair was more messy than usual. It looked like it hadn't been washed for a week or more, a spiky hay rack the color of sewage. Stubble lined his face like smeared mud. His sneer took them all in, well-practiced.

Rose yawned at him, and once again Johnny beat Kirk to the defense. "She's here to provide the elegance and intelligence you so obviously lack, Numbhead. And the only string you're good at plucking is the one between your thighs."

Kirk tensed when Rose gave Johnny that sweet smile again. The smile hurt. And it shouldn't, cos it meant nothing, surely? Kirk lost his thread, self-confidence slipping away. He stood up as if about to give a speech, but he'd forgotten the script. They were all watching him now, waiting for him to say whatever he had been about to say. Even Johnny managed to take his eyes off Rose for a second to focus on the singer.

The singer. The frontman. Leader of the band… Yeah, right. This band was a shambles. Did any of them *really* like each other? At this moment in time, that seemed a little doubtful, which was very sad, as they had all been close once. Even the slightly tubby Ned—one of Kirk's oldest and best friends whom he'd met at school alongside Johnny, and besides Rose, one of the only people he knew who could genuinely make Kirk laugh, and whom he admired greatly for not being beaten by his condition—could push the wrong buttons with his humor sometimes. And he was very critical of Kirk's songs, too. Kirk had a growing suspicion the multi-talented drummer was going to drop the band soon anyway and pursue either his stand-up ambitions or the less-stressful career of sound design. While he had a knack for twiddling knobs on a mixing board, Kirk felt the drummer was drawn more to comedy. Ned was hilarious on stage, where his firmly held belief in not trying to suppress his TS but manage it instead, and indeed use it as a comedy tool, really came to the fore. Whichever route he chose to eventually move down, Ned's boredom of the band was becoming more evident, as was his increasing indifference to Kirk's vision.

Kirk opened his mouth to speak, then paused. Why the fuck bother? He suddenly wanted to call it a day. He was getting too old for his dreams for the band to come true anyway. Thirty-three was practically geriatric in rock terms. If he—if *they*—hadn't made it by now, it was obvious they never would. He wavered on his feet, momentarily defeated.

Rose came to his rescue. "Kirk's written some new songs. Stuff you won't believe, it's that good." She beamed at him encouragingly. *That's* why he invited her to band meetings. He smiled gratefully and opened his mouth to elaborate, to tell them exactly why his new songs would go down so well live, why they should make a great new demo that would attract a manager, a deal. He was going to tell them how they would soon be playing to 200 people at their gigs instead of twenty, how they would soon be able to afford decent equipment, go on tour, hell, maybe even have a crack at America if the new album he had in his mind went according to plan, if only they could all pull together and make it work. He was going to tell them all this and more. And then just as he was about to start, Ned broke in instead with the mother of all Tourette's outbursts, his extremely loud shout of "NHS!" turning heads all around the pub, the drummer looking as completely bewildered by what was coming out of his mouth as the rest of them, and then they were all falling about laughing—all except Kirk.

His moment was gone. Rose had given him the stage, and Ned had taken it. Kirk wasn't even convinced the cry was a genuine TS tic (and felt ashamed to even think it).

"Whoah!" Johnny was clapping his hands. "Where the fuck did *that* one come from, Ned, old son?"

The drummer put his hands wide. His shaved head shone under the pub lights. "Fuck knows. New material to me, too!"

Davey was still guffawing, truly back in his comfort zone—he hated talking about the future of the band's music; he just wanted to play bass, fuck women, talk shit, and drink lots of beer. And now Ned was moving the conversation on to one of Davey's own pet topics, the state of today's music industry, and he and the bass player were almost in agreement for once, although it wouldn't last.

"That cunt responsible for the Z Factor should be hanged outside HMV for a start," Davey was proclaiming loudly, so loudly that some rock girls at the next table were smiling in agreement, which was dangerous. You should never encourage Davey Crooked. "He's turned music into puppy food for the brain-dead. Get a tramp to roast his fuckin' nuts in a brazier and sell 'em for 50 pence. Then he'd finally be contributing to society, the cum-bucket."

Ned nodded. "Set the music industry back thirty years. It's like punk never happened." When he got riled, the drummer's arm tics became a little more aggressive, which just made him madder. He could control them in the confines of a comedy routine when he was on stage, using his Tourette's to provide extremely refreshing and self-deprecating humor. But when he was angry, it became his enemy. "And as for Rap, don't even get me fuckin' started! Sexism with all the fun taken out. Calling girls bitches and lyrics about guns and gangstas…is that what kids should aspire to?" Ned's round face was getting redder by the minute. But now he had lost Davey, as the bassist liked lyrics about slapping bitches and fucking hoes. When he pointed this out to Ned, the drummer produced a physical tic that startled them both for a minute. Ned's arm tilted in a parody of a Nazi salute, while his head twitched manically.

"Cocks in orbit, man, that was a wild one!" Davey responded with his usual sensitivity.

Ned ignored both the drummer's remark and his own tic. "What do you know about music anyway, Davey? It's like talking to an eight-year-old. You've as much musical ability as a tapir. Hell, I'm sure a woodlouse knows more chords than you."

Davey's only answer was a belch that could peel the top off a beer can. It was at this point that Kirk walked away, heading for the toilet and a breath of fresh air.

By the time he'd returned, some idiot had put Cat O' Nine Tails on the jukebox and Johnny was chatting quietly to Rose while the other two argued with increasing ferocity.

He left the pub quietly and didn't turn back.

LEO DARKE

PANDEMONIUM

Book One in the *101 Ways to Hell Series*

Part One

The Guide Book

Chapter One
I Hate Pink Floyd t-Shirt

Billy was listening to an album of Pink Floyd cover tracks when the aggressive thumping at the door roused him from his chair.

He'd nicked the CD off the cover of the latest edition of *Mojo;* or rather, it had eased itself away from its meager gum fastenings and into his hand. Practically fell off. Listening to it now, to the various bands' interpretations of "Wish you Were Here" on this Tuesday in mid-April, he was reminded of two things: how much he loved the original tracks, and a t-shirt once worn by Johnny Rotten. He forgot all about these conflicting lines of thought when the ferocious banging on the door made him move to the laced net curtain to peep out. Another random thought occurred to him as he did so, about being caught "peeping," this one courtesy of material from Mickey Flanagan, the cockney stand-up comedian—because the lace didn't completely cover the left-hand corner of the lounge window and the "peepee" could see Billy peeping from his position outside the front door.

The sense of calm created by the music, vanished. He knew this visit must have something to do with Aura before he even reached the window and saw the thug standing there.

The man was in his early forties, stocky, wearing a scruffy, brown hoody and dirty jeans. His face was brutal and slightly deformed in a way that was difficult to pinpoint; there was something about the cast of the features that didn't sit quite right. And as he glared at Billy through the pane of glass, his expression certainly didn't hint that he was calling around to check the meter. The man jerked his head toward the door. *Open it, you fucker.*

If the man had something to tell him about Aura, then Billy wanted to hear it, despite his feeling that the man wasn't bearing good news. As he stepped into the short hall to open the door, he wondered if he'd pushed it just a little too far with her. As soon as he opened the door, he knew he had.

The man's dark hair was tousled and messy. It looked like he had a blotch of moss growing on one cheek, but it was probably paint, as he looked like a painter and decorator, albeit one potentially born in Innsmouth… His slightly askew eyes were menacing and dark.

"You Billy?" The voice was guttural, and a thick country accent dragged at the words.

Billy nodded, a clench of unease right in the middle of his gut. The Pink Floyd tribute album was still playing (a band he'd never heard of called Beak had reached "Welcome to the Machine").

The thug cleared his throat. "I'll tell ya this once. Don't try to contact Aura no more. No calls, no messages, nothin'." He ticked off the instructions on his fingers as he spoke.

Billy stood there in his socks and an insubstantial Judas Sinned t-shirt and bristled. "I just want to know she's all right," he protested. He sounded like a stalker, even to himself now, though he knew it wasn't like that.

The thug took a step closer. "I'll say it again: you keep away. You don't try to find her, you don't try to contact her."

He wasn't going to get any info out of this oaf. Billy's anger overcame his desperation to know more. "Who the fuck are you coming to my house and threatening me?"

The thug moved with terrific speed. He actually growled in fury as he lunged at Billy with demented eyes. The shock of the charge took Billy completely by surprise. He was bowled over and landed on his back in his own hallway while the thug slammed a big army boot down on his chest, effectively pinning him there. The man had wigged out big time. He tried to rain punches down on Billy's face and would have caused some real damage were it not for the narrowness of the hall impeding his blows. Unfortunately, the close walls prevented Billy from rolling away to either side, too, trapping him on his back beneath the boot that was now grinding viciously into his chest. He managed to deflect the majority of punches with his own hands, which just infuriated the thug even more.

The man was grunting and cursing as he gave in to his inexplicable hatred. "You cunt, you *cunt*!" he spat repeatedly as he stomped and punched. Billy strove unsuccessfully to push upward against the weight, "Shine on You Crazy Diamond" playing now through the open door to the lounge. Maybe the thug, like Rotten before him, hated Pink Floyd, too. Maybe Billy should have been playing the Cockney Rejects instead. At least he would have been in the mood for a scrap. As it was, he was only conscious of three things now: what in the name of hell the neighbors would be making of all this and what state his designer t-shirt would be in after the unprecedented wear and tear. The third consideration bothered him the most however: for Aura to send this animal around to warn him off (and there didn't seem to be any other explanation than that she'd sent him), he must have seriously pissed her off. There could be no going back after this. And that hurt more than anything this psychotic ape could do to him, and it also drained any desire to fight back. His anger and inability to accept the abruptness of her distancing herself from him had resulted in this. The flurry of unanswered calls he'd made to her mobile number certainly could be construed as unreasonable—and desperate. Nobody liked desperate. Billy had never before done desperate. This is what it tasted like. This was the fruit it bore. Billy was ashamed: this was conclusive proof that he'd blown it for good. She obviously never wanted to see him again.

"Get the fuck off me!" Billy managed to gasp as the boot continued to bear down on him, cutting off his breath. Then, a little more lamely: "The neighbors will have called the cops by now!"

The thug didn't respond to either utterance. His fists continued to try to mar Billy's unremarkable good looks, but the close walls continued to hamper him from getting a proper swing. Billy grasped the man's boot and tried to twist it off his chest, but his position gave him no leverage. "You *fucking* cunt!" the thug elaborated on his previous litany, and then suddenly lifted his boot and turned to go.

Billy pushed himself up on one elbow, stunned by the whole unpleasant, albeit surreal, experience. The man was about to step out of the house, his back to Billy. Billy jumped to his feet, adrenaline coursing through him, and shoved the man from behind, propelling him through the doorway. "Get the fuck out of my house!" he yelled this time. It was the thug's turn to be caught by surprise, and he stumbled over the doormat, allowing Billy to slam the door after him.

He stood there panting for a minute, trying to understand everything that had just happened. He jumped as a terrific crash jarred the wooden door in its jamb. That heavy boot had been put to good purpose again. Billy tensed, waiting to see if his assailant would repeat the kick, but there was silence from outside.

His thoughts were manic quicksilver crazy. He had not been prepared for a fight. He was in his socks, for God's sake! And Pink Floyd was not the most aggressive of soundtracks. He certainly didn't feel inspired to chase out after the man. But he knew he had to.

He darted toward the closet, searching for his All Saints mock army boots. He shouldered his way into a leather jacket for added measure, finished doing up the laces, and made for the door again, collecting a poker from the fireplace as he went. Surely the bastard would have disappeared by now, he hoped (and was that why he had taken so long to do up his boot laces? Was he actually just a coward who didn't deserve Aura in the first place?) and yet simultaneously didn't hope. With the thug gone, his last connection with Aura would be gone, too.

When he opened the door, there was no sign of the malevolent visitor outside on the street. But Billy could see his next-door neighbors approaching along the pavement. So they had missed the entire show then. That was something, he supposed. He really didn't want to have to explain why he was brawling with a stranger in his own doorway. The neighbors on the other side of Billy's terraced house were always out during the day, so that didn't matter.

He crossed the street to avoid the approaching neighbors, conscious of the poker clutched in his fist. He marched quickly to the side street on the right, wondering if the thug had nipped down there, but apart from the back of an old pick-up truck disappearing around the corner at the end, there was no sign of anybody.

He hesitated, realized his breath was pent up after the fury of the attack, and released it. He honestly felt more disappointed than relieved. Aura was gone. He'd lost her forever. All the phone calls to her voice mail over the last two weeks, the messages he'd left—his concern and agitation increasing with each one, until the dreaded "desperate" kicked in when she hadn't replied to any of them—had left him here, on this street corner with no answers, an aching chest where a size ten boot had ground, a bruise on his chin from the constant flailing fists, and a poker in his hand. What a hero.

He turned and made his way back to his house. The tumult of emotions the violent visitor had unleashed was beginning to ebb. The shock fading, replaced by despair. That was it then. Should he hate her for sending this (speed-fueled?) slightly deformed crazy to his house? Could he hate her? *Did he even know her?* The answer to that had to be no. He had no idea where she lived or any detail about her past whatsoever. The last time he'd seen her, two weeks ago in the elegant grounds of Tortworth Court, she had run away inexplicably. But if this attack proved one thing, it was that she had appalling taste in acquaintances. He remembered that afternoon, dusk creeping over the mansion house and the ornate gardens…and recalled what else he'd seen there among the gathering shadows of the trees. He remembered his unease, too. *No, it had been real FEAR, not unease; don't hide from the truth, sunshine.* He had been distinctly scared. And now this: violence and strangeness seemed to follow Aura around. Perhaps he was better off rid of her after all.

If only it was that easy, he told himself as he withdrew the keys to his house. If forgetting could only be that easy… His neighbors were letting themselves in next door. He nodded politely, his attention distracted by the dirty boot print on the white door. Was that to be Aura's legacy? Was that all he had to remind him of her charms? That, and the whistle of course… He could hear it now, as he closed the door behind him, and his overworked heart kicked into overdrive for the second time that day. The CD had run its course, and the house was otherwise silent, apart from the tuneless warbling. It was faint today. Sometimes it seemed to be coming from right behind him, loud and sharp, and, of course, there was never anybody there when he turned around. He froze in the hallway, the same hallway where ten minutes earlier he'd been sprawled on his back defending himself from a manic assailant, and listened to the indistinct whistle. It was always the same three notes, protracted, eerie, relentless. Right now it was trembling on the edge of inaudibility, wistful as a half-remembered dream, fading, fading… gone. He breathed again, the tension that seized him each time he heard the whistle easing away. There had been far worse times. He could handle it in the daytime. It was a very different matter when he heard it alone at night…

This was Aura's other legacy, of course. The one that had followed him since he had first met her, and which was beginning to drive him mad. The jury was still out whether the whistle was all in his head, just like the budding relationship with Aura seemed to have been.

He sat in his armchair and wondered where it had all gone wrong.

Chapter Two
Not the AA Guide Book to
101 Best British Walks

She was standing in the travel section, looking at a guide book to British Walks.

Billy had never seen her or the book before, and his attention was aroused immediately. Not by the book—he worked in a bookshop all day every day for God's sake and was surrounded by the buggers—but by the beautiful creature holding it.

She was slender as a water nymph, tall, maybe five-eight. Long, sleek legs in tight blue jeans and knee-length fawn boots. Her poncho was fawn, too, swaddled around her slight figure as if she was really feeling the late March chill. Her long, blonde hair fell in waves around her elfin face. She felt his gaze on her even from ten meters away and looked up.

Billy felt a shock vibration jolt him, as if he'd just stumbled into a live cattle wire. Her eyes held his for a moment, kaleidoscope-blue flecked with a mosaic of gray. The gaze was lost and wild, and even in that first moment of meeting, he saw the conflict there, an excitement mixed with sadness. She smiled shyly at him, dropped her gaze back to the book. Billy was already moving, stepping briskly toward her, no idea what he was going to say, just more convinced than he'd ever been about anything in his life before that he had to go and say *something*.

He paused at a loaded trolley that was next to her, waiting for the travel bookseller to shelve its contents. She looked up again and flashed that winsome smile, and Billy could see that her teeth were white and slightly sharp, although the side molars were slightly (ever so *slightly*) uneven. Now that he was close to her, he could see that her nose was a trifle prominent, too, though not unattractively so. It was shaped in a seductive curve rather than being oversized. And anyway, what was it they said about imperfection? It accentuated the beauty of everything else or some such bollocks. But it did in her case. It really did. And she was, startlingly, self-consciously beautiful.

Billy rested both hands on the edge of the trolley, trying to affect a nonchalant air. Now that he was here, he was a fish gulping on a beach. Stranded by foolishness, totally out of his comfort zone. Her electric eyes didn't waver, scrutinizing him…measuring him. But for what? But it was more than that, too. There was a quality to those eyes that stirred more than obvious attraction in him, teasing away at something beneath the surface of his memory that had been long buried. He could see the same suggestion of recognition in her gaze, too. But that was ridiculous. He'd never seen her before in his life.

"Hello," he said after the silence began to become unnatural, even if, for some reason, not awkward.

She smiled again in answer, her cheeks showing the slightest hint of a blush.

He wrenched his gaze away from hers and looked down at the hardback book in her hands instead. It looked old and battered, and he guessed it must have been in the shop a long time to be in such a well-used state. Her right hand obscured part of the title, but he could make out most of it: *The Olde British Guide to 101 Walkes through…* The rest was hidden. Were the extra E's a sign of when it had been written or just a postmodern affectation, he wondered. The book was fat, the dust jacket tattered, and she was holding it open at Walk No. 21, he noticed.

"Walk 21… Where does that take you?" he asked, and immediately felt foolish. It was his turn to blush.

Again the long, measuring gaze before she answered. And when she did, her voice was quiet and soft, with the slightest tremor of a West Country burr. "I expect it will take you exactly where you need it to."

He laughed. What kind of answer was that? Was she a little touched? Instead of deterring him, however, this hint of eccentricity only intrigued him more.

"And what does that mean?"

"It means whatever you want it to."

Ooookayyyy. He grunted in amusement. "Enigmatic, eh?"

She tilted her head coquettishly. "Me, or the book?"

Where the hell did he go from here? Everything she said seemed to pull the rug from under his feet. He realized a female member of the staff was watching them chat from the till by the door, but he refused to acknowledge her. *Julie, damn her.* Always watching him, flirting blatantly and sometimes inappropriately, and while normally he received her attentions gracefully but with no real interest, right now he really didn't want her interfering. In an effort to make it look as though he was helping a customer and not trying it on with an attractive female, he reached for the book as if to offer the blonde girl some advice.

"May I?" he said.

She handed it over readily enough without a word, and he glanced at the page she'd been studying.

WALK NO. 21. DEEPEST, DARKEST SOMERSET

Beneath the title there was a paragraph of text written in old-fashioned English, followed by a sketchy map of a circular walk, and beneath that, a step-by-step guide on how to follow the route.

"Interesting, isn't it?"

He looked up. She stepped around the trolley to peer over his shoulder at the book, and he breathed in her scent. A faint aroma of blossom clung to her. It stirred his senses, quickened his pulse, and again, there was a vague memory associated with it that was just out of reach.

She took the book from him, closed it, and looked up earnestly. "It's very old. How wonderful to find such a book in a shiny, new shop like this."

He was still trying to catch a glimpse of the rest of the title, but again, those beautiful, slender fingers were obscuring it.

For lack of anything better to say he mumbled, "It *is* very old. Obviously been thumbed through a lot. Looks more like an old library book than something we would stock. I shall have to order in some newer copies." As conversational gambits went, this one was pretty dull, so he pushed on with: "Do you walk in Somerset a lot then?" It was better than "Do you come here often?" but only marginally.

"Oh, yes. I spend all my time in deepest Somerset."

He felt another thrill at the delightful accent that furred her words. He suddenly longed to hold her, to breath that May blossom aroma in deep, and nuzzle the long, pale neck. She was so close he could snatch her in his arms right now and not care about what anyone thought. Not even Julie, who, he noticed, was still watching them, a look of intense irritation on her face.

"Maybe I'll take a walk there myself," he said.

Her smile dropped, and she stared at him earnestly. There was confusion in her eyes now. She pursed her lips. "Yes," she said hesitantly. Her gaze fell for a second. "Maybe you should."

"Maybe even Walk number 21," he added.

Her eyes locked on his again. There was no trace of playfulness now. She looked deadly serious. She said nothing but held his gaze until he looked away, puzzled by her intensity. Over the blonde's shoulder, he could see Julie moving around from behind the till, her attention still fixed on him and the girl, her expression dark. Over in the Sports section, Jerry was watching them, too, a cynical sneer on his face as he paused in his shelving task. The blonde was oblivious to the reaction she was causing amongst Billy's colleagues, however. She stepped away from Billy and over to the tall stack of Travel books. She popped the book into a vacant slot in the British Isles section (next to an *AA Guide to Country Walks*, he noticed) and turned to face Billy again. The smile was back, shy, tentative.

Julie Everly was watching Billy alright. Oh yes. The *fucker!*

Didn't take much to distract him, did it? Blonde hair, good legs, and blue eyes. In fact, everything Julie *herself* had. What was so special about this tart, she wondered as she moved out from behind the till, ignoring the old lady who was approaching with a book to purchase. She stepped closer to find out exactly how much flirting was going on. The bastard usually saved it for Julie, even if (being *brutally* honest with herself) she knew deep down he wasn't that interested. Didn't stop him from responding to her insinuations and obvious desire for him, though, did it? He'd given her enough signals that one day he might give in and take her out. Julie had persuaded herself that the only reason he'd deferred 'til now was because she had a boyfriend. But hadn't she made it clear what a waste of time and space this particular boyfriend was? She'd certainly told Billy enough times, for God's sake. How he never paid her attention, never took her anywhere, never treated her. Just came home from work and watched sports on the TV. What kind of relationship was that? Julie wanted more. She sensed that in Billy there was real potential boyfriend material. Billy wouldn't settle for watching the soaps and maybe once in a blue moon (or even once a fortnight, if she was lucky) slipping her a quick one before falling asleep, as if the act had bored him into unconsciousness.

She saw him break off his flirting with the "special" customer as he became aware Julie was watching him, and she marched quickly over to where Jerry, the tall, skinny Scouse was making a poor imitation of a bookseller shelving stock.

"Look at him," she hissed. "Bastard hasn't done any work since she walked in."

Jerry smirked. "Don't blame him. She's a belter."

Julie glared at him. "What's so special about her?!"

"Let me see..." Jerry paused dramatically. "Sophisticated, slim, great legs, long, blonde hair—"

"*I've* got long, blonde hair!"

"—pretty."

Julie gaped at him. That hurt. "You wanker!"

"That I am," Jerry agreed cheerfully, a wicked grin on his face. "And proud of it. But to be honest..." he trailed off as he studied Billy from across the shop. "I don't know why you're so into him. He's not exactly Josh Hartnett." Indeed, he wasn't. Billy was in his late thirties, tall enough, slim enough without being skinny (unlike himself, Jerry thought ruefully), and his face was pleasant and reasonably good looking, and yes, he still had his hair (unlike himself, Jerry thought even more ruefully.) But really, he wasn't all *that*. "Face it Julie," the Scouse continued cruelly, "he ain't interested."

"Fuck *you*!"

"No, thanks. We already did that, remember?"

"You really are a twat, aren't you?"

He smiled smugly at her. "I think you've got a customer."

She turned to see the old lady waiting patiently at the till. She sighed and stormed over to serve her.

Billy stared at the mysterious blonde. He didn't know what else to do or say. He couldn't move, couldn't think of anything beyond this beautiful girl who seemed to trigger so many impulses inside him, some of them completely inexplicable.

"What's your name?" he said simply. His attempts at flirtation were gone. He was serious now, as serious as she had been a moment ago when he mentioned the Walk. He *needed* to know.

"Aura," she said, and then she was gone.

It wouldn't be the first time she would walk out on him, and he would soon become familiar with her disappearances. That is, until the final, most devastating one of all. But right now, it felt like the sun had died in his world. He watched her leave the shop, walking past Julie without looking back, and everything in this corporate bookstore suddenly seemed meaningless and mundane.

She was gone, and Julie was heading for him instead. What kind of poor substitute was that? Then, ashamed of his lack of charity, he summoned a smile for his colleague. To his surprise, she turned her head away, blanking him, and strode purposefully away across the shop. Going to report him to the manager for flirting with pretty customers maybe? *Jealous mare.*

Billy sighed, and then he remembered the book. He crossed over to the shelf where Aura (and wasn't that a great name?) had replaced it. For a moment, he couldn't find it. There was the *AA Guide to Country Walks,* but next to it was a book on farming. Maybe he hadn't watched carefully enough when she put it back. He stepped back and scanned the rows of books. All sorts of walking guides—circular paths around Bath, around Bristol, even around Portishead, but none dedicated to Somerset. And they were all paperbacks, too. Not a hardback in sight.

He scratched his head. Weird.

Slightly confused, he turned away from the Travel section, ready for his lunch break.

It was as he was crossing the shop that he heard the whistle for the first time. It was faint, almost submerged under the classical music playing over the shop's speaker system, and he didn't think too much about it. It was probably some old fool whistling out in the central hub of the Galleries, the shopping mall complex the bookshop belonged to. So he promptly forgot all about it and hurried over to the staff room door before any customers could stop him with a request.

An hour later, as he let himself back out onto the shop floor, his stomach full of tomato soup and cheese sandwiches, he heard it again. A little louder this time.

He searched around for whoever could be producing it. The shop floor was fairly busy with Friday afternoon shoppers, but he couldn't see anyone whistling.

The flat, tuneless warble seemed to be coming from over by the Erotica alcove, where the dirty old men hid to read the pornographic photography books (Frank, the portly security guard attached to the shop had caught a middle-aged man actually pleasuring himself there once; it was no wonder the female staff were calling for the section to be moved to a more conspicuous location), but when Billy leaned over the balcony on the raised section overlooking the alcove, there was nobody there.

A little disconcerted, Billy put it to the back of his mind and headed for the Travel section again, thoughts of Aura more appealing than those of a bodiless whistle. He was determined to find the book now that lunch was out of the way, and this time, it didn't take him very long to track it down.

The classical music pumping around the shop came to a stop as the CD was changed, and in the sudden silence, the whistle was clearer, louder. It seemed to be coming from all around him, the three protracted notes changing interminably. Probably an electrical fault with the speakers, he decided and focused his attention on the book, the spine of which he could now see clearly—right next to the *AA Guide to Country Walks*, where it should be. He pulled it out carefully and glanced at the cover. It bore the illustration of a path meandering through typical English countryside, the meadows and hills simply sketched. But it was the title that riveted him. The piping whistle swelled in his ears as he read it:

THE OLDE BRITISHE GUIDE TO 101 WALKES
THROUGH…

And if he'd expected the location to be Somerset, he was in for a surprise. For some reason (maybe it was the creepy whistling), the word that was no longer concealed by Aura's slender fingers chilled him right down to the marrow. It was probably a publisher's whacky attempt at humor, maybe referring to the difficulties experienced by ramblers finding the right paths through overgrown terrains. Probably. Maybe. But (and he couldn't, for the life of him, explain why) he didn't think so.

The word Aura had hidden was HELL.

INTERLUDE ONE

ROMAN BRITON, 364 AD

"Enough of your complaints! We have a job to do, so let's do it before this squad is whittled away even more by Celtic demons."

The squad of battered and filthy legionaries regarded their centurion with distaste that bordered on rebellion. If it hadn't been for the fact they were stuck in this heathen island of dark forests filled with creeping, savage Britons and no way of returning to their homeland, they would have long ago gutted their leader with his own *gladius*.

The squad originally consisted of ten legionaries. The troop's original leader, the *Decanus* with whom they had exercised and drilled, not to mention shared every night in their squad tent for the last eighteen months, had been replaced for this mission by a more experienced centurion, and they were missing their erstwhile commander with each hour they had to spend in this new bastard's company. He wasn't a bad man, and that was his problem; he was far *too* dedicated. He obviously believed in this crazy suicide mission, probably because he had one eye on promotion. They'd already lost three men in sneak attacks, and while that wasn't the centurion's fault, it was clear to everyone but him that this mission was doomed to failure.

They glared up at him now as they sat on the damp grass and rocks of the small clearing, shivering from the cold and the gloom and the incipient threats of attack from the depths of the forest.

Laccus Sciro, a stocky, swarthy legionary with a foul temper and a cruel sense of humor, regarded the tall centurion with barely guarded contempt. Of course, this quill pusher of a centurion hadn't allowed them to light a fire. Their old *Decanus* would have. He would have brought an amphora of good Roman wine along for the trip, too. Which was probably why the poor bastard had been replaced with this Ceasar's arse-licking fucker instead.

Sciro turned to the soldier beside him, ignoring the centurion. "A real fucking mess," he muttered darkly, not quite loudly enough for the officer to hear. "This bastard's leading us to certain death. We just going to take it?"

His friend, Antoni Martus, shrugged, glancing at their leader hostilely. He was lithe, with sneaky features and a prominent nose. He spat in the grass without answering.

"What was that, Sciro?"

The centurion stepped toward the bulky legionary, one hand on the hilt of his sword. His face was set and hard. He would not take *any* more bullshit from this pack of lazy scum.

Sciro glowered up at his leader. "Nothin'."

The centurion stiffened. This was just another example of their disrespectful attitude toward authority. If they were back in camp and a common infantryman had addressed his officer in such a manner, he would have been cleaning the barracks for three months. Why the hell had they given him this bunch of insolent, not to mention indolent, gamblers and whoremongers to do such an important job? It was almost as if the *Pilus Prior* who had delegated them for this mission had known it was doomed to failure and didn't want to waste his best men. But what did that say about the centurion? He believed in this job even if nobody else did, and he was going to do his damnedest to prove the *Pilus* wrong and complete the mission as planned.

He kept his hand meaningfully on the sword hilt. There was a long silence while the two Romans glared at each other.

Eventually, Sciro lowered his eyes. "Nothing... *sir.*"

"Then get on your feet. Now!"

The seven legionaries climbed up slowly and reluctantly, their bodies tired and aching from the long march through this hellish forest and the incessant cold and rain.

Sciro was last up. He withdrew his sword from its scabbard as if to check it was clean and dry. His eyes met the centurion's as he did so, and they locked gazes for another handful of seconds. The officer's hand was still on the hilt of his own weapon. The other soldiers fell silent, watching the conflict of wills eagerly, wondering who would make the first move.

Sciro grinned wolfishly and then slowly, so slowly, sheathed his sword in its scabbard. He scratched at the two days' worth of stubble on his jowls and watched as the officer nodded abruptly, then turned away to continue the march.

He led them on through the dripping trees. Mostly oak and ash, thick boughs and trunks making the darkness of night that much darker, more threatening. Painted Celts could be lurking behind every bole, waiting to skewer them with their primitive javelins and swords.

Sciro, last in line, was no longer grinning as he glanced furtively around him at the impenetrable gloom. He hated Briton. Hated it with a passion. No wonder the indigenous people were so wild and barbaric, so utterly savage. They lived out their brutal existence squatting in mud huts and praying to dark Gods while Sciro's countrymen back home erected magnificent palaces, temples, and cities that were glorious testimonies to their advanced civilization. What did these pigs have that could rival those achievements? He gritted his teeth. Megalithic monuments and arcane stone circles. It was pathetic, and it stirred a deep hatred in his soul. If it hadn't been for the stubborn refusal to accept Roman civilization into their lives—to accept *sophistication*, for fuck's sake—he could have been deployed back to Rome years ago. Back to the warmth, the wine, the food, the women of Rome.

He thought of the women here. Mud streaked, clad in filthy, stinking furs, their hair crawling with lice, their teeth snaggled (if they had any), their bodies gristly and sharp-boned. It was no wonder some of the legionaries turned to each other for sexual comforts. Not that Sciro would ever stoop to *that*, of course. He would wait until he got back to Rome, and then he would spend all his *sestertii* on the elegant ladies of the most beautiful city in the world.

But right now he was squelching through mud, with a biting wind penetrating his tunic, his head aching from lack of sleep, his balls itching from wet leggings, and wishing the centurion would trip in the dark and fall down one of the various clefts and gullies that riddled this endless forest. Now *that* was an idea…

Ahead of him, the puny form of Aurelius Piccano halted momentarily to adjust his sandals, causing Sciro to walk into him. *Clumsy fuck!*

Sciro was tempted to push him over in the mud as the smaller soldier knelt to refasten his buckles, but he resisted the urge. He shouldn't waste his aggression on his friends… He patted the legionary on his head as he passed him. "You can pull rear duties now, Piccano, you useless prick," he said in what, for him, was an amiable tone.

Piccano straightened swiftly, blanching at the idea. "The centurion picked you, Sciro," he argued petulantly, his small, round face puckered up with anxiety.

"Fuck you, and fuck *him*," Sciro replied, walking on and leaving the smaller man to look nervously around and (especially) behind him.

At the front of the troop, the officer had heard the mutter of voices and glanced back to see what was causing the commotion. Hadn't he told them enough times to keep silent while they were on the march? Their enemies were all around them. These really were the most clueless cowherds he'd ever seen. He certainly wouldn't dream of calling them soldiers. He halted the file of legionaries momentarily with a raised hand, making sure the disturbance at the back was finished before beckoning them forward once more. Sciro, of course. Always Sciro. The way he'd played with his sword, openly mocking his officer—openly threatening him. The centurion half expected to wake from one of their infrequent rest breaks to find the evil bastard squatting over him with that sword blade resting against his neck.

As far as missions were concerned, this one really *was* going all the way…

…to Hell.

Chapter Three
Closing Time

It was closing time, and Billy was glad of that. The last customer was ushered out by the portly Frank, and as usual, the "loss prevention officer" (hey, Frank, fancy title for a security guard) nipped off sharpish, leaving three members of staff to close everything down.

Those three members consisted of Billy, a stout, former football hooligan turned philosophical bookseller named James, and the truculent Julie.

Billy wished he could have locked up on his own. At this time of the evening, he just wanted to get the hell out, not have to put up with Julie's weirdness or James's constant chatter. But tonight there was another reason he wanted a bit of privacy. He'd been thinking all day about the book Aura had been reading. He'd been too busy serving a flurry of Friday afternoon customers all eager to snag a good book for the weekend to get around to checking it out properly until now. He could see James up on the raised area where all the Mind, Body, and Spirit bullshit was, tidying up the mayhem customers had left it in. He couldn't spot Julie anywhere, thankfully.

He crossed to the Travel section, half expecting not to be able to find it again like earlier, or heaven forbid, discovering it had actually been sold. But no, there it was, in plain sight, wedged next to the AA guide book. He was pulling it from the shelf when Julie appeared from the customer orders office and, spotting Billy, immediately made a bee-line in his direction.

Billy groaned to himself but looked up with a forced smile.

It wasn't that he disliked her. How could he dislike someone who so obviously thought he was wonderful, even if he couldn't, for the life of him, work out why she felt that way. She was only 25 after all, and Billy was 38. There was a world of difference between them in terms of tastes, interests, and general character that could not be put down solely to the age gap. Her constant attentions toward him were kind of flattering, but they were, at times, a bit cloying, too. And she was very persistent. Like right now.

She glanced at the book in his hand, and irritation creased her freckled brow. She obviously remembered who had been looking at it earlier. Julie was pretty enough, Billy couldn't deny, in an anodyne, underfed, prickly kind of way. Her blonde hair was thin and a little lank despite the curler she obviously used to energize it. Her eyes were faded blue, sharp as a seagull's, as was her pointed nose. He wasn't really attracted to her—or maybe only slightly (he'd once almost kissed her at a colleague's leaving do, but that was after a fair few pints). If he might have relented before, however, the arrival of the ethereally beautiful Aura into his life had really put paid to any chances of any-thing happening between Julie and Billy now. She looked like a faded black-and-white photograph next to Aura's Technicolor glory.

"What's so interesting about that bloody book?" she asked him, un-able to disguise the note of petulance in her voice.

He shrugged, feeling caught out and a little cornered. He wished she would leave him alone. He felt a needling compulsion to investi-gate the book and whatever secrets it might hold.

She scanned the title and laughed mirthlessly. "Walks through Hell, huh? Sounds like a pleasant way to spend a Sunday afternoon. You planning to take your new friend for a stroll?"

He ignored the sarcasm, then indulged in some of his own before he could stop himself. "It's six-thirty, Julie. Your boyfriend will be expecting you."

Annoyance flared up in her pixie face. The end of her pointed nose crinkled. "You trying to get rid of me?" Then she added her own spin to his words, a spin that appealed to her, however far-fetched it might be. Her expression brightened. "You're jealous, aren't you?" She reached out a bony hand and touched his bare arm (he was wearing a standard branded corporate t-shirt emblazoned with the name of the bookshop franchise). When he didn't flinch, she took that as encouragement and stroked his skin in what she guessed was an erotic fashion.

"There's no need to be, you know," she said, lowering her voice huskily.

Billy detected the note of passion in it, and despite himself, he felt a little aroused. God, he was a man after all! Yet he gently pulled away and glanced at his watch demonstratively. His urge to check the book out properly was stronger than any lust Julie might stir in him, especially now that Aura had arrived on the scene.

"Time to close this baby up," he said jovially. He could hear James thumping down the stairs from the raised area. Julie heard him, too, and that spurred her on.

"You know there's someone in this shop I really like, don't you?"

Billy felt trapped. "Julie," he began, but she put her hand on his chest to stop him.

"Listen to me. There's someone who makes me feel more alive than I've ever felt before. Every time I hear him speak, I want to kiss him. When he's serving on the till and calls for the next customer, he always shouts out the same thing and..."

He almost laughed. "What thing?"

She smiled, and her hand moved down his chest a little, a subtle caress. "He calls out, 'Yes, please,' and..." She chuckled and flushed. Her cheeks looked like freckled bacon for a second. "And I go all weak at the knees..."

"Weak at the knees, eh?" James popped his head around the tall shelves of the Travel section and smiled broadly, his round, frameless spectacles reflecting the fluorescents above. "Who's causing that? Not Billy the Kid again, is it? When are you gonna make an honest woman of her, Bill?"

"For fuck's sake, James! Haven't you got a home to go to?"

"Too right. As soon as you two love birds have finished flirting, of course. Don't let me stop you though."

"Nothing for you to peep at here," Billy told him.

"James, you're a prick," Julie snapped angrily.

James beamed. "Is that any way to refer to your Assistant Manager?"

Julie shook her head in irritation and walked off toward the staff room.

Billy cleared his throat. "You might as well clear off, too, James. I just wanted to sort one more thing out and I'll follow on."

James glanced at him curiously. "What you up to? Not like you to linger after time."

Billy averted his gaze. "Just something I forgot to do earlier. You don't want to miss the start of the England game do you? Just leave me the keys. Won't be long." Billy knew exactly what buttons to push to decide it for James. He handed the shop keys over and turned to leave. "Cash drawers are all in the safe. And don't forget to check Goods In, for fuck's sake. You know what happened last week." Last week involved a rather daring but ridiculous plan by a rival bookshop owner (although, in this case, it was a stall on St. Nick's Market) who decided it would be a brilliant idea to hide in the parcel unpacking room until after the shop had been shut and then help himself to a sack load of free books. It wasn't so much that he forgot about the alarm as he was convinced he could get away quickly enough with his booty before anyone responded to it. If it had been left up to Frank, the shop's corpulent security guard, then he would have been right. However, he forgot one essential thing—the shop was part of the Galleries Mall shopping center. Every alarm alerted the 24-hour security staff for the whole complex, and they hadn't eaten as many pies as Frank over the years.

"I'm heading there now," Billy told James, and he walked across the shop, still clutching the guide book. He was aware of a curious niggling in his mind, almost like an urge for a fix, like a junkie wanting to be alone so he could find a vein. A silly analogy, he told himself, but the sense of compulsion stayed with him as he hurried to Goods In. He was just pushing through the double doors into the unpacking room when he caught sight of Julie out of the corner of his eye. She had her coat on and a grim expression and was heading for the main doors. He breathed out, and then the doors swung closed behind him and he was alone in the shop.

James had already killed the canned music, so the shop was eerily silent. Billy crossed to one of the PCs on the long desk and placed the book next to it, intending to check out the ISBN and gain a little more information about the Guide. He nudged the "stock analysis" key on the board and turned to pick up the book again. He frowned, scanning the back, then flipped open the inside cover. He flicked through to the publication info page, his frown deepening.

No ISBN. That was unusual. But not unprecedented. No barcode either. Just how bloody old was this book? It looked like one of the old books he used to take out from his local library back in the early eighties. He remembered a copy of the *Everyman Frankenstein* that had looked every bit as battered as this.

Even the pages were yellowed, for God's sake. But then maybe that was the intention, the faux antique-look marketing to match the kitsch title, which he could only assume was a postmodern attempt at humor.

Except this book looked anything but postmodern. And absolutely nothing about it hinted at any intentions toward humor on the part of whoever had compiled it. He examined the publication page more carefully. Published by Hobbemarke House, Somerset. The publication history was a real eye-opener: *first edition published 1610, derived from older texts.*

For the second time since he had found the book, a coldness spread inside him. He actually looked over his shoulder, something he hadn't done in many years. The Goods In room suddenly seemed larger than normal, with too many corners not illuminated by the one small fluorescent. Stacks of empty cardboard boxes and metal racks of books were obscured by gloom at the furthest end near the fire door.

He turned back to the PC and pulled up the book search page. He keyed in the title of the book and waited while the slow machine worked its wonders. Or didn't, in this case. There was no mention of *The Olde Britishe Guide to 101 Walkes through Hell …*

He refused to be beaten. He *needed* to know about this book for some reason. He checked the cover for the editor. Of course, there wasn't one listed, not on the flyleaf or title page either. He keyed in Hobbemarke House and came up with a similar blank.

He returned his attention to the book, and flipping through it again, a brief preface caught his eye:

> *The Wayes marked in this Booke Are not for*
> *All, though all those who touch it must follow them.*
> *Those who tread them would do well to tread them wisely.*
> *Trust unto the markers, though they may alter…*
> *For the Pathes may change for those who walke them.*
> *Lest ye not enter a wilderness of the mind, tread softly, tread with care.*
> *Man is lost… May you each find your Waye.*

The light flickered and then went out.

He was plunged into complete blackness. And silence. Even the hum of the computer had been cut off. He could hear his own breathing, though, and it sounded way too loud.

"Fuck," he said to break the quiet and bolster his nerves. Then something else disturbed the silence. Faint at first, then growing in volume, as if whoever was whistling was approaching the Goods In room from across the darkened shop.

Three notes in a descending key, long and trembling, pausing as the whistler took in a breath, then resuming, becoming clearer. Billy could hear the tuneless drone right outside the doors now. He stepped away from the desk, groping toward the wall beside the doors, intending to find the switches that operated the shop's lighting system, realizing as he did so that even if he managed to find them in the dark, they would not respond. He stumbled over a box of half-unpacked books left in the center of the floor and fell to one knee. His gasp of breath was loud in the sudden silence. The whistling had stopped. He strained his ears, remaining in a kneeling position, but all he could hear was the tinnitus in his left ear and the thumping of his heart.

Then the whistle started up again from just behind his right ear, as if whoever was responsible was leaning over him in the dark. Billy cried out and lurched to his feet, heading for where he hoped the double doors were located. The whistle followed him, *reached for him....* Billy's shoes clattered over the concrete Goods In flooring, but he heard no other footfalls pursuing.

He burst through the doors, and the haunting whistle was with him, just over his shoulder. It stayed with him as he scampered through the pitch dark of the shop, colliding with tables, spilling the immaculately piled books onto the carpet. It stayed with him as he blundered into the Erotica alcove, completely clueless as to where he was going. He felt the tight cul-de-sac of books pressing around him, the whistle trapping him from behind. The three notes grew more urgent, more violent in tone.

Then they stopped. And Billy's tinnitus was again the loudest sound in the shop.

And the lights flicked on.

And everything was normal again.

Everything was *normal* again.

And, from Midnight Machinations, don't miss…

LIGHTS!

A killer is targeting TV and Film extras on various productions throughout the South West of England. The murderer leaves a macabre marker at each crime scene—a VHS video nasty, while the murders themselves mimic the killings depicted in the tapes.

CAMERA!

While the police are drawn into both the seedy world of nasties and the hierarchical system that thrives in the film industry, the killer remains one step ahead.

CUT!

It's an A–Z kill list, and the cops are in a race to stop the slayings before the murderer can chop their way through the 39 titles on the list of banned films, from *Absurd* to *Zombie Flesh Eaters*…

WALKING SHADOW
A Stone/Darke Mystery